Carie Toeller

First Corpse the Appetizer

A Layne Stevens Novel

First Corpse: The Appetizer is a work of fiction. All names, characters, settings and incidents are fictitious. Any resemblance to actual events or people is strictly coincidental and not intended by the author.

Published in the United States by Cliff House Books
www.cliffhousebooks.com

Paperback ISBN 978-0-9970647-1-1
Digital ISBN 978-0-9970674-2-8

Library of Congress Control Number: 2018905905

First Edition

FIRST CORPSE THE APPETIZER

CARIE TOELLER

To all of the tenacious women who have inspired me throughout my life. And for my family and friends who have supported me unconditionally, even in my most erratic states. You know who you are. My gratitude and my love. Always.

C

1

In times of stress, Layne adhered to a strict diet of the four major food groups—wine, chocolate, cheese and more wine. This definitely qualified as one of those times. With dried mud covering her clothes, and hair matted to the side of her face, she lurked behind a potted palm, longing for a gigantic glass of buttery chardonnay. Hell, even Strawberry Boone's Farm straight from the bottle sounded good after her train wreck of a day. She glanced down at what had once been white jeans. Damned taxies. How could a single tire and one small pothole create so much sludge? Then she heard someone call out her name, and through spear-shaped leaves she scanned the hotel lobby, dreading what awaited her.

Layne adored her fans, but somehow they always managed to find her at the worst possible times. She steadied herself, took in a deep breath, slid from behind the decorative foliage, and plunged into the crowd. No one commented on her disarray as she smiled and mingled, uttered her thanks, and shook sweaty palms. In fact, they all seemed thrilled to see her. That is, all but one man, who caught her eye with a chilling glare.

She felt a tug at the hem of her tee shirt and shifted her gaze down to an older man, of shorter stature, pointing a black marker at the bald spot on top of his head. She chuckled as she signed the glistening patch of hairless skin. That was a new one, even for her. When she looked up, the chilly eyed man was gone, and she continued her expedition through the pack, autographing everything from crumpled tissues to bare biceps, with her sights set on the vintage style lift that would carry her to the sanctuary of her room.

Finally reaching the lift, the door closed, separating her from the chaos, and she collapsed against the far wall, letting her knees buckle beneath her and planting her exhausted behind on the glossy gray subway tile floor. But before making its ascent, the elevator door re-opened, and a well-appointed older couple joined her. No words were spoken, but Layne noted an echo of her mother's disapproval in the woman's stare—clearly, nice girls never sat on dirty elevator floors. Layne let out a sigh. Compared to her ass, the floor was pristine.

With a chug upward, the old lift creaked and moaned. She empathized. Sure, she exercised two or three times a week. When she wasn't traveling. Or too busy. Okay, maybe more like two or three times a month. Which explained why the day she'd spent battling San Francisco's steep hills and crooked slopes made her calves twist into painful knots. Nope. No surprise there. Her optimism often...well, pretty much always exceeded her actual physical prowess. And hitting forty, uh, something hadn't helped.

From his stilted position at the front of the elevator, the older gentleman shot a glimpse back at Layne, and then bent down to whisper to his wife. Of course, Layne heard every word.

"Darling," the gentleman said. "It's Layne Stevens. You know, from that food show."

The woman gave a scrutinizing tilt backward, and Layne responded with as much of a smile as she could muster. The woman sniffed her disgust, and then turned to her husband.

"It's difficult to tell, but I believe you're correct," the woman said. "What of it?"

"Well, I realize she looks a fright, but there's a beautiful gal under all that grime." The gentleman's gaze wandered toward an imaginary distance. "The wavy chestnut hair, and those gorgeous brown eyes.

Golden skin, like it's been kissed by the sun. And that smile...a man could lose himself in that smile."

Layne's chest tightened as she watched the gentleman's ardent gaze float to his wife's steely glare.

He stiffened and cleared his throat. "And she's a darned decent little cook."

The woman's face pinched. "Do you have a point?"

"Yes, I do. She'd be perfect for our Timothy."

"Don't be ridiculous. Timothy's divorce from that witch he called a wife left him completely emasculated. The last thing he needs is some entitled prima donna who thinks she can sit on an elevator floor, covered in remnants of something or other unholy...woman on woman mud wrestling or what have you."

The gentleman's gaze wandered off again, and Layne let her head drop. At least she'd dodged having to decline yet another pointless matchmaking attempt.

"And besides," the woman said, "overbearing women give poor Timothy a gruesome rash."

Layne cringed. Poor Timothy must have been rashy a lot as a child.

The gentleman forged on. "Look at her, darling. Neither of them is getting any younger. With her husband gone, she's clearly in need of some stability. And as a celebrity, we might even forego the wait on the urine sample and background check."

Had they forgotten she was right there?

"Oh, all right," the woman said. "But this is your last chance to select a suitable mate. If this doesn't work out, I'm taking charge."

The couple turned in unison to Layne. Damn. She'd been so close to getting out of this one. Lifting her head, she plastered on what she hoped was a somewhat friendly grin.

"Our son is aging." the woman said. "Not unlike yourself."

Layne bit the inside of her lip and tried to remember the woman meant well.

"And we don't want him to be alone after we die," the woman continued. "We have a great deal of money, which he will inherit, and on the days when his skin is clear, he's easy on the eyes. And to be frank, it appears you could use a good man. So, we would be willing to consider letting you date our Timothy."

Why did everyone assume she needed a man? Layne liked her life the way it was—a fantastic job, two reasonably well-adjusted grown children, supportive family and friends...on most days. There just wasn't space or time in her schedule for the complexities of an intimate relationship. Her world was as it should be—pleasant, and routine, and predictable.

"Well?" the gentleman asked, nudging her from her thoughts.

"Sorry," Layne said, "I...um...as tempting as the offer is, I'm afraid I'm not currently accepting romantic inquiries. There's the show to think about, and the mud wrestling. It's all very time-consuming. Thank you, though. And I wish you the best of luck finding a mate for poor Timothy."

Layne worked to squelch the completely inappropriate laughter bubbling inside her as the lift shuddered to a stop. But it didn't go unnoticed by the older woman, who emphasized her outrage with the severe tightening of her lips before she marched off. The gentleman gave Layne a reticent smile and trailed after his wife. Layne used the antique brass handrail to hoist herself to her feet, while every muscle in her body complained, and headed in the opposite direction down the hall, grateful to leave the conversation behind her.

The hallway's etched glass wall sconces offered plenty of light, but Layne still managed to bump into every carved wooden sideboard and embroidered settee in her path as she dug through her purse for the key to her room. And while she hadn't really noticed the antique furnishings, when she glanced up, it was impossible not to notice that the double doors to her suite were wide open. Her pace slowed. She had left the privacy request hanging from the knob, but the doors must have been opened by housekeeping. Right?

The little voice in Layne's head, always on alert for a way to help, answered. *Don't be an idiot,* it said. *Everyone knows housekeepers don't come after four. Ax murderers and armed robbers, maybe, but not housekeepers.*

Layne's little voice called her an idiot with staggering frequency, matched only by her will to ignore it. But had it muttered something about armed robbers?

"Shit," Layne said. "The diamonds." She searched frantically for someone to help, but she was alone. Flattening her back against the hallway's ornate turn of the century wallpaper, she chose to overlook the rapid thudding in her chest as she inched closer to the suite. Near the doorway, she stopped to listen for noises coming from inside. She waited to hear something. Anything? Nope. Nothing. She took a cautious peek inside. Still, nothing. No sign of anyone wielding a toilet brush, an ax, or otherwise but something felt off, and the goosebumps prickling on her arms agreed.

This won't end well, her little voice warned.

"Shut up," Layne whispered to her crappy little voice. But her pulse raced as she crept through the suite's sitting area toward the adjoining bedroom. She snuck to the opening and eased her head around the doorframe. Late afternoon sunlight slivered through lowered plantation shutters, playing tricks with her vision, and her eyes fought to adjust.

Her focus finally settled on the massive antique armoire in the far corner of the room. She'd locked her grandmother's diamond jewelry in the safe at the bottom of that old closet, and its door also stood ajar. A sudden surge of adrenaline and stupidity possessed her, and she raced to the armoire but stopped dead at a shiny silver tray on the floor.

Her brow lowered. Appetizers?

The armoire door drifted open, someone screamed, and Layne's predictable world went black.

2

Twenty-four hours earlier, Layne sat wedged between a young man, mostly leg, and a gourd-shaped person of unidentifiable gender with an incessant cat-like cough. Beads of sweat crawled down her forehead, and her stomach churned at the stale-air stench of body odor, sweet perfume, and fuel.

A flight attendant stopped at her row. "Ms. Stevens, I'm so sorry for the confusion, but it turns out there is an open seat in business class. If you'll please follow me."

Layne gathered her things and climbed over the mountain of legs into the aisle. Several rows ahead, two older women watched her approach.

"Oh my," one of the women said, reaching out a shaky hand. "I can't believe it. Look, Beatrice. Look who it is!"

Layne took the woman's hand and gave her a sly grin. "Shh. You'll blow my cover."

"Oh, we can't have that," the woman said, lowering her voice. "Would you mind signing my magazine? There's a lovely picture of you on the front this month."

Layne gasped when she saw the photo. Why had she let them

spackle her with makeup and tease her hair? And did the camera really only add ten pounds?

"I must say, you're much prettier in person, dear," the woman said as Layne signed.

The other woman shouldered in for a glance. "Why on Earth would you let those photographers do that to your hair?"

"Beatrice!" the nice woman said, then she turned to Layne. "It's a fine picture, dear. Don't pay attention to Beatrice. Her mouth goes like gangbusters, but her filter deserted her a hundred years ago."

Layne chuckled as she said her goodbye's, then continued up the aisle to part the curtain separating the privileged few from, well, everyone else. The attendant pointed her to an empty seat next to a man in a dark business suit, with eyes closed, mouth agape, cheek pressed into the small windowpane, and snuffles of warm breath leaving misty tendrils on the glass. Men, how did they do it?

After stowing her laptop bag overhead, she shoved her cell phone into the front pocket of her jeans, sank into a soft, roomy leather chair, and took a moment to compose herself. Then she felt for the under-seat life preserver, located the oval indentation that identified the oxygen mask above her head, fastened her seatbelt low and tight around her hips, and choked down four tropical fruit and drywall flavored antacids, before using her foot to stuff her purse under the seat in front of her.

She finally felt settled when a voice boomed through scratchy speakers, and her entire body clenched.

"Good evening, folks. This is your captain. On behalf of tonight's crew, I'd like to welcome everyone aboard. Our travel time from Los Angeles to San Francisco tonight will be roughly one hour and ten minutes."

Roughly? The rest of the captain's speech went unheard as Layne dealt with the closing of her airways.

After what felt like an eternity into the flight, the attendant came by with complimentary beverages and desserts. Layne didn't often eat processed foods, but the chocolaty goodness of one particular double fudge brownie spoke to her in a seductive, Barry White kind of way.

"You've had a rough night," the brownie said in an extra low, silky voice. "You barely escaped flying coach. You need me."

Turned out double fudge brownies could be very persuasive.

Layne glanced at her watch for the fourth time, swirled her wine in the clear plastic cup, breathed in the aroma—an herbal bouquet with a hint of oak—and took a sip. It felt spicy on her tongue, like satin going down, and it warmed her insides. Then she nibbled on her brownie. Oh yes, the unrivaled combination of chocolate and red wine.

She was in heaven until the plane hit a bump. She'd never understood how air could have bumps. But she forced herself to focus on the subtle undertones of the merlot and how they complemented the richness of the brownie. Then the cabin rumbled and shook. Pretentious wine snobbery would have to wait. She put her dessert and glass of wine on the tiny pop-out table and gripped her armrests.

If only the subtle undertones in the merlot contained a hint of Valium, her little voice mused.

A strong vibration penetrated her seat, a thunk came from below, and she squeezed her eyelids tight. The airplane rocked, first right, then left. Why had she gotten on that plane? Another bump, a sputter, and a loud ding from above. The nose of the aircraft lurched, then made a sharp descent, and her gut followed. Shit, shit, shit. They were all going to die.

"Pardon me, miss?"

Not now, Layne thought as her seatback shuddered.

"Miss, are you all right?"

Wait. That was not her little voice. And it wasn't Barry White. But it was undeniably male.

"I don't mean to inconvenience you," the male voice said. "But would you mind letting go of my arm? I've got a bit of a mess to contend with here."

Layne allowed her eyes to slice open and found herself clamped to the side of dark-suit man. "What's happening?" she asked.

"It looks like I have some cleanup to do."

She peered down at his slacks, covered in red wine and crumbled brownie. "Oh my gosh. I'm so sorry."

He gave her a sympathetic grin. "I'm pretty sure the worst is over."

What was he thinking? The worst would happen when they crashed. The plane quivered, and Layne let out a squeal.

"It's okay," dark-suit man said. "We're about to land."

Her focus darted around the cabin. "Land?"

"It's something planes do. At some point, they all land. One way or another."

A jolt struck them. She tightened her clutch on the man's arm, and he snickered.

This was so not funny. Daring a glimpse out the small window, she began to unclench as she realized the plane was actually on the ground. It slowed to a roll, she released her grasp on dark-suit man, slid her legs out from underneath his, and put her hands over her pounding heart. "Really, I'm—"

"Don't worry about it," he said. "That's the most excitement I've had on a flight in years. And the suit can be cleaned."

She reclaimed a modest amount of composure and focused on his face. He flashed her an amazing smile. Holy shit. Nausea played at the back of her tongue. Air travel, making a complete fool of herself, and gorgeous men—not a good combination. She turned away, unbuckled her seatbelt, and pried herself from her seat. Dark-suit man stood to help with her laptop bag, and she stopped to thank him.

"The pleasure was all mine," he said, in a rich, husky tone that reminded her of melted caramel.

"Uh...I've gotta go," she said, fumbling with her bags. "Thanks, so much." She managed a half-hearted wave as she barreled through the small business-class crowd, straight into another man who had moved into the aisle.

"Oh, jeez," she said. "Sorry. Are you all right?"

"No worries," the man said, pulling a backpack from the overhead bin.

Layne steadied herself against an empty headrest, hitched her computer bag and purse up on her shoulder, and puffed a wisp of hair out of her eyes. Then her little voice made an unwelcome appearance.

Well, if something had to crash and burn, at least it wasn't the plane.

3

Three thousand miles away, Hans Berger fumbled in the darkness for his cell phone. He propelled a small table lamp into the wall, sent his watch flying, and toppled an unread stack of espionage novels in search of the bellowing fiend, but still the blare reverberated from somewhere near his bed. One last slap at the nightstand connected, and he squinted against the glare of the screen, letting out a groan. No good could come from this call at two in the morning. He had wondered how long it might take for the fallout of her presence on American food television to blow back on him. It was amusing, in a sick kind of way. So much thought, so much worry spent on her, when she had no knowledge of his existence.

After a hasty discussion, he pulled wrinkled gray slacks over long legs, trim hips, and flannel sleep shorts. He rolled on some deodorant, slipped a clean black turtleneck over toned arms and chest, finger-combed his stubborn blond hair using water from the bathroom sink to flatten it a bit, sucked on an open tube of toothpaste, then assessed his angular jaw in the mirror, running a hand across a full day's growth of stubble. But there was no time to shave. He grabbed his jacket, gun, and badge, and left his apartment for the five-block trek to East Berlin's Federal Criminal Police Headquarters.

Berger rushed along the Elsenstrasse on a dark and empty sidewalk, shouldering the chill of a late frost in Berlin as it tunneled through his heavy wool coat. His pace and the freezing temperature ensured his fully awakened state when he arrived. Most of the time he loved his job. At that moment, not so much.

The elevator doors opened on the second floor of the Bundeskriminalamt building to a level of activity he had not expected at the hour, and he dodged more than one officer as he sped to the meeting room just off the main hall. The barbed flicker of a faulty overhead light amplified the tension in the room, where a secure voice transmission commanded all focus. Berger stepped inside, and it took only a moment for him to recognize the raspy male voice.

"I don't believe I can speak any more slowly," the voice on the secure line said. "Are you BKA clowns listening? I'm telling you, the damned thing is at risk."

The officers seated around the large conference table surveyed one another, then anchored their stares at BKA Counterintelligence Director, Dieter Braun.

"What are you saying?" The director asked. "That it is missing?"

"Do you know where the fuck it is?"

Quiet consumed the room.

"Shit," the caller said. "Is Berger on the fucking call?"

Berger tensed as all eyes turned on him. "I am here," he said.

"Where the hell is it, Berger?"

"I...I am afraid I do not know."

"Then I'd say the fucking thing is missing."

Director Braun pierced him with a penetrating stare. His tone was restrained, but Berger did not miss the underlying fury. "Officer Berger, do you know where Frederick Schatz is? Does he still have it?"

Berger struggled to release the hold on his breath. "I...I cannot tell you for certain. But I assure you he would not hesitate to kill for its security. I must believe it is still in his possession."

"Bring him in," the director said.

"Last we spoke, he was in San Francisco."

"He returned to the states? But we agreed he was to remain here until the situation was resolved."

"He communicated to me that he had been missing his family, Director."

"You have met most of his family. Did you find that a credible explanation?"

Berger chose to assume the question rhetorical and did not respond.

"Clearly, he has gone to see the Stevens woman," the Director said. "But why now? There is too much risk. This is unacceptable, Officer Berger."

"I apologize, Director. I take full responsibility."

"As you should. It is your responsibility. He is your responsibility." The director stared down at clenched hands. "Find Schatz. And if he does not have it, find the item. But remember, we don't want this in the public eye. If he is with her, you must manage it carefully. And for God's sake, make sure he does not kill anyone."

"Hey," the raspy voice on the line said. "Whatever it takes."

The line disengaged and Berger turned to go, but the glares of the other officers in the room felt like poisoned darts aimed at his back.

4

Layne raced through the jetway and into the glare of fluorescent lights bouncing off the bright yellows and blues of the terminal at SFO. She sidestepped other travelers and hoped she'd make it to the hotel without further incident. Of course, she knew better. As if on cue, the sound of warm caramel captured her attention.

"Layne? Layne Stevens, wait."

Crap. She turned as dark-suit man jogged toward her from across the concourse. When he neared, he held out a cell phone.

"Is this yours?" he asked.

"Oh, my goodness," she said as she took her phone from him. "I didn't realize I'd dropped it. Thank you, Mr..."

"Ryan," he said. "Ryan Cooke." He extended his hand.

She shifted her bags and reached out. "Ryan," she said. "Thank you."

It was a friendly enough gesture, but when her fingers touched his, a tingling sensation zipped through her to certain...unmentionable places. Places that hadn't tingled in quite some time. She let out a nervous chortle—an awkward noise that she hoped sounded like a coquettish laugh, but she was pretty sure came out more like a frog in heat.

He gave her a sidelong stare. "Did I miss the punch line?"

"It's just...uh...I'm sorry. You caught me off guard. And, well, your name..."

"My name?"

"Because I'm a cook. Isn't that how you recognized me?"

Decent save, her little voice commented.

"You're a cook?" Ryan asked.

"I guess we both are." Another stinted chuckle escaped her, and Ryan sent her another questioning glance.

"That's what I do," she said. "I cook. But I'm sure your busy, and you don't want to hear about being a cook. I mean, like in a kitchen, not as part of your family." She cleared her throat. "It's not important. Anyway, thank you, again, so much. Ryan, was it? That's twice now you've saved me."

I take back my earlier comment, her little voice said. *You're not an idiot. You're a blabbering idiot.*

"Well, I'm glad I found you," Ryan said. "If it were me, I'd be lost without my phone."

"Oh, my gosh. So would I. I can't tell you how much I appreciate you going out of your way like this."

For a moment, he just stood there, holding her hand, and her gaze. Fortunately, her mouth had run out of blabber. He gave her that awesome smile, and she returned a flirtatious grin. Then, before she could bridle herself, she lowered her lashes over what she assumed was a libidinous gaze that screamed *take me right here, right now. I'm all yours*. Shit. What the hell was happening? She couldn't remember the last time she'd been struck with the desire, much less the nerve, to flirt. In part, because as she'd just proved, she was terrible at it. But mostly, because no one had seemed worth the risk.

He moved closer. "It was a pleasure to meet you, Layne."

That damned caramel caressed her ears again. And the scent. The man smelled like...heaven. Or maybe it was fresh corn tortillas. Either way, she found it intoxicating.

"Yes, a pleasure," she said. "I mean, not for you to meet me. Or for me to meet me. I meant, for me to...uh..."

Ryan chuckled and slid his hand from hers. "I knew what you meant." He glanced at his watch. "Well, I need to get going. Better put that phone somewhere safe."

"Right. I will definitely do that," she said, flicking her index finger at him.

She immediately regretted the lame gesture, but didn't have time to dwell, as something came flying toward her, and smacked her on the side of her face before she could duck.

"Oh!" she said with a start.

"Are you all right?" Ryan asked, bending down to pick up a plump purple doll sporting a triangle on its head.

She nodded. "I'm fine, thanks. Teletubbies are pretty soft."

Ryan stared at the toy for a moment. "Is this what kids are playing with these days?"

"It's gender-neutral," Layne said, for lack of a better explanation.

"I can see that," Ryan said, still inspecting the doll.

Layne muffled a laugh. "Did you just look between its legs?"

They each took a step back when a young boy dashed between them, grabbed the doll, and kept running as he yelled, "Tinky Winky, Tinky Winky."

From somewhere in the seating area near the gate, a woman's voice bellowed, "Colby, you get back here right now. You are in big trouble, mister. Did you hear me, Colby? Get over here now!"

The young boy darted between them again making sputtering noises with his lips as he zigged and zagged the purple plaything through the air.

"I have to tell you," Ryan said. "This has me concerned for future generations."

Layne brought her hand to her mouth, unable to contain her laughter any longer.

"What?" Ryan said, laughing with her. "Am I wrong?"

As their laughter subsided, their gazes met again, and while his enticing blue eyes showed interest, Layne also caught a hint of regret.

"Well, Layne," he said. "I really enjoyed meeting you."

"I enjoyed meeting you too." She held up her phone. "Thanks again."

"Anytime," he said, flashing her one last glimpse of that killer smile.

When he turned back toward the concourse, she noticed a chunk of brownie smushed onto the back of his pants, and she debated saying something.

Like what? Her little voice chimed in. *Hey, Ryan, because of me, there's a big old piece of brownie stuck to that very fine ass. I don't think so.*

Her little voice was right. She was an idiot. Layne shook her head and turned to go, but still distracted by the encounter, she tripped over a small ridge in the carpet. Her purse and laptop bag launched several feet ahead of her as she fell, landing with a thud on her front side, her face buried in musty, formerly turquoise, indoor-outdoor flooring.

Oh, god. Had he seen that? She tried to appear casual when she peeked back. Well, as casual as a grown woman can appear when splayed on the floor of an airport terminal.

Smooth. Very smooth, her little voice said.

Layne let out a quiet sigh of both relief and disappointment. Ryan Cooke was gone.

SONNY WRIGHT POPPED a couple of beer nuts into his mouth and snickered. Layne Stevens was one clumsy woman.

He stood in plain sight, near enough to discern the expensive cut of the man's suit, and the soft blush of her cheeks when she smiled. Hell, he'd listened to their entire conversation, but they hadn't noticed him. And Layne wouldn't remember him from the flight. No one ever did. With lifeless brown eyes and dull blond hair, not clipped too short or left too long, he was tall, but not too tall, and lean, but not too thin. He didn't consider himself ugly, but no one had ever called him handsome.

He chose nondescript clothing appropriate to his work environment. He orchestrated the appearance of purpose. And his place as the middle child in a family of nine had honed his ability to blend. Sonny

Wright was a shadow. A skill he'd perfected, and one he leveraged to his very lucrative advantage.

His cell phone honked. He'd selected the obnoxious ringtone for this caller because it fit the irritating digitized voice. He pulled his phone from the side pocket of his backpack.

"I presume there were no complications, Mr. Wright."

The caller always used a voice modulator, and for some ungodly reason had made the conscious decision to adopt the voice of Siri. Sonny didn't get it, or the formality of these conversations with this person who called themselves The Employer. But then there were a lot of things he didn't get.

"Piece of cake," he replied.

"What about the other passenger slated for business class on the flight?"

"Some polite persuasion made the other guy a no-show."

"Exceptional work."

"Hey," Sonny said. "You didn't tell me that she's afraid to fly."

"I was unaware of her pteromerhanophobia. Interesting given the requirements of her profession."

"Yeah, well, whatever you call it, it worked in our favor."

"Please elaborate."

"I got to watch their interactions on the plane."

"Continue."

"You were right. They've never met before tonight," Sonny said.

"How can you be so assured on this point?"

"It's a long story."

"Then you are correct to withhold it. In regard to her cellular phone?"

"She had it in her front pocket, and she was so flustered by the time we touched down, making the switch was easy. A simple stop and drop."

"I beg your pardon?"

"The technique I used. I stopped her, took her cell, then dropped the duplicate on her seat. The guy seemed pretty happy to find the thing—"

"Again, if you will spare me the prosaic details. You are positive it is in her possession?"

Prosaic? Who the hell talked like that? "Yup, I watched him give it to her just now."

"So, you will proceed as planned?"

"Yup."

"Excellent. By the way, I have established personnel within the FBI. All the information you need on Ms. Stevens will be to you before the hour."

Sonny's back stiffened. "Inside the bureau? Can you give me a name?"

"Best this person's identity remains discreet."

"What makes you think you can trust them?"

"You let me govern that, Mr. Wright. Keep me posted as to your progress."

Sonny let his head fall back. He already regretted taking the assignment. Turning his attention back to Layne, he watched her pull herself up off the floor, dust off her front side, pick up her bags, and then meld into the terminal foot traffic like nothing ever happened. And he followed—not too close, but not far behind.

5

The call to the BKA had achieved its purpose, and had been oddly entertaining—the young German officers in their cheap suits, probably squirming in their seats, hanging on his every word. Were they on top of the microphones, or was there just that much heavy breathing? And damn, Officer Berger made it all the more sweet. Like a delicious mound of frosting on a red velvet cupcake. A more sensitive man might've felt sorry for the poor bastard, because Berger was royally screwed. Even better, Berger knew he was screwed. The stammering gave it away.

A raspy chuckle surfaced from deep inside. Laughter was rare these days. For that alone, the conversation had been worth it. Well, that, and the huge sum of promised cash.

He dialed another number, established a secure pin, and hold music drifted through the phone's speaker. Fucking classical hold music. An eternity in Mozart hell passed before The Employer came on the line.

"I presume there is favorable news," The Employer said in lieu of a greeting.

"I did what you asked. I spoke to Director Braun's team. Convinced them the thing is missing. But I don't understand what you fucking hope to gain from all this."

"If the Germans believe it misplaced, they are more likely to lead us to it in their quest to retrieve it. I want it, and if I need to manipulate them or anyone else to acquire it, I will."

"But we got word months ago that it might be in the wind."

The Employer snickered. "I am so relieved to hear the FBI received my message. However, my relentless pursuit to propagate the rumor went unnoticed by the BKA. Thanks to you, all players now hold squares on the board."

"But what if the Germans don't know where it is?"

"Then they will forage until they locate it. As will we."

"You realize if the thing is really gone, it'll be like looking for a fucking needle in a giant fucking pile of needles."

"I assume the BKA's mound of needles will not be quite so high. In fact, my consortia inform me one of their retirees is in San Francisco as we speak. That cannot be coincidence. I would like you to manage the situation. See what he knows. If that avenue does not prove fruitful, I will utilize my contingent in the field to track other potential leads."

"Yeah, they mentioned Schatz is here. I'll handle him. But what is so fucking special about this goddamned thing?"

"Must every other word out of your mouth necessitate an expletive? It is extremely off-putting. Regardless, I have neither the time nor the equanimity for a global economy lesson. So, we will need to defer that answer to another time."

"I don't really care anyway. But I am curious, why me?"

"Your role within the FBI provides you with distinct qualifications. All I require is the occasional task, such as you just performed, and some valid intelligence. My sources informed me you would be willing. Having completed your first assignment, can I surmise they were correct?"

"Oh, I'm willing. But it seems like a hefty sum for a little strong-arm and some intel. What's the catch?"

"There is no catch, as you assert. Procurement of the memory card is critical. And I will do or pay anything to guarantee that outcome."

"So, who's your primary in the field?"

"I am pleased you asked, because this is key. I have retained the services of Sonny Wright. His reputation precedes him. Does it not?"

"It does."

"He is unaware of your identity, and I would like it to remain as such. Stay out of his way. Do not contact him. Am I clear?"

"Crystal."

"Excellent."

"One more question."

"If you must."

"Why all this clandestine bullshit? The call transfer service. The pin numbers. And why the hell would you want to be called The Employer? Why not just go with The Riddler, or The Penguin?"

An audible sigh came through the line. "Highly amusing. It all serves a purpose. Do you know who, or where I am?"

"No, but—"

"Do you comprehend the reach and influence of my organization?"

"Well, not—"

"Are you able to discern whether I'm male or female?"

"Your choice for voice mod is an interesting touch. The Siri voice? Really? Do you have any idea how wrong that is?"

"You know nothing about me, yet I possess a full dossier on you. Your gender is obvious by your undisguised voice, as is your frequent indulgence in cigarettes. I understand you are victim to multiple food allergies which causes you irritable bowels. I am aware of your place of employment, of course, as well as your residence. In fact, I am privy to your location at this very moment."

"I suppose I should have fucking expected that. But do me a favor. Please don't start referring to yourself in the third person. That shit freaks me out."

"So, have we reached an accord?" The Employer asked.

"Hell, for this kind of money, I'm in."

"Outstanding. Now then, *The Employer* would like to know if you have obtained every scrap of information the bureau holds on Layne Stevens."

"Heh. I get it. Fucking hilarious. Yes, I sent you everything we fucking have on the foodie chick. The BKA idiots think Schatz is in San Francisco for her."

"And so the game begins."

6

Layne took in lush greenery lit by thousands of twinkling lights as her cab navigated a steep, winding, one-way drive. But the approach didn't compare to the grand Victorian building that emerged when the taxi rounded the last curve. She'd chosen The Riede Hotel for its reputation and its restaurant, which boasted a seasonal menu of locally grown, organic foods. The historic architecture and secluded location at the top of a hill above Union Square added to its appeal.

"This is incredible," Layne said.

"That'll be forty-two dollars," the driver said. "No cash, only credit."

She swiped her credit card, and the driver pushed a button on the dash to pop the trunk. She opened her own door, slid out of the car, hefted her suitcases from the back, standing the biggest on end, and donned the straps of her tote and laptop bag hoping to manage everything in one trip. A cushy couch, a generous glass of wine, and a refund of her tip to the driver all seemed in order right then.

Suddenly, a bellman sprinted from the hotel and dashed past her. Her gaze followed him to her largest bag, drifting down the drive, its wobbly roll fueled by weight, gravity, and momentum. The suitcase skirted the bend, and both the bag and the bellman disappeared from view. A few moments later, the bellman scaled the narrow road, red-faced, chest heaving, her luggage in tow.

He gulped for air, and sweat dripped from his forehead. "Ms. Stevens, I seized your travel case. Look at it. It is here."

"That was unbelievable," Layne said. "I can't thank you enough."

"You come with heavy baggage, but it was my honor to retrieve it for you."

"You went above and beyond, Mr..."

He bent at the waist and braced his hands against his knees. "My surname is Ajagaonkar, but most find it difficult to pronounce. Please, you must call me Deepshet."

"Oh, all right. Thank you, Dee... um, thank you again, so much. You are a lifesaver."

"I hope a cherry one."

"Pardon?"

"Life Savers, I very much enjoy popping the cherry."

"Oh, uh, well..."

"We are elated to have you here at The Riede," Deepshet continued. "And I am proud to provide you with excellent servicing."

Layne rifled through her purse for a tip that was well-earned, and jumped when the bellman accosted her. Before she could object, he'd untangled her from her belongings, slung them over his shoulders, and motioned her toward the lobby entrance.

"Please, register," Deepshet said. "I will couple with you in your room."

She chuckled as the slight man strode away, engulfed by her bags.

When Layne arrived at her suite, Deepshet opened the stately double doors and set her luggage near the entry to an adjoining bedroom. Then he positioned himself to one side, allowing Layne to take in both the room and the view beyond.

"Holy cow," she said.

"Yes, I believe the sacred cow adequately conveys your meaning. It is lovely, isn't it? We are newly remodeled, and this is our most exquisite suite."

Layne wandered through the lavish sitting area, decorated in white-washed country-French antiques and white, overstuffed furnishings. Throw pillows, bolsters, and decor in rich jewel tones accented the room, and elegantly sheered French doors led to a spacious balcony. Her lips parted in awe at the city lights sparkling through expansive windows, with the Golden Gate Bridge illuminated in the distance.

"Please," Deepshet said. "If I may have you in the bedroom?"

Awe interrupted. "I'm sorry?"

"The bedroom, may I present it to you?"

"Oh, of course."

Layne followed the bellmen to a private master bedroom with an elegant four-poster bed, its fluffy down comforter and oversized pillows almost too inviting to resist. A Queen Anne vanity with a grand mirror sat against one wall, and an enormous antique armoire with an immense door showcasing intricate scrollwork dominated the far corner of the room. The bedroom opened to a large bathroom, with cream-colored marble, thick, rose-scented towels, and a deep whirlpool tub, housing beeswax candles and aromatherapy bath salts.

"This is so luxurious," she said.

Deepshet nodded. "I am glad you approve."

Layne wouldn't have chosen the décor for her own home, but there, it made her feel like royalty. She re-entered the sitting room, kicked off her shoes, stretched out on the pillowy sofa, and let her lids fall shut. Then the enticing sound of melted caramel that had enveloped her on the plane teased her mind. "The pleasure was all mine," Ryan had said. The memory of that seductive tone caused her to crave a sinfully gooey dessert, amongst other things.

She pictured his penetrating blue eyes, recalled the secure feel of his hand when he'd taken hers and not let go, his easy manner, and the small lines around his eyes when he smiled. Wrinkles, she'd call them on herself. But on him, they were just...yummy. She replayed how he'd raked his fingers through his brown hair, cut short on the sides, but a little longer on top, with a touch of gray at the temples. She imagined those fingers—

"One thousand pardons, Madam."

Oh. Shit. She leapt off the couch. "I am so sorry, Deep, uh..."

"No need, madam. I was enlivened to see you in such engaging thought, and reluctant to interrupt."

She thanked the bellman several times, gave him a huge tip, and watched to be sure the door closed behind him before re-engaging with the couch. Then she groaned out loud. She did not need this—getting all wrapped up in school-girl fantasies about a man she'd just met.

She got up again from the couch and walked out to the balcony. A damp breeze nipped at her face, and she folded her arms as the salty aroma of ocean air embraced her. Then she moved closer to the railing to take in the bay, reflecting a brilliant gold from the lights of the bridge. She knew its history—the Golden Gate had earned its name as a lucrative gateway to trade with the orient years before anyone discovered gold in the area—but the vision before her certainly did the name justice.

The lights of the city also beckoned her gaze, but she couldn't shake visions of Ryan. Damn it. She would not get caught up in any more of those salacious thoughts. In fact, who was this person having those kinds of thoughts?

That was all you sister, her little voice said.

Okay, two things worked in her favor. One, short of stalking the San Francisco airport, running into Ryan again seemed unlikely. Two, and most important, she did not want or have time for a romantic relationship in her life.

Uh huh, her little voice said.

She puffed out a breath. First, she'd call for room service—she needed that wine, and a lot more chocolate. Then she'd unpack, map out her schedule for her time in San Francisco, and make her arrangements to go home. There. B-bye, Ryan Cooke.

Sonny climbed the stairs to the top-floor apartment he'd scoped out earlier in the day. Significant water damage to the ceiling and an off-premise landlord meant his use would likely go unnoticed. The lack of electricity didn't concern him, and he felt fortunate to be in the presence of a working toilet. Despite the pervasive smell of mold, this apartment offered the perfect vantage point from the busy street below The Riede Hotel.

True to his military training, he set up a small aluminum folding table, unpacked and assembled his gear, and placed each piece in its designated spot. Precise organization yielded efficiency, and had been the difference between life and death on more than one occasion. Satisfied with his work, he picked up his sniper rifle and panned the scope across the suites of the hotel. She stepped onto her balcony, and Sonny let out a low whistle. He knew she was twelve years older—in fact, he knew everything about Layne Stevens—but hell, what he wouldn't give for a woman like her to notice him, just once.

With careful precision, Sonny directed the gun's scope over every nuance of Layne's body. It wasn't perfect, but for forty-seven she looked damned good. And every curve, every imperfection, enticed him. He trailed her movements and expelled a frustrated breath. The only shot he'd ever have at someone like Layne involved the weapon he held in his hand. And the Employer didn't pay him to watch, or to question, or even to think. He got paid to follow instructions.

Narrowing the focus, he fixed the rifle's scope between her beautiful, unsuspecting eyes.

7

Despite the relatively easy day and the short flight from Los Angeles, exhaustion overtook Ryan during the ride to his condo near Fisherman's Wharf. The driver came around to open his door, and as Ryan got out of the car, he experienced a momentary bout of dizziness. He steadied himself against the car door and took a deep breath.

"Are you all right, sir?" the driver asked.

"Yes, thanks. I'm fine. Just a long day."

"Okay then, you have a nice evening."

Ryan climbed the stairs to his apartment, and nearly bowled over his long-time housekeeper, Sophia, as he walked through the door.

"Oh my, Signor Cooke," Sophia said. "You startled me."

"I'm sorry, Sophia. I guess I was lost in my thoughts."

"So much thinking in your work. You must rest the mind sometimes."

If she only knew. "You're here late tonight," he said.

"Three bambini, grandchildren, home sick today. I care for them while the others work the deli."

"Well, thank you for coming." He surveyed the room. "The place looks perfect, as always."

"Gracie, signor. Your mail is on the counter, and I left Coppa di Testa in the freezer. You have no food. You cannot live on beer."

"Coppa di Testa?"

"Si. Head cheese."

"Pardon?"

"Braised pig's head. Very good for you. It will keep you strong."

His expression remained polite, but his stomach rolled. "Very thoughtful. Thank you."

She turned to leave but stopped, and her eyebrows came together when she faced him. "You have something you want to ask me."

She was too damned perceptive. "I don't think so."

Sophia waited before she spoke again. "Okay, then, enjoy the evening."

"Sophia, wait."

"Yes?"

"This may sound silly." He hesitated. "But do you believe in fate?"

"Fate, signor?"

"Like when you sense you were meant to meet someone."

"Oh, Signor Cooke, you are quite pleasing to the eye, but I am a married woman. Besides, you are too young." Her face lit as she studied him. "Ah," she said. "All kidding to the side, signor. I believe this fate very much to be true. And when you feel it, you will know it as well. Or perhaps you have felt it already, yes?"

Before he could respond, she closed the door behind her. What just happened? He stared at the back of the door for a moment, then pushed the conversation from his mind and went about his routine. He put his phone, gun, and wallet in a wicker basket on the entry table, hung his jacket and tie on a suit valet near the door, and flipped through his mail.

Ryan lived in a one-bedroom condo, small by most standards, but roomy for San Francisco. Decorated in black and brown tones, with sparse but high-quality furnishings in dark woods and leather, it sat over Nakamura's fish market across the street from Pier 27. The odor from the market sometimes overwhelmed the place, but he didn't spend much time there, and he didn't entertain, so he chose to overlook it for a magnificent view of the bay.

He loosened his shirt collar, entered the small kitchen, and resisted a peculiar urge to inspect the pig's head resting in his freezer. Instead, he grabbed an amber ale from the fridge. Then he raised a window in the family room, letting the cool night air roll in, and sat on the couch to soak up the panorama of the Golden Gate Bridge lights shimmering on the water. Ryan often took this solace at the end of his workday. Most evenings, the lights, the beer, and the sound of the waves lapping at the pier pilings helped to clear his head, but Ryan couldn't relax.

Looking down at his pants, stained with red wine and brownie, he shook his head. Waking up with a woman clutched to his side...hell, she was lucky he hadn't shot her. But she intrigued him. She was tall, with a big, inviting smile, eyes like milk chocolate with tiny flecks of gold, and long, thick, wavy brown hair. But it wasn't just her looks that appealed to him. She had an energy and a genuine nature he found irresistible, and she smelled...amazing. He pictured her incident in the terminal, and the corner of his lips turned up. Was he a jerk for not going back to help? He hadn't wanted to embarrass her. He only hoped he'd ducked out the exit in time.

Then he recalled the flight attendant's surprise when he'd asked for Layne's name. Apparently, she was somewhat famous. He went to his desk, powered up his computer, and typed "Layne Stevens" into the search engine. Her picture appeared on the first results line—*Food Made Whole,* hosted by Layne Stevens, and presented by The Foodie Channel. Hunh. An entire channel dedicated to food. What would be next, a station for gardening? He clicked on the link and leaned in. A cook? Hell, the woman had her own top-rated show.

He scrolled down the page and skimmed the collection of articles, videos, and images—Layne with movie stars, Layne with children, Layne with athletes, Layne at charity events. All the pictures had one thing in common, the same thing he'd noticed at the airport. No ring. Damn it. What the hell was he doing? Even if Sophia had been right, he couldn't act on a random attraction. His job allowed room for the occasional date, but not some sort of foolish attachment. He didn't need this. He would not get hung up on Layne Stevens. He returned to the couch. But while he fended off thoughts of Layne, his head tipped back, his eyelids drooped, and her smile captured his mind as he drifted off to sleep.

Several hours later, something in Ryan's subconscious woke him. Groggy, he hoisted himself off the sofa, switched off the family room lights, and headed toward the bedroom. His collapse on the bed seemed imminent until a faint noise caught his attention.

He glanced back. Through the darkness formed the outline of a man standing near his entry table. The man turned, and Ryan rushed at him. A hand lashed out, and too exhausted to defend himself, Ryan felt the familiar pain of skilled fingers pinching the carotid pressure points on either side of his neck. His vision blurred, his body sagged, and Ryan's world went black.

Sonny made decent time returning from Fisherman's Wharf and arrived back at the abandoned apartment just before midnight. He resumed his post, training his binoculars on Layne's suite, and indulged in a small grin. She was still awake. He found most reconnaissance assignments grueling, but not this one. He could have watched Layne Stevens all night. She shifted her activities to the bedroom, where, fortunately for him, the shutters were tilted open, and more than his interest rose as she undressed.

She unbuttoned her blouse and walked to the dresser on the far wall. Sonny put down the binoculars and picked up his rifle, counting once again on the gun's scope for a more precise image. He followed, and then lost her for a moment. She returned wearing a white lace bra and orange panties with Saturday printed across the behind. He snickered, wondering what she'd done with Monday's underwear. With her shapely Saturday ass to the window, Layne took off her bra, assessed herself in the bureau mirror, took a healthy pinch of skin at her waist, and shrugged.

Layne's backside shielded her reflection, but Sonny felt certain the shrug wasn't justified. She slipped into an oversized t-shirt and turned to face him. Damned shirt. Then she walked toward the windows and peered through the shutters at the street below, before tipping them closed. Just as well. A need had arisen that demanded his attention, and he couldn't take care of that need with a sniper rifle in his hand. His phone honked. He'd expected the call, but the timing stunk.

"We're on schedule, I presume," The Employer said.

"Yup."

"Is something wrong?"

Sonny cleared his throat. "Nope."

"There were no issues at Cooke's residence?"

"I had a situation, but I handled it."

"Then everything has been managed? Including Cooke's phone?"

How many times did he have to go over this shit? "Yup. I made the switch."

"Excellent. Is your location acceptable?"

"Oh, yeah. I have an awesome view of Ms. Stevens."

Several seconds elapsed. "You are not there for the view, Mr. Wright."

"Sure," Sonny said. "But I'm curious, why the active surveillance when both of their phones are tagged to record?"

"For exactly what the term implies—circumstances may dictate a necessity to take action."

"And by action you mean..."

"I am not paying you this kind of money simply to play peeping Tom, Mr. Wright."

"I get that. What circumstances?"

"Answers will be disclosed when I choose to disclose them."

"Okay, it's your dime."

"And, I'm confident a dime well spent."

The line went dead, and Sonny bit back a growl. He couldn't let The Employer get to him. Checking one final time on Layne's suite, he noted that her lights were out. He hoped she would rest well. She'd need it.

8

Layne exited The Riede to brilliant sunlight casting off a wispy morning fog. A crisp breeze met her face, and she inhaled the invigorating scent of ocean spray mingled with spring blooms. Eager to distract herself from the events surrounding her airport belly flop, she flagged a cab.

The Kebab House topped her list—a Mediterranean cafe known for its organic falafel and grass-fed beef and lamb kebabs. Her taxi pulled to the curb, and she rolled down the window, taking in an aromatic whiff of braised meat and savory spices. Then she spotted the flashing neon sign: "Proudly Serving Osama's Extra Big Kebabs." Hmm. Would her viewers want to see Osama's big kebabs? She stayed in the cab.

The Whole Jelly Deli came next. A chalkboard perched outside the door advertised use of all natural, freshly prepared ingredients, with over twenty different sandwiches, on organic, sprouted, whole-grain breads. A peanut butter with bacon and fig jam on fermented sourdough tempted her. It didn't suit the "Appetizers to Die For" theme she'd planned for her upcoming episode, but she'd try to get back there for lunch.

On the way to her next stop, the taxi traveled past Ghirardelli Square. Nowhere close to a fit for the segment, stopping there didn't make sense. But the aroma of chocolate permeated the cab. Nope, she had a long list of places to visit. She glanced at the cute shops. Focus, Layne. Stick to the plan. Oh, hell. For several hours, Layne basked in the luxury of upscale boutiques, fine dining, and the unrivaled aromas and tastes of Ghirardelli chocolate. She missed lunch at the Whole Jelly Deli, but oh, yes, she'd died and gone to chocolate heaven.

Drawn to unique small businesses, Layne stopped at a tiny store just off the square. Choco-Latte specialized in pairing Ghirardelli certified kosher chocolate creations with various types of organic coffee. She polished off four dark chocolate and almond clusters with sea salt, and sipped on a fair-trade, organic, hazelnut mocha, reveling in the pure decadence. A contented sigh escaped her. Layne loved her job. And a woman did need her energy for such tough work.

The sun eased its way toward the coastline, and what had she accomplished? Well, nothing on her list. But she had confirmed that Ghirardelli Square ranked well above that theme park as the happiest place on Earth. Reluctant to leave the chocolate wonderland, but several miles from her hotel, Layne set out at a decent clip to hail another cab. She traversed the slants and slopes of the city with no taxi in sight, and finally stopped to lean against a lamp post. Her thighs ached, her lungs burned, and of course, her damned little voice had an opinion.

If you worked out more, this wouldn't be an issue, it said.

Layne flicked her little voice into a muddy pothole and continued her pursuit of a taxi, leaving the voice in the street to drown.

Her cell phone buzzed in her pocket.

"Hey, Maggie," Layne said. "Are you here?"

"Finally. Two hours late—damned airlines. How was your flight last night?

"Uh..."

"Sweetie, did you toss your cookies on some poor stranger again?"

"No. It wasn't the smoothest flight I've ever had, but it wasn't the worst."

"I knew I should have gone with you."

"I don't need a babysitter, Mags. I appreciate the concern, but it was fine. I'm here, and that's all that matters."

"I can't picture myself as a babysitter. Although there was that one guy that wanted me to—"

"Maggie."

"Oh, all right, miss tighty panties. Are we ready for tonight?"

"All set. Where are you now?"

"I'm at...wait a minute, what's with all the heavy breathing? Were you having sex?"

"Oh, please. Think about who you're talking to."

"Good point. Then why are you panting like a rabid dog?"

"I'm walking."

"Like, for exercise?"

"Because I can't find a cab."

"That's a relief. For a second, I thought you'd lost your mind."

"Jeez. What is it with you naturally skinny people? Some of us have to exercise, Mags. I work out three times a week. Usually. I do yoga. Sometimes. I walk. Like right now. And I took kickboxing once. I exercise because I need to. Not everyone can channel the curves of Mae West like you do."

"Okay, okay. Don't get your ta-ta's in a tangle. But I'll tell you this, if I keep producing your show, I'll be channeling the curves of Harriet the Hippo sooner than later. I am so dreading my forties."

"We're already in our forties, Mags."

"Shush. Someone might hear you."

A gust of wind whirled around her, and Layne swept her hair off her face to scan the area. "There's no one here, and at this rate I may never get a cab."

"See? If you'd stayed in and had sex, not only would you not need to exercise, you'd be having a hell of a lot more fun, and you'd already be at the hotel."

"There isn't anyone I'm interested in having sex with." Layne's mind darted to Ryan.

"Because you're a prude?" Maggie asked.

Damn it. Why was Ryan still in her head?

"Layne, are you there?"

"Yes. And I am not a prude. I'm just..."

"Just what?"

"We've talked about this, Mags. I'm not ready."

"It's been five years, hun. What's it gonna take?"

Layne didn't want to have this conversation again. "Besides," she said. "Ghirardelli Square might actually be better than sex."

"You know how I feel about chocolate, but better than sex?"

"And, if I'd been having sex, I wouldn't have any research done for the show."

"True. So, you found some places that will work?"

"Uh, okay, Mags, see you tonight." She tapped to end the call.

Layne wasn't good at lying, and hanging up meant she didn't have too. She glanced down to ensure her phone made it back into her pocket just as one of those elusive taxis passed her by. It veered close to the curb. Too close. And muck from a pothole splashed from the cab's tire, soaking Layne's entire right side. She stilled—a slimy, soggy statue of her former self. It didn't happen often, but when it did, little voice payback was a bitch.

LAYNE ARRIVED BACK at The Riede at a little past four with mud caked to her skin and clothes, still wet undergarments pinching at her more covert parts, and jeans that had transformed to moist sandpaper against her inner thighs. She regretted it the minute she entered the hotel lobby without first taking a peek inside, and made a bow-legged dash to hide behind a decorative tree. From there, she scrutinized every inch of the Victorian parlor for a way around the crowd, and then resigned herself to her fate. She searched her purse for a hair band, peeled the crusty wedge of hair off her face, raked her fingers through the stringy chaos, and fastened it into a messy bun at the back of her head. Then she plastered on a smile and waddled into the crowd.

9

Layne woke on a hard surface, with a fuzzy mind and a painful lump on the back of her head. A cool cloth blotted her face, and vibrant green eyes set off by curly, flaming-red hair were distinct against the blur of people talking above her. Someone called her name, urged her to focus, and Layne's memory came back to her.

"Oh, god. There's a dead guy in that beautiful armoire."

"Yes, honey," Maggie said. "Are you all right? You passed out. Let me help you up."

"Why?"

"So you can rest on the couch, hun."

"No, I mean why is there a dead guy in the closet?"

"Here, let's get you out of this room." Maggie helped her off the floor, and did her best to steer, as Layne weaved her way to the sitting room sofa.

"How did you get in?" Layne asked.

"You left the doors open. That funny little bellman saw the body and called the police."

"I heard someone scream."

"Yes, sweetie, that was you. Layne, honey, is there something you want to tell me?"

"It wasn't me, I swear. I didn't do it!"

"Not that, I'm talking about your...well...this new look. Sort of grunge meets grungier. What the hell happened?"

Layne looked down at her clothing and felt the sting of tears forming in her eyes. "It hasn't been a very good day."

Maggie wrapped a firm arm around her shoulders. "I'm so sorry sweetie. You don't need to talk about it now. How about I get you a nice cup of hot tea?"

"Tea? Okay. Tea is good."

A few minutes later Maggie handed Layne a steaming mug of hot black tea. She inhaled the calming aroma from just above the rim and took a soothing sip. Then one of the uniformed men sauntered over, and her jaw dropped. The man looked more like an old Mountie than a San Francisco police officer. He wore a wide-brimmed hat on top of course, unruly gray hair. A Mounties-style uniform strained over a belly that had seen its fair share of pints. And a full, predominantly gray mustache hid all evidence of lips.

Maggie let out a snort. "What happened? You forget your horse?"

The man twirled a toothpick with his tongue, giving him a slight drawl. "My mount retired," he said. "Lord only knows why I couldn't have gone with it."

Layne flashed on her research, and a vague recollection of police officers riding horseback in Golden Gate Park came to her.

"Ms. Stevens, I'm Sergeant Temple. Nice to meet you, ma'am. I'm sorry we can't give you more time."

His tone said otherwise.

"More time?" Layne asked.

"Do you have any idea what happened here?"

Tears pooled again. "There was a dead man in the closet."

"Uh huh. We know that. Anything else?"

"All that blood."

"Yep, there was a boatload of blood."

Maggie glared at the Sergeant.

"And he was so...blue," Layne said, squirming a little.

"Yeah, happens when you're dead," Sergeant Temple said.

"Oh, I almost forgot the silver tray!"

"Oddest damn thing I've ever seen. Ma'am, can you tell us anything we don't know?"

Maggie cut in. "Apparently, you don't know, Sergeant tactful, that women prefer to have men gawk at their faces when conversing with them, not their breasts. And would it kill you to be the slightest bit sensitive? She's had a traumatic day."

Sergeant Temple leered at Maggie. "And you are?"

"I'm Maggie Malone, Layne's producer, and her best friend. And I'm your worst nightmare if you don't stop undressing her with your eyes."

His gaze fixed on Layne's face. "Ma'am, did you recognize the man?"

"I didn't get a great look at him, but I don't think so."

"That's what we suspected." Sergeant Temple scratched his mustache. "Turns out this incident may be linked to some federal case. We'll need to wait for the F-ing, uh, I mean, the Federal Bureau Agent in Charge before we ask any more questions."

The hair stood on Layne's arms. "Federal Bureau?"

"FBI Counterintelligence, ma'am. Gadgets, secret spy stuff. It's all counter-intelligent if you ask me."

Her vision swam. "Can I lie down?"

"Now see what you've done?" Maggie said. "I finally had her calm."

"Sorry, ma'am. But I'm on the clock."

"Don't you ma'am me," Maggie said. "And go be on the clock somewhere else."

Sergeant Temple's eyes meandered from Maggie's face to her chest and all the way down before he strolled away.

Maggie glowered at the sergeant's back, then turned to Layne. "All right, honey, ignore him. Everything's gonna be fine."

"You know," Layne said in a daze. "If you didn't wear such low-cut sweaters, that might not happen so often."

"Jeez, Layne, I'm not stupid. Mammary obsession is a universal male weakness that I use to my advantage whenever possible. And it's well worth minor inconveniences like farmer Joe Friday over there."

"Uh huh. What's an aneurysm?"

"I'm no expert," Maggie said. "But I think it's a blood clot that makes your head explode."

"That's it. That's what I have. Is there a doctor in here somewhere?"

"You'll be fine, hun. Just lie down for a bit. Okay?"

Layne examined the room as she lay on the couch. White dust coated various surfaces in the suite, and masses of people shuffled in and out despite the cross of yellow crime scene tape flapping in the entry. Hotel staff talked of plans to pack up her things, and Maggie flirted with men in uniform, while ensuring Layne wasn't unduly disturbed. She couldn't see the door through the crowd, but she observed that everyone snapped into action.

It's about time, her little voice said. *The f-ing agent in charge.*

Layne wavered to an upright position and attempted to secure her balance, sketchy on a normal day. A well-dressed man stopped to talk with some of the other suits, then headed for her.

She froze. "Ryan?"

His brow wrinkled. "I'm sorry, have we met?"

10

Outside the glass walls of the meeting room, the central area of BKA headquarters hummed with activity, but Berger ignored it. He'd had no luck with his usual contacts and time ran thin. So, he called the only other person he could think of to call. He hadn't made contact in some time. But he hoped she would understand the urgency. His knee bounced at a rapid pace, and his chest tightened with every unanswered ring that sounded through the speaker of his unregistered cell phone. His thumb moved to end the call, but someone came on the line.

"We require your help," Berger said in place of a greeting.

"What the hell?" a tired female voice said through a yawn. "It's frickin' midnight in California."

"The memory card appears to be missing."

"You're a little late to the party, Hans. Word is, your man, Schatz, lost the damned thing."

"Do you know where he is?"

"We know he's here. Don't worry. We'll find him. And hopefully, he'll lead us to the card."

"Sherry, there is concern he may attempt something...rash."

"Okay. But there's nothing I can do in the middle of the night.

"You understand how important this is?"

"Hans, I get it."

"Thank you. About how we left—"

"Oh, jesus. Please stop while you're not too far behind."

He paused, uncertain what to say next, so he shifted back to the topic at hand. "This must happen quickly."

"Hans, if Schatz is here, it won't take a bloodhound to find him. Trust me. I will handle it. In the morning. After I've had my coffee. Can I go back to bed now?"

11

Layne's mouth hung open. She had clung to Ryan Cooke like an octopus. He'd chased after her to return her phone. He'd...lingered! How did he not remember?

Maggie rushed to Layne's side. "Sweetie, do you know this man?"

Layne couldn't respond.

"You'd better not be some crazed fan," Maggie said to Ryan.

His lips pursed, and Maggie turned a critical eye to Layne. "Hun, what the hell is going on?"

Layne answered Maggie's question, but her focus remained on Ryan. "We met last night on the plane." There was the brow-wrinkling thing again. Did he really not remember her?

Maggie's stance relaxed as she leveled an obvious once-over at Ryan. "Oh, my. You are one delicious man."

Layne pressed her fingertips to her forehead. Even her stupid little voice had no comment. But she did hear an annoying drawl.

"I see you two have met," Sergeant Temple said. "I've been informed that Special Agent Cooke here, and his band of merry men, will act as your twenty-four-seven until the FBI can sort through this mess. So, the SFPD will be moving out."

"Excuse me, my what?"

"Your around the clock bodyguards, ma'am."

Layne felt a swoosh of all color draining from her face, and raised her hand to speak. But before she could form a coherent sentence, several more men in dark business suits entered the suite, and Sergeant Temple scurried for the door.

"I'll be right back," Ryan said.

Maggie watched Ryan walk away, her eyes settled unapologetically on his ass. "Oh, I can't wait to hear this story," she said.

"What story?"

"The one about you and that hunk of Special Agent in Charge. I'd be his babysitter. Hold on, is that why you sounded so distracted earlier?"

"I was not distracted."

"Jesus, Layne, there's nothing wrong with showing a little interest. It's okay to have needs."

Layne cast her gaze to the ceiling. "Oh my god. Can we please not talk about this here? Or anywhere? Ever again?"

"You know, Dr. Matthews told me that he and his hot new girlfriend are doing the horizontal mambo every night."

"As in, seventy years old, Dr. Matthews?"

"Says he feels like a new man." Maggie's eyebrows bobbled.

"And now I'm going to need a new dentist. You are such a bitch. It is not easy to find a good dentist."

"Someone's got to add sizzle to your life." Maggie's attention floated to a crime scene tech with bulging biceps.

"I have sizzle," Layne said.

Maggie wandered away.

"I order fajitas at least once a week," Layne called after her, shaking her head as Maggie disappeared into the crowd. She frowned. Maggie would have found the fajita comment funny if she wasn't so preoccupied. She wrapped her arms around herself and took stock of her situation. There really wasn't anything funny about it. Her skin felt tight, her lungs strained for air, and stabbing knots had taken up residence between her shoulder blades. This would all be okay if she could just go home.

She scanned the room. Ryan had vanished, and Sergeant Temple was likely in Oregon at the pace of his departure. The whole thing made her uncomfortable. Ryan made her uncomfortable. Hell, even Maggie was making her uncomfortable. A very tall, very slender, very stiff man in a navy polyester suit walked by.

"Pardon me," she said, reaching for his sleeve.

"Oh, Ms. Stevens. I apologize for not introducing myself earlier. I'm Special Agent Kirby Short, Senior Investigative Agent responsible for the crime scene and forensics. And I'll be handling your room transition."

Layne craned her neck to study the agent. She noted a prominent chin, dirty-blond hair cemented into place by an abnormal amount of hair gel, and an unusually beige pallor.

"Are you all right?" the agent asked. "You seem…muddy."

"Oh, that," Layne said. "Happens all the time. You're very tall."

"Yes, ma'am."

"I'm sorry, your name was?"

He hesitated. "Special Agent Short, ma'am."

"Oh." She suspected a deficiency in the sense of humor department, and chose to let the irony pass. "Is all this room stuff necessary? I really should be getting home."

The agent stared over her head as he spoke. "I'm afraid that won't be possible."

"What? But why?"

"We understand it's not ideal."

"I'd like to know why I'm being detained."

"I'll leave those details to Agent Cooke. He went to check on a few things, but he'll be back momentarily. We have two rooms reserved down the hall, one for the security team and one for the two of you."

"The two of us?"

His gaze remained steadily above her. "Yes, you and Agent Cooke."

Her throat closed. "Me and Agent Cooke."

"He'll stay with you in your new suite, on the couch of course. We feel it would be best all around."

"All around where? He's not going to follow me into the bathroom, is he?"

"Not unless it's deemed necessary."

"You're joking, right?"

"I assure you, I never joke about a crime scene, Ms. Stevens."

Suspicion confirmed. Layne inhaled deeply through her nose. "What if I declined?"

"I don't understand," he said.

"What if I chose to leave?"

"I'm afraid leaving is not an option."

"So, you're forcing me to stay."

"Force is a strong word. We're providing you with secure accommodations while we investigate. It may only be a few days."

Her jaw dropped. "A few days?"

"I apologize for the confusion, but I assure you, you're in good hands with Agent Cooke. Perhaps he'll be able to shed more light. It was very nice meeting you." The agent continued toward the bedroom, but called back over his shoulder to her. "Be sure to let me know if you need anything."

She did. She needed several shots of tequila and a truckload of chocolate.

Maggie edged her way near.

"Not a word," Layne said.

"Oh, honey. There is too much material to work with. Between Mr. Tall, who is actually Agent Short, and sharing a room with Special Agent good hands, I wouldn't know where to begin."

Layne narrowed her eyes at Maggie. "Thank you for your restraint."

"Sweetie, I've never seen you this uptight."

"There's a dead man, Maggie, in that bedroom."

"But still."

"I'm a hostage!"

"And your captor is a hot guy with handcuffs."

Layne clamped her lips together.

"Okay, calm down," Maggie said. "This sucks. But they can't keep you here against your will, can they?"

Agent Short passed by again, and this time Maggie stopped him. "You can't make her stay if she wants to go home, can you?"

"No, of course not," Agent Short said. "I mean, not me personally. But the FBI can detain her for as long as necessary." He glanced at Layne and rushed off.

When Maggie turned back to Layne, her eyes popped. "Whoa, sweetie, that nostril flare thing is very unattractive."

Layne growled.

"Hmm," Maggie said. "I've seen that look before. Whatever you're planning, I want in."

SONNY'S PHONE honked at him for the fourth time in thirty minutes, and his eyes flicked to the popcorn ceiling of the run-down apartment. Frickin' Employer. At least this conversation had clarified his objective. But he didn't like it, and he hoped Layne wouldn't force him to do something they would both regret.

He found Layne in his scope and noted that she looked a little less fresh than she had that morning, but she still looked totally hot. He watched her pace her suite, gnaw at her fingernails, wring her hands. He'd seen it before. The unease caused by lack of control. The itch to run and hide. But he wouldn't need to act, because Layne Stevens wouldn't run. No, she'd do as instructed and trust the pretty boy to protect her, not grasping the gravity of her situation until it was too late.

She moved across the room, and he lost her as she passed between two windows. He followed the wall and waited for her to appear on the other side. Then he panned back. What the hell? Did she take a seat at the table? Unlikely in her state, but possible. Shitty walls. He broadened the focal range of the rifle scope. She'd be back in his sight soon enough.

12

Loud conversation, organized commotion, and the pungent aroma of strong coffee filled the suite down the hall at The Riede, as tactical agents hooked up equipment, performed sound and video checks, verified tracers on phone lines, and planned strategic placement of security personnel. Ryan expected no less, having handpicked his unit.

He noted a large flip-chart page stuck to the far wall and frowned. Betting pools were a normal diversion for the surveillance team, meant to ease the tension of an often-grueling job. This pool, titled "Layne Stevens," offered three wagering options: "Foreign Op," "Ex-Girlfriend," and "Just Damned Unlucky." Votes were cast in all three columns, indicated by agent initials. Smarter agents had not yet voted.

"All right, listen up," Ryan said, and all heads turned his way. "Let's get a few things straight. Many of you heard Ms. Stevens address me by my first name, but she is not an ex-girlfriend."

Ryan spotted the lean build, dark brown hair, and dark eyes of his senior equipment technician, Agent Chance Rusk, behind the server racks, with his hand raised.

"Rusk?"

"You gotta admit, boss," Rusk said. "She is hot. Too hot to be on the Home and Garden Network, or whatever the hell it is."

"I understand this is all in fun, but let's try to show some respect," Ryan said. "Did you say there's a garden network?"

"I don't know," Rusk said. "I don't watch that shit."

"Hunh. Where are we with systems?"

"Ready to go," Rusk said. "Securing the last of the cables now."

"Great work," Ryan said. "Hawk?"

"Yeah, boss?"

"Last I heard you were in charge of muscle. And please keep your update professional, or you and Rusk will be on latrine duty for the duration of the op."

Agent Jeron Hawk's eyebrows lifted. Something about the young agent always lifted Ryan's mood. He had curly, dirty-blond hair that preferred a state of disarray. Mischief danced in his hazel eyes. And the kid never had a bad day. Or if he did, he didn't show it.

"Before you sentence us to the fancy latrine," Hawk said, "you should know that yesterday I caught Rusk switching back and forth between the Garden Channel and the Shopping Network."

Rusk swung his head out from behind the racks. "That's bullshit."

"Hey, don't blame me if you can't keep your sensitive side in check," Hawk said.

Rusk used his middle finger to rub the side of his nose, and Hawk responded with a cocky grin.

"Okay, Hawk," Ryan said. "Security detail?"

"Right, boss. Hansel and Gretel are your primary muscle, like always. And I got two men sleepin' in the hall, two watchin' the hookers out front, four loadin' up on caffeine in the lobby, and two guys in the alley under the balcony hoping to get a view under her skirt."

Ryan's voice rose over the laughter. "What part of professional are we not grasping here?" The laughter stopped. "Marco, give me the rundown on tech."

Technical specialist and surveillance team lead, Special Agent Marco Viorantelli, oozed the confidence of a man who could secure a room in his sleep. In his mid-fifties with black, wavy, slicked-back hair, and leathery skin, he carried a small build but the strength of men half his age, with enough energy to make a toddler seem lazy.

"All set, boss," Marco said. "We got multiple ears in both rooms and eyes on the TV room, on the balcony, and in the hall. We also got eyes on the lobby and all the entrances."

"Perfect," Ryan said. "What else?"

"No eyes in the bedroom or the crapper, and no ears on the balcony. Too much road noise. Got a tracer on her cell, but like always we'd need time to track. Wired the hotel landline, but hell, no one uses 'em anymore."

"Nice job, Marco." Ryan scanned the room. "Anything else?"

"With respect, sir," a female voice said. "You've told us she's not an ex, but I don't see an approach that assumes she's a foreign op."

Ryan took in the six-foot-tall frame, short blond hair, all-business attire, and severely attractive features of Special Agent Sherry Rennick. She had no discernible body fat and no apparent social skills. But she knew what she wanted, and had the determination to get it. She'd graduated with honors from Cornell University Law School after a four-year stint in the military.

Senior by rank but junior in experience, she carried a reputation for being a little over the top, and no man on Ryan's team screwed with Rennick unless he wanted his ass kicked. But he'd requested her for his unit because of her eagerness and her tenacious attention to detail. She also told it like she saw it, which, given recent events, he feared may work against him.

"Continue," he said.

"Well, sir, it's too coincidental. They reseated Stevens next to you on the plane, and she lands in the center of our investigation. Appears to be the biggest break we've had, but it feels contrived, almost like a setup. And all things considered, sir, you went pretty easy on her just now."

Rennick had done her homework. In fact, she knew more than he did. If she'd disclosed the information accurately, they had one hell of a coincidence on their hands. And Ryan didn't believe in them. He had never encountered a legitimate coincidence. There was always some connection. Too bad. Layne Stevens seemed like a nice woman. And he liked her smile. But the karmic rule of coincidence meant she was somehow involved. The room fell silent while the agents waited for his response.

"Okay," Ryan said. "Let's talk about approach. I am reiterating, on the record, that Layne Stevens and I have not met before this week. We will pursue the two remaining angles. Either she's a foreign operative, and she's damned good, or she's incredibly unlucky to have stumbled into this thing. I want her personal history—relatives, living and deceased, where they came from, where they are now, and who they're connected to. Friends, acquaintances, neighbors, co-workers, businesses she frequents, and anything else you can find. Get me a detailed biography of Layne Stevens by tonight. Got it?"

Ryan waited for the request to sink in before he went on. "I will continue to go easy on Ms. Stevens," he looked at Rennick, "and play the sympathetic bodyguard. If she's an op, I don't want to raise suspicion. And either way, I need to gain her trust. Remember, solving this murder would be a bonus, and it may even help with the investigation, but it's not our primary focus. Our sights are still set on finding that memory card. Any other questions?"

Rusk snapped a panel onto the back of a server, and the sound bounced through the stillness of the room.

"What are we waiting for?" Ryan asked.

The team erupted into action, and Ryan pulled Marco aside. "Do we have information on the vic, or any more intel on the missing card?"

"Nothing new on the card, boss," Marco said. "And we don't have an ID on the vic yet, but it's gotta be him."

Ryan let out a breath. "All right, keep me posted. What prelims do we have on Stevens?"

Marco went over the initial details he'd gathered on Layne.

"Good. More digging, Marco," Ryan said. "We need more to go on. And I want you to do something else for me, but this is between us."

"Sure thing, boss."

"Track the movement of this cell number for the last twenty-four hours."

Marco studied the sticky note with Ryan's phone number scribbled on it. "What's going on?"

"I honestly don't know. But until we find out, I'll just have to fake it."

13

Layne peeked out to the hall. Two enormous agents stood several feet away, distracted by the charms of Maggie Malone. Well, that, and Maggie's blatant display of ample cleavage. A group of crime scene technicians headed toward the double doors. Layne merged into the crowd and left the suite.

It killed her, but she didn't turn back to see if anyone noticed. The group stopped at the elevator, and she passed them to head for the stairs. At the bottom floor, she eased open the stairwell door, and then pulled it shut. The bellman who had helped with her luggage was headed straight for her. Her pulse quickened. Think, Layne. But instead of rational thought, her little voice accosted her.

What the hell are you doing? You are not following the rules. Return to your suite, right now.

Layne turned toward the steps, then stopped. No. If they wanted to reach her, they could call her cell. Besides, it was three full flights of stairs, and she did not intend to pant and sweat in front of Special Agent Ryan Cooke.

The bellman didn't enter the stairwell, and Layne peered out again at the lobby. Only a few guests strolled through the ornate Victorian parlor. She put her head down, pushed the door open, and hurried toward the main exit.

A familiar voice called to her. "Ms. Stevens, hello."

She kept walking while she spoke. "Deepsh... Hello. So nice to see you. But I'm in kind of a rush."

He followed. "I am acquainted with the happenings upstairs. That must have been horrendous for you. Are you faring well? I notice that you are leaving crumbles of soil in the path of your behind."

"Yes, yes, I'm fine. Thanks. But I really need to leave."

"Oh, you cannot go out the front."

She stopped. "What? Why?"

"The entrance is blocked by very wide men. No one in or out without a lengthy and, might I say, thorough search."

She scanned the foyer. Damn. Federal security men everywhere.

"Come," Deepshet said. "I will take you in the kitchen. From there is a path through the garden to the main thoroughfare, on which you may hail a cab. If you are in a hurry, it would be the fastest way."

She touched his arm. "Thank you. You truly are a lifesaver."

"This time I prefer to be one that is Deepshet flavored."

He smiled as he led Layne to the back of the hotel and ferried her through the busy kitchen to the rear door. After he'd gone, she waffled. It wasn't too late to turn back. Yes, yes, it was. Through a small window in the service door, Layne saw two men standing guard at the exit. But a restaurant shift had just ended. Waitresses, bussers, and prep cooks, all dressed in street clothes, began leaving together. Again, she submerged herself into the crowd. The security detail, more interested in people going in than out, regarded them with a passing glance. She was halfway down the path when one of the men said, "Hey, aren't you Layne Stevens?"

Layne stared at the ground. "No. No, I'm not." She had always been a terrible liar.

"Oh, yes, you are. What happened to your hair?"

Unsure if anyone else had heard the exchange, and not caring to find out, she bolted into the thick, tall brush that edged the narrow path.

~

SONNY'S PHONE quacked at him as he searched the windows of the suite with his scope. The duck call signaled trouble, but provided a welcomed break from The Employer. He tapped his bluetooth. "Talk."

He listened as he put his weapon in its assigned spot, grabbed the binoculars, and moved closer to the window of the apartment to focus on the street below. Layne tumbled from the bushes onto the sidewalk, with twigs and leaves sticking out of her hair. Had she lost her ef-ing mind? He had to hand it to her—the woman had balls. But the situation triggered a directive he didn't want to carry out. Layne was not to leave protective custody. Not alive. With his eyes still fixed on Layne, he placed the binoculars back on the table, reached for his sniper rifle, and with his finger on the trigger, once again sighted Layne in his scope.

14

A substantial man with an earpiece and a tight gray suit intercepted Layne's path on the sidewalk below The Riede. She spun around to walk the other direction, and another suited giant blocked her way. Within seconds, a hotel golf cart pulled up. No words were exchanged as she climbed into the back, and the two men sandwiched Layne into the minuscule vehicle like oversized bookends. She longed to go back to the happiest place on Earth, but the cart zipped toward the narrow road to the hotel.

"Wait," Layne said to the driver. "Was that a pub?" The driver didn't respond.

Layne re-entered the suite to an empathetic grimace from Maggie. Then she perched on the edge of the sofa and awaited the repercussions of her attempted escape. At least she'd avoided taking the stairs.

Ryan returned and stopped to speak with Mr. Tall. Then Layne heard the pale agent clearing the room. She listened to Maggie accept a dinner invitation from the young, bicep-flexing crime scene tech. She overheard staff in uniforms and suits grumble about needing more time, and she watched Ryan come to sit beside her. His lips moved, but she didn't hear a word he said.

"Ms. Stevens, are you listening?"

She peered down at her hands.

"I realize this has been rough on you," Ryan said. "But there are a few things I'd like to discuss."

She corralled her thoughts and looked him square in the eyes. "All right, Agent Cooke. You have my attention."

"Thank you," he said. "First, I'd like to know what happened here?" He waved his hand over the general disarray of Layne's clothing and hair.

"An evil taxi driver and a pothole full of muddy water conspired against me."

Ryan's eyebrows lifted. "Oh. So, nothing to do with the current situation?"

"As it affects you, I guess not. But it is definitely affecting me. In more ways than I'm willing to share."

"Is that why you left?"

"Finding a hot shower wouldn't be the worst idea I've had today, but I left because being detained against my will isn't high on my bucket list."

His tone softened. "I apologize. I should have gone over the arrangements with you myself. I'm very sorry about all this."

She let out a sigh. "I shouldn't have just gone. I get that. But I told the Dudley Do-Right Sergeant everything I know, which, by the way, isn't much. Why do I have to be here?"

"Because we can't keep you safe if we let you go."

"Safe from what?"

"We're not sure. Until we understand what's going on, we don't want to take any chances."

"So, Agent Cooke, I'm supposed to believe I'm being held hostage for my own protection?"

The corner of his lips turned upward. "That's the story I had planned to go with. And please, it's Ryan. Can I still call you Layne?"

"Then, you do remember me?"

A voice called from across the room. "Agent Cooke, we need a moment."

Ryan gave Layne an apologetic frown. "Don't go anywhere," he said.

Very funny, she thought as she constructed a polite smile. "I'll be right here." She so longed to go to that pub.

A few minutes later Ryan returned. "I'm sorry, Layne. What were we talking about?"

She stared down at her hands.

"Damn," he said. "I did it again. Of course I remember you. I work long hours with too little sleep and too much coffee. Out of context I...I didn't expect to see you. That's all. Can you forgive me?"

"Well, at least I'm not going insane. I started to wonder if I'd dreamt the entire thing. I hope your pants aren't ruined."

Ryan hesitated. "No worries. Now, about the reason you left. I understand you're uncomfortable with this, but that can't be all. Tell me what's going on."

Layne fidgeted. "Uh..."

"Layne, I need you to be honest with me."

"Well, this may sound odd given my career, but I'm not comfortable being the center of attention."

He nodded. "That is somewhat surprising."

"And I felt a very strong urge to get out of this room."

"Okay."

"So, I went."

"Wow," Ryan said. "Not what I expected."

"Yeah, me neither. I never do stuff like that. Now, Maggie? She would have left in a heartbeat, and her exit would've had flair. She's the wild one. I'm the responsible one. But I had a good rationalization going."

"I'd love to hear it."

"I was in the wrong place at the wrong time. I had no useful information. I was in everyone's way. Then, when Mr. Tall—"

"Mr. Tall?"

"I'm sorry, I meant Agent Short. Anyway, when he told me I couldn't leave...well..."

"Please go on," Ryan said.

"Well, I know this may seem stubborn, but when I'm told I can't do something, like leave, that's exactly what I want to do."

Ryan grinned. "Sounds a little like me."

"I work to keep those impulses under control," Layne said. "To keep my life under control. But here, I don't have any control over anything. And I guess...I mean...well..."

"Layne?"

"Oh, all right. Your reaction when you first saw me. With everything else, I...uh—"

"No need to continue. Again, I apologize. I want to assure you, this murder investigation is our highest priority. As soon as we can confirm that you're not in any danger, you'll be free to go."

She breathed a sigh of relief. How long could it take?

"About the other thing," Ryan said. "Can you and I start over?" He shifted on the couch to face her and took her hand with his. "I'm Special Agent Ryan Cooke," he said, giving her hand a gentle squeeze. "It's a pleasure to meet you, Layne."

That annoying and at the same time exhilarating tingle shot up her arm, and a warmth enveloped her.

"Layne, honey," Maggie said as she approached them. "You're beet red. Are you feeling all right?"

"Excellent timing, as always, Maggie," Layne said. "And thanks for your concern, but I'm fine."

"Oh. Ohhhh," Maggie said. "I'll come back."

"Wait," Ryan said. "I'd like to ask you both some questions. If you don't mind, Ms. Malone."

"Of course, sugar."

"Could each of you please tell me what you observed when you first entered the suite?"

Layne described approaching the room and seeing the open doors. Then she remembered the safe. "My diamonds! They belonged to my grandmother. Are they gone?"

15

Berger's eyes flicked from his cell phone to the clock on the meeting room wall, then back to his cell. Both devices agreed—it was two in the morning. He turned up the volume on his phone to ensure he wouldn't miss the call, but still jumped when it blared, the assault on his senses only magnifying his tension.

"Berger," he said.

"We found Schatz," Agent Sherry Rennick stated.

"We know," Berger said.

"That was classified."

"You Americans, such arrogance. Contrary to what you may think, you are not the only government with counterintelligence."

She made a small snort, and Berger's grip on the phone tightened. "Tell me. Does he have it?"

"No."

"But this is not possible. Are you sure?"

"Yes."

"Does he know where it is?"

Rennick hesitated for a moment. "He's not talking. And your counterintelligence people don't know as much as you think they do."

"What do you mean?"

"Forget it. Our team is tasked with retrieving the damned thing. Do you have any leads at all?"

"I am afraid I do not. But you must find it."

"That might take some time."

"Time we do not have."

16

Another piece of news coming at Ryan like a one-two punch. Why had no one told him about the diamonds?

Maggie rubbed Layne's arm. "No worries, sweetie. Earrings, bracelet, necklace, all accounted for. You should go through the rest of your jewelry, but everything seems to be there."

"Where were the diamonds?" Ryan asked.

"I keep all of my jewelry in the hotel safe when I travel," Layne said. "And the safe is at the bottom of the armoire."

"Was the safe open when you came in?"

"No idea. I didn't make it that far."

"It was locked," Maggie said. "Officer beer belly wanted to look inside, so I gave him the code."

Ryan sent Maggie a wry smile. "You mean Sergeant Temple?"

"That's him."

"How did you know the code, Ms. Malone?"

"She uses the same one every time."

Ryan raised a scolding brow at Layne.

"It never seemed like an issue before," Layne said. "What if I forget the code? A woman's gotta have backup."

Maggie nodded her agreement and Ryan shook his head. "Let's get back to the details of the room," he said.

"There isn't much else to tell," Layne said. "The bedroom seemed normal outside of the open closet door. Oh, wait a minute. The silver tray."

"The platter of food?"

"Yes. On the floor, in front of the armoire. Really bizarre."

"I assume you didn't order it?"

"No. It was there when I arrived. I darn near tripped over the thing trying to reach the safe. That's when I saw the dead..."

Ryan sensed Layne's composure crumbling. "That's enough for now," he said. "We're analyzing the tray, but please let me know if you remember anything else."

"Do you think this was some sort of weird robbery gone bad?" Layne asked.

"Right now, that's as good an explanation as any. You'll need to go through your belongings, make sure nothing is missing or out of place."

"But...most of my things are in the bedroom."

"That's right."

Maggie's eyes widened. "Are you out of your flipping mind? This woman just found a bloody, disgusting, dead body in the closet. And you want her to go back into that room?"

Ryan let out a breath. "I suppose you've got a point. I don't like doing this, but we'll ask housekeeping to move everything to your new room, and we can go through them tomorrow."

"Tomorrow? My new room? But you said as soon as you knew there wasn't any danger I could go home."

"That's correct."

"How long is that going to take?"

"I wish I could give you a definite answer, but we just don't know. I'm sorry, but you'll need to stay until this is resolved," he said. "That means no more sneaking out. All right?"

Layne shrugged, but the resigned expression on her face told him she wouldn't try to escape again. And her reaction when he'd taken her hand meant he had her right where he wanted her.

"This whole thing is creepy," Maggie said. "Can you blame her for how she reacted?"

"And you," Ryan said to Maggie. "Stop distracting my agents."

Maggie donned a satisfied grin.

"But you're right, Ms. Malone," Ryan said. "It's a difficult situation. All the more reason for Layne to be where we can protect her. By the way, Layne, we took your clothes from the closet into evidence."

Layne's face squinched. "So, I'm stuck here, and I don't have anything to wear."

"We left the items in the dresser," Ryan said.

"Alrighty, then. At least I have undergarments."

"It's okay, hun. I'll bring you a few of my things."

Layne tried to picture herself in a leather miniskirt and thigh high leather boots. "That's sweet, Maggie. But don't go to any trouble. I think I have some jeans and tee shirts in the dresser."

"Well, then," Maggie said, "my phone has been ringing like a doorbell at a brothel, and the press is threatening to make stuff up if I don't get back to them."

Ryan caught Maggie's arm. "You know none of what happened here can be exposed to the media?"

"Yes, I do, sugar. Agent tall, blond and dreary read me the oath. But if anyone is going to fabricate stories, I'd rather it be me. At least then they'll have something spicy to report."

"Thank you for your help, Ms. Malone."

Maggie turned sympathetic eyes to Layne. "I hate to do this. Will you be all right if I go?"

"I'll be fine," Layne said. "But can you take the diamonds with you? My mother would kill me if anything happened to them. And she swears my grandmother would come back to haunt me."

"Of course, hun." Maggie turned to Ryan. "Is that all right with you?"

"We'd prefer not to have the liability, so that works for me. I'll talk with Agent Short."

Maggie gave Layne a long hug, and then turned again to Ryan. "Very Special Agent Cooke, I could use an escort to the door."

Hesitant, Ryan allowed himself to be guided toward the double doors to the suite. Then Maggie moved in close, placed her hands on his chest, and gave him the sweetest of smiles.

"I am holding you personally responsible for the safety of my best friend," she said. "And I don't care how delectable you are. If one freckle on her fanny is harmed, I swear, I will hunt you down, and I will hurt you."

Ryan fought back a smirk. "I promise, I'll do everything in my power to protect Layne. You have my word."

"I will hurt you," Maggie said again.

"I understand."

Ryan verified the forensics unit had processed the diamond jewelry and case, entrusted them to Maggie with her signature, and then took the opportunity to check in with the rest of his team. He entered the suite down the hall and spoke in private to Marco.

"Got anything for me on my cell phone?"

"Here's the trace log, boss. Nothing out of the ordinary. Was it stolen?"

"Not that I'm aware of," Ryan said.

"What are you not telling me?"

"When I figure that out you'll be the first to know."

Ryan took the log into the bedroom, closed the door, and scanned over the data on the GPS trace for his cell phone. The short list looked accurate. It showed his phone in every location he remembered being in the last twenty-four hours. After a series of meetings at the Los Angeles field office, followed by a late recap with the office director, a town car had taken him to LAX. He'd gone through expedited security, sat in the gate area for a few minutes, and approached the jetway to board with the business class passengers. That's where his memory faltered. How had he gotten home from SFO? And why couldn't he remember meeting Layne on the flight? He had no doubt about her involvement. He just couldn't figure how. He needed more information, but first, he had to deal with his gap in time.

He took out his cell. "Yes, this is Very Special..." He cleared his throat. "This is Special Agent Ryan Cooke. I need to see Dr. Hanley as soon as possible."

17

Layne hadn't heard their entire discussion, but she could read Maggie like a campy novel, and she had to admit, she found watching her best friend threaten the life of a federal agent highly gratifying.

For several years, Layne went without a best friend. Her husband had filled that role, and when he passed, it just felt wrong to replace the closeness she'd shared with him. Then Layne met Maggie, and adored her. Sure, Maggie's moral code made Layne look like a nun. But Layne cherished Maggie's directness and her confidence, her compassion and her honesty. Maggie found humor in almost every situation, she embraced life, and she'd give anyone the shirt off her back if they needed it. Particularly if they were an attractive male. And with Maggie, you always knew where you stood.

She watched Maggie leave the suite, followed by Ryan, then hugged her arms across her chest as a shiver ran through her. What she'd seen in that bedroom, being stuck at the hotel, the reality of it folded around her like a blanket of ice. After a few minutes, Ryan came back and took a seat on the sofa beside her.

"Maggie's a good friend," he said.

Layne nodded, but she fought back the tears that had been building since the moment she'd woken up on the floor.

"We need to establish a few ground rules," Ryan said. "Are you up for that?"

She nodded again.

"First, and most important, you go nowhere alone."

She shifted in her seat. "Even the bathroom?"

He grinned "No one is going to follow you into the bathroom, but someone will be in the suite with you at all times."

Her spirits lifted a little. "That's a relief."

"Regarding the bathroom..."

Layne opened her mouth to speak, then closed it, and hid her face in her hands. Her spirits had lifted way too soon.

Ryan lowered his voice. "Don't be embarrassed, Layne. Lots of women have them."

She whimpered.

"It's not a big deal," he said. "But I wanted to mention it before you overheard anything."

Her hands dropped to her lap. "People are talking about it?"

"Well, most of us are men. We see something like that, we talk."

Oh. My. God, her little voice said.

"If it makes you feel any better, some of the men didn't know what it was. The shape of it was...unusual."

She grimaced. "Maggie bought it for me."

"Ah."

"So, only a few of them know?"

"Well, I explained it. But I made sure to use the politically correct term."

Layne shut her eyes. "Yes, because heaven forbid my humiliation should be anything but politically correct."

"I can tell you're uncomfortable with this."

Her eyes popped open. "You think?"

"You left it out on the bathroom counter where housekeeping would see it. We assumed..."

Oh. My. God, her little voice repeated.

"I keep the privacy sign on my door when I travel," Layne said. "I don't like people in my room. Not that it matters now. Everyone but the Pope has been in this suite."

"Yes, well, the Pope called to say he was running late."

"That's not funny," she said trying not to smile.

He put a reassuring hand on her shoulder. "I'll make sure there's no more talk, okay?"

That damned tingle returned, racing from the point of the arousingly direct physical contact, all the way down her spine. "Thank you," she said, as she attempted to ignore it.

Then Agent Short approached them with the intimate object of discussion dangling between his latex-gloved thumb and forefinger.

Oh. My. F-ing. God, her little voice cried.

Layne scoured the room to see if anyone was watching.

Not anyone, her little voice shrieked. *Everyone! Everyone is staring at the damned rabbit!*

Agent Short spoke to Ryan. "It cleared, sir. I thought she might want to place it somewhere more private."

Layne didn't wait for Ryan's response. She jumped up, snatched the item from the agent's hand, whirled around looking for someplace to hide it, stuffed it under a couch cushion and sat on top of it.

Agent Short's lips opened, but the flat of Layne's palm flashed up at him.

Ryan interjected. "Thanks, Short. I'll come check on things in a few minutes."

"Yes, sir." Agent Short made a rapid departure.

Ryan turned to Layne, and her palm went up again. "Next ground rule, please," she said. He suppressed a grin, and Layne leveled an icy stare at him.

"Okay, let's talk about phone protocol."

"Yes," Layne said. "Phone protocol."

"We'll need you to engage the speaker on either the room phone or your cell phone, no matter who the caller appears to be."

"All right. Wait. Even for personal calls?"

"If you are in some way related to this incident, your friends or family might be at risk. I'm fairly skilled at determining if a person is under duress, but I need to hear them."

"I am not involved in this. How can you even say that? I've never seen that man before today."

"Does that mean you got a good look at him before you passed out?"

"Well, no, but—"

"Layne, until we have a better handle on what happened, and why, we can't make any assumptions."

She slumped back on the couch as Ryan continued.

"Also, and this is very important, we'll need you to keep your phone on vibrate."

"But then how..."

He looked down, hiding a smile behind his hand.

She gasped. "I cannot believe you just said that! You're making fun of my...my..."

"I'm sorry," Ryan said on a laugh. "I couldn't resist."

"Oh, my. You're a terrible person," she said, but her own laughter welled until she had to let it out. "You should be ashamed of yourself."

"I am. Very ashamed," he said, still chuckling.

At the other end of the couch, AC/DC's "Highway to Hell" rang out from Layne's purse and her laughter stopped. "Oh, god. It's my mother."

"Perfect timing," Ryan said. "Be sure to use the speaker."

Her face puckered. "Do I have to?"

"Yes, you do."

"Can't we make one exception?"

"Are we going to have a problem here?"

Layne frowned, reached for her purse, pressed the speaker button on her phone, and faked more composure than she felt. "Hi, Mom."

"Layne! Thank the Lord you're all right."

Layne's mother, Helen, had the slightest hint of a German accent left from a childhood spent in Berlin. And at seventy-eight, she was as shrewd as ever.

"You couldn't be bothered to call and tell an old woman you're still alive?"

"I'm sorry, Mom. I didn't want to worry you. How did you find out?"

"It's all over the news. A murder. It's so exciting. Now that I know you're all right, of course. Did you do it? Did you whack the guy?"

"Mom! I found the man in my hotel room. That's all I know."

Layne sought Ryan's expression to determine if she'd said too much, but his gaze was once again aimed downward as he attempted to contain his laughter. She glared at his hair.

"Well, that figures," Helen said. "You just don't have it in you." The line grew quiet, and then her mother called out, "Yes, Karl. Layne's fine."

Layne pictured her father, settled into his favorite chair, in his favorite undershirt, the edge of the newspaper balanced on his belly, smoking his favorite pipe.

"And she didn't kill anybody," Helen said to Karl, disappointment clear in her voice.

Layne's dad bellowed in the background. "I told you before. It's all them damn liberals mixed in with those bastards at that Bohemian Grove. It's like oxygen and matches. Shit is bound to explode."

Layne stared at the ceiling. "Mom, please ask Dad to stop."

"Layne says to shut the hell up," Helen called to Karl.

"She said no such thing," Karl replied. "My Layne would never talk to me that way, you nasty woman. You tell her to get the hell out of that godforsaken shit hole before somebody does her some real damage. Now, where's my dinner?"

Layne pinched the bridge of her nose. "Mom, I need to go."

Her little voice thoughtfully pointed out that those should have been the first words from her mouth when she answered the call.

"What about your grandmother's diamonds, baby girl?" Her mother asked. "And her locket? Do you still have them?"

"Yes, Mom. As far as we can tell, nothing was stolen."

"Thank heavens. You'd have gone straight to hell if you'd lost that jewelry."

"Yes, I know. Hauntings from the grave. I got it. Thanks for calling, Mom."

"Your father and I love you, dear."

"I love you too."

"Be careful, baby girl."

Layne ended the call and put her head back into her hands. On a scale from one to ten, between the politically correct, rabbit-shaped, vibrating accessory, and the conversation with her parents, her level of embarrassment hovered at around twenty.

"Wow," Ryan said.

Layne chose not to look up. "Don't."

"But—"

"Un-uh."

"I just—"

"Nope."

18

"Hey," Ryan said. "Why don't we go downstairs and grab some dinner while they make up your new room?"

Layne couldn't bring herself to meet Ryan's gaze.

"You know, food?" Ryan continued. "It's common in some countries to eat at this time of day."

Her eyes flew to her watch. "Shit!"

"Hunh. Not the reaction I normally get when I ask a woman to dinner."

"I'm sorry, it's not you. It's...I'm...uh...I have a nine o'clock reservation at Rue de Rêves, and I can't go like this."

"Rue de Rêves?"

"It's French for street of fate. Or, street of dreams. Damn, it's a restaurant, okay?"

"All right, calm down. I'm familiar with the place. What do you mean you can't go like this? Layne, you're not leaving the hotel."

"You don't understand. I have to go."

"I'm sure they'll reschedule your reservation given the circumstances."

Layne stood and began to pace. "How can I explain this? Did you ever have one of those moments where you were positive the next action you took would make or break your career?"

He nodded. "I have those often."

"Well, this is one of them. But not so much for me," Layne said. "Last year I visited San Francisco at the request of the head chef at Rue de Rêves. I hadn't done many international whole foods venues, and it seemed like a great fit for the show. He created a spectacular menu—a program outlining several courses with organic wine pairings—and the first course, the appetizer, oh my gosh, amazing. But then the soup arrived, and I found a fly."

"A fly?"

"You know, buzz, buzz...a fly...in my soup."

Ryan's forehead creased.

"Anyway," Layne said, "the waiter got nervous and started making fly-in-my-soup jokes with his cute little French accent. The staff panicked, and patrons started leaving the restaurant. It was a huge mess. It should've been no big deal—I mean, really, flies happen—but it turned into a fiasco. Unfortunately, my team got the whole thing on film, and somehow the footage leaked. The chef was devastated."

"Leaked? Like on the internet?"

"It went viral. Poor Chef Degasse is such a nice man, and he was horrified at the incident. Then to have the video all over the web..." Layne shook her head. "He filed a lawsuit against the network, but I'm certain his lawyers pressured him into it. Then things calmed down. He remodeled, rebuilt his business, and this is the final item for resolution to the pending lawsuit—my agreement to come back and feature him on an episode. But I have to do it tonight. Critics, other chefs, columnists, they're all waiting for something to go wrong. I joked with Maggie that I'd break my leg or something. I totally jinxed myself."

"I don't believe in jinxes," Ryan said. "But this is pretty ironic."

"Then you understand why I have to go?"

His lips curled. "No."

"This isn't funny."

"Oh, all right. I suppose we need to eat either way. But French food is so small. Can we go somewhere good afterward?"

"We?"

"Rule number one, remember?"

"Oh, no. That is not happening."

"I'm not that bad of a dinner companion."

"It's not you. It's that...taking...uh...well, a date, that would be big news in this circle. It isn't done."

"Okay. Here are your choices. Invite the witty and charming, and might I say devilishly handsome federal agent to dinner, or stay at the hotel. Your call."

Layne stopped pacing to come to terms with the ultimatum, then let out a sigh. "All right. I guess I'll just have to deal with the aftermath. You can come with me to dinner."

Ryan lifted one brow. "I'm sorry, but that didn't sound even a little bit like an invitation. If you expect me to go on a date with you, I'll need a proper invitation."

His smile was both enticing and aggravating. "Okay. Special Agent Cooke, would you do me the honor of accompanying me to dinner this evening?"

"I thought you'd never ask."

"But this isn't a date.

"Uh huh."

"It's an arrangement."

"We'll see."

Ryan gave her a sly grin, but Layne couldn't let herself be distracted by butterfly generating innuendo and a few sexy smiles. There were details to work out. She scrutinized him from head to toe. "The suit will work," she said. "How do you feel about being on camera?"

"I don't," Ryan said.

"You don't have a feeling about it?"

"I don't appear on camera."

"Oh, right. Secret spy stuff."

He smirked.

"How about this? I'll make sure all the shots are from behind you," she said. "They'll only film me, and, of course, the food. Will that work?"

"I'll want to see the footage before it airs."

"Scouts honor." Layne held up two fingers.

"It's three fingers."

"Don't go getting all grumpy on me now."

He shook his head. "I can't believe I let you con me into going out for French food."

"I guarantee it'll be the best meal you've ever had. Now, if you don't mind, I should start getting ready." A horrible realization hit her. "Oh my gosh. Your people took my clothes."

"My people are thorough. Look, Layne, I admire your sense of obligation. But are you sure you want to go through with this?"

"Honestly, I feel like a fire truck ran over me, then backed up to do a better job. But Chef Degasse will be a laughing stock if I don't go. I can't do that to him, not again. A hot bath and some new clothes, I'll be fine."

"I don't like the thought of taking you out of the hotel."

Layne raised pleading eyebrows at him.

"And I think it's a bad idea in general."

She tilted her head a little and gave him an expectant grin.

He sighed. "All right. There's a spa-salon-thing and a dress shop off the lobby. I'll arrange for someone to take you down for...whatever women do, and I'll finish up here."

She beamed at Ryan. "Thank you."

He picked up his radio. "Rennick, I need an assist."

While Layne waited for her escort, she phoned the restaurant to confirm her reservation. Then she called Dennis, her camera crew lead. After assurances regarding both her physical and mental state, she agreed to meet the crew at the restaurant and asked Dennis to call Maggie. A few minutes later, a blond, well-postured amazon of woman stood at the doorway to her room.

"Special Agent Sherry Rennick," Ryan said. "This is Layne Stevens. Rennick, please take Ms. Stevens to the spa and the dress shop downstairs. The concierge is waiting. Do not let her out of your sight. And take Hansel and Gretel with you. They need the exercise. Also, I'd like a new a tie. Can you handle that while you're there?"

"Yes, sir," the agent said, eyeing Layne's appearance as if she were looking at the contents of a dumpster.

Layne stiffened at the female agent's scrutiny. Then she glanced around her at the two enormous bodyguards Maggie had distracted during the attempted escape. They were built about the same—like massive brick walls with huge biceps. But the one Ryan had referred to as Hansel had a narrow face, with a strong chin, and dark, almost black hair, while Gretel sported boyish features, a round face full of freckles, and strawberry blond hair.

Lovely, Layne's little voice said. *We get to try on dresses with Drill Sergeant Rennick and the incredible hulks. Will the fun never end?*

SONNY'S BINOCULARS had been trained on Layne's suite for several hours, and it relieved him to see her go. Because the longer he watched, the more frustrated he became. He figured the blond dominatrix for a first-rate bitch. But what was the deal with the tall guy waving that sex toy around? Did they plant it in Layne's room to humiliate her? Shit. Her alleged protectors. She didn't know them like he did.

He supposed without the audio, things might be taken out of context. But even from a distance, the pretty boy, Cooke, seemed full of himself. Sure, he played nice with Layne. But the minute she left he had turned her room upside down looking for the damned card. She would trust that asshole until he finished using her. He wasn't good enough for Layne.

Sonny put the binoculars down. Thankful to have avoided taking action earlier in the day, he felt confident there would be no repeat escape attempt. He saw it on her face. She was resigned to her fate—what she knew of it. He wanted to warn her, to show her that her protectors were actually the enemy. But like Layne, he too was resigned to his fate.

19

Excitement and activity charged the suite down the hall as Ryan stepped inside. He observed for a time, satisfied with what he saw. They were an exceptional team. The best he had worked with. A team he knew would solve the puzzle posed to them, or die trying.

"Listen up," he called to the room. "I assume you all heard the exchange. I'm aware we weren't prepared for this, but we might as well use it to our advantage. If anyone's going to make a move, either to threaten Ms. Stevens, or to contact her, this would be the logical time."

Rusk grinned. "So, we're using the hotty as bait?"

"We're playing the hand we've been dealt, and we need to be ready for anything. Hawk, we're gonna want more manpower. Let's have a small contingent of men stay here at the hotel. The rest will come with us."

"Will they get to eat snails?"

"No," Ryan said. "And neither will I." He noted most of the team had folders in front of them. "Remember, it would be helpful to apprehend someone, like the person responsible for our John Doe, but the memory card is still our primary mission. I performed another cursory search of her suite, looking for anything we might have missed, but came up empty. And if she took the card, it's unlikely to still be here.

We don't know who she interacted with when she left the hotel. We'll have to be on our toes for possible assailants, but observation is key. What we need, more than anything, is information. Any questions?" He heard mumbling and talk, but no questions. "Then get to work on plans for transportation and security."

Marco pulled Ryan aside. "I distributed the report, boss, but there's a couple of other things." He turned his back to the team and handed Ryan a small evidence bag.

"What's this?"

"They found it in the vic's stomach. It was a locket until HQ ripped it apart. Nothing inside. But the vic ID'd as the German op we fingered, retired and hiding in the states, just like we thought."

"Excellent." Ryan studied the bag again. "I'm going to take this with me but let's keep it quiet for now. It must mean something, or he wouldn't have swallowed it. But the less people that know, the better. Did you follow up on the silver tray?"

"Yup. Someone ordered it from room service during the lunch rush. The hotel was hosting a large conference, so the woman who took the order didn't know whether they talked to a man or a woman. Hell, she barely remembered taking the call."

"But somebody delivered it to the room."

"A bellman. I wrote down his name—a Mr. Agokoka...or, I don't know. I can't fucking pronounce it. Funny guy though. Big fan of Ms. Stevens. He helped her with her bags when she arrived. He recalled the order because he was hoping to see her again, so he volunteered to take it up. Gave us some decent intel about who came and went. I think he might've been stalking her room, but he stopped watching after she left this morning."

"What time did she leave?"

Marco looked at his notes. "He has her leaving at 8:52 am."

"Very precise."

"Like I said, funny guy."

"And she came back for lunch?"

"He assumed she did until he saw her walk into the hotel at 4:03 pm."

"And he's certain he saw Layne this afternoon?"

"He said some fans got wind that she was staying at the hotel, and they made a big scene in the lobby when she arrived. So, yeah, it was her. But that doesn't mean she didn't sneak in during the middle of the day."

"You said the bellman delivered the room service tray. He must have seen her."

"The caller asked for the service cart to be left outside the door."

"And your certain the person who took the call doesn't know anything?"

"Talked to her myself. Like I said, pretty useless."

"Hmm. So, what was on the tray?"

"Something wrapped in bacon. But you couldn't tell exactly what from looking at it. I asked room service for the name, and I still don't know what it is. It's in the report. We sent the entire thing in for analysis and prints."

"More questions than answers, Marco. Fix that, and keep me updated."

"One more thing, boss." Marco handed Ryan a folder. "Not great news for the nice TV lady."

Ryan skimmed through the report. Her background seemed standard enough. She'd been married, widowed several years back, and had two grown children. Nothing unusual in her job history. Lived in Los Angeles most of her life. But the further he read, the less standard it became. Not great news was an understatement.

20

A flamboyant Russian accent greeted the group as Layne and her funky entourage exited the hotel elevator at the lobby.

"My, my, you look so tense," the concierge said.

Rennick threw the man a nasty glare and nudged her chin toward Layne.

"Oh, poor lamb," the concierge said to Rennick. "One could never mistake you for Ms. Stevens. I was merely making an observation." He turned his attention to Layne and scooped both of her hands into his. "Sweetheart, such a day you have had. Come. An invigorating sugar scrub with peppermint and almond oil will perk you right up. And we will go without the mud and the twigs, eh?"

"Twigs?"

"The leaves and twigs stuck in your hair, my darling. Do not worry. All will be fixed."

Why hadn't anyone bothered to mention the twigs? She sensed her little voice might say something, but it was too busy laughing at her.

The concierge led them to the spa, where Hansel and Gretel secured the area, and then left Layne with a muscular massage technician and Rennick. Uncomfortable didn't begin to describe the effect of

Rennick's presence in the room. But after a full body scrub, an oily rub down, and a wonderful citrus facial, Layne felt rejuvenated. And her skin glowed. She made a mental note to pamper herself more often, next time without an audience.

In all her fresh-from-the-spa radiance, fluffy white slippers and a plush white spa robe, Layne padded next to the salon. She explained where she'd be dining and that she would be on camera. Three stylists attended to her hair, makeup, and nails, while Rennick stood off to the side, looking impatient and annoyed. Layne's little voice found this amusing, and truthfully, so did Layne.

The result of her salon experience delighted her. Her thick, long hair had been washed, blown straight, parted in the center and twisted back on either side into a full ponytail at the nape of her neck, and then secured by a large pearl-studded barrette. A touch of cinnamon blush, earth tone eyeshadows, Audrey Hepburn style liner with thick black lashes, and rosy lip shine completed her makeup. It was more than she would usually wear, but ideal for the camera. A natural French manicure and spa-tacular pedicure rounded out the visit. For the first time since starting at Foodie, Layne felt like a celebrity. She presented herself to the group. "Is it too much?" she asked.

"Yes," Rennick said.

Hansel and Gretel stared. Neither said a word.

"So much for that movie star glow," Layne mumbled.

"Nonsense, my dear," the concierge said, stepping in. "You are stunning. Now, on to the boutique?"

He escorted Layne to a ladies fine shoes and apparel store, where a personal shopper greeted her with three potential outfits, all in black.

Layne checked the sizes on the tags. "How did you know?" she asked the concierge.

"Oh, my darling. I have an eye. You are a perfect size eight."

She wasn't sure if she'd ever heard the words perfect and size eight used together, but she'd take it. The fairy tale twins posted themselves at the door to the small boutique, while Rennick completed her scrutiny of the tiny area along with a not so internal rant. Then Layne carried a sequined black pantsuit, a formal black evening gown, and a simple black cocktail dress into the fitting room. She settled on the cocktail dress with a classic hourglass design, wide princess neckline, and cap sleeves. Handing the other two outfits to the shopping assistant, she whispered her sizes for black bikini underwear, bra, sheer black thigh-high stockings, and a pair of black heels.

After some shimmying and a few adjustments, she put the final touches in place and assessed herself in the mirror. Not bad for a forty-something mother of two who just found a dead man in her closet.

~

WHILE KEEPING one eye on the dressing room, Gretel watched Rennick sniff out the loudest, ugliest tie he had ever seen. She signed for it and brought it to him.

"Cooke's not gonna like this," he said.

"All that mock innocence from Stevens is bullshit," Rennick said. "She's an op, and she needs to feel some heat. Wire the tie, give it to Cooke, and tell him little miss cooking show chose it. He'll wear it. And when he asks her about it, she'll know the game is on."

Gretel shook his head. "You're playing with fire, Rennick. I wouldn't want to be you tomorrow."

He took the tie up to the surveillance suite, waved it at Ryan, and then handed it over to a wire tech.

Ryan stared at the tie. "What the hell is that?"

Gretel pulled at his shirt collar and made a conscious decision to avoid the eruption certain to happen when Ryan learned the truth. "Rennick told me to tell you the babe picked it out."

"You've got to be kidding. I can't wear that."

Gretel shrugged.

"Give it to me." Ryan tore the tie from the hands of the tech—who had barely completed his task—and then stormed into the bedroom. When he returned to the main room of the suite, Gretel noted the polished hair and the faint aroma of cologne. He fought back a smirk. "Not bad, boss, except for the ugly ass tie."

"Let's go," Ryan said.

~

LAYNE PULLED HERSELF TOGETHER, both her outfit and her wits, and walked out of the dressing room dreading Rennick's response. To her relief, the concierge stepped forward, grabbed her hands, and swung her arms wide for a full appraisal. "You look ravishing my dear."

Rennick tapped her foot. "Whatever. We need to go."

Layne headed for the elevator, security detail in tow, and the old-style lift door opened to Gretel, returning from the surveillance suite. As Layne moved into the lift, she caught her heel on the edge of a raised subway tile and stumbled face first into him. She sputtered several apologies as Gretel helped her to regain her balance.

Rennick scoffed. "Maybe our focus should be on keeping everyone else safe from you."

Layne's brows jumped. "Excuse me?"

Her little voice rallied with support. *Oh, nice comeback. Super clever.*

"I'm simply pointing out," Rennick said, "that maybe a woman your age shouldn't be wearing such high heels."

Real voice found. "Hmm, let me think about that. Oh, yes. My shoes were under a dead man and are most likely covered in blood. And they've probably been shipped out as evidence. But thank you, so much, for your concern over the age appropriateness of my attire. In the future, perhaps a woman your age should keep their childish comments to themselves."

Rennick stared at the elevator door without further remark. Hansel studied the ceiling. And Gretel struggled to contain his laughter. That made Layne grin.

As the lift scraped past the second floor, she sensed a faint itching sensation in her eyes, and she let out a blood-curdling sneeze. Then another. And another. She glanced around. "Does someone here own a cat?"

No one spoke.

"I'm allergic to cats," she said.

Rennick fine-tuned her glare at the elevator door. Hansel searched the ceiling as if it divulged the meaning of life. And Gretel shook his head.

The elevator stopped at the third floor. Thank god.

21

Berger updated Director Braun, and then watched him leave the conference room as a shrill chime filled the space. He blinked back his fatigue and engaged the line.

"Hans Berger here."

"You'd sure as hell better have something for me," the irritating raspy voice said. It made Berger want to clear his own throat.

"We are close," Berger replied.

"Shit, Berger. We both know that's not true."

"Then why did you contact me?"

"I need you to understand something."

Berger's voice cracked as he struggled to curb his anger. "What is that?"

"This is a warning," the caller said. "BKA made promises. Braun made promises. You, senior fucking BKA Officer, Hans Berger, made promises. Your ineptitude has cost the American government more than you can imagine. But if you can't secure this thing, it's going to be disastrous, and that will fall on you."

"Do you believe I do not comprehend this?"

"I don't care what you fucking comprehend, Berger. Find the damned card."

22

The elevator creaked open, and Rennick exited, marching toward the surveillance suite. Hansel and Gretel escorted Layne to her suite, where Ryan waited, and a speechless moment lingered between them. Layne had never seen a tie quite so bright, and she couldn't get a read on Ryan. Was he hiding disappointment? Or was his face set in stunned amazement at her transformation?

Ryan broke the silence. "You look incredible, Layne."

Her ankle wobbled a bit as she smiled at the floor. "Thank you," she said, at a volume even she could barely hear. Shit. Flattery from other men didn't cause this reaction. Sure, she wasn't the most beautiful woman on the planet, but plenty of men found her attractive. And over the years, she'd taught herself how to gracefully accept a compliment. So, why did this man make her feel like fifteen with braces all over again? She reminded herself that this was not a date. It couldn't be a date. She didn't want it to be a date. She'd decided long ago that there would be no more dates. And this definitely was not a date. She chose to focus her attention on his hideous tie.

"You okay?" he asked.

"Pardon?"

"You seem distracted. Is everything all right?"

"Of course. I mean, what's up with drill sergeant Rennick? She's a total bi—" Layne caught herself. "She's not a very nice person."

Ryan's brows lowered. "What happened?"

She hesitated. Rennick had been indelicate, but she also may have been right. The shoes were higher than normal for her, but had she really passed that point? Was she too old for four-inch heels?

"Layne?"

"What? Oh. I'd rather not talk about it. Are you ready?"

Ryan turned a quizzical stare to Hansel and Gretel. They both looked away.

"Okay, then," Layne said. "Let's go."

"Hunh." Ryan glanced at his watch. "There's a little time, and I'd like to discuss something with you before we leave."

The concern in his tone made her uneasy. "What's going on?"

He motioned Layne to the couch and sat down next to her. "Layne, is there something you're not telling me?"

"Can you be more specific?"

"You need to be honest, Layne. You can tell me anything. You know that, right?"

Layne's internal alarm system blared. "I have told you everything. My life is an open book."

"Is it?"

She glanced down. "I guess there are some things I'm private about. Things I don't discuss. But if you think it will help, I'll tell you anything you want to know."

Well, almost anything. There were some things she only shared with people she trusted, and regardless of the tingle he evoked, she still felt uncertain about Ryan.

"First, let's talk about grilled rumaki."

She laughed. "Wow. I did not see that coming."

Muffled eighty's music streamed out of her purse. Specifically, "8-6-7-5-3-0-9."

"That's Jenny," Layne said.

"Right," Ryan said. "Rick Springfield."

"It's Tommy Tutone. But I meant my daughter, Jenny."

"Are you sure?"

"Yes. I recognize my daughter's ringtone."

"I was talking about Tommy Tutone. You have a daughter?"

Layne gave him a furtive glance and then placed Jenny on speaker. "Hi, sweetheart," she said.

"Mom! O-M-G! Why didn't you call me?"

"Oh, Jenny. I'm so sorry. I didn't want you to worry. It's not a big deal. I'm surprised it even made the news in San Diego."

"It didn't. Grandma called me."

A pain stabbed at Layne's temple. "Why does she do those things?"

"You were involved in a murder. Why shouldn't she call? What I can't understand is why you didn't call. Are you in danger? Are you okay? Did you see the body? O-M-G. Have you talked to Dean?"

"I'm sure Grandma already did."

"Oh. My. God. I cannot believe this."

Layne whispered to Ryan, "She's twenty."

"Who are you whispering too? Is someone there? Are you being held hostage?"

"Slow down, Jenny. You're wearing me out. I'm fine. Everything is fine."

"You always say that."

A vein in Layne's temple began to twitch as Ryan motioned with a crook of his fingers for the phone. She shook her head. He shot her an I'm-in-charge expression and put out his hand. She clenched her lips. Had he not seen her use the universal gesture for no? He moved his hand closer to the phone, and with narrowed eyes, she gave it to him.

Ryan turned off the speaker and spoke into Layne's cell. "Jenny? This is Special Agent Ryan Cooke with the Federal Bureau of Investigation."

A moment passed while he listened.

"I assure you, your mother is fine."

He paused.

"No, she isn't a suspect. Should she be?" Playfulness laced his voice, but the tirade on the other end of the line was clear even without the speaker engaged.

"Jen—," Ryan said.

Layne chuckled. What was the phrase? Be careful what you ask for?

Ryan's volume went up a notch. "Jenny." The tirade stopped. "I'm sorry," he said. "It was a joke, but it was inappropriate. I apologize. We're just keeping an eye on your mom until we can get a handle on what happened."

Another pause.

"Yes, it's strictly a precaution."

Ryan continued. "Dean is your brother? Sure, you can tell him everything I've told you." He nodded. "Of course. Dean can call his mother any time." He nodded. "Sure, you should feel free to call anytime as well. I'm certain she'd enjoy hearing from you."

He listened a little longer.

"Yes, she's at the same hotel...Uh huh, I'm the agent in charge of the investigation and also acting as your mother's personal bodyguard. Yes, in her suite."

Layne heard a squeal.

"No. On the couch." He nodded again. "Of course I will. Here's your mom."

Ryan handed the cell phone back to Layne. "Definitely not under duress."

"Okay, sweetie," Layne said into the phone.

"Mom, he sounds so hot. How old is he? What does he look like?"

"I'm hanging up now," Layne said.

"He's staying in your room?"

"Goodbye, Jenny. Give Dean my love, and tell him everything is fine."

"Oh, all right," Jenny said. "I love you, Mom."

"I love you too, sweetheart. I'll call you when I'm back in LA."

When the conversation ended, Ryan looked at her with a raised brow. "Do I really sound hot?"

"Good hearing. And thanks for running interference."

"Comes with the job. And you're welcome." He inspected the couch. "Hey, do you hear a buzzing noise? It seems to be coming from the—oh."

Layne's cheeks warmed as she subtly explored the crevices of the cushions beneath her. "What were we talking about before Jenny called?"

"Grilled rumaki. Does that mean anything to you?"

"Yes. It's my favorite appetizer." Layne stopped her search. "Oh my goodness. The silver tray!"

~

RENNICK PAID careful attention to the audio coming through to the surveillance suite from Ryan's tie. At least Stevens hadn't ratted her out, but something else troubled her. Marco peered over his monitor as she approached.

"What's up, Rennick?" he asked.

"Doesn't it concern you that Cooke is sharing everything we've got with that foodie chick?"

"That wasn't everything."

"Besides the rumaki, what else is there?"

"That's need-to-know. But you'll find out soon enough."

"Like hell. We're either all on the team, or we're not."

"Ah, young Luke Skywalker," he said. "Much to learn, you have."

"Who the hell is Luke Skywalker? And why are you talking like that?"

Marco barked out a laugh. "You're kidding. Star Wars?"

"It's a movie, right?"

"Shit, Rennick. What the fuck do you do in your spare time?"

Rennick stormed away from Marco's desk. It was none of his damned business what she did with her personal time. But she couldn't worry about Marco. The situation needed some serious damage control, and clearly, the task had fallen to her.

23

Ryan waited for Layne to process what she'd remembered. But he wondered...was she just now recalling what she'd seen on the tray, or had she known all along? Another coincidence. And this case held far too many where Layne was concerned. He hoped her reaction to the news he planned to share would be telling.

"Was it grilled rumaki on the tray?" Layne asked.

"Yes. Someone ordered it from room service during the lunch rush. Were you here?"

"No. I ate at a chocolate shop in Ghirardelli Square."

"You had chocolate for lunch?"

Layne half-smiled, half-grimaced.

"And you didn't order the tray before you left?"

"No. But now that I know it's on their menu..."

Ryan frowned. "How many people know it's your favorite appetizer?"

"My entire family. All my friends. Everyone I work with. My viewers."

"Your viewers?"

"I've got a great recipe for grilled rumaki on my website. It's called Layne's Favorite Appetizer."

"Wonderful. What is it, exactly?"

"Water chestnuts and chicken livers, wrapped in bacon and marinated—"

He wrinkled his nose. "You lost me at chicken livers."

"I think you'd be surprised if you tried it."

"Yes, I'd be very surprised if I got anywhere close to trying it."

She chuckled. "What makes this recipe so delicious is that the appetizer is threaded onto skewers and cooked on the grill. Have you ever eaten grilled bacon? It's to die for." Layne's hand flew to her mouth. "Crap. I'm so sorry. That was terrible."

Ryan concealed his growing discomfort. This was not going to be easy. "Is that how bacon is normally prepared?"

"No. It's usually pan-fried."

"What about the rumaki?" he asked. "Is it always skewered?"

"That's not the normal prep, but it's worth the extra effort."

"Hmm. Well, we sent the tray to forensics. They'll analyze the contents and check for prints." Ryan slid a small evidence bag from his pocket. "Does this look familiar to you?"

Layne examined the bag, and her fingers went to her neck. "My locket! What happened to it?"

"Our forensics team pulled it apart."

"Pulled it apart? It looks like they beat it with a sledgehammer."

"They believed something might have been hidden inside the locket."

"Like what?"

"I was hoping you could tell me."

"You took this from my jewelry case?"

"No. They recovered it during the autopsy of the dead man's body."

Layne's posture stiffened.

"They found it in his stomach," Ryan said.

"That can't be. It was in my jewelry case. Remember? Nothing was stolen."

"We checked for the diamonds, but you never went through the rest of your jewelry."

Layne sat quietly for a moment. Then the vibration from under the cushions resumed, and she shoved her hands into the nooks and crannies of the couch, her method not as subtle as it had been earlier.

"So, you think the dead man ordered the rumaki, but ate my locket."

"We're not sure what happened." As Ryan spoke, he worked to keep his eyes from following Layne's exploration of the couch. "Do you recognize the name Frederick Schatz?"

Layne stopped foraging. "Of course. But why—"

The buzzing noise grew louder, and the intensity of the vibration built until a high-pitched whirring sound filled the room, followed by a distinct click, and then silence.

She cleared her throat. "What were you saying?"

"What?" Ryan asked. "Oh. There's something I need to tell you, Layne."

"All right."

"This is highly classified information."

Her brows came together. "Okay."

"And it can't leave this room. As much as you might want to, you cannot tell anyone. All right?"

"Will you spill it already?"

Ryan folded Layne's hands into his. "I'm sorry, Layne, but we identified the dead man in the armoire as your uncle, Frederick Schatz."

The buzzing resumed, but Layne didn't appear to notice.

"I know this must be difficult for you," Ryan said. "I'm very sorry."

She didn't respond.

"Layne?"

"I…that's not possible."

"Has it been a while since you've seen your uncle?" Ryan asked.

Confusion crossed her face. "I've never seen him. He lived with us in South Dakota, but I was only two at the time, and he stayed there when we moved. But he never forgets my birthday, and we talk every Christmas."

"He didn't visit?

"No. He's afraid to fly, like me. So he doesn't travel. And my mom and dad have this thing about South Dakota—they won't go back. I never got to meet him in person. But lately he's called every few months. Poor man. Never married. No children." Her face paled. "I...I don't understand, Ryan. Are you sure it's him?"

"We're piecing the facts together, but yes."

Her lips tightened. "Let's be certain I've got this straight," she said. "My Uncle Fred, who hates to fly, flew to California, somehow managed to find me in San Francisco, broke into my hotel room and ordered my favorite appetizer, but ate my locket. And after all that, some psycho murdered him and crammed him into the closet. Then the FBI had the foresight to autopsy my uncle's stomach, and when they found my locket, they smashed it to bits."

"I realize it sounds somewhat unbelievable."

"No, Ryan, it doesn't. It sounds insane. All of it. Completely insane."

"The autopsy of the stomach contents is routine. But I'll admit, the rest has me stumped."

Tears filled Layne's eyes.

"Layne, we need to locate the item your uncle thought was hidden in the locket. You won't be safe, no one will be safe, until that happens."

A soft buzz resonated from the couch. Layne stood, flipped up the cushion, grabbed her rabbit vibrator, turned it off, stuffed it into her purse, and sat back down.

"Are you okay?" Ryan asked.

"I'm fine. I'm totally fine. We should go."

SONNY NOTICED the activity in Layne's suite and reluctantly put down his chocolate-filled croissant and venti macchiato to aim his binoculars toward the hotel. "Holy shit," he said to the empty apartment. "That is one hell of a dress."

He had a weakness for three things—little black dresses, beer nuts in the can, and sweets. He knew his taste for sugary temptations made him look like a pussy. He'd seen the sidelong glances from other men at the coffee shop when he'd ordered four extra pumps of vanilla, but he didn't give a crap. He had no one to impress.

But his dessert paled to the vision of Layne in that marvel of a dress, and his groin twitched as he watched her. The pretty boy handed Layne a clear bag. Sonny zoomed in on her face as her expression changed. Shit. What was going on over there? Sure, their conversations were being recorded, but he wouldn't gain access to the recordings until later. Hell, he may never hear them. Damned Employer.

She seemed confused by the bag's contents. Sonny re-focused, but he couldn't make it out. Had they found the card? He continued to observe their interaction. Shit, no. Don't cry. He could tolerate a lot of things. A woman in tears was not one of them. Fortunately, the tears didn't come.

"That's my girl," he said. "Hold it together, Layne. It'll all be over soon."

He checked his watch. According to The Employer, Layne had reservations at nine. He was cutting it damned close.

24

Layne stared out the window as the town car pulled away from the hotel and merged into the bog of city traffic.

"I'm sorry, Layne," Ryan said. "I should have waited for a better time. Sometimes I get too focused on the work. I wasn't thinking. Can you forgive me?"

"It's all right," she said, her gaze cast at the passing row houses that lined the busy streets of the city. "I can't imagine there would be a good time to hear that someone you cared about was murdered in your hotel room."

"Layne?"

She turned to look at him.

He held up his arm for her to slide under. "We don't know each other very well, but if you need a shoulder..." She leaned into him, and let the tears fall. It wasn't fair. Why Uncle Fred? And why now? Why did the people she love keep leaving her?

When they arrived at Rue de Rêves, Ryan gave her shoulders a gentle squeeze. "Are you still up for this?"

She sniffed and nodded, and then used what she thought was Ryan's handkerchief to dab away her tears. Then she pulled down the small mirror housed above her seat, and her shoulders sank.

So much for Audrey Hepburn eyes, her little voice grumbled. *And do men still carry handkerchiefs?*

Layne glanced over at Ryan's empty suit pocket. "Oh my gosh. Your tie. I'm really sorry."

Ryan looked down at the brightly patterned material. "It's hardly noticeable."

Layne did what she could to repair her makeup, and braced herself for the night ahead. The valet opened the car door, and Ryan got out first, taking her hand to help her onto the sidewalk. They were instantly engulfed by agency muscle fending off a hoard of fans and photographers. Ryan's arm encircled her waist as he guided her through the crowd toward the restaurant. It was a comforting and protective gesture. One she needed. She had this odd sensation, like she was walking a tightrope with his arm her only safety net. But would he leave her too? He was funny, and charming, and sexy as hell. But he was a man. Also known as a complication. A distraction. A disappointment waiting to happen. She shook off those thoughts and focused on getting from the sidewalk to the restaurant with her sanity intact.

"This is a madhouse," Layne said, catching glimpses of her camera crew unloading equipment, and of Maggie amongst the news cameras and reporters, gracious and glowing, totally in her element.

"You were right," Ryan said. "If you'd canceled, your chef friend would be a laughingstock."

Layne spotted him the moment she entered. Chef Philippe Degasse looked just as she remembered—tall, slim, and tan, with silvery gray hair pulled back into a short ponytail, a closely trimmed silver goatee, and eyes that glinted with spirit. A classic chef's toque crowned his head, and he wore a well-starched, white chef's coat over traditional black and white checked pants.

"Madame Stevens!" Chef Degasse said as he swept Layne's hands into his own and kissed the backs of both. "Always the most beautiful woman in the room. You poor thing, what a distressing day. It was so gracious of you to come. And with a date. Unheard of, my dear. I love it."

"Chef Degasse," Layne said. "It's so nice to see you again. I'd like you to meet my...friend, Ryan Cooke." Okay, it did feel a little bit like a date.

Instead of shaking Ryan's offered hand, the chef grabbed him by the shoulders, pulled him close, and planted sloppy kisses on both of Ryan's cheeks.

"Such a handsome gentleman, and the tie, so courageous," the chef said, then he lowered his voice. "You are a lucky man tonight, no?" Degasse turned to Layne and gestured toward the dining room. "What do you think, ma chérie?"

"It's spectacular," Layne said, taking in the black and white theme with crystal accents sparkling from wall sconces to window coverings to elaborate chandeliers. "I've never seen anything like it. No wonder it's the hottest restaurant in town."

"Oh, you are too kind. Please, follow me."

On the way to their table, Layne spotted a framed article from the *San Francisco Chronicle* placed in a prominent location on the wall, and she moved in for a closer look. "Holy shi—" Her hand flew to her mouth.

Ryan leaned in to look at the contents of the frame and quickly cut away his gaze.

Chef Degasse let out a hearty chuckle. "Ah, my shining moment."

Layne's jaw dropped as she stared at the newsprint photo. "You're...you're naked!"

"Oui, Madame. I have always desired to run in the Bay to Breakers. This year I did it. I joined with a group of seniors, and nude is how they run, so this is how I ran."

"I'm sorry, you ran naked? With everything...uh..."

"Oui, all the good parts bobbing about. It was truly liberating." He extended an arm. "Please, Madame, after you."

"That is so...I mean...I'm speechless."

"Many before you have made the same comment. Ah, here we are. The best table in the house."

He held out a chair for Layne, while Ryan seated himself with his back to the cameras. Then Degasse whipped open white linen napkins and patted them onto their laps. Layne couldn't help chuckling as Ryan's lips clamped together at the generous pat.

"This evening we start with the aperitif," the chef said. "I would not normally begin as such, but the nastiness of the day requires a bit of cheer, no?"

"Oui, monsieur," Layne said. "Some cheer would be wonderful."

Degasse waved his arms and barked orders in French as he moved toward the kitchen. Within seconds, a small army of waiters swarmed their table providing moist, warm cloth napkins to cleanse their hands, iced water with thin wafers of cucumber and lemon, and a basket of sprouted whole-grain sourdough baguette, still hot from the oven.

The army departed, and Ryan leaned toward Layne. "Chef Degasse is not at all what I pictured."

"You mean you didn't picture him naked?"

Ryan grinned. "Didn't you say he was in his sixties?"

"He is. What were you picturing?" Layne covered a warm slice of bread with creamy butter and breathed in the essence of sourdough. Her mouth watered, and she took a bite, enjoying the tangy flavor of the freshly baked bread.

"I guess someone more like Santa," Ryan said, fumbling to spread butter on his own piece of baguette with his tiny knife.

Layne took another bite, and Degasse reappeared at their table. "The butter is encroyable, no? We culture and churn it here in our kitchen. We have the cows in the back."

Ryan's eyebrows shot up, and Layne covered her mouth to keep from spraying chewed bread all over the table.

"I make a joke, no? Can you imagine such a thing? Cows, in the middle of San Francisco." Degasse laughed. "True, we have no cows, but we use only the finest organic cream, raw, of course, from nearby Petaluma, with a pinch of Fleur de Sel to enhance the flavor. What do you think?"

"It's excellent," Ryan said. "I've never tasted butter this good. But then, what I eat is bright yellow and comes in a plastic tub."

"Monsieur, that is not butter. How can you think to put that rubbish into your mouth?"

"But the tub says it's heart healthy."

"Your tub, monsieur, she lies. Please, no more. I will send some of this home with you." He hurried off without waiting for a response.

Ryan eyed the butter dish. "Raw cream?"

"Delicious, isn't it?"

"It doesn't sound delicious." He took another big bite. "So, your show. Food Made Whole. That's a reference to cooking with whole foods?"

"Yes. You're familiar with the concept?"

"I've heard the term. Whatever it is, if the picture on the wall is any indication, it's working for the chef."

Layne chuckled. "I agree. It's amazing what the human body will do for you when you feed it nourishing foods and give it exercise. Chef Degasse is a perfect example of that."

"Now you've got me intrigued. What, exactly, are whole foods?"

"They're foods as nature intended."

"As opposed to?"

"That tub in your fridge. My guess? If you read the ingredients, there wouldn't be any actual foods on the list."

"Yeah? What would be there?"

"Chemicals, preservatives, artificial flavors, processed fats, dyes, fillers. Trust me. It's not pretty."

"And not actually good for me, I assume."

"Excellent assumption."

"Then how can they label it as healthy?"

"At one point the fat they used, like pure olive oil, for instance, might have been very nutritious. But the label isn't required to account for the processing. If the original ingredient was heart healthy, it's legal to slap that on the side. But, to be honest, I don't understand how they get away with adding in all the other crap and still calling it healthy."

"Crap. That's a technical term?"

She laughed. "Thanks for being such a good sport about all this."

"The chef's not going to kiss me again, is he?"

She lifted a brow. "Not until we leave."

"You do realize your fate is in my hands."

"Point taken."

Generous snifters of warm Cognac arrived at the table, and Ryan held his glass to Layne's. "To a most intriguing evening."

Sonny watched them enter the restaurant accompanied by a swarm of federal brawn. The chef showed them to their seats, a few tables over from his, and the pack of suited wolves positioned themselves in strategic spots around the room. He shook his head. Amateurs.

A waiter dressed in formal attire handed Sonny a fancy menu scrawled in French on one side, and in English on the other. A busboy placed a basket of bread on his table and filled his water glass. Cucumber. Nice touch. The waiter outlined the format for the evening, but Sonny ignored the well-rehearsed speech while he scanned the dining room. All tables full. Three exits if he counted the kitchen. Approximately twenty-five feet to Layne.

Once the wait staff had gone, he took a swig of his water, slathered butter on a hunk of hot bread, stuffed it into his mouth, and made a discreet check of the back of his waistband. Under the circumstances, it would prove inconvenient to have the handle of his weapon sticking out.

Damn, that was some tasty baguette.

25

Ryan's team spread themselves throughout the dining room, as Hansel and Gretel took positions in the restaurant foyer on either side of the main door. A slight maître d' approached them, and a low-volume but heated discussion ensued. Ryan considered intervening, but Degasse marched over and leveled a stern glare at the three men.

"What seems to be the trouble?" Degasse asked.

The maître d' spoke with urgency. "Ces hommes l'intention d'être plantés ici comme hideux gargouilles tous les soir."

Degasse narrowed his eyes at Hansel and Gretel. "Gentlemen, is this so?"

The two men looked at each other, then back at Degasse.

"Jacques informs me you intend to be planted here like hideous gargoyles all evening," Degasse said.

Gretel widened his stance. "We're here to ensure the safety of Ms. Stevens."

"All right, then do what you must," Degasse said. "But please, no disturbances. This dinner is very important. And at the end, I have a special treat for the two of you rugged beasts. Oui?"

Both men nodded.

"Jacques," Degasse said. "I expect only the most courteous behavior toward our guests."

Jacques pressed his lips together and huffed back to the reception stand.

After Degasse had gone, Gretel directed his attention back to the maître d'. "Hey, Jock."

Jacques rolled his eyes. "Qu'est ce que c'est?'

Gretel stared.

Jacques put his hands on his hips. "What is it?"

"Nobody gets in without a reservation. Got it?"

"I assure you, you behemoth of a man, that no one ever gets in without a reservation."

A few minutes later, Maggie waltzed through the restaurant lobby.

Gretel nudged his chin at Jacques. "Hey, Jock. Did that woman have a reservation?"

"Do I seem like an idiot? Anyone can see this woman is Maggie Malone."

Again, Gretel stared, and again Jacques rolled his eyes. "Ms. Stevens' producairre."

"I knew that," Gretel said.

Maggie approached the table full of life and excitement, in a silver shimmer of dress that hugged her curves so well, and dipped so low in both front and back, that it left little to the imagination. It was difficult for Ryan not to stare. She gave them a vivacious greeting and then bent down to caress Ryan's tie.

"My, my," she said.

In a feeble attempt to turn his focus away from her silky white cleavage, Ryan also looked down at his tie. "Do you like it?" he asked.

"My mother always told me not to speak when I couldn't find something nice to say. I rarely listen to my mother, but for Layne's sake, I'm going to decline to comment on the tie."

"Maggie!" Layne said.

"No offense taken," Ryan assured.

"It's hard to tell," Maggie said. "But isn't that mascara smeared all over it? Oh, Layne, you've made me so proud."

Layne shook her head. "No. I was... and I thought it was...It's been a rough day, and I..."

"You should be proud of her," Ryan said. "She's been amazing given the circumstances."

"Ooo, this one's a keeper." Maggie turned again to Ryan. "Now remember, hun, it's been a while since Layne—well, you know—so be gentle with her."

Ryan choked back a laugh, and Layne covered her face with her hands.

Maggie whispered in Layne's ear, "you can thank me later." Then she turned toward the lobby. "Well, I've gotta run," she said. "My audience outside awaits. Extra Special Agent Cooke, always a yummy treat."

Ryan watched, almost mesmerized, as Maggie flitted back through the restaurant, stopped to peruse Hansel from head to toe, gave his bicep a flirtatious squeeze, and then headed out the door.

"She's really something," he said.

"Is she gone?"

"Yes. She's not staying for dinner?"

Layne dropped her hands. "Dinner isn't her thing. Maggie only comes for the PR and the spotlight. About her comment—"

Ryan held up a hand and gave Layne a warm smile. "No need."

After a few sips of cognac, Layne rose from her chair.

Ryan also stood. "Going somewhere?"

"Yes, to talk to my crew. Give them guidelines so you don't end up on film. They're five feet away. I don't think I need an escort."

"I apologize," he said. "Please, just warn me next time."

Her words sounded strained. "No, don't apologize. It was my fault. With everything that's happened, I'm just a little on edge. But I'm glad you're here. And I'll be right back. Okay?"

Ryan noted Layne's deft avoidance of questions from her camera crew. Then a younger man pulled her aside. He had a relaxed style about him, but the conversation looked tense, and Layne seemed apprehensive when she returned to the table.

Ryan stood. "What's wrong?"

"I spoke with Dennis. He's my crew lead."

"Yes?"

"It's...it's about the tie."

"What about it?"

"The cameras are set up a little off to the side for a decent angle on the food, and to avoid you in the shots."

"Sounds right."

"But, I guess, the...uh...vivid colors of the tie are bleeding into the frame."

"And?"

"Would you mind taking it off?"

"Of course not," he said. "If it affects the camera, I'd be happy to remove it."

"I have to ask," Layne said. "And I don't mean to offend you, but is that really your taste in ties?"

"Pardon?"

"The tie. It...well, the style of it surprised me."

Ryan struggled to control the irritation rising inside him. "Looks like we've been the victims of a prank. I was informed that you selected this tie."

Layne's eyes widened. "You thought I picked that out?"

"That's what I was told."

They both laughed, but Rennick didn't joke, and that concerned him.

As a result of the kissing chef, the napkin incident, the Maggie episode, and then the tie, the conversation and laughter in the surveillance suite forced Rennick to strain for what little she could glean from the wire. But the gist came through loud and clear. Her play at little miss cooking show had failed.

"That was genius, Rennick," Rusk said with a sardonic smile.

Rennick fumed. Good thing she'd already initiated plan B. She left the suite.

26

"Ah, we are without the tie, Monsieur," Chef Degasse said as he approached the table. "C'est bien. The boldness of the tie, it overwhelmed the Romanesque features of the face."

Ryan chuckled, and he was happy to see Layne's tension easing a little too.

"The two of you make such a lovely couple," Degasse said as he gave them each a scripted menu for the evening. Then with a flourish of his arms, he announced, "The seven corpse meal."

Ryan eyed the chef. "Pardon?"

"The meal. It has seven corpses. As is tradition in France."

"Excuse me, Chef," Ryan said. "But I believe you mean course."

"Oui, this is what I said. Madame, are we ready for the first corpse?"

"We are," she said with a warm smile. Then she nodded to the film crew, who took their places for the shoot.

Ryan studied Layne as Degasse rushed toward the kitchen. "Haven't you had enough corpses for one day?"

Her eyes followed the chef through the dining room, and warmth lit her face. "It's doubtful you're going to undo sixty years of French inflection in one evening," she said. "Thank you, but I can handle it."

"You're a good person, Layne Stevens."

Several silent minutes passed. Small talk just wasn't Ryan's thing, and he dreaded what came next—the drudge of pointless banter in search of any nugget of useful information. He'd read the report, knew Layne's story, understood who she was, but did she?

"So," he said, "have you always wanted to do a cooking show?"

"No. I never imagined I'd be where I am today. I got my degree in hospitality, and landed my first job after college at the Omnivance Hotel in Bel Aire as an assistant to the Concierge."

"That's interesting."

"Not even my parents find that interesting."

Ryan seized the opportunity. "I'd like to hear more about your parents."

Degasse returned to the table, surrounded by a swarm of waiters, and declared, "Les hors-d'œuvre, or how to say here, the appetizer."

Ryan's jaw tightened. The chef had terrible timing.

"Because the appetizer is to be featured on your upcoming show," Degasse continued, "I have prepared three instead of only one. All roasted. The first is a lovely blend of mixed organic olives, roasted with fresh herbs and garlic. It is unusual to roast the olives, I know, but this method truly brings out the flavor of the different varieties. And the roasted garlic, this is heaven."

It surprised Ryan to see Layne admiring the bowl of small green and brown lumps in the middle of their table.

"Next," Degasse said, "we have organic roasted fig. The fig acts as a delicate vessel for the finest organic French brie, all wrapped in bacon —naturally cured, of course, and crisped to perfection—with a drizzle of crème de cassis reduction."

Hot fruit filled with cheese? Ryan struggled to maintain a neutral expression.

"Last but not least," Degasse said, "I introduce Beurre Brun le Crabe en Champignon. In English? Mais oui, Brown Butter Crab Stuffed Mushroom. The king of the crab ensconced in exquisite baby bella mushroom with artisan asiago cheese, melted to bubbly perfection." Degasse stepped back and opened his arms. "I present the trio of roasted appetizers all together as a symphony for the palette."

Ryan considered the symphony and his palette regretted his lack of foresight. They really should have gone to a drive-through beforehand.

After the waiters retreated, the sommelier moved in for approval of the wine. Ryan read the label, nodded, and the wine steward poured a small amount of organic Semillon into his glass. Ryan swirled the wine, watched the legs trickle down the inside of the globe, smelled the fruity aroma, and took a sip. "Very nice, thank you," he said. Then he caught Layne staring at him. "What?"

"Impressive," she said.

He grinned. "I'm not all guns and bad guys."

While Layne sampled the appetizers, Ryan watched a group of men enter the restaurant. They were obnoxious and overbearing. Jacques appeared not to find a reservation for them, but one of them slipped Jacques a bill, and he led them to a table.

It disturbed Ryan that the maître d' had been so easily persuaded. But he assessed the men, taking in more detail. Well-groomed, dressed in suits, expensive watches, polished shoes, American accents. Loud, drunken American accents. He disliked this type of profiling, but his ability to perform his job depended on it. If he marked everyone as a suspect, he couldn't narrow the pool of possible threats, and this compromised his focus.

A heated discussion developed at the newly seated table, and Ryan noted his team's attention to the group. Jacques rushed to the side of the big tipper and leveled heavily accented warnings along with small amounts of spittle at the man's neck. The man stood, bent toward the center of the table, and spoke with urgency to the other four men. Ryan's team relaxed, and he realized some time had passed since he'd acknowledged Layne. But before he could turn to face her, one of the men got up from the table and headed for them.

27

Berger went home to get some rest, but sleep would not come, and the first traces of dawn slipping through the edges of his window shade did not help. He reeled in his bed, desperate to gain the comfort of a position that would allow his body and his thoughts to quiet. Three hours later, his eyes had not closed, and his mind continued to thrash. He got out of bed, took a searing hot shower, shaved, applied toothpaste to his teeth, this time with a toothbrush, and went back to work.

When he reached the BKA building, disturbing news about Frederick Schatz awaited him. Berger ran up the steps to the fourth floor, stormed past Director Braun's assistant and into the director's office without warning.

"Ich muss nach California gehen," Berger said.

"Was können Sie auf eigene Faust tun?" The Director replied.

"Er war..."

THOUSANDS OF MILES AWAY, an American translator echoed the conversation coming through the device hidden in Director Braun's office...

"I must go to California, Berger says.
What can you do there on your own? The director asks him.
Frederick Schatz was my responsibility. And he was a fine man. I owe it to him, and to you, to find out what happened. I will bring his killer to justice, and find the memory card. That's Berger again.
Very well. Assemble a team, Braun says to Berger.
I must act quickly, and a team would only hinder my progress. I must do this alone, Berger says.
But this is suicide, Braun says. He sounds upset.
I will risk it, Berger says."

A DOOR CLICKED SHUT, and an audible sigh could be heard before the recording ended.

The translator peered at the two-way glass on the wall which allowed The Employer to see him, but not the reverse.

"That was the end of what we captured yesterday," the translator said. "Director Braun left the office after that."

"It is specious, is it not, that all roads lead to San Francisco?"

"It is," the translator agreed. "Can I be of any further assistance?"

"That will suffice for now," The Employer said.

The translator hadn't fully understood The Employer's comment about San Francisco, and he wouldn't dare ask. But he did hear the smug grin that accompanied the remark.

28

The man from the boisterous table hurried past them toward the restroom, and Ryan turned to find Layne staring at him. "I'm sorry, Layne. You were saying?"

"What's going on?"

"Just being cautious. Nothing to worry about."

She nodded, but concern mantled her face.

"Really," he said. "Everything's fine. Let's concentrate on these wonderful..." He studied the appetizers. "On the food. Okay?"

"If you're sure."

"I'm positive. Now, which of the fifty utensils do I use for this?"

Ryan fumbled with his tiny appetizer fork as, one by one, Layne put green and brown lumps into her mouth, reveling in each bite. He hadn't touched the shriveled nuggets inhabiting his plate, but he found himself jealous of those on hers. It had been some time since a woman had looked at him with as much desire as Layne showed those olives.

She glanced over at him. "You're not eating?"

"Do I have to?"

Her eyes narrowed.

"All right, I'll try them." He stabbed at an unappealing green orb and tasted it. "Hunh. I have to admit, that's not bad. So, back to our conversation, I believe you were talking about your parents."

"I don't think so. I generally avoid that topic. Wait, you asked about my job."

"Oh, right. From Assistant Concierge to food diva—that's quite a jump."

"Hey, I am not a diva. I'm a foodie."

"With her own top-rated show on one of the most watched channels in the country."

"Well, yes. But I don't think that qualifies me as a diva. Maggie, now there's a diva. I'm not sure what kind, but the title definitely suits her." Layne sampled another appetizer. "Holy cow, you've got to try these figs."

He frowned.

"Trust me, they're wonderful."

He tried a bite. "Hmm. They're surprisingly good."

"Good? Are you kidding? The blend of flavors—the fig, the brie, the bacon, the glaze—they're amazing."

Becoming more adept at his use of small utensils, Ryan contemplated another bacon fig thing before he continued his line of questioning. "How did you end up with your own show?" he asked.

"It's a long story."

"Aren't there six more courses?"

"I wouldn't want my protector to die of boredom during dinner."

"I suspect there is nothing boring about you, Layne."

Her cheeks turned a soft shade of pink, and he was gratified at having made her blush again. Besides the food, things were off to a good start.

Ryan inspected a stuffed mushroom. "Finally, something I recognize," he said. "But why are the appetizers all shriveled?"

"It's the roasting. I can understand how you might be put off by the appearance, but when I see shriveled skin, I know there's going be something tasty inside."

He lifted his eyebrows, and Layne cleared her throat.

"Let's just concentrate on the appetizers," she said.

"Of course, but no more naughty talk at the table."

"I'll try to control myself."

"You'd better, or I may have to get out the handcuffs."

Layne's eyes grew wide, and it was Ryan's turn to clear his throat.

"You're right," he said. "We should concentrate on the appetizers."

Ryan didn't typically pay much attention to his food, but with the tone set by Layne, he took a bite of mushroom and savored it. "The crab is so..."

"Sweet?"

"Yes. How did Degasse do that?"

"It's the brown butter."

"Don't tell me—it comes from brown cows he keeps out back."

Layne chuckled.

"I'm sorry I interrupted you earlier," Ryan said. "Please, go on with your story."

"Let's see. I guess I sometimes have difficulty containing my opinion."

"You don't say."

She dropped her jaw in feigned dismay. "Anyway, in hospitality, when you have a big mouth, promotions tend to come like puppies."

"Puppies?"

"You know, something you think you want until you have to deal with the mess."

"Ah. But I imagine there's also higher pay."

"You don't get a ton more money, but they give you a fancy title and a little more control. Anyhow, I worked my way up through the ranks, and finally became the hotel's Executive Food and Beverage Director."

"Wow."

"Yeah, you'd think, right?"

"Not wow?"

"Our restaurants stunk. People would go out for fast food rather than eat at the hotel."

He frowned. "Wow."

"Exactly. The food scene in downtown LA is very competitive. But with my new found authority, I considered the types of foods I enjoy when I dine out, did quite a bit of research, and made some significant changes—added more locally grown produce, took on some artisan suppliers, eliminated most of the processed ingredients—and it worked. The food got better."

"Sounds like a clever move."

"In hospitality, no clever move comes without issues."

"How so?"

"No one understood it. We brought in lots of fresh ingredients, and with all the different terms...natural, organic, non-GMO, sustainable, allergen free...well, you get the idea. Guests would ask questions about ingredients, like gluten or lactose, and our serving staff couldn't answer them."

"And now I'm confused too."

"Then I'll be certain to send you my cheat sheet."

"Your what?"

"From all that research, I put together a cheat sheet for the employees. We used it for training, and eventually everybody got on board. The staff, management, the customers...everyone was happy. It felt incredible."

"It seems like you were perfect for the job."

"Well, I'd come into a difficult time in my personal life. But throwing myself into the new position saved me. I set my mind to making it work, and in the process, I developed a passion for whole foods—the flavors, the health benefits, the entire concept really."

Ryan opened his mouth to ask a question, then stopped himself.

"What is it?" Layne asked.

"I assure you it was nothing intelligent," he said.

She laughed at the comment, but he'd decided that before he pursued the information in her file, it might be best for her to have more wine.

THE LAST-MINUTE FINE dining directive still irked him as he tore off another hunk of bread, scraped it across the top of the small container of butter, and then perused the pretentious menu. Sonny had nothing against French food. He just hated the French—pompous snobs with their fancy cigarettes and skinny jeans. And the suit—how did guys wear these things all ef-ing day? The shirt collar scratched at his neck. The pant legs constricted his thighs. And the tie brushed over his bread plate whenever he moved. But he supposed the irritations could be tolerated for the pleasure of watching Layne. And so far, the free meal had been pretty tasty.

He smirked. He hadn't anticipated dinner and a show. But these highly trained professional bureau thugs damned near took out an inebriated dumb ass, who from the expression on his face, might not have made it to the urinal in time. And the best part? They hadn't noticed the only real threat in the room. Shit, he was good.

He popped the last bacon-wrapped fig into his mouth and allowed himself to shut his eyes for a moment. The incredible combination of flavors fascinated him, unlike anything he'd ever tried. For smug bastards, the French could spin a dish. He put down his fork, took a swig of his wine, and swiped at his lips with the fancy napkin. He understood his orders. No interaction with the target. Observation only. But she sat so close he could smell her perfume. He previewed the next course on the menu. Soup. That should give him time to figure out how to get to Layne.

29

As they ate, Ryan considered what Layne had told him about his heart healthy spread, and took a mental tally of the processed foods in his kitchen. "Oh, wait. I have a tomato," he said.

"Excuse me?"

"That's a whole food, isn't it?"

Layne crinkled her nose. "Nope, sorry."

"What do you mean?"

"Is it organic?"

"I don't think so."

"If it wasn't grown using organic methods, then it's been compromised. Not everyone would agree, but by my definition, that's not a whole food."

"Someone compromised my tomato? That just sounds wrong."

She nodded. "It is. The average grocery store tomato is grown from genetically modified seed, in soil depleted of nutrients..."

Ryan ate another olive. "Uh huh."

"With polluted water, chemical fertilizers, and toxic pesticides—"

"I think I understand."

"It's harvested before it's ripe, waxed to make it shiny, travels hundreds of miles, then sits in the market for weeks."

"I've got the picture."

"By then, there are hardly any nutrients left in the thing. Lycopene my ass. And don't get me started on the taste..."

"I wouldn't dream of it. There's a lot of information swimming around in that beautiful head of yours."

She grimaced. "Sorry."

He put his hand over hers. "Never apologize for your passion."

Her gaze fell to his hand.

"Layne," he said.

"Yes?"

"There's something I want to—"

"Madame et Monsieur. Are we ready for the next corpse?"

Layne slipped her hand out from under Ryan's to focus on the chef. And he wasn't sure whether to be relieved or disappointed. That spark he'd felt might help to win her over, but he wasn't supposed to be the one feeling it.

"For the second corpse," Degasse said, "may I present Le Crème Consummé du Poireau un Petoncle. This is a creamy, roasted leek soup with wild baby bay scallops and crème fraiche," Degasse said. "This corpse is paired with a lovely organic Côte du Rhône which will bring out the sweetness of the roasted leek. And I have personally ensured no extra little surprises in this dish." He cast a small grin at Layne.

"I'm sure it will be perfect," she said.

Degasse stepped back, and they were each given a wide, shallow bowl with flat edges, sprinkled with minced herbs. The creamy broth had a green tinge, segmented by fine white lines that swirled away from a dollop of crème fraiche in the center of the dish. Degasse stood by as Ryan approved the wine, then he gave Ryan's shoulder a squeeze. "Please...enjoy."

"You seem to have made quite an impression on Chef Degasse," Layne said.

"I'll admit I'm a little out of my element, but I appreciate a nice wine. I need to stay sharp though. If there's a pairing with every course, I'll take just a sip of each."

"Maybe I'll drink yours," Layne said with a chuckle.

"I'll bet you could use it."

Layne tasted her soup and her eyelids closed. "Yum. Perfectly caramelized scallops, and the sweet tang of the roasted leeks combined with the richness of the cream...it's an incredible combination."

Ryan gazed at Layne's expression as she savored her soup. When she opened her eyes, she glanced over at him, her eyes enlarged, and then she bent forward, clutching her throat. Ryan leapt from his chair, her crew raced toward the table, and Degasse pushed his way through the crowd.

Layne held up a hand. "I'm okay. Really, I'm fine. I just need some water."

Ryan put her glass in her hand, and she took a few sips. "Seriously, I'm fine. I...uh...swallowed wrong. Chef Degasse, I am so sorry I worried you. The soup is heavenly. In fact, it's so delicious I forgot how to swallow. You know me. Always so graceful."

Relief spread over the chef's face as he dabbed his forehead with a cloth napkin. "What you lack in grace, my dear, you make up for in charm."

The crowd dispersed, and Ryan took his seat. "Are you sure you're all right?"

Layne leveled a stern whisper at him. "What the heck? When I saw you staring at me like that, I just about fell off my chair."

"Like what?"

"Like...like...never mind."

"Hunh. I hadn't realized I was so obvious. Let me be honest with you, Layne."

Her eyes darted around the room as if scanning for the nearest exit. "That really isn't necessary," she said. "In fact, honesty is way overrated. Couldn't we pretend you were staring at something caught in my teeth and move on?"

Ryan grinned and leaned in close. "You're a beautiful woman, Layne, and even more beautiful when you lose yourself in some exotic flavor. A man would have to be blind not to notice. Hell, a ninety-year-old man with trifocals ogled you on the way in."

She muffled a laugh. "I think that might be an exaggeration, but thank you."

"I'm not kidding. But he didn't see what I do."

Her eyes finally met his, and he leaned closer. "I see a woman so incredibly beautiful both inside and out, that the beauty is impossible to overlook."

"Wow," Layne said on a breath. "That was...wow."

He settled back in his chair. "See? A wonderful dinner companion and two sips of wine, and my guard is already down. But that's no excuse for making you feel uncomfortable. Can you forgive me?"

"Of course. I'm sorry I snapped at you. I guess the day is wearing on me. And I'm still anxious about tonight, especially this course."

"Understandable. So, we're okay then?"

She nodded. "By the way, I wasn't kidding about my lack of grace. It's a well-known fact about Layne Stevens, cooking show host and stunt maven. You're protecting a klutz."

"Stunt maven, huh? I'll keep that in mind."

The sommelier poured more wine, and with their equipment set aside, the camera crew took the opportunity for a short break. Layne continued to sip at her soup, and Ryan slathered more creamy butter on another piece of warm baguette. "Isn't butter bad for you?" he asked.

Degasse re-materialized before them. "Please, allow me," Degasse said. "In fact, Monsieur, fat is essential to vibrant health. Other cultures have thrived for centuries on whole saturated fats—butter, lard, tallow, and my personal favorite, duck fat. Only in America is the food supply so damaged that even foods once considered healthy do harm."

"That's disturbing," Ryan said.

"It is indeed. This is what motivates me each day to do what I do. Now, please, tell me your assessment of the soup."

"It's excellent," Ryan said.

Degasse eyed Layne.

"Oh, Chef, it's exquisite."

He beamed. "I am so pleased you enjoyed it. On to the next corpse, then?"

Ryan spotted the rapid movement of a figure coming toward them, and within seconds, he was up with gun drawn and aimed at the assailant. Several of his team tackled the man to the ground, searched, and cuffed him.

"He's got a piece, boss," Gretel yelled over the commotion. "You want us to take him in?"

"No. We need to understand the threat. Take him to a town car."

Ryan turned to Layne, but she was gone.

30

Ryan scanned the dining room for any sign of Layne, and when he didn't see her, he called out her name.

A muffled voice came from beneath him. "Down here."

He lifted the side of the tablecloth and exhaled a relieved breath. "Are you all right?"

"Uh huh."

He knelt, extending his hand to help her out.

"No, thanks. I'm good here."

"Layne, we've got him."

She bit at the corner of her lip.

"It's okay," Ryan said. "We've got the guy."

She inched her way out from under the table, but between the shoes and the skirt, Ryan didn't envy the process. Then the edge of the tablecloth caught on Layne's heel, and everything on the table shifted —plates, silver, recently filled water glasses.

"Uh oh," she said.

Ryan tried to hide his grimace as most of a glass of water, including the ice and soggy wedges of lemon and cucumber, landed on his sleeve. "No big deal. Let's get you out of there."

He helped Layne up, took off his jacket, wiped it down with his napkin, and hung it on the back of his chair. Then he patted his shirt sleeve. Dry enough.

"At this rate," Layne said, "you'll be naked by the end of the night." Her hand flew to her mouth.

"Now I know your true intentions," he said with a sly grin.

She took her seat with an air of composure, but her grip on his dry sleeve revealed it as a thin disguise.

"Was that part of the stunt maven act?" he asked.

She let out a half-hearted chuckle.

"Listen, I've got to go outside and talk to this guy. I'll only be a few minutes, and I'll leave Hansel with you at the table. Will you be all right?"

Layne shook her head, but her mouth said, "Sure."

Why were women so damned confusing? "Layne?"

"Yes, I'll be fine. Go."

"I'll need my arm."

RYAN CLIMBED into the back of the town car and eyeballed the man, still in cuffs, babbling in drunkenese about the constitution and his lawyer.

"Name?"

"I'm a...I know my rights," the man said.

"This is a matter of national security. You have no rights."

"Huh?"

"What were your intentions when you approached Layne Stevens?"

"They paid me."

"Who paid you?"

"The guys."

"What guys?"

"The damn guys at my table. Who'd ya think?"

Ryan expelled an exasperated breath. "What were you supposed to do?"

"Look, unless you tell me...ah shit, wait for my lawyer. I know stuff. I get a call."

"You get nothing until you explain why you rushed our table."

"That woman, she ruined everything. It was my buddy wanted to come here. Frickin' French food. I knew it was gonna be bad, but he said we gotta come. I guess I had... hmm, few too many, but we get here, and there she is. Layne frickin' Stevens."

"The food's actually very good," Gretel said from the driver's seat.

Ryan sent Gretel a sharp glare.

"Sorry, boss, but the chef hooked us up."

"I am kinda hungry," the man said. "Got any left?"

Ryan turned his attention back to the drunken idiot. "I will only ask this one more time before I shoot you. What was your intent?"

"I told ya. The guys paid me to go tell her. She ruined my marriage, but man, she's so hot."

"You came at us like a freight train with a concealed weapon to tell Ms. Stevens she's hot?"

The man belched. "I always carry. I'm a PI."

Ryan shook his head.

"You know, private investigator, as in private eye." The man gave an exaggerated wink. "That's my eye. Was gonna point to it. It's what I do. But these damn cuffs. Catchy, don't ya think? PI?" The man winked again.

"Yeah, catchy." Ryan turned to Gretel. "You have his wallet?"

"Running it now, boss."

"Who are your pals?" Ryan gestured with his chin to the lineup of all American men, now all in handcuffs, standing on the side of the building.

"Buddies from college. It's a frickin' bachelor party. The guy on the left, he's getting married. Wanted to come here. Can you believe it? Never, in a zillion years, would I pick this place for the last rights. But he wanted this snooty sh—"

"That doesn't explain why you came at Ms. Stevens with a loaded weapon."

"How many times do I gotta tell it?" The man attempted to wriggle out of his handcuffs. "Look, a couple three years ago some woman hires me to find out who her husband is hammering. Turns out he was sneaking off with his frickin' laptop. Ha. Streaming episodes of *Food Made Whole*. Well, I gotta see this thing for myself. Ya know, research. And I frickin' get hooked. But I gotta go and do it right in front of my main squeeze. I mean, ex... Anyway, that show is like food porn. Once you start watching, you can't stop. Then we see her here, ya know, that close. The guys, they're all giving me a bad time. Next thing there's four hundi's on the table if I go confess to the lady that I think she's hot and she ruined my marriage."

"And you didn't notice the camera crew, or the strategically positioned men in dark suits?"

Confusion crossed the man's face. "What camera crew? The news? I'm gonna be on the frickin' television?"

Ryan's fists tightened. "So, this was a dare."

"Jesus. That's what I been sayin'. Can I take a piss?"

"Why bring a gun to a bachelor party?"

"It's always there." The man tried to look behind his back. "I don't even notice it anymore. Hey, where is it? I didn't scare her, did I? Shit. I would never. The last thing I wanted..."

Ryan eyed Gretel. "Well?"

"It's all here, boss. He's a PI straight up. Recently divorced."

"All right. Go check in with the friends. Verify the story. I'm going back inside."

"You got it, boss."

The man tipped toward Ryan. "I really gotta piss. Hey, can you get me her autograph?"

Ryan slammed the car door and went back to the restaurant to talk with Jacques.

"I'm curious," he said to the Maître d'. "Why did you seat that group without a reservation?"

Jacques curled the corner of the reservation book as he peered down. "They did have a reservation."

Ryan stared. "Excuse me?"

Jacques stiffened. "I pretended I could not find their reservation because they were filthy drunk. But the tall one, he made it worth my while. I assumed more money for the restaurant and a bonus pour moi. Any other night, no harm done."

Ryan's lips formed a tight line. Could the evening get any more complicated? He turned to their table, where Hansel occupied his seat, and a crowd of people waited to talk to Layne. She spoke to a man of average height, with a medium build and blond hair. Nothing about him stood out, but something about him jabbed at Ryan's gut.

31

The nondescript man bent down to shake Layne's hand, and Ryan observed him wrapping his other hand around her upper arm. The familiarity of the gesture irritated him, and he keyed in on their conversation as he worked his way across the room.

Layne smiled at the man. "Well, after the day I've had, I may need your services."

"It would be my pleasure to meet all of your needs, Layne," the man said.

Ryan moved in next to Hansel. "How's everything over here?"

Hansel stood. "Autographs, boss. Keep forgetting she's a celebrity. The line formed right after you left."

Ryan studied the man standing next to Layne's chair.

"Ryan," she said. "This is..."

The man straightened and his expression seemed to carry a hint of disdain. "It's Sonny."

"Yes, Sonny," Layne said. "He works in private security. He happened to be here for dinner and saw the, uh, incident."

Sonny turned back to Layne, and his face warmed. "It was wonderful to talk with you, Layne. I'll leave my contact information on your website. Someday soon you'll need me."

"Let's hope not, for my sake."

"Oh, you will. Until we meet again." The man walked away and took a seat a few tables over.

"Are all your fans that...odd?" Ryan asked.

"What do you mean? I thought he was kind of sweet," Layne said. "Although the last part was a little strange."

Ryan scrutinized the man, then returned his attention to Layne. "What was with all the touching?"

"Why, Agent Cooke, if I didn't know better, I'd say you were jealous."

Something behind Ryan appeared to catch Layne's eye.

"Look at poor Gretel," she said. "At that rate, he's never going to make it."

Ryan turned to see Gretel shimmying his oversized frame through crowded tables and chairs. It was several minutes before he reached them.

"Story checks out, boss," Gretel said. "I contacted the fiancé. Guy's getting married on Saturday. Just a drunken boys' night out, and they left the four hundred they bet the PI on the table."

"All right, let them go," Ryan said. "But make sure they understand why they were detained. And tell them to continue their festivities elsewhere."

"Will do, boss. But if the fiancé had anything to say about it, I'd guess the festivities are over."

Ryan turned to Layne. "You sure you're okay?"

"I am, thanks. What happened outside?"

"Just an over-exuberant fan. Don't get me wrong, but you're a hard woman to take out in public."

Layne nodded. "I'm a hard woman to be me out in public...I mean...oh, screw it. You know what I mean."

He chuckled. "How much wine have you had?"

"Not nearly enough."

Degasse joined them. "Shall we proceed, Madame?"

"I'm so sorry, Chef. I can't believe everything that has gone wrong. Well...I can...it's me. But poor you."

"No need, my dear. My only disappointment is this time Dennis did not capture the incident on film. Unlike the other nastiness, this would have been exceptional marketing. Such bravery and rigorous action by the fine officers. But no matter. I am sure another opportunity will come about. You always bring a liveliness to our city."

Layne laughed. "I think I'm going to take that as a compliment."

"As indeed you should." He waited for a signal from Dennis before resuming the meal. "Now, may I introduce the third corpse, a table-side tossed salad."

A large, hand-carved, cherry wood bowl sat on a wooden stand at table height in front of Degasse. Several waiters stood behind him with different ingredients. "We use only organic produce, local and in season," Degasse said as he layered mixed greens, half rounds of thinly sliced red onion, wedges of tangerine, slivered almonds, and a blend of wild mushrooms into the bowl. "Ah, the mushroom, food of the gods. And an aphrodisiac as well, no?"

Next, he began adding ingredients to a small mixing bowl with one hand while whisking with the other. "For the dressing, I begin with the aged Balsamic vinegar, then a dab of stone ground mustard, a bit of raw, unfiltered honey, some celery seed, a pinch of Fleur de Sel—the queen of the sea salt—and a grind of the white pepper. Now I blend in some organic avocado oil until emulsified. The oil is key. So rich and fruity." The restaurant grew silent as all patrons watched Degasse. "I pour this over the vegetables, toss et Voila! Heritage salad with mustard vinaigrette."

Degasse stood aside to allow the cameras and other customers view of his creation. Then he tilted the bowl to give Layne and Ryan a glimpse. "We will partner this with a fruity, organic Pinot Gris as a balance to the tanginess of the salad."

Layne reached her hand toward the bowl, and Degasse swatted her away. "Oh, Madame. You feisty creature."

"Can't blame a girl for trying." Layne bobbed her eyebrows at the chef.

Degasse leaned toward Ryan. "You may have your hands full this evening, Monsieur."

THE CREW CAPTURED the entire course as Degasse plated the salads himself, added a sprinkle of Camembert to each plate, and placed them in front of Layne and Ryan. But Dennis noted Layne's eyelids narrowing, so he instructed them to focus in on the dish, and on Degasse.

With the third course complete, Dennis walked over to Layne's table. "It's been one hell of a day," he said to Layne. "Are you sure you want to keep filming? We can take a few shots of the outside and in the kitchen, and be done with it."

"That's thoughtful, Dennis, but Chef Degasse would be so disappointed. Keep it rolling and the editors can work their voodoo magic afterward." Layne fluttered her fingers in the air.

Dennis shook his head and stepped off to the side to make a call, keeping his voice muffled. "She shouldn't be here," he said into his cell phone. "This was a mistake."

He listened to the response, but his back tensed as he struggled to maintain his composure.

"No," he said. "And I'm not being dramatic. Look, this is not how it was supposed to go down. Things are getting out of hand."

He frowned.

"Understood. I'll do whatever you ask, but I don't like it. We could compromise everything."

32

"You haven't finished your story," Ryan said after Dennis left the table.

"I was kind of hoping you'd forgotten," Layne said.

He snickered. "You were talking about your cheat sheet."

"Right. Well, eventually the Omnivance turned my whole foods cheat sheet into a nationwide program. It received a fair amount of press, and the Foodie Channel got wind of it. Public interest in organic foods and sustainable farming was at an all-time high, so they asked me to do a guest spot."

"There's public interest in this stuff?"

"You'd be amazed," she said. "It's a hotly debated topic. Anyway, I sat in as a guest on the Foodie Review. Have you ever seen the show?"

"Nope, somehow I missed that one."

"It's foodie news but with a comic spin. The show went well. Stu and I—he's the host—we had a great time bantering back and forth, and the episode got excellent reviews.

"Wait. Are you telling me there's a food show with a host named Stew?"

Layne swallowed her gulp of wine and laughed. "It's short for Stuart."

"Got it."

"So, they signed me on for a permanent guest spot, and that's when I met Darren."

"Who's Darren?"

"Darren Chase. He's the President of the Foodie Channel. He's kinda stuffy and formal, so it surprised me that he liked our bit on the show. But he asked me to pitch."

"Wild guess. He wasn't referring to the network softball team."

"Nope. I had to pitch an idea for a new show. Darren is a huge proponent of whole foods, and he's very influential in the industry, so it was a lot of pressure."

Layne stopped talking long enough to take a big bite of her salad, giving Ryan time to locate the correct utensil. He was enjoying their conversation, and the lack of unexpected intrusions in this course held promise. He tried the salad. For a bowl of wet vegetables, it far exceeded his expectations. And after an aperitif and some wine, Layne finally seemed to relax and enjoy the evening. He hoped this would yield some new information, but if he was being honest with himself, he felt glad to see Layne's tensions ease, information or not.

"So, about your pitch," Ryan said.

Layne swallowed. "Let's see. I had three days to come up with an idea and put together a presentation."

"Sounds difficult."

"That's where Stu was a godsend. He worked with me day and night to help me prepare. Then on Monday morning, exactly as Stu coached me, I walked into the executive conference room at the Foodie Channel, went through my PowerPoint with authority and a sense of humor, and just like that, my show was in the Fall lineup. It was a whirlwind. I gave my notice at the Omnivance, trained my replacement, and here I am. I still can't believe it. I feel so fortunate."

Ryan studied Layne. "And Stu?"

"We've been inseparable ever since. I couldn't have done it without him."

Ryan hadn't factored in a relationship. That made things more difficult. "Well, Stuart's a lucky man."

A throng of waiters moved in to clear salad plates, used crystal, and silver, and it relieved Ryan to note his utensil selection shrinking. "I'm sorry to interrupt your story again, but please tell me the next course isn't snails."

"Snails?"

"The intermezzo is next on the program, isn't that snails?"

Layne chuckled. "Snails are called escargot."

"That's a relief. I don't think I could've done it. What's an intermezzo?"

As if on cue, a waiter slid between them offering two small crystal dishes filled with a scoop of something orange, followed by slim pilsner glasses containing a clear, bubbly beverage, and garnished with a slice of lime.

Ryan stared at the small bowl in front of him. "Ice cream?"

Once again, Degasse appeared from behind his staff. "No, no, monsieur. Mango sorbet and sparkling mineral water. To cleanse the palette for the heavier corpse to follow. Please enjoy."

"That word is driving me crazy," Ryan said after Degasse had gone.

"That is so sweet of you. But it's kinda funny if you think about it...corpse...ha. Don't we get more wine?"

"I believe you drank all the wine."

She gave him a playful slap on the arm. "Don't be silly. The French never run out of wine."

"We're cleansing," Ryan said.

"Ah yes, cleansing." Layne dipped into her sorbet, and with her mouth full said, "Mmm, this is delicious. Don't you think this is delicious?" Then she raised her wine glass into the air. "Excuse me, anyone, I seem to be out of wine."

Ryan let out a laugh, and Layne's lips formed a pout. "What?"

Fifteen minutes later, the camera crew ambled back into the dining room, and Chef Degasse approached the table. "Ah, I see we are ready for the main corpse."

Degasse's infantry moved in, and after much fanfare, pointing, and final instruction, he announced the dish. "May I present the Crème du Sole. This is a most tender fish, seared on the grill with special seasoning, and finished with a lemon crème beurre blanc. It is presented with honey-roasted gorgonzola beet, kohlrabi hazelnut pilaf, and confetti of Brussels sprout. It looks exquisite, no?"

Degasse placed their entrees in front of them, and Layne took in the aroma while Ryan gaped at his plate. No. Exquisite was not the description he would have used.

"Oh, this smells amazing," Layne said.

Words eluded Ryan. An entire fish, complete with head and tail, flopped off the ends of the oval plate. It looked as though Degasse had swiped it from the window of the market below his condo, dumped it onto his plate, and decorated it.

The sommelier poured the wine, and Layne raised her glass. "To new friends."

Ouch. First a boyfriend, then a whole fish, and now the F word? Much like the dish, this course officially stunk. He didn't get it. Seducing female suspects was sort of his thing. Something he had a reputation for at the agency. Why was he having so much trouble with Layne? Ryan contemplated the fish. It stared back, but it didn't seem to have any answers.

"Don't you think this is taking whole foods a little too far?" he asked. "This thing might as well be swimming."

"You should drink more wine," Layne said.

Ryan followed Layne's lead and clumsily navigated his fork under the skin to find something similar to the fillet of sole he recognized.

"See? It's not so bad," Layne said.

The parts he'd been willing to try were okay. The pilaf tasted great. And although he never imagined himself anywhere near a Brussels sprout, they weren't terrible. He looked at the fish again and decided instead to move on with his line of questioning.

"So, you were born in South Dakota?"

"Uh huh," Layne said between enthusiastic bites.

"That explains the slight German accent I heard in your mother's voice."

"I know I've had some wine, but you've got me there. First, that you noticed an accent, but how do you tie that to South Dakota?"

"That's need-to-know," he said with a toying grin. "How did you end up in California?"

"I'm not sure why we moved to LA," she said. "But I've never lived anywhere else. It's one of the reasons I love this job. I get to spend time in so many places I wouldn't have seen."

"You do a lot of flying?"

"Yes. And I know what you're thinking. But for the most part, I have my fear of flying managed. I booked this trip at the last minute. Then I barely checked in on time, and I was nervous about the shoot. I had a rough start with my seat assignment, and the turbulence...I guess it all got to me. Can I apologize again for spilling my dessert all over you?"

That explained the stains he'd found on his slacks. "Don't worry about it. You know, I fly quite a bit, and I can't imagine doing that if it was something I dreaded. You must be a very strong woman."

Layne put on a gratified grin.

"So," Ryan said. "If your mom and dad are German, how did you come by this exotic complexion and dark hair?"

"Wow. Exotic. I like it. I could brush the question off to a skilled colorist and time in the sun, but I'm sure you'll find out anyway." Layne adjusted her napkin and lowered her voice. "I'm adopted."

Grateful she'd brought it up on her own, Ryan pretended to be surprised. But he felt confident some encouragement and a little more wine would get him what he needed.

33

Ryan scrutinized a pile of dark red cubes on his plate. He isolated one with his fork and pushed it around. "So," he said. "Have you ever met your biological parents?"

"No. But it's not a big deal," Layne said. "The couple I know as my parents adopted me after my first birthday, and I didn't learn I was adopted until my late thirties. I found my real birth certificate when I helped my dad clean out his office."

"You have a counterfeit birth certificate?"

"I don't think counterfeit is the right word. My mom told me adoption agencies provided the documents to protect children who weren't emotionally ready to handle it."

"Hmm. I wasn't aware of that." An interesting fib, he thought. The government didn't take well to forged official documents, unless they were for government use.

"What about you?" she asked. "Are you a native Californian?"

Ryan glanced around. None of his men were within earshot. And sharing a piece of personal information might help move the conversation along, but he didn't intend to do that on film. Fortunately, the camera crew was headed to the kitchen for their cream of whole fish on a platter.

"Ryan?"

"Sorry. No. I was born in Virginia. My father was military, so I've moved dozens of times and lived all over the world."

"As an adult that sounds exciting, but as a child I imagine it would be kind of rough," Layne said.

"A little. I learned a lot about the nature of people, both good and bad. Overall it's been a plus for the job."

"What makes a person choose work like this?"

"It's hard to say. I don't have any siblings, and I lost my parents when they were relatively young, so I have no family ties to maintain. I guess with my childhood as a Navy brat, this job just felt like home."

"I'm sorry about your parents."

"Thanks. It was a long time ago."

"What happened?"

He stared down at his plate, uncertain how much he was willing to share.

"I'm sorry. That was a very personal question. I shouldn't have asked," Layne said.

"No, it's okay. We were stationed in China Lake. I was seventeen at the time. My father had shore duty that year, so it was like we were a regular family. One morning my father was still at home when I got up, which was unusual for him. He had an amazing work ethic. I heard him moving around in the bedroom, but I just assumed he wasn't feeling well. Anyway, I said goodbye to my mom, left for school, and when I got home, the place was trashed, and my parents were gone."

Lane's hand went to her heart. "Oh my god, Ryan. That's terrible. Did they ever find them?"

He shook his head as the memories flooded his mind. "I can still picture my mom's face, her smile as I walked through the kitchen that morning. But my dad...well..."

"You didn't get to say goodbye."

He looked over at her and saw his anguish mirrored in her eyes. "Hey, I'm supposed to ask the questions here."

"And you still don't know what happened to them?"

"After this long, odds are I'll never know."

"You were only seventeen. What did you do?"

"I took my GED and joined the Navy. I had big plans to help with the investigation. You know how teenagers think. Of course, the Navy wouldn't let me anywhere near their investigation, but I pursued it on my own for several years. Picked up some skills. And here I am, sharing way more than I intended. I'm not sure how you did that, but stop it."

"Yes, sir," she said with a teasing smile.

The reminder of Rennick propelled him to the present, and he raised a brow at Layne. "So, now I get to ask you a question."

"Of course."

"What are these red things?" He stabbed at a scarlet cube with his fork and held it up.

She chuckled. "Those are beets."

"Really. I tried beets at a salad bar once."

"And?"

"They were slimy."

"Trust me. They didn't taste like this. These are awesome."

"Awesome seems like it might be an overstatement," Ryan said. "Hey, since we're on the subject of family, do you know what happened to your biological parents?"

"Only that they were both killed in a car accident in a town not far from where my parents lived. I needed a home, and my parents weren't able to have children. In hindsight, they may not have chosen to have kids, but they did what they felt was right."

"Then you're an only child?"

"Actually, I'm not. I have a brother who is two years younger than I am. And no, he's not adopted. My mom called him the miracle baby they never wanted. Don't get me wrong. She said it lovingly. For her."

Ryan had missed the information on Layne's brother in the report, but he'd go over her file in more detail when they returned to the hotel. They continued to talk and eat. Ryan sipped his water, while Layne drank more wine. As they finished their entrees, Ryan detected a distinct slowness to Layne's speech, along with the occasional slur.

After the plates were cleared, Layne reached across the table, took one of Ryan's hands into hers, gazed into his eyes, and said, "There's something I need to tell you."

Ryan waited for Layne to speak. Instead, she laid her forehead on the table.

"Layne?"

She rolled her head to face him. "Huh?"

"Are you okay?"

"I'm fine. Always fine."

The four wine pairings had been modest, but he assumed after the day's events, they took their toll. "You had something you wanted to tell me?"

She whispered loudly, "I need to go to the powder room."

Ryan chuckled and motioned for Hansel. "Ms. Stevens would like to use the ladies' room. Can you secure the area?"

Hansel nodded, then spoke into his radio and headed toward the bathrooms. He reappeared, gave another nod, and Ryan assisted Layne with her chair.

"Such a gentleman," she said, wavering to an upright position.

Ryan caught her as she lost her balance, and put his arm around her for support.

"I'm okay," she said, letting him lead her through the dining room and down the hall. She tipped her head back and looked up at him, her eyes wide and innocent. "I say that a lot, don't I?"

Ryan pushed the women's restroom door open with his shoulder, guided Layne inside, placed her in front of a stall, balanced her, and then stepped aside. "I'll be in the hallway if you need me."

"No!" Layne grabbed the edges of the stall and twisted around to look at him. "You can't go. Stay right there. Both of you." She closed one eye and looked at the wall to the left of Ryan. "You. Stay. Right. There."

He snickered. "All right. We'll both be right here." He folded his arms and leaned against the wall behind him as Layne entered the stall and shut the door behind her. A loud bang came from the tiny enclosure, along with some mild cursing.

"I'm okay," she said. "God, I love thigh highs. Don't you love thigh highs? What would women do without thigh highs?"

Ryan could have gone all night without picturing Layne in sheer, black, thigh high stockings.

A rustling noise came from the stall, and Layne called out to him again. "Hey, I found my polite...ha...my political connect...ha-ha...my vibrator! It's here. In my purse."

Another picture to erase from his mind. "You might want to tuck that back into your bag."

"You... are so...very, probably right."

More rustling, then a flush, and the stall door opened. To Ryan's relief, Layne emerged fully dressed, with all articles of clothing, and otherwise, returned to their appropriate spot. But she appeared to be stuck. After some finagling, she pushed off the doorway, stumbled, and landed flat on Ryan's chest. He caught her around the waist, and she anchored against him. When she tipped her face up, her lips, courtesy of her heels, were mere centimeters from his.

"It would be so easy to kiss you right now," she said. "If I could figure out which one was you."

Ryan took a moment to put his testosterone in check. "Are you all right?"

"I'm fine, thanks." Her body melted into his. "Are you all right?"

"I'm..." He cleared his throat. "If we don't leave the ladies' room soon, my entire team is likely to join us."

Layne crinkled her nose. "This isn't a very good place for a party."

"I agree."

Layne stared up at him for a moment, tilted her head, and then she slid her tongue along his jaw bone.

His eyebrows jumped. "Did you just lick me?"

"Did I? Hmm. I missed it. Can I please do it again?"

He fought his laughter. "Don't you want to wash your hands?"

"No."

"Yes, you do. Come on." Ryan maneuvered Layne to a vertical position and guided her to the sink to rinse her hands.

She turned and used his shirt sleeve to dry them. "You know," she said, "I'm trying really hard, but it is very difficult not to...well, you know."

“What do I know?” Ryan asked.

“You know. This is not a date. There is no dating. I don’t go on dates. But you’ve been so...sweet, and so...nice, and so...charming. And protective. Very protective. It makes me feel...”

She teetered to the side, then steadied herself with both hands on his chest and slanted toward him. “Ryan?”

Despite his best efforts, his nerve endings sizzled every time she touched him. “Yes?”

She peered at him from under heavy eyelids. “I love you.”

He stared down at her.

She tipped closer. “Well?”

34

For the first time in years, Ryan froze. He knew the way out. Say the words and move on. Just spill them. He could do that. He'd done it before. They were only words, and clearly, there would be no movement on Layne's part until she heard them.

"I..." he said.

Layne smiled.

He let out a breath. "I love you, too."

Her smile grew as she turned toward the door. "That's what I thought."

He doubted she would remember the exchange. But either way, it would work to his advantage.

Layne steadied herself, slunk through the ladies' room door, then slid her backside along the wall of the narrow hallway. She knocked a few pictures to the floor before stopping to sit in the container of a Ficus. Then she continued down the wall. When it ended, she gazed in the general direction of their table. Ryan linked his arm around her waist, ferried her through the restaurant, and helped her into her chair, where dessert and a bottle of French champagne awaited them.

Dennis approached the table and extended his hand to Ryan. "Well, man, that's a wrap for us. We got a final shot of the dessert, and all that's left is the fancy French coffee. Nobody wants to watch a plastered Layne Stevens drink snooty coffee, so we're outta here. You got this?"

Ryan shook the camera lead's hand. "Yes, I do. Thank you."

Layne slid down in her chair, and both men jumped to grab her under the arms, pulling her back up.

Dennis smirked. "Good luck with that."

"Yeah, thanks."

"This could've been a nightmare," Dennis said. "But it was a decent shoot."

"I'll be sure to let Layne know."

Ryan moved his chair closer to Layne's, hoping it would be easier to catch her that way. After one sip of champagne, on her insistence, a few forkfuls of something sinfully sweet, and several jolts of what Degasse described as finest quality, French press, fair trade, organic espresso—whatever that was—Layne had enough composure to say her goodbyes.

Chef Degasse made his way to their table. "The poor dear, such a day for her. I can only hope the food and the wine helped her to forget her worries."

"Dinner was exceptional, Chef Degasse," Ryan said. "Really, thank you."

"The pleasure was mine. And it warms my heart to see her so happy. I believe you are responsible for that. No? Here is your butter, Monsieur. I will make more for you at any time. You need only call. And please take care of our Layne."

Layne sat up a little straighter. "Yes?"

Degasse bent down to kiss the backs of Layne's hands. "Until next time, mon amie."

"Thank you," she said. "Thank you so much. It was wonderful. Thank you so much."

Degasse shook Ryan's hand, then turned to leave.

"Wait," Layne said. "Wait, master excellent chef. There's something I need to tell you."

Ryan dreaded any words that might come from Layne's lips.

Degasse again took Layne's hands in his. "Oui, ma chère?"

"Le repas était superbe."

"Madame, my thanks for the lovely compliment, but you told me you did not speak Francais."

"Was that Francais?"

The chef chuckled. "Always a delight, ma chère."

Layne eased her head back down to the table, and Ryan frowned. He'd been well-trained to return sniper fire, subdue attackers, and out-think his opponents, but nothing had prepared him for the minefield disguised as Layne Stevens.

He and Degasse helped Layne to her feet, and Ryan scanned the room for Hansel and Gretel. Each held several gold-foil doggy bags with frilly gold bows. They looked ridiculous. He motioned with his chin, and they handed off their bounty to assist with the departure. Gretel stepped out of the restaurant first, while Jacques propped the doors open for Layne and Ryan. Hansel followed. The masses had retired for the evening, except for one man.

Sonny approached them. "I wanted to say goodbye, Agent Cooke."

"I don't recall giving you my name."

An unsettling grin emerged on the man's face.

35

Cool air washed over Layne. She stirred, sensing someone next to her, but her mind fought it, retreated to the haze that engulfed her. Her body floated on a soft, fluffy surface, and a light breeze tickled her thighs, her stomach, her breasts, caressing her bare skin. She felt movement again, closer this time, then the brush of fingers against her cheek. She sighed. A finger traced the outline of her jaw and trailed down her neck, and she shivered at the agonizingly slow touch as it slid downward.

Lips skimmed over the rise of her breast. Her breath caught, and her nipples firmed. A hand smoothed down her sternum, and she arched in response as it swept past her waist and over her abdomen. A moist heat blossomed between her legs, as the hand lingered on her lower belly, fingers gently circling the line where fine hair met her skin. Layne's body blazed, but muddy thoughts darkened her mind.

"Wait. I can't," she said.

"Layne."

"Please...wait."

"It would be my pleasure to meet all of your needs, Layne."

She'd heard those words before. "No, stop...please."

Firm hands grasped her shoulders, pulling her up, and then something gripped her like a vise. She wanted to fight, to pull away, but her arms were pinned at her sides. Through the fog that enveloped her mind, a voice called to her. She broke into a cold sweat, and her body shuddered.

"Layne, I'm here. It's okay, Layne. You're okay."

She fought to open her eyes, and her breath came in rapid bursts. "Where am I?"

He pulled her close. "Shhh. You're safe. I'm right here."

She choked back a sob. "What's happening?"

"I've got you, Layne. Everything's going to be all right."

She buried her face into his chest and clung to his shirt as he stroked her hair. "You're all right, Layne. No one can hurt you now."

Layne's body conceded to his embrace, and the haze overtook her once more.

36

The next morning, Layne woke with her tongue glued to the roof of her mouth, her head pounding, and hot tar bubbling in her stomach. As her vision cleared, she became aware that she faced windows she'd not seen before. Careful to move only her eyes, she noted her heels near an accordion style closet, and her little black dress draped over a chair at a desk in the corner of the room. She took in what she could without moving. The bedroom wasn't familiar. Then she registered a weight pressing down on her side, and dread gripped her chest. Warily, she tipped back.

Ryan lay facing her, on his side, breathing out soft snuffles, with his head on her pillow and his arm flopped over her. A vague rush of memories from the previous evening battered her mind, and a wave of nausea washed over her along with a distant sense of events she couldn't recall. She strained to remember how she'd gotten to the hotel, how she'd ended up in a bed with Ryan, and why her dress hung on a chair across the room, but the memories eluded her. So did the answer to her most pressing question. Should she be thrilled or mortified about her situation?

Ryan rolled away from her and stretched. "Good morning," he said.

Layne eased onto her back. "Good must be relative."

"How're you feeling?"

"Like crap." Despite a headache and blurry vision, Layne couldn't help admiring Ryan's broad shoulders and well-defined chest. "Why are you here?"

"Bodyguard, remember?"

"I mean here in the bed."

"It was easier to guard you from here."

"Without a shirt?"

He flashed her a sexy smile. "You noticed."

Her brows knitted together.

"My tee shirt had...um...an incident," he said.

Her eyes narrowed.

"Look, the couch is too short. And to be honest, in your condition, it's fortunate I didn't leave you alone."

"Was I that bad?"

"I'm talking about the nightmare you had last night."

"What nightmare?"

"You don't remember me comforting you in the middle of the night?"

"Last night is all a big blur."

"That hurts," he said. "It was a sensitive moment for me."

She managed a small grin, but it faded fast. "Oh no, poor Chef Degasse. He must be humiliated."

"You have nothing to worry about. The chef took everything in stride. Besides, they'd finished filming when you...well, anyway, the customers were gone, and his only concern was you. You were right, he's a very nice man."

"When I what?"

"What?"

"You said they had finished filming when I..."

"Oh, you had a little too much wine. It was no big deal and entirely understandable. Dennis and his crew got shots of the dessert while we were in the bathroom, then we left. End of story. By the way, Dennis asked me to tell you that all things considered, it was a decent shoot."

"Lovely." Layne pressed the heels of her hands to her eyelids. "I am so getting fired."

"It wasn't that bad. Everyone understood you'd had a rough day, and no one faulted you for overindulging a bit."

She recalled what Ryan had told her early in the evening about her uncle. Heck yeah, she deserved to overindulge. But she wished she hadn't done it at that dinner. "Did you say we were in the bathroom?"

"Don't worry, I stood outside the stall."

Layne moved her hands to press at her temples.

"A hot shower and you'll be good as new," he said.

"Right."

"Well, you'll feel better than you do now."

A familiar sensation revealed itself, and that damned little voice roared in her head. *Lower level, ladies' undergarments. Slippery when wet. Please watch your step.*

Oh dear god. She wanted to know, but she didn't want to ask. Or, she wanted to ask, but she didn't really want to know. Shit. Either way, she was screwed.

"Ryan?"

"Yes?"

"Be honest, did I do anything last night I should be aware of?"

"Nope. I told you. You have nothing to worry about."

Not enough information. "My dress?"

"Oh. That was pretty funny."

"What? What was funny?"

"You, working your way out of that dress. You were determined to take it off by yourself and insistent that I not watch."

"So, you didn't watch?"

"Of course I did. You stumbled so many times I thought you might hit your head on the desk. But here's the funny part."

That clinched it. She didn't want to know. "What?"

"After you'd been so adamant, you announced you were done and said I could look."

She lifted the covers and peeked down at her lacy bra, panties, and stockings, and her mouth fell open. "And you looked?"

"I tried not to, Layne, I really did, but...wow."

She forced herself to ask the next question. "Then what happened?"

"I helped you to the bed."

"And?"

"You passed out."

She pulled a pillow over her face.

"Would it make you feel any better if I told you that you have outstanding taste in lingerie?"

"Please shoot me," Layne said through the pillow, and then she peeked out at him. "What about you?"

"What about me?"

"Did you do anything you might regret?"

"I didn't drink, remember?"

"Right." What hadn't he told her? She lifted the pillow and stared into his eyes for a sign...a clue. Nothing. "Does this room have a bathroom?"

Ryan pointed to the door next to the closet. "All of your things should be there. I'll stay out here this time."

Layne grunted as she sat up, pulling a blanket up with her. She waited a few seconds for the spinning to stop, groaned, then wrapped the blanket around her, and staggered to the bathroom, locking the door behind her. She thanked the ghost of hangovers present when she found her toiletries all laid out as she had placed them in the other suite. Grabbing the Ibuprofen, she turned on the hot water in the shower, and then glanced in the mirror. "Jesus Christ!"

"Are you all right in there?" Ryan called.

Hell no. Her tangled hair stuck out in all directions. Her mascara was smeared like inkblots around her eyes. And she owned pearls with more color than her skin. Had she been struck by lightning?

Her little voice chimed right in there for support. *Ooooh, that's super sexy. I'm sure he was all over that.*

"Layne, is everything okay?" Ryan said through the door.

Her shoulders dropped. "If you call looking like Edward Scissorhands okay, then everything is peachy."

He chuckled.

"I heard that," she said.

"Is there anything I can get you?"

"Not unless you've got a new head out there somewhere."

"Sorry. None of those. But I will have my special hangover cure waiting for you when you're ready. I'm going to station Hansel in the sitting room while I get in a quick shower and a change of clothes. Lock the bathroom door, and don't open it until I come back. Okay?"

"Way ahead of you." Thank god she had some time alone to wallow in her misery.

"Enjoy your shower." His voice trailed off, and the bedroom door snapped shut.

What an incredibly thoughtful, and kind, and gorgeous man, she thought. Damn it. Focus on the goal, Layne. You get through this thing and go back to LA. Without him. That is the goal.

What? Her little voice protested. *But I like this one. That can't really be the goal. He's one of the good ones. He should be the one we keep.*

Layne really tried to ignore her damned little voice as she stepped into the steamy shower enclosure, but it might have made an atypically valid point. She shook her head and let the hot water wash over her, shoving all thoughts from her mind. The tension gripping her body subsided, and she allowed herself to relax. But the respite didn't last long. Memories began to trickle back, and her eyes popped open.

Oh. Shit.

37

The first leg of Berger's flight to San Francisco carried a young couple arguing non-stop in the seats in front of him. The second leg featured a colicky baby wailing in its mother's arms a few rows behind. Sleep had eluded him again. But no matter, sleep could wait.

At SFO, he rented a small blue Geo and set out for The Riede. Parked across the busy street below the hotel, low energy streetlights flickered on and off, casting shadows in the early morning mist as he fiddled with the buttons and knobs on the dash. Finally, she approached, and Berger got out of the car.

"What the hell are you doing here?" Rennick asked.

Berger glared. "Why did you not tell me Schatz was dead? You knew. You knew it when we spoke."

"It was confidential. Besides, you have your own counterintelligence. Remember?"

Berger's fists tightened. "Things are not moving rapidly enough. And it has attracted too much press with his niece involved. We are receiving pressure from your agency. Other agencies are now searching for the card. We must heal the wound."

Rennick snickered. "I think you mean stop the bleeding."

"Yes, yes. There is too much at stake. The card must be found."

"That is exactly what we're trying to do. But you and me? We can't be seen together."

"In American English, the more correct statement would be you and I."

"I don't give a shit if it's you and banana slugs. No one can see us like this or *I* will lose my job, and then where will you and *I* be? This is under control. Go back to Berlin. Let me handle it."

"But—

"Hans. I've got this."

She turned and headed toward The Riede with an arrogant stride that felt unwarranted to Berger given the status of the situation. They had worked the problem from inside the FBI, and it had yielded them nothing. But perhaps the answer lay outside the hotel. Other interested parties were certain to be there. He would sit and observe. This would lead him to something. It had to.

38

Ryan entered the surveillance suite ready for answers. "Report," he called to the group.

Marco spoke up. "We're having trouble pinning down an address for Ms. Stevens' parents, but we're working on it."

"Okay, keep me posted. Anything on agency ties for Layne?"

"Besides her relationship to the vic? Nothin' boss. No intel, no whispers. I'm telling you, if she's an op, she covered her tracks."

"All right." He surveyed the room. "What else?"

"Agent Cooke, sir."

Ryan eyed her as she approached. "Agent Rennick."

"You should be advised, sir, that early in the evening we lost communication with the wire contained in your tie."

"I'm aware of that, Rennick," he said. "I was asked to remove the tie because of the glare it created on camera." Ryan ignored the snickering and remarks. "What the hell were you thinking?"

She responded with an overconfidence that annoyed him. "Sir, I hoped if she knew we were playing her, she might get nervous and make a mistake."

Ryan worked to contain his anger. "Rennick, you have potential to be a damned good agent, but there are times when I need you to think, and times when I need you to follow orders. If I can't count on you to discern the difference, I'm going to send you home. Is that clear?"

"But, sir..."

"No buts. And stop calling me sir, damn it."

"Yes, sir," she said to his back as he walked away.

Gretel strolled past Rennick. "I'm not one to say I told you so, but did I not call that from a mile away?"

"Go screw yourself," Rennick shot back.

"If only I could." Gretel flashed her a nasty smile as he went for the door.

The hot shower calmed Ryan's nerves and renewed his focus. But he needed more information from Layne, and he needed it fast. He exited the bedroom wearing jeans, a brushed cotton tee under a long-sleeved chambray shirt, and a well-worn pair of hiking boots. The attire received applause and whistles from the more seasoned members of the team. Rennick stood quietly in the corner.

"Here we go, ladies," Ryan said. "The time has come for a full court press." The statement garnered more cheering and some catcalls. "No one, whether they're an operative, an ex, or just damned unlucky, pulls one over on Ryan Cooke. Marco, get a copy of the report to Seth. Tell him I'd like the profile back today if he can do it."

"You got it, boss."

"Rennick."

"Sir."

"What did we talk about earlier, Rennick?"

Her gaze lowered. "Not calling you sir, sir. I mean—"

"If I give you another assignment, do you think you can manage not to screw it up?"

"I'll do my best, sir. Shit. Agent Cooke."

"I want you to think like a woman, Rennick. Can you do that for me?"

"I'll...I'll try."

"Find me a picnic basket, something you would enjoy having a man put together for you."

She stiffened. "I don't understand."

"Rennick, Ms. Stevens and I are going on a date. She needs to be impressed by a tempting assortment of picnic items that I will tell her I selected myself."

"A date, sir?"

"Hawk, what's my success rate with the picnic ploy?"

"It's gotta be ninety-nine percent, boss. But there was that one..." Laughter and muffled remembrances filled the room.

"Are you with me, Rennick?" Ryan asked.

"Yes, sir." Her brows pinched. "I mean...I'm not quite following you."

"Look, Rennick, I'm no James Bond, but if I can make 'em fall for me, they'll usually tell me anything I want to know."

Surprise spread across Rennick's face. "So, you think she's an op?"

"Jesus, Rennick, where have you been?"

"Sorry, sir."

Ryan eyeballed the ceiling.

"Damn it. Agent Cooke, sir."

He gave up. "Go find me a picnic, and please touch base with Seth later about the profile."

"Yes, sir."

At least she was sort of with the program.

"Marco, I'm taking the locket," Ryan said.

"You're the boss, sir." Marco walked away with a chuckle.

When Ryan returned to Layne's suite, Hansel nudged his chin toward Layne's purse.

"Thinking about getting one like that for yourself?"

"It's that damned song, "Love Shack." Keeps playing from her damned bag," Hansel said.

"Love Shack?"

"You know, B-52's."

"I'm familiar with the song."

"Thing blares damned near every five minutes."

"Thanks. Why don't you take a break?"

Given Layne's fondness for acquaintance-appropriate ringtones, Ryan pondered the assignment of the "Love Shack." Sorry, Stu. You've got competition.

He took some time to gather more details from the report on Layne. Then he bolstered himself for what might prove one of the biggest challenges of his career. After a quick internal pep talk, Ryan walked through the bedroom and knocked on the bathroom door. She didn't respond.

"Layne?"

~

RENNICK STRUGGLED WITH HER ASSIGNMENT. Should she go to a grocer? What about a flower shop? Where the hell was she supposed to buy a picnic basket? She dialed the nearest florist, and they gave her the number for a business called Perfect Picnics. Really? Entire stores dedicated to this shit? She mapped the route to the shop on her phone and then sat down at her laptop. After typing her password into a secure database, she downloaded a document onto a flash drive, dropped the drive into her purse, and left the suite.

The girl behind the counter at Perfect Picnics had long blond hair and appeared to be in her mid-twenties. "How can I help you today?" she said in a bubbly way that made Rennick want to shoot her.

"I need a picnic basket," Rennick said.

The girl mimicked Rennick's serious tone. "I'm sorry, we don't carry those here."

Rennick glared.

"Joking." The girl's cheerful smile went unreturned. "Okay, for a man or a woman?"

"Both. Wait, what do you mean?"

"Is the person being surprised with the basket male or female?"

"What makes you think it's a surprise?"

The girl wrinkled her nose. "Aren't all picnic baskets a surprise?"

Rennick cast her eyes at the ceiling. "It's for a woman."

"Hmm, lucky girl. Just the two of you?"

Rennick ignored the innuendo. "Yes."

"All-righty, here's our selection for women." The girl handed

Rennick a menu of several basket options. "What type of woman would you say she is?"

Rennick scanned the list: athletic, outdoorsy, romantic, gardener, junk food junkie, chocoholic... She snickered and made her decision.

The girl arched a brow. "Excellent choice. Does she have any food allergies or definite dislikes?"

Rennick didn't know, and she didn't care. "No."

"Wine?"

Tempting. "No, thanks."

"All righty then, I'll make the basket up now. There's coffee and cookies along the back while you wait."

Ten minutes later the girl emerged with a picnic basket and went through the contents, assuming Rennick cared. Rennick paid and headed toward the door, but the girl called after her. "If the date doesn't work out, feel free to come back and visit."

Rennick shook her head as she left the shop, and then stared down at the basket and the ridiculous piece of patchwork sold to her as a picnic blanket. People totally sucked. She looked at her watch. Cooke had talked a good game back in the surveillance suite, but her instinct told her she still needed to prepare for plan B.

39

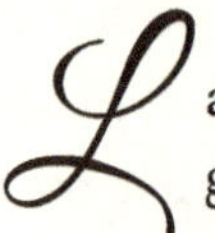ayne heard the handle jiggle on the bathroom door. Thank god for locks.

"Layne?"

She couldn't face him. Not after what she'd remembered.

"Layne, what's going on in there? Are you okay?"

She spoke to Ryan through the door. "Besides the fuzzy sweaters on my teeth? I'm fine."

"I know just the thing," he said. "I'll be right back."

"Wait..."

She heard the bedroom door click shut, and she knew there was no way out of it. She'd have to face him eventually.

When he returned, she braced herself and cracked the door open. With her face still flushed from the heat of the shower, her hair wet, no makeup, and bare shoulders, only a thin towel separated her from the door, and from Ryan. A knot formed in her stomach as she secured her towel with one hand and reached out with the other to take a small packet from him.

He averted his eyes. "Make a paste out of the sugar with some water," he said. "Then use it to brush your teeth. It's like magic."

"Thank you. I still need a few minutes. Obviously."

"No rush. I'll be in the front room. Wear something comfortable."

Crap, her little voice said as she closed the bathroom door. *Of course he can't look at you. Hell, I can hardly stand to look at you after last night.*

Layne enjoyed the vision of shoving her little voice out the third-floor window, and then proceeded to get ready. Mercifully, most of her casual clothing had not been in the bloody closet. She chose a light-weight, yellow, short-sleeved sweater, jeans, and yellow strappy sandals. She dried her hair and pulled it back into a wavy ponytail, stretched the skin around her eyes tight to avoid the over forty eyelid speed bumps that would sabotage her application of eyeliner, then swiped on a coat of mascara and some light pink lip-gloss.

When she entered the front room, Ryan's gaze lingered on her. Not what she'd expected. She slid her hands into her pockets. "So, what's the plan?"

"We're going to eat a hearty breakfast and then do some sightseeing. I already left a message for Maggie. Are you feeling any better?"

Layne's attention drifted downward. "Somewhat. But while I showered, I had the stupid idea to count the number of times I've humiliated myself in the past twenty-four hours. It was pretty darned high, even for me. And that's just from what I remember."

"You humiliated yourself?"

She let out a weak laugh.

He moved toward her, tipped her chin up, and brushed a loose strand of curls from her face. "Hey," he said. "No dwelling. Today is going to be a fun and relaxing day. Besides, I find your stunts kind of cute. Come on. Let's eat." He placed a hand on the small of her back, and the familiar tingling sensation charged through her body as he led her to a table full of breakfast items.

She scanned the spread. "My goodness, you're spoiling me."

His hand slid up her back to land with a gentle caress of his thumb at the nape of her neck, and she swallowed the lump forming in her throat.

His lips brushed close to her ear. "I wasn't sure what your stomach would tolerate, so I got you a bit of everything."

Goosebumps spiked the hair on her arms, and she had to admit, she kinda liked being spoiled. She was also starting to enjoy this tingling thing. He handed her a glass half-filled with a cloudy white liquid.

"What's this?"

"It's my secret hangover tonic. Best to do it like a shot."

Layne took a sniff, grimaced and downed the liquid in one pass. "Yuck," she said.

He chuckled. "You'll thank me later."

Ryan stayed by her side as they filled their plates, and she thought she could get used to that too.

"By the way," he said, "it seems to have stopped now, but your cell phone played "Love Shack" several times this morning."

"Love Shack?"

"Uh huh."

Layne scrunched her lips to the side.

"Let me guess," Ryan said. "Stu?"

She felt her eyes widen. "What? No. You thought Stuart and I..?"

"Am I wrong?"

"Stu is in his mid-seventies. He's more like a protective father. He's a good friend, but nothing more."

"Hmm. Then who's set to that ringtone?"

"I'm not seeing anyone, if that's what you're implying. I like the song, so I use it as my general ringtone." Layne picked up a slice of perfectly crisp bacon. "It's odd though."

"What's odd?"

"I have all sorts of custom ringtones, so "Love Shack" rarely plays anymore. My song for Maggie is perfect."

"Oh yeah? What is it?"

"You'll know it when you hear it."

He smiled, but his expression also held unease.

"After we eat, why don't you check your phone," he said. "See if there's a number attached to all of those calls."

She didn't like the sound of that. "Sure."

They finished their breakfast, and Layne realized she no longer felt hungover.

"What was in that drink? It really worked."

"Don't tell the guys, but it's just baking soda and water. My roommate back at the academy told me about it. Been using it for years. Works like a charm every time."

"That's funny. My brother drinks something like that for hangovers. You remind me a little of him."

"Maybe someday I'll get to meet him," Ryan said. He pulled the small evidence bag from his jeans pocket. "Do you feel up to looking at this again? Anything you can tell me about the locket would be helpful." Then his radio squawked—their car was ready. "On second thought, we'll look at this later." He stuffed the bag into his back pocket.

Layne went for her purse, peered inside, and frowned.

"What's wrong?" Ryan asked.

"There's not much about last night that I recall. Even some of what happened during the day is a blur. But one of the things I remembered in the shower was finding my politically correct accessory. It's still here."

Ryan grinned. "Nope. There is nothing politically correct I can say."

She shuffled through her purse and came up with her phone. "Five calls from a blocked number," she said as she handed it to Ryan.

"It's probably a reporter," he said. "Nothing to worry about." But, again, his expression said otherwise.

She put the phone back in her bag and followed Ryan out to the hall, where Hansel and Gretel waited to escort them to the lobby.

"Where are we going?" she asked.

"That's need-to-know."

She leveled her best scowl at him.

"Needs more practice," he said.

"Yeah, I know."

SONNY UTILIZED his idle time by systematically taking apart and reassembling his equipment, until his bluetooth quacked in his ear. "Yup?"

"It's me," the caller said.

"No shit. Are they on the move?"

"They are headed for you now."

He picked up his rifle and directed the scope. "I got 'em."

Sonny watched two gorillas in tight gray suits secure the area outside the lobby doors, and then Layne exited the hotel with pretty boy at her side. She wouldn't run again, she felt secure with that idiot. This saved Sonny some grief, but he wished he could change the fate he knew was inevitable.

Three town cars waited in the valet area, all with black tinted windows. Pretty boy escorted Layne to the middle vehicle, opened her door, and offered his hand for assistance. Layne looked vibrant, excited, and something else. Hopeful? Sonny sneered. He couldn't deny his reaction to seeing Layne. Worse, his response to seeing her with him. His jaw tightened. He wasn't getting paid to worry about her fate or her social life. Stay focused, Wright.

The town cars lumbered down the narrow drive and into the congestion of the traffic below. He'd bet, with all of their well-trained muscle, no one noticed the small blue Geo pulling into the lane behind them. Sonny packed up his gear and left the apartment.

40

As their driver navigated the scrum of downtown traffic, the iconic voice of Madonna sang to them from Layne's purse. "Like a Virgin..."

"You're kidding, right?" Ryan asked.

The corner of Layne's lips curved upward as she rummaged through her bag, then pulled out her phone and put it on speaker. "Hi, Mags."

"What the hell?"

"That's a pleasant greeting."

"I can't wait around forever, Layne. I understand there's a dead body and all, but we have work to do."

"It's complicated. It...I...let me talk to Ryan, and I'll call you back."

"There'd better be a hell of a lot more than talk going on if you want me to wait."

"Maggie."

"Just sayin'."

"I'll call you back."

"Uh huh."

"I promise, Mags, I will let you know, but it won't be until later today."

"Fine. I'll make an appointment with Eduardo at the spa. He's got an extra big—"

"Maggie! Too much information."

"You really are a prude. Speaking of that, how are things going with the federal hotty?"

"Goodbye, Mags."

"Oh, all right. Call me later, sweetie. Ciao."

For several minutes after the conversation, Layne inspected the interior of the car. "I feel like the President," she said, glancing back at the town car behind them. "Is all this security necessary?"

"Trying to distract me from your call with Maggie?"

"Is it working?"

"Federal hotty, huh? I've got to admit, guarding you has been excellent for my ego."

Layne shot him a derisive grin.

"New subject. Got it." Ryan said. "You feel presidential because we're not taking any chances with your safety."

"My safety? So, this outing has nothing to do with catching my uncle's killer?"

Ryan stared at her for a moment, as if weighing his options.

"Beautiful and smart. Okay, here it is. I've planned a relaxing day for us, but I wouldn't be disappointed if, in the process, we drew out someone who could help us—someone with information about what's going on, or about your uncle."

Layne stared out the window past Ryan. She wanted to catch whoever killed her uncle, and the team seemed well-equipped to protect her, but her stomach churned at the thought.

Ryan placed his hand over hers and she jumped. "Shit, sorry. I guess I'm a little freaked out."

"You're not in any danger, Layne. We have complete control of the situation."

She nodded, but her attention drifted. "I always try to find the silver lining, but I can't find one here."

The town car came to a stop.

"I see a silver lining," Ryan said. "But given the circumstances, it's somewhat selfish."

She lowered her gaze to her lap, but Ryan slid the tip of his finger under her chin and turned her face to his.

"What is it, Ryan? What is the silver lining in this crappy mess?"

"This has been hard on you. I know. But if you hadn't fallen into our investigation, we might never have seen each other again."

"What are you saying?"

"That I care for you, Layne. It's not something that happens often for me, and it sure as hell shouldn't be happening now. But it is."

She tried to read his eyes. "You mean, as a friend?"

Ryan leaned in, moving his lips close to hers. "Absolutely not."

Then Gretel's voice boomed over Ryan's radio. "Hey, Romeo, we gonna go look at the flippin' zebras or what?"

Ryan's head tipped back. "Perfect timing, Einstein," he said.

"Oh my gosh," Layne said. "Your men were listening this entire time?"

"You let me worry about them."

He took her hand in his, helped her out of the town car, and when it pulled away, he didn't let go.

RENNICK PERUSED the surveillance suite and shook her head. At least the dimwits were alert as they monitored the conversation, but the op wasn't their only concern. They all had money riding on the latest pool.

She'd seen Cooke leave in well-worn jeans that accentuated a firm backside, the snug t-shirt, ultra-masculine hiking boots, and that loose fitting, woodsman-like, long sleeved shirt with buttons undone. He looked like the fricking poster boy for Plow and Hearth, not that she was into that kind of thing.

And she understood what the idiots had told her. According to the plan, Gretel would interrupt their special moment to build anticipation, and to show Stevens the entire team had heard Cooke's confession. He would charm her as they ogled the cute little red-tailed monkeys, and woo her over a surprise lunch. He would seduce her to gain her trust. How could she resist? It was all very Lifetime television, and all bullshit. It didn't matter what Cooke said. She smelled it on him. He had fallen for Layne Stevens. But since the rest of the assholes she worked with had dicks, they didn't see it. She couldn't sit there any longer. She needed to act.

Marco glanced over. "Hey, Rennick. Where ya going?"

She ignored him and walked out the door.

41

Layne and Ryan set out for a leisurely tour of the zoo. They admired the animals and talked about their lives. Several times Ryan took her hand or put a caring arm around her. Layne hadn't realized how much she'd missed that sense of comfort. It felt...nice. And while the logical part of her brain begged her to resist the rapidly growing attraction to Ryan, her little voice, and the chemical concoction of hormones that sent tingly zips of electricity through her body every time he touched her, won out.

They approached the elephant enclosure, and a loud shot rang out. Layne covered her head with her arms and tried to duck, but lost her balance. She thrashed, kicking her leg into the air and falling backward to land flat on her ass.

Ryan knelt beside her. "Jesus, Layne, are you all right?"

"Was that a gunshot?"

"Yes, it was. They're demonstrating a wild west shootout over there." He pointed.

"Oh my god. I'm such an idiot," Layne said.

Thank you for saving me the trouble this time, her little voice contributed.

Ryan squelched his grin. "The gunshot did sound very realistic. Are you hurt? You fell pretty hard."

"I'm okay. Thanks. I try to keep a fair amount of padding back there for this very reason. At least that's what I tell myself."

"That was...really spectacular." His grin spread. "I wish you could have seen it."

"Believe me, I have."

He helped her up, and she brushed off the seat of her jeans.

"Are you sure you're not injured?" he asked.

"My bottom and I are used to it." She looked down. "Hey, where'd my other sandal go?"

A crowd formed around a nearby habitat, and a young boy's voice rang out, "Mommy, mommy, that elephant is eating a shoe!"

Layne turned to see an inquisitive elephant grazing its trunk over her sandal, which was lodged in the branches of a bush just inside the enclosure.

Ryan's head tilted to one side. "Hunh. It must have flown off when you did that scissor kick thing."

Layne grimaced. "Scissor kick thing?"

The elephant snuffled, and one of the straps caught on the end of its snout.

"Well, at least we know your feet smell good," Ryan said.

Layne lifted a brow.

"That didn't come out well. I only meant—"

She put up a hand. "No need."

The crowd near the enclosure grew. Children pointed. Parents snapped photos. And a line formed around Layne for her autograph. Ryan's team moved in to ensure order, and Ryan stayed close to Layne. Then a zookeeper weaved his way to them through the mess.

"Ms. Stevens, wow. I'm a huge fan." The zookeeper gave her hand a fervent shake. "My sincerest apologies for the incident. I promise you, we will retrieve your sandal."

"No, no, it was my fault. And I'm not worried about my sandal. Please just help the poor elephant."

The zookeeper patted her hand. "Don't you fret. We'll take care of it." A jeep trudged through the habitat toward the sandal-faced mammal. "I need to go assist," he said. "But please meet me in the administration office. It's around the corner to the right." He rushed off.

"What are the odds?" Ryan asked.

"You'll find they increase the longer you're around me."

Ryan took Layne's hand and led her to the administration building. The zookeeper entered through a back door as they arrived.

"Ah, Ms. Stevens, you'll be happy to hear that Evelyn is unharmed. Not a scratch on her. However, your shoe..." He held up Layne's sandal, with the straps cut and covered in elephant snuffle goo.

"Oooh. Yuck. Well, like I said, I can always buy another sandal. But I'm so glad Evelyn is all right."

"On behalf of the staff, please accept these souvenir Evelyn flip-flops as our gift. We wouldn't want you wandering the zoo barefoot."

"Oh my...um...goodness. Those are...amazing," Layne said.

Ryan half-coughed, half-laughed as the zookeeper handed Layne a pair of gray sandals with big floppy ears fanning out from either side, and elephant trunks standing five inches tall from the point between the toes.

"And they're my size," Layne said.

The zookeeper stood a bit taller. "I checked your sandal."

"Well, thank you, so much." She slipped them on. "I feel...much safer with Evelyn protecting my feet. And if anyone should turn in footage..."

"I'm familiar with the routine," he said.

Layne gave him her business card, but he slid it back to her with a pen. "Would you mind?"

They left the office with ears flapping and two long trunks pointing the way.

"Hey," Ryan said. "What was that about footage?"

"Footage? I don't recall that." She turned toward a small pen. "A Chacoan Peccary. It looks like a cross between a porcupine and a pig."

Ryan moved in beside her. "You're right," he said. "Poor thing."

"But pigs and porcupines are cute."

"Well, that thing isn't cute."

"No...no he's not. He looks sort of like Sergeant Temple. Kind of round and bristly."

Ryan laughed and weaved his fingers through hers, drawing her close to his side as they continued to walk. "So," he said, "the footage?"

She glanced down. "Be careful not to step on my ears."

Ryan's eyes narrowed.

"Oh, all right. I used to show up a lot on YouTube. People would catch me on film, pulling stunts like the one with the elephant. Stunt maven, remember? They'd ridicule me in the tabloids, and my credibility would go straight down the toilet, along with the ratings. But Maggie came up with the idea to put them on the show."

"You mean like bloopers?"

She nodded. "It was one of her better ideas. People saw me laughing about my blunders, and I guess I became more real to them. Now, instead of posting footage on the internet, they upload it to our site. We leave them all posted and pick a few to feature on a show each month. They're some of our highest rated episodes."

"And that doesn't bother you?"

"It did at first. Now it seems normal."

"Hunh. Maybe I'll check them out."

"Uh...I think they're password protected."

"I'd need a password to access the bloopers?"

She turned her attention to another enclosure. "Are those Chilean Flamingos over there? I really wanted to see those."

He nudged her with his shoulder.

"All right, you don't need a password. Just my permission."

"Do I have your permission?"

"Um, no."

They wandered past Komodo Dragons and California Sea Lions, and Layne shared some very personal things. She boasted about her children, now young adults and living their own lives. She revealed the still painful memory of her husband's heart attack during the annual Ominvance Wienerfest several years back. She spoke of her apprehension to pursue other relationships. She talked about experiences she and her husband had shared, everything from cooking classes to scuba diving. And she confided that she'd not yet slept with another man. Ryan was a good listener, caring and supportive, but he seemed to distance himself from her the more she spoke. No big deal. It wasn't really a date. Was it?

"The Omnivance has an annual wienerfest?" Ryan asked.

"Not anymore," Layne said. "And it's probably for the best. People enjoyed the event, but the name..."

As they approached the exit, Ryan radioed for the town car to pick them up for lunch.

"Where are we going?" Layne asked.

"That's—"

She held up her hand. "Need to know," she said. "Got it."

42

Most of the surveillance team dressed in business-casual attire, but not Rennick. She exited the suite at The Riede wearing regulation FBI. For her, that meant a white button-down shirt covered by a tailored gray jacket, a fitted gray skirt that hit at the knees, sheer hose, and low, gray pumps. Her military-short haircut and minimal makeup complemented the severity of the look. It didn't get her a lot of dates, but it made her comfortable. And since most men were imbeciles, she had no need to date.

There wasn't much time before the cheesy romance brigade would reach it's happily ever after, and she needed to keep that from happening, so she placed a call to Seth from her car.

He answered on the first ring. "Hey, Sherry," he said.

Seth didn't like the formality of last names. It was very irritating.

"Is the Stevens sheet done?" she asked as she swerved around a car traveling at the posted speed limit.

"Just finished up. How are you on this fine day?"

She ignored his pleasant mood. "I'll be there in ten."

"Looking forward to it."

Rennick could all but hear Seth's stupid grin through the phone. Moron. He was consistently too happy to see her. So, when she arrived at headquarters, she badgered him until he coughed up the reader's digest version of the profile. Then she snatched the confidential envelope, signed for it, and made her escape. But instead of going straight back to The Riede, she went to her loft and changed into sweatpants, a gym shirt, and running shoes. She plunked a baseball cap on her head and sat down to think through her plan. The moment she hit the couch, a rotund ball of orange fur flew into her lap.

"Hello, Uzi," Rennick said. "How's my girl? Are you having a nice day?"

Uzi purred as Rennick stroked the cat's thick fur. "What's that? Oh, you are such a good kitty. Don't tell anyone, but I need to go clean up a huge mess. The pinheads I work with...well, sometimes I think you're smarter than they are. Will you be a good girl while I'm gone?" Uzi nuzzled Rennick's chin. "Of course you will. And I promise to bring you back a treat."

Rennick gave the cat a vigorous back scratch, and Uzi reciprocated the affection by peeing in her lap. She frowned—just another mess to deal with. Fortunately, Uzi's advanced age allowed for only modest amounts of piddle. She placed the cat on the floor and stared down at her sweatpants. "Was that necessary?"

Uzi replied with a gut-wrenching cough.

Rennick put on clean sweats, threw the damp ones into the washer, and then pulled a hefty platinum case from the top shelf of her coat closet. She laid it on the kitchen table, rolled the numbers on the combination lock until it clicked, took a quick inventory of the parts that made up her sniper rifle, then left the apartment, taking the case with her.

An hour later she arrived back at her loft and checked the kitchen floor for puddles of urine. Satisfied with her inspection, she dropped a catnip-stuffed mouse on the floor and placed her briefcase on the kitchen table. Uzi pounced on the mouse as Rennick broke the seal and removed the profile Seth had given her from the confidential envelope. She ran the official sheets through her shredder, and then pulled the pages she'd produced at the Copy Mart out of her bag, slid them into a new confidential envelope, sealed it, and smirked.

Then she headed to her bedroom for a quick transformation back to regulation bureau attire. But when she returned to the kitchen, the distinct odor of cat urine wafted through the room. She re-examined the floor. "There has got to be some kind of pill for that. What do you think Uzi? Would you like mommy to buy you some drugs?"

Uzi meowed.

No longer dressed to crawl around on her hands and knees, Rennick sprayed the engineered hardwood with pet enzyme, grabbed an old towel from the Uzi stack, dropped it on top of the puddle, patted it with the flat of her shoe, and left it for later. "Bye-bye, Uzi. I've got to get going," she said. "Please try to use your litter box while I'm gone." She tucked the new envelope under her arm, picked up her purse, and left for Golden Gate Park.

FROM ACROSS THE BUSY STREET, Sonny examined all paths leading into the park. Then he scanned the sidewalk and scoffed—no shortage of agency goons. But he questioned his location. If this was the drop for Layne and pretty boy, why had he seen the bitchy blond on the other side of the park? He popped several beer nuts into his mouth and took a swig of cherry cola. Three town cars came to a stop across the street, double parking near a pathway entrance and forcing all other vehicles to go around. The blue Geo idled by and disappeared into traffic. It would probably return, but that didn't concern him. He shook his head. Berger—where did the agencies come up with these guys?

Layne and pretty boy exited the middle town car, and the prick put his hand on Layne's back as he guided her toward the path. Sonny finished his last few nuts, grabbed his backpack, got out of his car, and crossed the street.

43

Berger passed the town cars and scanned the street for parking. His rental was small, but in this situation, size did not matter—the area surrounding Golden Gate Park was gridlocked with tourists. He had little choice but to move with the flow of traffic and soon found himself on the opposite side of the park from the location where he'd seen the town cars pull up. A parked car signaled to turn out, and Berger stopped. He slipped his car into the space, disregarded the parking meter, and headed out at a jog to find the FBI entourage.

As he approached a large polo field, he slowed and took a moment to get his bearings. A good distance ahead, he observed a police officer on horseback, and to his surprise, his also saw his contact, Agent Sherry Rennick, carrying the platinum case he had given her as a gift several years before. The case she had told him had been modified on the inside to hold her sniper rifle.

He broke into a sprint.

44

Ryan deftly avoided generous amounts of duck excrement along with Evelyn's ears flapping against the gravel path. He led Layne past a children's playground, lush botanical gardens, an immaculate Japanese tea garden, and a considerably sized pond with an island covered in dense foliage and hundreds of ducks, geese, and birds.

Layne looked around. "It's incredible. All the times I've come to San Francisco, and I've never been here. Are there restaurants?"

"Something like that," Ryan said.

She looked down. "Wow. It's bigger than I expected."

"Yes, the park is quite impressive."

She chuckled. "I meant the duck poop. But the park is big too, and so beautiful."

They came to a grassy area surrounded by enormous conifer and eucalyptus trees, and she didn't mask her excitement when she spotted the quilted blanket and picnic basket Ryan's team had placed below a huge old pine.

"Is that for us?" she asked.

Ryan had executed this move a dozen times and never before been nervous. Why had Layne's response mattered? "I hope you like picnics," he said.

She rewarded him with a glowing smile. "Who doesn't like picnics?"

Damn it. It was just a smile. He needed to get it together.

When they arrived at the blanket, Layne removed her Evelyns, settled on her knees next to Ryan, and reached for the basket.

"Wait," Ryan said. "Don't open that."

She backed away like it was a wicker time bomb.

"I'm sorry," he said. "I didn't mean to frighten you. It's just...Agent Rennick handled the basket. I had hoped to impress you by taking the credit, but to be honest, I have no idea what's inside that thing."

"How bad could it be?"

"The tie."

"I have yet to come across a food I totally hated. Think of it as an adventure."

"I realize I denied this last night, but you really are braver than I am. Okay, go for it."

Layne opened the basket and lifted out a long cylindrical tube wrapped in plastic. She unwrapped it, set it upright on the grass, and then slid a bottle of sparkling cranberry cider down through the middle of the ingenious ice mold.

"I've never seen anything like that. It's good you're here," Ryan said.

Next, she pulled out heavy-duty disposable dishes, silverware, stemware, and thick paper napkins, along with an assortment of sandwiches, fresh fruit, salads and kettle chips.

"There are even condiments," she said, holding up a small jar of mayonnaise. "It's like room service in the park." She took a final peek into the basket and fumbled to shut the lid.

"What is it?"

"Nothing. Just closing it up so it doesn't get dirty. Let's eat."

"Layne."

She opened the basket and tipped it toward him, giving him a view of the grape-flavored sensual massage oil and the purple finger massager tucked inside.

"Agent Rennick is now zero for two," Ryan said. "It's too bad. She was close on this one."

"It could've been worse."

"I planned to tell you I put the basket together myself. After what happened yesterday, I'm not sure how it could've been worse."

"All right, that might've been awkward. I mean for you. Can we eat?"

Ryan grabbed his radio. "Let me fire Rennick, then we can eat."

Layne's eyes widened.

"I'm kidding. Sort of. Dig in."

After lunch, they stretched out on the blanket and gazed through tree branches at a light blue sky dotted with puffy white clouds. Ryan linked his fingers with hers, and she looked over at him.

"It's been a wonderful day, Layne," he said.

Her eyes seemed to be searching his, then she frowned.

"Hunh. Not the response I expected."

"Sorry. I was just thinking about my uncle. Even though we never met in person, I...I can't believe he's gone. And my mom. I know I can't tell her, but she is going to be devastated when she finds out."

"I apologize for you having to deal with all of this."

"But that's just it. I'm not. I'm not dealing with anything. I can't shake this feeling that I should be doing something to help catch whoever did this. Something besides waiting for someone to approach us in the middle of Golden Gate Park."

"I know you're going through a lot right now, but you need to trust me. We have everything under control, and we will catch the person who killed your uncle. I promise."

Layne gave him an unconvincing grin and then focused back on the clouds. And again, Ryan found himself uncertain about what he should do. Should he try to console her, or just let her be? Damn it. Something was throwing him off his game. But it didn't matter what Rennick thought, it wasn't Layne. And he would prove it—to himself and to his team.

Layne let out a loud sigh and then turned again to look at him. "I hope I didn't make you uncomfortable with everything I shared today."

"No, no, not at all," he replied. But the words sounded insincere, even to him. "Well, we should get back to the hotel. I've got work to do, and didn't you want to call Chef Degasse?"

Her brow lowered for a moment, but she got up and dusted herself off. "Hey, do you still have my locket?" she asked.

Ryan reached into his pocket and handed her the bag. She propped herself against the immense trunk of the old pine to inspect the remains of her necklace while Ryan folded the blanket. When he glanced over, she was staring at him, and she didn't divert her eyes. Instead, she gave him a flirty smile. He dropped the blanket, moved in close to Layne, put a hand on the tree above her shoulder, and swept several wisps of hair back from her face.

"I'm sorry, Layne."

Her soft brown eyes seemed to stare straight into his soul.

"Sorry for what?" she asked.

He trailed the tip of his finger along the line of her jaw. "For giving you mixed signals."

"These signals seem pretty clear."

His finger skimmed down her neck and over her collarbone. "This could be complicated."

"I know," she said, sliding her hands around his waist.

He moved closer. "Are you sure about this?"

Her reply came out on a silky breath. "Yes."

He brushed his mouth over hers, her lips parted, and then his radio screeched, "Cooke!" and the thunder of horse hooves descended on them.

Ryan pressed his body against Layne's to shield her from the attack, and her muffled shriek rang in his ear as a mounted patrolman galloped for them at full stride. The massive stallion swiped by, then raced toward the trees at the far end of the park. Several of Ryan's men chased the horse, while others rushed at him and Layne.

"Where the hell were you?" Ryan spat at Gretel as he approached them.

"He looked like a fucking cop for Christ's sake," Gretel said, chugging for air.

Ryan calmed himself, and realizing he still had Layne pinned to the tree, stepped back to give her some room. "Are you okay?"

"You saved me."

"They weren't after you."

Ryan's radio squawked. "Hey, boss, got something over here."

Ryan studied a grove of tall pines in the distance and then turned to Gretel. "Can you take Layne back to the car?"

"You got it, boss."

Ryan jogged across the expanse of grass toward the horse with an SFPD logo on the saddle blanket. A familiar full-bellied figure in a Mounties style uniform stood beside it.

"Sergeant," Ryan said.

"Special Agent Cooke," Sergeant Temple said. "That was one heck of a show y'all put on out there."

"I assure you it was no show. This your horse?"

"I told ya, my horse retired. I was on foot patrol in that quadrant over there when I saw the assault." Sergeant Temple pointed.

"Did you see the rider?"

"From behind when he took off his mask. Sat tall. On the thin side. Blond hair. That's about all I got before he disappeared."

"You didn't get a view from the front?"

"No, sir."

"Then the rider could have been female?"

Sergeant Temple snorted. "Yeah, right."

Ryan shook his head. "Any idea which way they went?"

"Nope. And the pine needles are damn thick. So, no tracks. No way to tell."

"Did you check in with your men? Anyone else witness the incident?"

"Our man scheduled for this quadrant called in sick. That left us with a gap in our rotation."

"Does the sick patrolman ride this horse?"

"Can't say for sure. We'd need to see the mount assignment log."

"Why are you here, Sergeant?"

"I'm a floater today on account of the gap."

"And you knew we would be here?"

"Yeah, we got word."

Ryan's agitation strained against his control. "We'll need your report—information on the sick officer, details on the mount assignment, what you observed, and anything else you can give us that would explain how the hell a rogue rider ends up on an SFPD mount."

"Will do." Sergeant Temple scribbled something in his notebook and wandered off.

Ryan headed toward the town car and called Marco. "I'm sure you heard. Whoever it was, we lost them. Temple was here. Claims he got eyes on the rider. Tall, lean, blond hair. I don't like it. Temple doesn't feel right."

RENNICK RETURNED to the surveillance suite and tossed the confidential envelope on Marco's desk.

Marco glared at her. "What the hell took you so long?"

"He was putting the packet together when I got there, I had to wait."

His eyes narrowed.

"And you know those analysts," she said. "They never come out of their caves. So they always want you to hang around and make small talk."

"You expect me to believe you hung out at HQ and made small talk with Seth?"

"I didn't want to be rude."

Rusk appeared from behind a rack of computers. "Since when?"

Rennick sent Rusk an icy stare, and Marco stood. "Seriously, Rennick, where the fuck were you?"

45

The Employer sat in an espresso-brown, leather executive chair behind a grand mahogany desk with the speaker on his office phone engaged. He examined a small, see-through, resealable bag. "Is this it?"

"No," came the raspy reply on the other end of the line.

"Help me to understand, then."

"It's Stevens' locket. The damned thing must have been in there at one point, but it's not there now."

"Correct me if I'm wrong," The Employer said. "But this means we are no closer to acquiring it than we were before."

"Look, I'm doing everything in my fucking power to find the thing. At least we know the bureau doesn't have it."

"And we surmise this how?"

"Really? I think I'd fucking know if the bureau had it."

The Employer cleared his throat.

"Okay, maybe they don't tell me everything. But if they had it, why would they still be screwing around with the locket?"

"How did you obtain this?"

"I snatched it out of her hand."

"So, she's aware of your identity?"

"I'm not an idiot. I rode a damned horse, dressed as a Mountie, and I wore a mask. There's no way—"

"Spare me the details," The Employer said. "I surmise a pat on the back is in order. I would have preferred the item, but at least we have some solid intel regarding its status. Satisfactory work, I suppose."

"Yeah, thanks."

"I don't need to reinforce how critical this is, do I?"

"I fucking get it. I don't want the thing falling into the wrong hands any more than you do. I'm doing everything I can to find it. Trust me."

"If only it were a matter of trust."

46

They were nearly back to the hotel, but Layne could still feel the rush of adrenaline pumping through her veins as the town car weaved through downtown traffic. "Is being attacked by a wild horseman what you meant by complicated?" she asked.

"Nope," Ryan said. "But it does add another layer of complexity to the situation."

"What do you mean? Wasn't that what we wanted? To draw someone out? I know we didn't catch them, but they'll try again. Right? We could set another trap. And this time, we'll catch the son of a bitch."

Ryan turned his gaze to the window.

"Ryan? What is it?"

"We'll be back at The Riede in a few minutes. We can talk there."

Layne felt like someone had mainlined a gallon of caffeine straight into her veins. She wanted to act, needed to ramble, to expel all of the thoughts whipping through her mind. But she suspected any thoughts she spewed would land like yesterday's omelet on the seat between them. So, instead, she closed her eyes and focused on her breathing, as her yoga instructor would have advised. She decided her yoga instructor was full of shit.

"Who's full of shit?" Ryan asked.

"My yoga instructor," she said with her eyes still closed. "Did I think that out loud?"

"Either that or I can read your mind."

"What am I thinking now?"

"I'm too much of a gentleman to repeat that, but thank you."

Layne suppressed a smile. "You're both full of shit."

"But you love me anyway. At least that's what you told me last night."

Layne's eyes popped open just as the town car came to a stop in front of the hotel. Before she could question Ryan's comment, the door next to her swung wide, and several agents waited to deliver her to her room. Once inside, she plopped on the sofa, and stared out at the city, suddenly uncertain whether she wanted more information on the casual bombshell Ryan had dropped.

Her little voice, on the other hand, tugged at her like a Terrier begging for a treat. *Ask him. Go ahead. What did he mean? We need to know. C'mon. Ask him now. Please?*

"Hey, I have a question for you," Ryan said.

She let her head fall back and groaned. "How could you possibly have more questions?"

"Why did you ask to see the locket?"

"Oh, I almost forgot. I wanted to look for the pictures."

"What pictures?"

"It would be easier to show you."

"Yes, it would. But I don't have the locket."

"What?"

"The rider took it as he passed by."

"How? I was holding it and...oh no."

"It's not your fault, Layne. With all the commotion, you couldn't have known. What were you saying about the pictures?"

"Well, before you distracted me at the park," she lifted a brow, "I was looking for the ring with the two tiny pictures. They were photos of my grandmother and grandfather. But I don't think I saw the ring in the bag."

"Hmm," Ryan said. "Excellent work. That may help us."

"Why would someone go to those lengths to take the locket after the FBI destroyed it?"

"Just something else for us to figure out. You mentioned wanting to phone Chef DeGasse, and I have a few things I need to take care of. Are you going to be okay if I leave for a bit?"

"I think I'll manage."

"I'll be back as soon as I can, and I'll ask Hansel and Gretel to come inside."

"Is that what I should call them?"

Ryan walked toward the door. "I wouldn't recommend it. By the way, there's some cream of brool in the minibar fridge. Degasse sent extra home with us last night. He didn't want you to miss dessert."

"I think you mean crème brûlée."

"Like I said," he called over his shoulder.

"Wait."

"Uh huh?"

"In the car, you mentioned something I'd told you?"

"You told me I was full of shit."

"No, the other—" The door to the suite closed.

Half an hour later, Layne took the last sinful bite of the most decadent crème brûlée she'd ever eaten, and she couldn't wait to talk to the chef.

He answered on the first ring. "Ma chérie, how are you feeling?"

"I'm fine, Chef. Thank you so much for your concern, and for the wonderful dinner. I want to apologize if I made a spectacle of myself last night."

"No need, my dear. It is the norm in Paris. Please think nothing of it. Did you try the brûlée?"

"Oh my goodness. Only you would think to add such an indulgent ingredient to crème brûlée. It was amazing. With your permission, I'd like to feature that recipe on one of my shows."

"I knew it. I knew you would love it. Shall I give you the recipe now?"

"If you can take the time. I'll need the appetizer recipes, too."

"Time is made, ma chère, not taken. For you, I will make the time."

Layne spent the next half hour scribbling out the chef's amazing recipes for candied bacon crème brûlée with caramel sauce, and the three appetizers she had tried the night before. Then the door to the suite opened, and Maggie breezed in wearing a skin-tight, cream-colored cashmere sweater, a short, black skirt, and knee-high, black, spike-heeled boots. Layne finished her call, and Maggie sent her a shrewd stare.

"Despite the rumors, it sounds like you had a successful dinner at Rue de Rêves?"

"Rumors?"

"Dennis called me from the restaurant last night. Goodness, that boy is protective. He was very concerned. Said you were three sheets to the wind, and he wanted to stop the shoot. Damn, I can't believe I missed it."

"I might've had one too many glasses of wine."

"Only one too many?"

"Truthfully, I have no clue how many. Did you see the footage?"

"Yes," Maggie said. "Dennis emailed it to me. Thanks to some tricky camera work, it came out great. And, of course, they'll edit the hell out of it. So, no worries."

"That's a relief."

"And," Maggie said. "It seemed like you were having a mighty fine time with that mighty fine agent."

"Maggie." Layne nudged her chin toward Hansel and Gretel, who avoided looking at the two women.

"Well, well," Maggie said as she strolled over to Hansel. "This is an unexpected pleasure."

Hansel stared straight ahead.

"I was hoping I'd run into you again," Maggie purred.

He didn't respond.

She moved to within inches of him. "So, you're the strong, sexy, silent type?"

"Comes with the job," Hansel said.

"Can you do a job for me?" Maggie peered up at him, her nose almost touching his chin.

"That depends."

She rose onto her toes and inclined against him to whisper into his ear. Hansel finally obliged her and bent down. When Maggie finished, a slight smile spread across his face. Layne couldn't recall ever seeing Hansel smile. Maggie backed up a bit, placed a kiss on the tip of her index finger, and pressed it to Hansel's lips. Then she let it trail over his chin, down his neck, and to his chest, before she turned and sauntered back over to Layne.

"I cannot believe you did that," Layne whispered.

"Of course you can. And I think I'm going to be very glad I did."

"Sometimes you make me so..."

"Envious?"

"Maybe."

"Anyway, since you never called me back, I came by to see how long you'd be cooped up with agent hotty. Not that I'd want a little thing like work to interfere with your sex life."

"I'm sorry, Maggie. There are...things."

"Things?"

The pitch of Layne's voice rose. "You know...things. Horses. My locket. Ice molds. Things. Things I'm not supposed to talk about."

"That's an intriguing list," Maggie said. "But enough about you. If I plan to deliver on my promise to Mr. tall, dark and yummy, I need to get ready." She stopped to study Layne. "You really like this guy, huh?"

Her best friend knew her too well. "What makes you say that?"

Maggie smirked. "We can chat later about the work stuff, but at some point, I will hear this story. Horses and ice molds. Sounds kinky." She turned, allowing Hansel to ogle her ass as she strutted toward the door, while Layne attempted to shove all lurid speculation about Maggie's promise to the colossal bodyguard out of her head.

"Ms. Stevens."

Layne looked over at Hansel.

"Can we keep the date with me and your friend between us?"

"Of course."

"Thanks. She's not a witness, but dating someone involved in the case is sort of against protocol."

"Got it." Her thoughts flashed to Ryan. "Wait, what did you say?"

Back at the run-down apartment, Sonny waited to hear if the royal fiasco in the park had produced the card. He focused his binoculars on Layne's windows and let out a low whistle as her curvy friend entered the suite. His mind wandered to the image of an oily threesome, then his phone honked. He tapped his bluetooth, hoping for good news.

"Yep."

"It's time," The Employer said.

"So, the bag didn't contain the card?"

"Would I be directing you to act if it did?"

"I guess not," Sonny said. "Should I do it now?"

"Wait until Cooke finds his way into the room."

"Got it," Sonny said.

47

Ryan inspected the small room—the padded table, the laminate countertops, the cabinets, the rolling stool—all of them, a lifeless shade of gray. His back tensed, and his nose wrinkled at the lingering smell of antiseptic. He didn't dislike doctors, exactly, but he wished he were somewhere else. Anywhere else. He paced until the door opened.

"Thank you for fitting me in, Dr. Hanley," Ryan said.

"Hello, Agent Cooke. It didn't sound like something that should wait. Tell me more about what's going on?"

"I seem to have a gap in my memory, from the night before last at about nineteen hundred hours, until I woke up yesterday morning."

"What is the last thing you remember before the gap?"

"I boarded a plane at LAX."

"Do you recall boarding?"

"Yes. But after that, nothing."

"And the first thing you remember afterward?"

"Waking up at my place. A driver logged my trip home from SFO, but I don't have any recollection. It's just...gone."

"How did you feel when you woke up?"

"My neck felt a little stiff. But other than that, good. Great, actually."

"And you functioned normally?"

"Ate a healthy breakfast, went to the gym, had a decent workout, ran five miles. I was fine."

"Please tell me your healthy breakfast wasn't frosted flakes with skim milk."

"I'm out of milk, but I added craisins to my cereal. I used to think that was a fruit. Now I'm not so sure."

Dr. Hanley frowned. "When did you become aware of the lost time?"

"Yesterday afternoon. The primary in my case mentioned meeting me during that period, and I have no memory of the event."

A nurse took his blood pressure and temperature while the doctor scrutinized Ryan's eyes with a penlight.

"And you didn't notice anything unusual yesterday, or the day before? Anything out of the ordinary?"

"There's something strange in my freezer."

The doctor looked at him. "Something to be concerned about?"

Ryan shook his head. "Honestly, I don't know. It's an odd shape. But it has cooking instructions, so I have to assume my housekeeper left it."

"You didn't eat it? Whatever it was?"

"Definitely not."

"Then what was the last thing you ate or drank before the gap?"

"I had the special at the field office in LA."

"Their cafe?"

"Yes."

"What was it?"

"Carne asada street tacos with chips and salsa, and a soda."

"They have a nice cafe. How was it?"

"It was very good. I really like that chopped onion mixture they put on top."

"You didn't get the guacamole?"

"What is it with you Californians and foods that are green? Green things should not go into a person's mouth."

"What about lettuce?"

"Iceberg lettuce isn't green."

Dr. Hanley chuckled. "Someday your eating habits will catch up with you."

"So I've heard."

"You didn't have anything at LAX?"

"Nope."

"Not even water?"

Ryan shook his head.

"I assume the airport was crowded."

"Yes. LAX is always heavy with commute travelers in the evening."

"Hmm. Okay, I'll need you to strip down."

"I'm sorry?"

"You heard me. Everything off."

The nurse made a hasty exit, leaving Ryan with the attractive young blond he knew as Dr. Hanley. She'd been his doctor for the last several years, but there was some amount of modesty he hoped to maintain. "No gown?"

"Listen, Ryan, either you were drugged, or there's something else going on. The something else scenario gets you a full battery of tests and suspension from active duty. Today, I'll take blood to analyze for drugs, but those results won't be back until tomorrow. Since you didn't eat or drink anything right before the lapse, the more likely explanation for drug-induced memory loss is injection. If we can find an injection site, then we've narrowed it down." She handed Ryan a flimsy, folded paper blanket, and opened a tall narrow cabinet. "You can hang your suit in here, and use this blanket to cover up until I get back. I give these to female patients for annual exams, but it'll work. I will see you in a few."

Ryan's eyebrows jumped. Dr. Hanley had a way with words.

Several minutes later, Ryan's chest tightened as he stood in the center of the cold examination room, naked, with his arms straight out at his sides and the flimsy blanket at his ankles on the floor. He felt ridiculous, and it didn't help that Dr. Hanley was examining his body with excruciating deliberation.

"Jacket?" she asked.

"Are you offering?"

"Were you wearing a suit jacket?"

"Yes, I was."

The doctor lowered the focus of her investigation, and every muscle in Ryan's body tensed. He fixed his gaze on the gray laminate cabinets above the sink.

"You don't have anything I haven't seen before," Dr. Hanley said.

"You certainly know how to make a man feel special."

Far too many minutes passed before she brushed the tip of a gloved finger over the side of his thigh, just over his right knee.

"There, on the lower part of the anterior quadriceps," she said.

Ryan looked down to inspect the tiny puncture wound developing a scab. "Damn."

"Actually, this is good news," the doctor said. "I won't be forced to pull you from duty. Tomorrow, we'll have details on the drug make up, but from what you've described, I have a fair guess."

"Can I get dressed?"

"Oh, of course. Anyway, I believe you were given a high dose of something in the Benzodiazepine class. In low doses, they're prescribed for anxiety. In high doses, they cause a suppressive action in certain parts of the brain for a limited amount of time, targeting those areas related to memory. As I said, we'll have specifics tomorrow. If I'm right, there won't be any permanent physical side effects, but the memories are gone. Somebody went to a lot of trouble to make sure you lost that time, and I'd guess by the location, at one point the person sat right next to you."

Ryan wasn't surprised. He had too many years on the job for that. But something didn't track. The case had been cold for months, and someone had drugged him before the murder occurred. Layne flashed through his mind, and he reminded himself that in his line of work there were no coincidences. He checked his tie in the mirror and headed back to The Riede.

48

On paper, the operation was going as planned. But in Ryan's head, the pieces didn't fit. What had he missed? Despite his thoughts on coincidence, he felt confident of one thing—an unfortunate relationship tied Layne to the case, but she did not kill her uncle, and she didn't have the card. He strode past her suite to check in with the surveillance team, where an odd combination of laughter and tension filled the room.

"What's going on?" he asked.

"Rennick's got a crush on young Seth," Rusk said.

Ryan flashed a questioning glance at Rennick.

"Absolutely not," Rennick said. "Rusk is an imbecile, sir."

Hawk wiggled his eyebrows. "You were gone for quite a while, Rennick. What did you say? Making small talk?"

"Yeah," Rusk said. "We know what they were making." He laughed at his own joke, along with several other agents, as Rennick's cheeks turned a furious shade of red.

Ryan put up a hand. "Recess is over. Issues with the profile, Rennick?"

"No, sir. I had to wait. That's all."

"All right. Marco, any word on Temple?"

Marco skimmed over his notes. "Ex-mounted patrol officer, Sherley Vincent Temple, forced into basic patrol when his horse retired."

Rusk choked on a sip of coffee. "Surely, you didn't say Shirley Temple."

Laughter filled the room.

"I said Sherley, spelled the guy way," Marco said. "And yes, his name is Sherley Temple. But he goes by Vince."

Hawk lowered his brow. "There is no way to spell Shirley in a guy way."

"Surely, you didn't mean that," Rusk said, nodding to his chuckling audience.

"All right, children," Ryan said. "Can we have a little focus?"

The room calmed, and Rusk grinned. "Surely we can, boss."

"Marco, please continue," Ryan said.

"Well, this guy's got a sketchy history at best," Marco said. "Written up several times for insubordination. Never played well with the other mounteds. Has made his dislike of basic patrol clear to his uppers. Seems to be biding his time until he retires next year. And get this, he wasn't assigned to park patrol today."

"What? Are you certain about that?"

"He signed out a car for basic patrol at the University."

"Well, I'll be damned," Ryan said. "What about the horse?"

"The patrolman for that mount worked another quadrant of the park. A gardener found him locked in a tool shed, blindfolded, tied up and stripped to his skivvies. He said someone jumped him from behind, so he didn't get eyes on the assailant, but the SFPD will take an official statement later today."

"Shit. Then it could be Temple."

"Could be aliens, boss. We don't have enough to go on, which leads me to the prelim autopsy report on Schatz."

"And?"

"It's not much. Death was caused by a single puncture wound to the heart."

"So, a skewer from the rumaki."

"That's a negative, boss."

"How can that be?"

"Forensics ruled it out. There were three skewers centered on the tray. That's how the appetizer is plated, and they hadn't been tampered with—not moved, not taken apart, not reassembled. We got plenty of prints, but so far they all match hotel staff or Schatz."

"So far?"

"They're still working through partials. We were all kinda hoping for death by rumaki. Sounds cool, doesn't it? But, no go."

"Then what the hell was the murder weapon?"

Marco read from the autopsy report. "Cause of death: sharp force injury, two-millimeter puncture wound to the heart causing systemic shock and rapid internal bleeding. Weapon to be determined."

"Two millimeters, like the size of a skewer."

"What can I say, boss? If it was a skewer, it didn't come from the platter we found in the room."

"Damn it, all right." Ryan started toward the bedroom, then stopped. "It doesn't make sense, Marco. If the bleeding was internal, how'd we end up with all that blood in the closet?"

Marco flipped through the document. "According to this, somebody squeezed him."

"Come again?"

Marco again quoted the report. "External blood loss due to circumferential constriction of the thorax and position of the body."

"Hunh."

"It says here that forensics detected a heavy-duty cleaning solution on the carpet in the area leading from the tray to the closet, but no traces of blood."

"So, somebody grabbed Schatz around the middle, dragged him across the floor, lifted him into the closet, and then cleaned up after themselves."

Marco nodded. "This is a pro, boss. There's no way the Stevens chick does that on her own."

Ryan rubbed his chin. "No way Temple manages that either."

"The cleanup left Short's team with nothing. It's a forensics nightmare."

"There has to be a partner," Ryan said.

"And the partner has the memory card?"

"I don't think so. If they'd found the card, why come back? Damn it, Marco, we need more to go on."

"Working on it. By the way, nice move—sliding in that little tidbit from last night's bathroom incident. Nothing like the power of suggestion. I'll bet she's squirming and over analyzing as we speak."

"Yeah, thanks." He'd planned to use it. His team had expected it. But why did it feel so wrong? He turned again to go, wanting time alone to think.

"Wait, boss. Seth's profile is in." Marco broke the seal on the envelope and removed the packet. He scanned the top page before handing it to Ryan. "It's all here. Looks like we're on the right track."

Ryan looked over the analyst's summary. Seth had misstepped only one time on a profile, and the circumstances were ambiguous—something about an emergency appendectomy and considerable doses of morphine. But the muscles in Ryan's jaw tightened as he read. He tossed the packet back to Marco and strained to regulate his voice. "Usual procedure. Hand out copies to the team, and we'll meet back here at twenty-one hundred hours to go over the game plan."

"Man," Marco said. "I honestly wouldn't have guessed. She's fuckin' good."

After several minutes spent pacing the hall, Ryan stormed into Layne's suite and headed for the door of the adjoining room. "Bedroom. Now," he said.

Layne's gaze shot up from her issue of Cook's Illustrated. "I'm sorry, what?"

He attempted to control his tone, but his words came out clipped. "I need to talk to you in private. Now. Please."

She put down the magazine, gave him a weary, "Okay," and followed him into the bedroom.

Once inside, Ryan slammed the door behind them and advanced on Layne with barely contained fury. "What are you not telling me?"

She stepped back from him. "What do you mean?"

Her apparent confusion only fueled Ryan's rage. "Cut the act, Layne. I've got your profile. I know who you are."

She turned toward the bedroom door, but Ryan grabbed her wrist and yanked her toward him. With his face set inches from hers, he glared into her eyes. "This is not how it works," he said. "You do not get to decide how this game is played."

"What game? What profile? What the hell are you talking about?"

He tightened his grasp on her wrist. "You know damned well what I'm talking about."

She tried to squirm away from him. "Ryan, you're hurting me."

For several seconds he didn't move, or speak, or lessen his grip. And the harder he worked to contain his anger, the more agitated and confused he became. He wrenched Layne against him, clamped his arm around her waist, and consumed her mouth with his. Then, as abruptly as he'd taken her, he shoved her away. He looked at the floor, clawed at his hair, and tried to recover, to find words, but none came.

He turned and left the suite.

As Rennick listened to the exchange, the surveillance suite buzzed with agents debating the probability of success with this new approach. She didn't partake in the banter, but she guarded a triumphant grin as she watched Marco, with brows furrowed, tap a nervous beat on the desk.

49

Ryan stepped off the elevator and paced the hotel lobby for several minutes. He no longer had control—of the operation, of himself, of his emotions. What the hell had he been thinking? And what would be the result? He didn't need to go to his condo, but he couldn't stay at The Riede. He radioed for a town car to take him home, then he called Marco.

"I want to get a few more things from my place," Ryan said when Marco picked up. "I'll be back within the hour."

"You're the boss." It was Marco's usual response, but his voice held noticeable concern.

Ryan arrived at his condo and went through his routine on rote—gun and keys on the side table, beer from the fridge, computer on. He sat on the couch, staring out at the bay, and a lightning bolt of realization hit him. He had disregarded his own karmic rule—there are no coincidences. Rennick had been right all along. Not only had Layne played him, she'd done it with expert precision from the start.

She had drugged him for reasons he still didn't understand. She'd handed off their only piece of evidence. And despite being her uncle, when Frederick Schatz either couldn't, or refused to point Layne to the card, she and a partner had eliminated him with the knowledge that the best federal counterintelligence team in the world would finish the search for them. The blushing, the flirting, the attempted escape, it had all been a goddamned act.

Ryan set his beer on the end table and tried to funnel his anger toward working through the investigation. The profile left no question, but something nagged at him. He went for his phone and called Seth.

"Dude," Seth said. "Thought you'd forgotten about us peons."

"Never," Ryan said. "Just too buried to breathe."

"So, then, to what do I owe the pleasure?"

"I'm calling about the Stevens profile."

"Man, she is so cool. That's like my favorite show on Foodie. Did you actually get to meet her?"

"Yes, I've met her."

"Dude, is she totally awesome, or what?"

"She's nice enough."

"Nice? You gotta be kidding. She's like a goddess."

"This must have been a tough write up for you then."

"No way, man. Easy, peasy. It's not like I let my feelings cloud my judgment or anything. That's not what you think, is it? Because this was pretty straightforward."

"Oh yeah?"

"One of my easiest profiles yet."

"Good to know. Hey, I'm sorry if Agent Rennick pressured you into getting it done before you were ready."

"No worries. I had it finished before she called."

"Hunh. Listen, Seth, I'm aware this isn't normal protocol, but I'm at home, and I spilled coffee all over the summary page. Would you mind sending it, soft, to my home e-mail?"

"I don't see why not. You got the sealed packet, right? And the file's password protected, so it should be cool."

"Thanks, man, I owe you one."

Seconds later an email from Seth arrived, and Ryan used the password he'd seen on the hard copy to open the file. Shit. He tipped back in his desk chair and contemplated the screen. Then his cell phone rang, replacing his confusion with unease.

"Hello, Mitch," Ryan said.

"Evening. Thought I'd check in on the Stevens op. How's it going?"

Ryan frowned. FBI Counterintelligence Director, Mitch Hall, did not call simply to check in.

"I'm at my condo now, picking up some things," Ryan said. "Unless you've heard otherwise in the last hour, the operation is moving ahead as planned."

"Glad to hear it," Director Hall said. "You're not too emotionally involved with this thing, are you, Cooke?"

The director hadn't called him by his last name in years, and he'd never questioned Ryan's judgment. "No, sir. But I believe I made an error in my request of a junior agent who doesn't truly appreciate the full court press technique you passed down to a few of us."

"Ah, yes. I think you tied my record with that approach."

"And I intend to beat it with this op. All due respect, sir."

"I'd expect nothing less. Do you need assistance with that junior?"

"Not necessary, Mitch. I'll handle it."

"Very well, then. Oh, by the way, I received a call from Darren Chase, President at the Foodie Channel. Called my direct line."

"He has your direct number?"

"Apparently anything can be bought these days. Anyway, he wants us to release Ms. Stevens."

"She's our prime suspect. That's not happening."

"He handed me some bullshit about a production schedule and how time is money. The network is threatening to sue for her release in a very public way. I've got it managed, but I figured you'd want to know."

"Thank you, Mitch. And thanks for calling."

Ryan pressed end on his phone and shook his head. The network thing might prove inconvenient, but he had bigger wrinkles to iron out —his outburst in Layne's suite with his entire team listening in; Rennick fighting him at every step; and Marco, the one person besides himself with access to Director Hall. Hell, he and Marco had been friends for twenty years. They'd risked their lives for each other numerous times. No way Marco betrayed him. But Director Hall stuck to protocol. He wouldn't talk to a member of Ryan's unit outside the chain of command. Not without unique circumstances. Like, for instance, hiding his own involvement.

Ryan stood at the windows and stared at the water. He didn't know who could be trusted, or what this particular game entailed, but only one course of action guaranteed the outcome. It was risky, but it supplied a way to earn back Layne's trust. And only then could he finish it. He organized the items on his desk, made a few calls from an untraceable cell phone, packed a duffle bag, and left.

50

Layne stood alone in the bedroom trembling with anger and disbelief. She couldn't imagine what might have caused Ryan's outburst, and the more she considered it, the more enraged she became. How dare he yell at her like that. How dare he kiss her like that. But his behavior paled to her frustration at her own reaction. The kiss was brash, and controlling, and completely unacceptable. But she hadn't fought it. Worse, she didn't regret it. She'd been waiting for him to kiss her. And although the circumstances were, quite frankly, crappy, her heart had raced, and her mouth had conceded to his without resistance. What a complete and total idiot. She'd let herself get caught up in a fantasy, and she'd broken her own damned rule—no involvement. Idiot, idiot, idiot. But still. Could she have seen that coming?

Her little voice added it's two cents. *I'm gonna cut you some slack on this one, because that shit really did swoop in from nowhere.*

"Right?" Layne said to the empty room. "What the hell?" She sat down on the bed and put her face into her hands. "Think, Stevens." But nothing came to her. Dropping her palms to her sides, she straightened her spine and took in a deep breath. But the breath didn't work. It never worked. "What the holy hell?"

She picked up the pillow Ryan had used, and as she committed pillow strangulation, Hansel's voice came through the bedroom door.

"Ms. Stevens? Is everything okay in there?"

With a tight grip still on the pillow, Layne rushed to open the door. "Damn it, Hansel, what the hell happened in here?"

He stepped inside. "I...I'm not sure, ma'am."

"Don't you dare call me ma'am."

"I'm sorry, but I don't know what you want me to say."

"Are you telling me," she stopped to catch her breath, "that you don't know why Prince Charming turned into Mr. Hyde?" She put a hand over her racing heart. "Were you following those breadcrumbs, Hansel? Huh? Were you?"

Hansel froze.

"Tell me! What is going on?"

Another man stepped into the room. "I got this," he said to Hansel.

"I'm sorry, ma'am," Hansel said as he turned to go.

"Sorry my ass. And don't call me ma'am!"

Hansel sped for the door, giving a slight jump when the pillow hit him on the backside.

"Ms. Stevens," the man said.

Layne glared at the pillow on the floor.

The man tried again. "Layne?"

She turned her glare to the man. "Who are you?"

"I'm Special Agent Marco Viorantelli, the surveillance team lead for this operation. May I call you Layne?"

Tears flooded her eyes. "Only my friends call me Layne, Special Agent Vior...whatever it was you said. Are you my friend?"

A sly smile spread over Marco's face. "Well, after observing you for the last couple of days, I wouldn't want to be your enemy. And please, call me Marco."

Layne emitted a small part-laugh, part-sob. "Can you tell me what's going on, Marco?"

"Yes," Marco said. "I believe I can."

~

The sun glowed copper over the bay as Ryan returned to The Riede. He entered the surveillance suite to a solemn group and not much time to turn things around. He could tackle his uncharacteristic outburst at Layne head on, or he could ignore it, position it as part of the plan. He chose the latter.

"Listen up," Ryan said to his team. "Let's keep this short. Here's the challenge. We need more information, and we need someone to screw up, whether it's Ms. Stevens, Temple, their agencies, or any other damned agency that might be after this thing. The easiest way to draw everyone's attention is to be out in the open again, preferably the wide open. But if we force our hand, I want to position us in better control. I'm proposing the Santa Cruz Beach Boardwalk."

Ryan scanned the room as talk and murmurs spread through the team. "Thoughts? Questions?"

Rusk raised his hand. "Will we have a food allowance? They sell the best-damned corn dogs at the boardwalk."

"Valid thoughts or questions?"

"Sir."

Ryan checked his irritation. "Yes, Agent Rennick."

"Wouldn't the chaos put us at somewhat of a disadvantage?"

"Hawk, please field that."

Hawk droned as if reading from a textbook. "In the game of cat and mouse, controlled chaos is your best offense. It places your opponent in an unprepared, defensive position, leaving more room for error, blah, blah, blah...do I have to continue, boss?"

"No, I think that'll do. Rennick, I'll need you to stay here and monitor the coms." Ryan didn't acknowledge Rennick again, and her body language told him he'd accomplished his goal. "Anything else?" he asked the group.

"Time?" Marco asked.

"I'll plan to arrive with Ms. Stevens at thirteen hundred hours. That should give you enough time to ensure the logistics. Until then, I'll apply more pressure. Maybe she'll slip up with something we can use, or she might try to contact someone. Either would be a step forward, but we can't count on it. This boardwalk plan has to work."

"Okay, you heard the man," Marco said. "Pull the maps, talk to the local PD, get me building and land layouts for the boardwalk and surround, start collecting equipment. We've got a lot to do, ladies, let's move." Marco searched the room. "Rennick?"

"Over here," Rennick said.

"We're gonna need donuts and lots of fucking coffee. Rookie buys."

Rennick shook her head, grabbed her purse, and left the suite muttering obscenities.

Ryan attended to some items, and then started for Layne's suite as he contemplated the potential consequences of his plan. He had one last obstacle to contend with. And she, most likely, wasn't speaking to him.

51

Layne sat with Hansel and Gretel at the dining table on the far side of the sitting room. Room service leftovers and playing cards were spread across the table, and both men graciously humored her as she used the gin rummy game for distraction from the evening's earlier incident. They were starting a new hand when Ryan walked into the suite. Layne chose not to acknowledge him.

Gretel glanced at Ryan. "Hey, boss."

"Now there's something I haven't seen before," Ryan said. He looked at Layne. "Either you have blackmail material, or you have superhuman powers of persuasion to get these two into a game of cards."

He was being all friendly and lighthearted. She found that very irritating.

For a change, her little voice rallied in support. *Who does he think he is, waltzing back in here like nothing happened? Go ahead. Kick him in the nuts. He deserves it. I'll do it. Maggie would do it. Come on. You know you want to.*

Okay, some version of support.

Layne made a point to focus anywhere but on Ryan when she replied. "Triple fudge lava cake with mocha icing," she said to a pricey still life portrait on the wall.

"Come again?" Ryan said.

Gretel elaborated. "The deal is, we wanna eat cake, we gotta play."

"Cake is highly motivating," Ryan said.

Hansel looked at Layne. "It's your play, Ms. Stevens."

She hesitated. "Thank you for putting up with me. And for letting me win at cards. But if you don't mind, I think I'll turn in."

Surprise crossed Gretel's face. "You knew?"

"It was very sweet of you both."

She pushed her chair back from the table, as did Hansel and Gretel. But as she stood, a window near the table shattered, and shards of glass sprayed the suite like snowflakes on a gust of wind. Ryan came at her from the side, and the room spun as he knocked her to the ground. As if in slow motion, she watched Hansel drop and reach for his gun, while Gretel crouched, moving toward the windows with determined, tiger-like precision. Other agents burst into the room with guns drawn, and a war waged over Layne's head, followed by an eerie silence. After a long, still moment, masses of people began scrambling around her, and she could hear the commotion from down on the street below. A sharp pain stabbed at her side, and through blurred vision, she watched the beautiful white carpet saturate into a dark pool of blood red.

WITH A LARGE DUFFLE slung over one shoulder, Sonny strolled through a poorly lit parking garage under a tavern next to the old apartment building. He stashed his gear in the trunk of his car and hopped the short flight of steps to the back entrance of Mulligans Irish Pub and Grub. Pulling a stool close to the bar, he ordered an Irish cream coffee with extra whipped cream, along with a double helping of bread pudding. Then he focused on the wide screen television nestled within the hundred or so whiskey bottles that embellished the wall.

Tattered mahogany wood blinds created a dark venue for the rugby match booming from speakers on either side of the screen. Amidst the piercing volume of the game, and the heated enthusiasm of the bar patrons, the several uniformed officers who entered through the front door went unacknowledged by most.

Sonny stole a glance in their direction and subtly tracked their progression through the room. They signaled the bartender to turn off the television—an act met with boos and groans—then they scrutinized the customers and posed predictable questions as they moved between the tables. All patrons told the same story; the match was in overtime, the volume was high, and the blinds were closed. No one saw or heard anything, and few were interested. They wanted to get back to the game.

Sonny's bread pudding arrived, and he asked the bartender for another drink. The officers moved in on either side of him as he gazed at the blank screen. Son of a bitch, he'd been set up.

"Pardon me, sir."

Sonny turned on his barstool to face the officer, who stared at him for a moment, then nudged his chin back toward the tables. "Do you mind?"

"What? Oh. No problem." Sonny picked up his coffee and bread pudding, and slid off the stool allowing the officers space to talk with the bartender. The nearest table overflowed with burly men and stocky freckle-faced women, all wearing dirt-encrusted Irish League rugby jerseys. A redhead with prominent front teeth removed her cleats from a chair and pulled it out for him. He thanked her and took the offered seat.

After a brief conversation, the officers excused the bartender and went out the back door leading to the underground lot. A few minutes passed, and they returned to the bar. They checked both bathrooms, peered into the kitchen, examined the patrons one last time, and left through the front.

Only then did Sonny fully release his breath. He'd had a moment of doubt, but his talents had served him again. He ordered another Irish cream coffee, bought the redhead a black and tan, and settled in to enjoy the end of the match.

52

Layne cracked her eyes open to bright lights and the frenzy of people around her. A host of memories rushed through her mind—the blast of gunfire, the spray of glass, the sea of blood. But those thoughts were muddled, much like her vision, and a bitter smell permeated the air. Sirens blared nearby, and that same sharp pain still penetrated her side.

Holy shit, her little voice said. *If this is heaven, I'd like to check out the other options.*

Layne grimaced. "Am I dead?"

"Nope."

Not her little voice. She pried her eyelids open further. "Where am I?"

"In your suite at The Riede."

"I'm not in the hospital?"

"Nope."

"But I got shot."

"Nope. Johnny got shot. You got side tackled."

She squinted at the voice, settled deep into an overstuffed chair beside her. "Gretel?"

He snickered. "I prefer Tom."

Voices yelled outside. Sirens continued to wail on the street below. And a flurry of activity filled the room with new window panes being installed, the cleanup of glass, and the whir of an industrial-sized carpet cleaner drawing a liberal stain from the rug. She tried to sit up.

"You don't want to do that," Gretel said.

Layne reached down to where a relentless ache plagued her side. "I'm not shot?"

"Nope, but you took a respectable hit from the boss."

"But, the blood."

"Johnny's."

"Who?"

"Hansel to you, I suppose."

"Oh god. Is he—

"Nope. He's not too happy, but he's not going to die."

Layne eased back on the sofa. "Johnny. I like that name. Thank goodness he's all right. Where was he shot?"

"Over there by the table."

Layne narrowed her eyes at Gretel.

"Only trying to lighten the mood," he said. "We wear pullover Kevlar, which means our sides are unprotected. Just Johnny's luck, the bullet hit him in the side. What are the odds? I been riding him a lot about those love handles, but the damn things probably saved his life. Either that, or the shooter would've missed if Johnny wasn't so darned chubby."

"That's not very nice."

"It's not a nice business."

Layne startled at a presence looming over her. "Oh my gosh. Mr. Tall."

Gretel smirked, and the towering agent's gaze flicked away from her for a moment.

"It's Agent Short, ma'am."

"Oh, right, sorry. You took me by surprise and—"

"Not necessary," he said. "How are you feeling?"

"I'm a little woozy, but I'm sure I'll be fine. Thank you for asking."

"Well, then. We're almost done here. I just wanted you to know that everything will be taken care of."

"Everything?"

The pillar of agent walked away, and she sought an explanation from Gretel.

"He's an odd guy," Gretel said. "But he's a good forensics agent. Doesn't miss a thing."

Ryan approached the sofa, but Layne couldn't bring herself to look at him.

"Tom," Ryan said. "Can you check in with Marco? It seems Temple made an appearance in the mess down there, and we've got something on an apartment across the street."

"Will do, boss."

Gretel left the suite, and Ryan knelt beside her. "Are you okay, Layne?"

"I guess I'm doing better than Johnny."

"Not that I'd wish for anyone to get shot, but I'm glad it was him and not you."

"Are you sure he'll be all right?"

"He'll be like new in no time, but his date won't be as interesting as he'd hoped."

"You know about the date?"

"Tom asked me to call Maggie."

"What about the protocol?"

Ryan shifted. "It's more like a guideline."

"A guideline, huh?"

Ryan didn't respond.

"So, where is Maggie?"

"I asked her if she wanted to come visit with you, but she said she'd never..." He cleared his throat. "She's at the hospital with Johnny."

Layne eased to a sitting position. "That's my best friend."

"Are you feeling any better?"

"Other than a few bruises, I'm all right."

"Sorry about that. I guess I came at you a little hard."

"You saved my life. Again." She frowned.

"I would love to let you believe that, but even saving your life wouldn't compensate for my behavior earlier today. And to be honest, I'm not sure how to—"

"Marco explained," she said, hoping to sidestep the conversation.

"You spoke to Marco?"

Layne pressed at her temples. "Here's the thing. I feel kind of fuzzy. I'm exhausted. And you are really high on the list of people I'd rather not talk to."

"Always direct. I like that about you. And I understand," he said.

But he didn't leave. Why wouldn't he leave?

"It's not only me, then?" he asked. "You have a list?"

"It's a short one. You're tied for first with Drill Sergeant Rennick."

"Ouch."

She ignored the weak attempt to gain her sympathy. "Apparently, you're staying. So, what did you say about not saving my life?"

"The truth is, there isn't a shooter at any agency who is that bad. They weren't aiming for you."

"But why would anyone want to shoot Hansel...uh, Johnny?"

"I wish I knew."

"Love Shack" rang out from Layne's purse, and Ryan handed over her bag. "Remember, on speaker."

Layne fished for her phone and then answered with as much composure as she could manage. "Layne Stevens."

The line crackled with static, and the service faded in and out. And although garbled by a faint echo, they all recognized the voice.

"Make this easy on yourself by making it easier on us," Siri said.

Layne stared sideways at her phone. "I don't understand."

"That was no accident, Ms. Stevens," Siri continued. "We will continue to eliminate those you care about until you give us what we want."

"But—"

The static ended, and Layne froze. Ryan was right. The shooter hadn't been aiming for her. A knot twisted tight in her gut. "Oh god. My kids."

~

Marco's team raced to secure the apartment complex across the street. They had identified the unit used by the sniper, but after scouring the building, they came up empty. He wasn't surprised. The location gave the shooter the advantage of both time and turmoil. Marco needed all hands on deck, and he was in desperate need of more coffee.

He looked around the suite. "Rennick?"

No response.

He stood. "Has anyone seen Rennick?"

"Yeah," Rusk said. "I saw her down on the street after Johnny got shot."

"Did she have donuts and coffee?"

"I doubt it. She was carrying a big-ass silver briefcase and walking away from the hotel."

"Well, that sucks," Marco said. "She was supposed to get the coffee. What kind of briefcase?"

"Hard to see through the crowd. It looked like one of those steel currency carriers. But who knows with Rennick? She swims in a different lane most of the time."

"Yeah, well, whatever lane she's in, it needs to include following orders. And coffee." Marco tried Rennick's cell phone. It went straight to voicemail. Then he tried Gretel. "Tom, where the hell are you?"

"I'm still looking for fucking Temple," Gretel said. "Are you sure it was him?"

Marco called over his shoulder, "Rusk, you sure you saw Temple down there?"

"Yep," Rusk said. "Right before I saw Rennick. They were headed in the same direction—East, up the sidewalk."

Marco turned back to his phone. "Did you get that?"

"Yeah," Gretel said. "I've gone up and down a couple of times, but Temple could've ducked in anywhere."

"All right. Come back in. We'll try to ping his cell. If he even has one. Did you see Rennick?"

"Nope. No sign of her either."

"Damn. Would you mind bringing me a cup of coffee?"

A rustling sound flooded the line.

"Tom?"

The call disconnected.

"Fuck. Rusk, take a team and find Tom. We may have trouble."

53

Layne's hands shook. "I need to talk to Jenny and Dean."

"We have protective detail on them," Ryan said. "But you're right, it can't hurt to check in."

She took her phone into the bedroom and called Dean. It rang several times as she willed him to answer, but it went to voicemail.

"Dean, honey, it's Mom. You need to call me right away. All right? I love you. Please call me. Right away. I love you."

She tapped to end the call, but her gaze lingered on the phone as she listened to Ryan making inquiries on his radio in the other room. He joined her in the bedroom.

"How many roommates does Dean have?" Ryan asked.

"He lives in a house with three other boys. Why?"

"Let's not jump to any conclusions."

"What is it? What's going on?"

"Chico PD checked on Dean. Three young men were home, but Dean is gone. They told the officer he went out a few hours earlier. It seems Dean noticed the police detail and didn't want to be followed, so he went out the back."

Her eyes widened. "He's missing?"

"He's not missing, we just don't know where he is."

"How are those different?"

"I'm sure he's fine."

Layne pulled up Jenny's number and put the phone on speaker.

"Hey, Mom," Jenny said. "Are you finally home?"

"Thank goodness I reached you," Layne said.

"You don't sound so great."

"Listen, Jenny. Listen carefully. I don't want you to freak out, but you may not be safe."

"What do you mean? I thought you said everything was fine."

"It's complicated, sweetie. Police officers are there to watch over you and your roommates, but you should be extra careful, all right?"

"Someone is watching us?"

"You don't see them?"

"Wait." Her voice lowered. "There's a man on the back patio."

"Is it an officer?"

"No, he doesn't have a uniform. Mom, what should I do?"

"Are you alone in the apartment?"

Jenny's voice wavered. "Yes."

"Honey, is the sliding door locked?

"Y-yes."

"Okay, do not open it. Lock all your windows. Keep me on the line, okay?"

"Okay."

Ryan shot orders into his radio as Layne waited for Jenny to secure her apartment.

"Jenny?"

"I'm here, mom. I checked all the windows. Everything is locked."

"You're doing great, hun. Agent Cooke is talking with the San Diego police now."

The call went silent.

"Jenny?"

No response.

"Jen, talk to me, sweetie."

A distant scream echoed through the phone.

"She's not there, Ryan. Did you hear her scream?"

"San Diego PD is watching the place. I'm sure everything is okay."

"But she's not answering."

Ryan spoke into the phone. "Jenny?"

A whoosh came through the line, then a man's voice. "Mrs. Stevens?"

"Where's my daughter?"

"Ma'am, this is Detective Revine, SBPD. Your daughter is fine."

"Oh, thank god."

"It was my mistake, ma'am. We received an escalation for this location, and I checked the perimeter. I looked in a few windows, and I must have startled her. She dropped her phone, screamed, and ran down the hall. I had an officer kick in past the lock on the front door. We searched the apartment. There's no one here besides Miss Stevens."

"Revine, this is Special Agent Cooke. Have you seen anything unusual?"

"I just arrived, sir, but my officers inform me everything has been quiet. I apologize again for frightening her."

"Not your fault, Revine. Thanks for taking the extra precaution."

"Yes, sir. We'll have the lock repaired and keep someone outside the apartment at all times until we're notified otherwise. She'd like to talk to her mom."

Ryan handed the phone back to Layne.

"Mom?"

"I'm so sorry, Jenny. I didn't mean to scare you like that. The officers will be right there if you need them, okay?"

"Mom, what's happening? Why are they here? Are you all right?"

"I'm fine, sweetie, but it's complicated, and I can't talk about it now. I promise I'll explain everything when I get home. For now, just stay safe."

"I will if you will."

"Of course I will. I love you, Jenny."

"Mom?"

"Yes, sweetie?"

A loud sigh came through the line. "I love you, too."

Layne ended the call and buried her face in her palms. "Please tell me this is a bad dream."

"At least we know she's okay."

Ryan tried to put an arm around her, but her worry spun into rage. "What is all this about?"

He attempted again to console her, but she pushed him away. "Tell me, Ryan. What the hell is going on?"

"You must understand how sensitive this information is."

She glared at him through angry tears. "I don't care how sensitive it is. What is happening here?"

"I didn't want to put you in any more danger by exposing you to this, but I suppose that's a moot point." He focused on her eyes. "We believe there may have been an NSD card hidden inside your locket."

"A what kind of card?"

"A nano secure digital memory card. It's an extremely tiny unit, smaller than a grain of rice, with the capacity to store enormous amounts of data." Ryan took a moment. "This particular card is high risk because of the information it contains."

"What kind of information?"

"It's rumored to contain evidence of a corporate conspiracy against the American public."

"All this over a damned conspiracy?"

"From what we understand, it's a doozy. Several years ago, the card went up for auction on a darknet site, but the German government acquired it before it could be purchased. I don't fully understand their intent, but an agreement between Germany and our government suppressed the contents. A few months back, we got wind the card was no longer contained. My team took the assignment to retrieve it."

"What does any of this have to do with me?"

"I know this is a lot to take in, but your uncle, Frederick Schatz, was an agent for the BKA—that's Germany's equivalent to the FBI."

"Uncle Fred? A German agent?" She let out a scoff. "That's ridiculous. Do you know how old he is? I mean, was?"

"Yes. His age, and the fact that he already lived here in the states made him the perfect choice. We believe your uncle agreed to keep the card hidden. Now he's gone, the card is missing, and for those following its trail, the most likely person to have it is..." his eyes flicked downward.

Layne's mouth went dry. "You can't be serious."

54

Berger watched the commotion from his rental car, parked again down the street from The Riede. The FBI secured the apartment building, and all those who passed by on foot were stopped for questioning. Local businesses were searched. Helicopters circled low. And officers swarmed the area. It reminded him of a police state on high alert.

No one noticed him, and he didn't dare move his car for fear he might draw unwanted attention. So, he waited, and he observed. But what he saw troubled him. The turmoil would fade, and when things settled, he would take his leave. Then he would place a call to Agent Sherry Rennick to find out why she'd run from him in the park, and why she had been in that apartment building, still carrying the platinum rifle case.

55

Layne fumbled to answer her phone when MC Hammer's "U Can't Touch This" blasted from the speaker. "Dean? Dean, honey. Where are you? Are you okay?"

She listened as her firstborn whined that he was twenty-three years old, capable of taking care of himself, and didn't need his mommy or any stupid policeman watching over him like a toddler. Layne explained the situation as best she could without giving away too many details, and as she tapped end on the call, she was somewhat convinced he wouldn't do anything stupid, but she still felt a tightening in her chest.

"I've never been a parent," Ryan said. "But this can't be easy."

"I'm just relieved they're both all right."

A long moment passed before Ryan spoke again. "Listen, Layne. Could your uncle have hidden the memory card in your locket?"

"Ryan, this whole thing is absurd."

"Yes, it may be hard to believe, but the fact remains that we need to find it."

"But it's insane. Even if my uncle was some kind of spy, I haven't seen him in forty-five years. And my grandmother gave me the locket three years ago."

"Would that be your mother's mother?"

"Yes."

"And therefore also your Uncle Fred's mother?"

"Well, yes."

"Did your grandmother ever see him?"

"She visited South Dakota every—" Layne stopped to process the thought. "So, you think my uncle hid this nano-memory thing in my grandmother's locket."

"It would appear so."

"Which means I've been wearing a conspiracy, worth killing over, around my neck for three years."

"Stranger things have happened."

"No, Ryan. Stranger things have not happened. I've never heard of anything remotely stranger than that." She shook her head. "This can't be right. Why? Why would he do it?"

"The BKA agreed to keep the card hidden, and that job was tasked to him. What we don't know is where the hell it went. By the amount of attention you're getting, we feel confident no other agency has it."

"Right. Because they think I have it."

"Do you have it?"

The pitch of her voice rose. "The nano thing? Of course not."

"Are you now, or have you ever been, an operative for any government agency?"

"You've spent the last couple of days with me. What do you think?"

"I think you're beautiful, intelligent, and in sound physical condition. All desirable traits for a female agent."

You gotta admit, he's a charmer, her little voice said.

"Oh my god. I mean, thank you. But shit, Ryan."

"Layne, I need to know."

But I believe he could use an introduction to your middle finger, her little voice amended.

"I'll give you need to know," she said, squeezing her hands into fists.

"Please. It's important you answer the question."

"No, damn it. I have never been a government agent. Happy?"

She turned for the bedroom door, but Ryan grabbed her arm.

"Ouch!" she said, looking down at his hand.

"Did that hurt?"

"Yes. Let me go."

"I want to look at it."

"Look at what?"

"The back of your arm."

"Why?"

"Because I felt something there."

"I don't think a bruise on my—"

"Do you remember signing autographs last night?"

"We've been through this. The whole night is a big blur."

"Not the entire night. Tell me the last thing you recall."

"A man rushed for the table, and your men pinned him to the floor. Then you left me with Hansel. I mean Johnny. And a line formed for autographs."

"And after that?"

She shook her head. "Nothing. It's like I wasn't even there.

"One of the men who asked for your autograph, he touched your arm. Can I please look at it?"

She lifted her gaze to the ceiling and turned around, allowing Ryan to slide his fingers along the back of her upper arm.

"Damn it," he said.

Layne peered over her shoulder. "What is it? What's wrong?"

Ryan took Layne's hand and led her to the nightstand. Picking up the hotel notepad and pen, he wrote as he spoke. "Why don't you take some time to freshen up, and we'll talk more later," he said, steering her across the room.

"What? Where are you—"

He put the note into her hand, nudged her into the bathroom, and closed the door behind her. Layne stared at the paper. Oh hell no. She had a million questions, and she was damned well going to get some answers. She turned the tub water on high and peeked out of the bathroom door. "I need to regroup," she said. "You don't mind if I take a bath, do you?"

His brow lowered. "Pardon?"

"Will you stay there until I'm done? I'll feel safer knowing you're close by." She waved Ryan inside.

"Oh, of course," he said, slipping through the door and closing it behind him. "I thought you didn't want me to follow you into the bathroom."

Layne shook the note in his face and spoke in a muffled shriek. "My room is bugged?"

Ryan grimaced. "No jokes. Got it. Don't worry. There aren't any bugs or cameras in here."

"Cameras? What happened, did you run out of equipment?"

"We didn't set up for video in the bedroom, only sound."

"Why didn't you tell me about this before?"

"We don't have time to go into it now, but I've made arrangements for us to talk in private tomorrow. I promise I will tell you everything then. Can you please just play along for tonight?"

She eyed him warily. "You want me to play along."

"It would be helpful."

"You mean like where you guard me from between the sheets again?"

"That would be both helpful and nice."

She found his grin way too adorable, and mentally kicked herself for noticing. "What was that whole thing with my arm?"

"Remember the first time I came to your suite, and I didn't recognize you?"

"Yes. But then you said you did."

"Well, I lied. I don't recall anything about that flight."

She let her jaw drop. "But, how? How is that possible? I attached myself to your side like a piece of plastic wrap, and I spilled my wine and brownie all over you. People don't usually forget that sort of thing."

"Yes, you mentioned my pants during dinner. But here's the thing, I learned today that I was drugged either right before or right after I got on the plane."

"But in the airport terminal, you...we...I thought..."

"Did I lead you to believe I was interested in you?"

"Well, in a way. It's difficult to say. I mean—" She frowned. "What does any of this have to do with my arm?"

"You were drugged, too."

"Excuse me?"

"The man in the restaurant, you introduced me to him, said his name was Sonny. Does that sound familiar?"

"Not at all."

"You have a small injection mark on the back of your arm. That's why you can't remember anything after the man approached you."

"An injection?" She craned to peer over her shoulder. "I think I would have noticed a needle, or at least felt something."

"Not a small pen needle. That would have fit in the palm of his hand. And the combination of the pressure he applied to your arm, along with the distraction, well, let's just say he's very good at what he does. But it doesn't make any sense. What could have happened last night to warrant inducing a memory lapse?"

"I'm confused," Layne said.

He shook his head. "It just doesn't add up."

"Ryan."

"Though it does explain how you went from sober to drunk so quickly."

"Ryan!"

"I'm sorry, Layne. Just trying to piece all this together."

"Piece what together? I'm totally lost."

He stepped closer. "What you sensed at the airport, Layne, and at the park—you were right. I am interested in you. In fact, I care very much. I have a job to do here, and it involves linking you to this investigation. But I don't believe you've done anything wrong, and I don't want to see you hurt. I can't give you all the answers now. So, I'm asking you to please overlook my earlier behavior, and trust me. I want to help you out of this mess, but I can't do that without your trust and your cooperation."

Layne studied the bathroom floor.

"Hey," Ryan said. "Tell me what's going through that beautiful head of yours."

She searched for the right words. “It’s...It’s too much. I’m tired, and I’m scared, and confused.”

“I get it. This is a lot to handle.”

Ryan reached for her, and this time she let him fold her into his arms. For several minutes, she soaked in the warmth and security of his hold on her. Then she looked up at him with tears threatening again. “How do I know this isn’t an act, like before?”

Tension scored his face. “You don’t. But I’m the only person here who thinks you’re on our side. Trust me, Layne. Please?”

56

Rennick returned to the third floor of The Riede with three big box-containers of coffee and several dozen glazed donuts. She thumped on the door with the toe of her shoe, and Hawk let her in.

"It's a cluster down there," Rennick said. "What's going on?"

"Johnny got shot," Hawk said. "And we've got a five dollar buy-in for the pool. The boss made it into the bedroom. What do you think? First base? Home run? Or do you think he'll strike out?"

"What do you mean Johnny got shot? What's his status?"

Hawk smirked. "His status? He'll be fine. It was clean—right through the baby fat."

Rennick scanned the room for a place to set down her load of caffeine and sugar. Hawk made no attempt to help.

"Clean, huh?" she asked. "What's the damage?"

"He gets out tomorrow," Hawk said. "But he'll be off duty a couple weeks. So, you want in or what?"

"In?"

"On the pool?"

"That's idiotic."

"Don't be so sure," Hawk said. "The boss has a pretty good track record."

"I meant the pool, you moron. It's juvenile and unprofessional."

Many heads nodded unapologetically, but no one offered to help her.

"So, you're in?"

Rennick ignored Hawk and walked further into the suite.

Marco eyeballed her as she moved through the room. "This is the second time you've been MIA today. Where the hell were you, Rennick?"

"Can you not see the coffee and the donuts?"

"What were you doing down on the street?"

"What street?"

Marco lifted a brow. "You weren't on the street below here after the shooting?"

"Again, I was out getting the fricking donuts and the fricking coffee. Is there somewhere I can put them down?"

"Really," Marco said. "Then why did Rusk see you with a big old silver briefcase by the apartment building?"

"What apartment building? Rusk is an idiot. I don't know who he saw, but it wasn't me. Rookie buys, remember?"

"Hmm," Marco said, pursing his lips.

Rennick muttered several choice four-letter words and headed for a folding table in the back corner of the room.

Hawk chuckled. "Sounds like Rennick's got something stuck farther up her ass than usual."

Rennick put the coffee and donuts on the table, then went for her workspace and sat down to collect her thoughts. Her actions had been warranted, but the day's events left her tense and uptight. And she couldn't believe Rusk had fingered her in that mess on the street. She needed to pull it together. Maybe watching the imbeciles figure out how to open a box of coffee would brighten her mood.

~

RYAN ENTERED the surveillance suite to heated discussion.

"What the fuck, dude?" Marco said to Gretel.

"Sorry, man," Gretel said. "I didn't think you were gonna go all search and rescue on me."

Marco's hands went to his hips. "The situation down there is out of control. I hear a rustling sound, and the line goes dead. Of course I'm gonna respond. What were you thinking?"

"I was thinking I didn't want to walk two blocks to get your fucking coffee."

"Damn it, Tom," Marco said, and then he glanced over at Ryan. "Oh. Hey, boss."

Ryan looked sideways at the two men. "Everything okay here?"

"It's nothing." Marco flashed a glare at Gretel. "Sounds like things are going well with Stevens."

"Better than I expected, but we may have a problem."

"How so?"

Ryan pulled Marco and Gretel off to the side. "Remember when I asked you to trace my cell phone?"

"Yeah, that one was hard to forget."

"I went to see Doc Hanley this afternoon, and it turns out someone drugged me. There's a gap in my memory from the time I boarded the plane at LAX until the next morning."

"No shit," Gretel said.

"You think it was Stevens?" Marco asked.

"She had the best opportunity, but I'm struggling with the timing. Why drug me before the Schatz murder occurred? And here's the other thing. I noticed the same injection mark on the back of Stevens' arm. She experienced total memory loss from about halfway through dinner last night."

"That would explain why the wine hit her so hard."

"That man at the restaurant," Ryan said. "He introduced himself as Sonny. Said he had a private security company."

"Johnny mentioned him," Gretel said. "Thought he might be a little whacked."

"Well," Ryan said. "He held her arm long enough to place the injection, and Johnny was right, his behavior was odd. He acted like he knew me, then waited outside until everyone left. Wanted time alone with Layne—as if that was gonna happen. Anyway, the information he provided probably won't pan out, but get a description from Johnny, find out if he remembers the man's conversation with Layne. And talk to the Maître d' about the reservation, track down anything you can."

"On it, boss," Marco said. "But it doesn't make sense. If she drugged you..."

"It does if her agency thinks she's been compromised. I'm worried they may sacrifice her, then we'll be back to square one."

"I'll see what I can dig up."

"I need to get back over there, but let me know what you find."

Marco called after him, "Hey, we experienced a break in the audio before you came back. I'm gonna check the mic in the bedroom."

Ryan flashed the two men a sly smile. "Trust me, the mics are fine."

57

Layne peered out of the bathroom. Ryan lay in the center of the bed with his hands clasped behind his head, and his eyes fixed on the ceiling.

"Close your eyes," she said. "I need to get my pajamas out of the drawer."

Ryan lowered his eyelids. "Why? Are you naked?"

Layne hoped he was performing for the microphones. "No. But I'd prefer that you not see me like this."

"Like what?"

"In this big old hotel robe." She eyed him as she shuffled to the dresser. "Hey, I asked you not to peek."

"I've seen Amish women dressed in less. What didn't you want me to see?"

"It makes me look...well...not thin."

He laughed.

"Would you stop looking at me and do whatever FBI agents are trained to do?"

"Such as?"

"Secure something. Investigate something. Do something that doesn't involve looking at me."

"I am investigating something."

Layne grabbed a t-shirt and flannel pajama pants from the dresser and padded back into the bathroom in her fluffy hotel slippers. When she came out, Ryan read her shirt. "A morning without hot—"

"It used to say hot tea," Layne said. "Then Maggie got hold of it."

"So, a morning without hot sex is like a morning without sunshine," Ryan said. "It makes an excellent point."

"Why are you on my bed?"

"Don't you mean our bed?"

She crossed her arms and tapped her slipper. Just how far did he expect her to go for the sake of playing along?

"Let's be realistic," Ryan said. "I slept here last night, and it didn't kill you. In fact, it might have saved your life."

Layne arched a brow.

"Okay," Ryan said, "here's the thing. Normally, I can be awake at the slightest sound, but I can't do that if you're in here, and I'm out there. With the events of the last couple of days, it's just not safe."

Layne cast her eyes upward.

"Besides," Ryan said, "the couch is too short. And it's hard. And lumpy."

"I suppose the floor is out of the question?"

"Sure, you can sleep on the floor if it will make you feel better."

She growled at him. "Oh, all right. Sleep on the bed. But no funny business."

"Scouts honor." Ryan held up two fingers.

Layne narrowed her eyes at him, then sat on the bed and placed her slippers next to the nightstand.

"You can't sleep on that side," Ryan said.

"But I always sleep on this side."

"You don't sleep in the middle?"

"No. I got used to this side, so this is where I sleep. Do you sleep in the middle?"

"Yes, I do," Ryan said.

"Then why do you want my side?"

"Because it's closest to both the door and the windows. I'm concerned about possible intruders."

She let out an aggravated breath, picked up her slippers, moved around to the other side of the bed, and flipped back the covers, ignoring his soft chuckles. Ryan got up, pulled off his shirt, and began to unbutton his pants.

Layne choked back a gasp. "What are you doing?"

"I'm not sleeping in my jeans."

"But—"

"I have boxers on under here. They're just like shorts." His gaze followed her. "Where are you going?"

"To the bathroom."

"Weren't you just in the bathroom?"

"I'm going again." She averted her eyes as she walked past him. "And when I come back, you'd better be under a blanket."

Ryan called after her, "They're just like shorts."

When Layne re-entered the room, Ryan lay in bed, on the agreed upon side, under the blankets.

"You can't sleep there," she said.

He groaned. "Haven't we been through this?"

"I mean under the covers."

"You told me I needed to be under the covers when you came out of the bathroom."

"I said under a blanket. We can't sleep under the same covers."

Ryan adjusted his pillow. "I'm not moving, do whatever you need to do."

Layne contemplated her options, grumbled, and huffed to her side of the bed. "Prepare to lose any body part that crosses over to my side."

"Layne?"

She plopped back on the bed. "Now what?"

"About my outburst earlier today."

"Yes?"

"I want to apologize again for my behavior. I don't know what came over me, but I am truly sorry."

"Thank you. I think I understand."

"Oh? I'm curious," he said. "What did Marco tell you?"

"First he tried some baseball analogy. It was impossible to follow. Then he switched to hockey. I don't watch sports, but I don't think anyone—"

"Layne?"

"Basically, he said you were new to all this feelings bullshit, and it made you behave like an ass."

"Feelings bullshit?"

"Uh huh."

"And you were satisfied with that explanation?"

"No, but he..."

"Did he say something else?"

"You know what? We don't need to talk about it anymore."

He looked over at her. "Are you sure?"

"If it keeps me from having to listen to any more half-assed, male psycho-babble, then yes. But it better not happen again."

"The outburst or the psycho-babble?"

Layne rolled away from him, hiding her grin.

"Hunh," Ryan said.

58

Sunlight formed patterns on the bedroom floor, and Layne squinted at the clock on the nightstand. Seven-thirty. Late for someone who was normally up by five. She felt a weight across her waist and turned to see Ryan's entire body occupying her side of the bed, with his arm dangled over her. And was he...spooning? Really?

The position prompted all sorts of emotions—thrill, panic, arousal, panic. Should she deliver a sharp elbow to the ribs? Or snuggle into the safety of his embrace? She settled on lying still for a bit, and tried not to enjoy the warmth of his chest pressed against her back. Then his arm curled tight around her, drawing her close, and she delighted in the pleasant tingle it evoked. She turned her head toward him, and the sound of warm caramel filled her ear.

"Don't worry," he said. "I'm too tired for any...what did you call it? Oh yeah. Funny business."

She lay content in his arms until he spoke again.

"Are you ready to go to the beach?" he asked.

"Pardon?"

"We're going to Santa Cruz today."

"Under normal circumstances, I'd say it sounds fun," Layne said.

"But that won't be possible since I'm not leaving the hotel. Like, until you catch all the bad guys."

"I'd be happy to stay here and do this all day. No. I take it back. I couldn't stay like this and not be tempted to do other things. Come on, we have places to be. Get that sexy ass out of bed."

Her little voice woke up. *Oh, Layne, you are in big trouble.*

He trailed the tips of his fingers down the side of her arm. "Do you trust me?"

Crap. "Maybe." She buried her face into the pillow. "Maybe it's me I don't trust."

"I heard that."

She tipped back against him again. "Why, exactly, are we going to the beach?"

"We're using you as bait."

Layne's eyebrows jumped. "What?"

"This game of cat and mouse will continue until whoever called gets what they want. But I'm not willing to let that happen. So, we're going to force the issue. We'll fish for them until they find us."

She turned over to face him. "So, I am literally the bait."

"Yes, you are."

"And I'm supposed to be okay with that?"

"You're braver than you think, Layne."

"But—"

His expression grew more serious. "This is the fastest way to end it, with the least amount of risk. Otherwise, they keep coming at us, and more people get hurt."

"But—"

"Trust me. Please?"

She let out a half-hearted whimper. "Okay. I can do this. I can be the bait. The one bait in all of eternity that doesn't get eaten."

Ryan pinched back a small grin. "I took the liberty of buying you a few beach items," he said. "I left them in the closet. Why don't you get ready while I check in with the surveillance team. I'll shower over there. Will you be all right here alone?"

"I know the drill—lock the bathroom door and don't open it until I hear your voice."

"You're a quick study." He kissed her on the forehead, got out of bed, and bent down for the jeans he'd left on the floor.

Oh man. Layne Stevens, don't you dare look.

Her little voice protested. *Don't you dare turn your eyes away from that firm backside.*

He slid his jeans up, buttoned them low on his hips, then turned around and grabbed his t-shirt off the nightstand. Holy shit.

Holy shit doesn't begin to cover it, her little voice added. *Look at those pecs.*

Layne tried to maintain a neutral expression as he slipped his shirt over broad shoulders, a muscular chest, and lean abs. Damn.

You said it, sister. Her little voice wasn't helping.

He walked toward the bedroom door, and her little voice called after him. *Wait. Come back.*

Layne sat up. "Ryan?"

He turned to face her.

"You're sure about this?" she asked.

"About what?"

Her little voice beat her to it. *About leaving me all alone after that spectacular display of the male form?*

Layne fiddled with the blanket. "About the beach thing?"

"I'm sure. Trust me."

"Okay."

Her little voice had a fit. *Okay? What do you mean, okay? You're letting him go? And did you just agree to his suicide mission?*

He flashed that amazing smile. "See you in a bit," he said. Then he closed the door behind him.

Wow.

You really need to grow a pair.

She got out of bed, retrieved the shopping bag Ryan had left for her, and focused on what he'd said about being brave. "He's insane," she said as she locked herself into the safety of the bathroom. Inside the bag, she found a flower-print beach tote and a matching beach towel.

Then she pulled out a one-piece bathing suit, and her little voice laughed.

You're gonna be totally hot in that. Like grandma hot.

~

A BARRAGE of boos and shaking heads assaulted Ryan as he walked into the surveillance suite. He waited impatiently for the heckling to stop.

"Sometimes you've just got to take things slow," he said. "If I'd pushed any harder, her closed-for-business sign would've gone up." Ryan studied the flip chart page on the wall. "I hope the pool didn't apply only to last night."

Conversation and banter spurred by a buzz of excitement filled the suite as the team prepared themselves to execute on the plan.

"Are we ready for this?" he asked.

"We have men on their way now," Marco said. "Here's the position map." He pointed to a detailed schematic hanging from the wall. It showed tactical teams placed in strategic locations throughout the beach and boardwalk. "We can sight any area from these vantage points. If someone approaches you, they're ours."

"I assume you wired the bag?"

"Lovely floral print," Marco said. "Pick that out yourself?"

Ryan ignored the comment. "Remember, bullets only if necessary."

"We heard you the first time, boss. We'll use tranqs unless the situation escalates."

"What about the dance hall?"

"What about it?"

"Is it covered?"

"Gonna take her ballroom dancing?"

"I may attempt to tango my way into the good graces of my date."

"I'll put some men inside, but mostly to protect the TV lady's feet."

"Let's keep the manpower in there light. I'm hoping that's when she'll open up, and I don't want to spook her with a parade of muscle."

"Hey, boss," Hawk said, "we've seen you dance. Maybe you should try a different approach if you want her to give you information."

Laughter coursed through the room.

"Thanks for your input," Ryan said. "I need to get ready. Have a car downstairs at twelve hundred hours."

"One more thing, boss," Marco said. "We got some info on Temple."

"Let's hear it."

"Temple had one tour in Vietnam—US Army Staff Sergeant. His weapon of choice was the M24 Sniper Rifle, which—"

"Which uses the 7.62 caliber round," Hawk said. "Damn, that redneck jackass shot Johnny."

"Jesus," Rusk said. "Is anyone not looking for this thing?"

"Hold on, now," Ryan said. "There are a lot of weapons using that round. Rennick, isn't the academy training on sniper rifles that use the 7.62?"

"Uh..."

"Rennick?"

"Uh...yes, sir. Sorry, sir."

"If our agencies are using them, it's a reasonable bet other agencies are too," Ryan said.

"C'mon, boss," Rusk said. "We gotta be able to nail Sherley for something."

"I'm afraid a name is not enough to convict."

Marco looked up from his computer. "What about a print, boss?"

"A print?"

"Just confirmed, they found a partial print matching Temple on the silver tray."

59

A knock sounded on the bedroom door. "Layne?"

"I'm almost ready," Layne called to Ryan. A few minutes later, she walked into the front room wearing a short black skirt, strappy black sandals, and a fitted black tank, revealing hints of her new bathing suit underneath. She'd pulled her hair back into a curly ponytail, and her skin glowed golden brown—the effect of time spent outdoors and a fresh application of lotion. She may have looked half-decent, but she would've felt a lot better without the swarm of bees in her intestines.

Three agents stood in the front room, along with Gretel, all wearing beach attire. "Good Morning," one of them said to Layne. The others nodded.

Layne returned a tentative grin. "Morning."

Ryan greeted her with an expression somewhere between overprotective and overtly libidinous. It made her heart skip a beat.

"You look...nice," he said. Then he cleared his throat. "We're going over the layout of the boardwalk."

"Nothing to worry about, ma'am," one of the agents said. "We'll have the entire area covered."

Someone knocked at the door, and a thickly accented male voice sang out, "Room Service."

More agents filtered into the suite as the room service attendant pushed an ample, dual level, rolling table into the room. The attendant's face lit up when he saw Layne. "I am elated to visit with you again, Ms. Stevens. I hope you are well."

"Yes, I am. Thank you." She glanced at the cart. "Is there anything you don't do?"

"I am a man of many talents." He took a low bow, then addressed Ryan. "Deepshet Ajagaonkar at your servicing, sir."

Ryan cast a warning glare at his men as Deepshet expanded the table, laid out a variety of breakfast items, and then swept his arm over the spread. "All that you ordered, sir. Will there be anything else I may help you with?"

"That should do it," Ryan said as he signed for the order. "I appreciate the efficiency on such short notice."

Deepshet nodded at Ryan, and then directed a toothy smile at Layne.

"Bye Deepsh..." She waved as he left the suite.

Ryan smirked as Layne watched Deepshet close the door behind him. "I am going straight to hell," she said.

"Please don't get these guys started on the name. The level of immaturity they're capable of is sometimes staggering."

Layne eyed the trays of food.

"Dig in before it gets cold," Ryan said. "Or before it's all gone."

"You treat your team pretty well. For a tough guy, that is." She followed Ryan along the table and filled her plate with cheesy scrambled eggs, thick cut bacon, and delicate crepes with strawberries and yogurt. Then she poured hot water into a mug and sifted through an assortment of teas. "Yum."

"I would have expected that more from Maggie, but thanks," Ryan said over his shoulder.

"Organic Assam."

"Was that a breakfast prayer?"

"It's my favorite tea."

"You said yum in reference to tea?"

"Yes, I did. Is that so bad?"

"You're a fascinating woman, Layne Stevens."

"Thank you," she said.

After the indulgent meal and a thorough review of the plan, Ryan walked over to Layne's new beach bag. "How's the clarity, Marco?"

A voice boomed over Ryan's radio. "It's like you're right here with me, boss. Damn, I rock. My work here is done, so I'm heading out. See you at the boardwalk. "

Ryan turned to Layne. "You won't need your purse. You can put your things into the bag. That's how we'll communicate with the team."

Layne nodded.

"And I'll wear an earpiece instead of this radio so they can talk with us." He addressed the group. "Okay. Final check. Did we miss anything?"

"I hope not, boss," Gretel said. "Or we're gonna be in deep shit."

The room erupted in laughter.

"So close," he said, moving to stand next to Layne. "You all right?"

Her throat constricted. "I'm a little nervous. You know, things don't normally end well for the bait. But I'm fine. I'm sure I'll be fine. Everything will be fine."

"I promise, I will not let anything happen to you." He lifted her face to his. "Are you with me?"

She nodded.

"Good. Then let's go."

"You mean now?"

"It's time."

"Perfect. I can do this," she said as her heart threatened to pound out of her chest.

"Layne?"

"Yup?"

"In order to leave the suite, you'll need to move toward the door."

"Ryan, I don't think I can do this."

He rubbed her arms and looked into her eyes. "You've got this, Layne. I know you do."

Damn, there was that caramel again. "Okay. But I want to be clear that I'm not going through with this because you remind me of dessert. I'm doing it for my uncle."

A look of surprise crossed Ryan's face. Crap, had the words actually come out of her mouth?

Her little voice snorted out a laugh. *Hell, yeah, they did.*

But there wasn't time for embarrassment. She was being shuffled out of the suite, which called for bravery. Unfortunately, she didn't have any of that. All she had was serious panic. "Is there a bulletproof vest for me somewhere?"

Ryan chuckled.

Her voice rose an octave. "You think I'm joking?"

"Trust me. You won't need it. As long as we're with you, it's all of us who are at risk."

"That seems to be a theme."

Ryan shepherded her down the long hallway with a protective arm around her waist, surrounded front and back by agents. As they neared the elevator, he leaned in close and said, "I remind you of dessert?"

Her cheeks seared, her brain disengaged, and her ankle twisted beneath her. She stumbled, clutching at whatever would help break her fall. About halfway down, she realized Gretel's board shorts were falling with her. She squeezed her eyes shut and prayed he had something on under those shorts.

RENNICK LISTENED to the exchange in Layne's suite long enough to ensure the team would not return to the surveillance suite. Then she sauntered over to Rusk.

"Hey," she said.

His brow lowered. "You want something."

"What makes you say that?"

"I don't have time for this, Rennick. Spit it out."

"If you must know, it's that time of the month."

"Jesus Christ, Rennick. That is the last fucking thing I needed to know."

"Yeah, well, I feel like shit. I'm supposed to monitor the coms, but I'm low on tampons, and these nasty cramps—"

"Go."

"What?"

"Go. I'll cover the coms. Just stop talking, and go."

"Thanks, Rusk. I owe you one."

Funny the things that made her smile.

60

The group came to a halt, and laughter boomed all around, while Gretel grumbled above her.

"Oh my gosh. I'm so sorry," Layne said squeezing her eyes tight.

"You can open your eyes, Layne," Ryan said. "Boxers. Best invention ever." He helped her up. "Are you all right?"

"No, I'm not all right. I'm going to get someone killed. This is not a good idea."

"I think I'm with her, boss," Gretel said. "Is it okay for me to dress now?"

"Yes, Tom," Ryan said. "Feel free to pull those up any time."

"This is really not a good idea," she said with more emphasis, turning her gaze to avoid looking at Gretel's behind as he bent over to hike up his shorts.

"Layne," Ryan said. "Everything will be fine. Well, everything besides Tom's shorts."

She stole a glance at Gretel's ripped pocket. "Oh no. I insist on paying for a new pair."

"No worries, Ms. Stevens. Happens all the time. Women just can't keep their hands off me."

Again, laughter filled the hallway, and someone called out from behind them. "That's the most action Tom's seen in months. He should pay you."

The laughter subsided, and the group made their way to the lobby without further incident. Gretel and another agent checked the entry and held the doors open while Ryan escorted Layne to a waiting town car. When she turned back to the hotel, the rest of the team was gone.

"What happened? Where did everyone go?"

Ryan helped Layne into the car before answering her question. "Too much cover would've drawn attention," he said. "We want to be followed, but we don't want anyone to know we want to be followed. Make sense?"

That made about as much sense to Layne as leaving the hotel. Thirty minutes into the trip, she'd spoken to her mom and dad, her pal Stu, Dean, Jenny, and, of course, Maggie. Nothing earth shattering she had told them. Just checking in. She dialed one last number and after a few moments tapped to end the call.

"No answer?"

"My brother," Layne said. "He never answers." She sniffed. Maybe after I'm dead, he'll think twice about sending people straight to voicemail.

"Layne," Ryan said. "No one is going to die today."

"You never know. We could get hit by a bus."

"Certainly not before you've had dessert." He grinned. "What do I remind you of? Is it some kind of chocolate?"

"I believe we were talking about my imminent death."

Ryan squelched his chuckle when she tasered him with her eyes.

"I meant what I said, Layne. There is no death in your near future. There are no busses on the beach. And the best field team in the world is protecting you. We've done this hundreds of times."

"Hundreds? Did you always have totally freaked out bait?"

"Sounded like some interesting phone conversations. What's going on with everyone?"

She sighed and conceded to Ryan's deflection. "The big topic of conversation was our sleeping arrangements. Maggie is sure we're having sex, and she wanted all the details. Stu heard from Maggie that we're sleeping together, and he gave me the old why-buy-the-cow speech. My parents also talked to Maggie. I don't want to know what she told them, but they asked about a date for the wedding."

"Spending time with you is never dull."

"It would be if I were dead."

"Why do I get the feeling you'd come back to haunt me?"

"That's an excellent suggestion."

"Come over here." Ryan held his arm out for her to slide underneath.

She shook her head.

"Come on." He made a fair impression of sad puppy eyes.

"That's not going to work."

"Yes, it is. Just move over a little."

She moved over a few inches.

"Not quite far enough." He pulled her closer. "Ah, that's it. Much better, don't you think?"

Tears threatened as she settled her cheek against his shoulder.

"I promise, Layne. Nothing bad will happen to you on my watch."

"I'm sorry I'm such a wimp," Layne said.

"Funny. I was just thinking what a strong person you are. You stumbled, somewhat literally," he let out a snicker, "into a life-threatening federal investigation, and you're still able to laugh and joke."

"It's either that, or curl into a fetal position with wine and chocolate and ball my eyes out." Her head popped up. "Oh no."

"What is it?"

Layne pointed to the beach bag and whispered, "Everyone heard our sleeping arrangement conversation."

"Marco asked me to tell you he could hear that too," Ryan said. "Yes, Marco, you're the man." He turned to Layne. "He also said thanks for giving the team a good chuckle."

"Please, just shoot me. This whole thing would be so much easier if you just shot me."

"Marco says they'll make every effort not to shoot you."

"He did not."

"Scouts honor." Ryan held up two fingers.

A belly laugh erupted from somewhere deep inside her. Maybe she'd tipped over the edge. Maybe she just no longer cared. But she couldn't control it. Laughter engulfed her like quicksand. And as it subsided, she caught a glint in Ryan's eyes. He brushed his knuckles down her cheek, and then his lips moved to hers.

61

With Rennick refusing to take his calls, Berger sat once again in his car outside The Riede. What else could he do? He had thought about going inside, talking with anyone in the FBI who would listen. But relations were strained enough, and he wouldn't risk causing further damage by interfering in another agency's investigation. He unlocked his phone and swiped through his emails. Then he checked his weather app. At least San Francisco had warmer temperatures than Berlin.

He considered abandoning his position, but then Rennick's car pulled out of the hotel parking garage. Finally. He would follow until she stopped, and then he would demand answers. He signaled with the intent of making a U-turn, but a trio of town cars pulled out of the hotel drive, headed in the opposite direction from Rennick. After the previous day's tour of the city, he could predict the routine. They would dangle Schatz's niece like a shrimp on a hook, in hopes that someone would bite. And if someone did? What then? Would she become a victim as well?

But rather than concern himself with conjecture about future events, he needed to decide. Quickly. Follow Sherry, or follow the shrimp.

62

Layne wanted desperately to know what it felt like to be kissed by Ryan when he wasn't in a homicidal rage. He'd gotten so close, so many times that she ached for it. She shut her eyes, and his lips brushed across hers, but he didn't kiss her.

"We're here," he said.

Ohhh myyy goddd...her little voice whined.

Layne was determined to stay in the car, to block out everything happening around them. But Ryan tugged at her hand, pulling her from her seat, and she clutched the beach bag under her arm as he rushed her toward the amusement park. When his pace slowed, she dug in. "Why are we going so fast?"

"Sorry about that," Ryan said, turning to face her. "But now that we're here, I'd like to finish what we started." He drew her to him, took her face into his hands, and kissed her. Finally. And it was better than she could have imagined. Unlike back at The Riede, this was a tender, passionate, heart-stopping, breath-stealing, mind-blowing, entire body on fire, holy shit kind of kiss. The intensity of it took her off guard, and every inch of her responded with a longing she hadn't felt in years. As the kiss ended, he wrapped his arms around her and pulled her tight against him.

Then he whispered into her ear, "I've been dying to do that for two days. And I plan to do a lot more of it. But right now, we've likely got distance mics aimed at us. Stay with me, follow my lead, and everything will be fine." He slowly let go of his embrace, took her hand, and laced his fingers with hers. "Okay. Where to first?"

Layne stared, unable to process anything but the clash of desire, estrogen, and fear racing through her.

"How do you feel about roller coasters?" he asked.

"What?"

"They're rides. They go up and down and around. Some people think they're fun."

"Rides?"

His expression told her to play along. "That's why we're here, isn't it?"

She tried to pull herself together. "Uh...oh, of course. Maybe later for the roller coaster. Is there anything a little more tame?"

"There's Dumbo the Flying Airplane."

She shook her head.

"How about bumper cars?" Ryan asked. "It would make my day to see Tom in one of those things. He'll hate it."

Layne remembered what he'd told her about some of the men stationed in plain sight. "That is really mean," she said. "Where do we buy tickets?"

On the way to the ticket booth, Layne noticed a food vendor, and she grabbed Ryan's arm, pulling him toward the stand.

"They don't sell tickets there," Ryan said.

"Who cares about the tickets? We're in the artichoke capital of the world. These will probably be the best artichokes we'll ever eat."

"Call me crazy," he said. "But I'm not a fan of vegetables that look like they were grown in outer space." He took Layne's hand and set them back on a path toward the ticket booth.

"But..."

"After the bumper cars."

"Oh, all right."

When they entered the bumper car arena, Layne started toward a turquoise car with huge yellow flowers, but Ryan reached for her. "Where do you think you're going?"

"To grab that car. See how bright and cheery it is?"

"We'll ride together."

"Can I drive?"

"Wouldn't have it any other way."

Ryan and Layne squeezed their adult-sized bodies into a kid-sized orb and buckled in, while Gretel attempted to station himself at the arena entrance. A lanky, pimple-faced teen in a red staff vest approached him. Gretel showed the boy his badge. The teen shook his head. Gretel glared at the boy who pointed at a sign posted on the wall. Gretel's lips pinched as he searched for an empty bumper car. The boy followed, and more words were exchanged. Gretel dug into his pocket and tossed a handful of tickets at the boy. Then he jammed his king-sized frame into a tiny, pink polka dot car.

Layne chuckled. That was one gutsy kid.

When the start bell rang, Layne gunned her flowery, floating disc and aimed for Gretel. For a moment, confusion filled Gretel's eyes. Bam! She slammed into him from the side. Then she backed up, turned a full circle and came at him from behind. Boom! Not wanting to frighten any children, she stalked Gretel for the duration of the ride. When the cars powered down, Layne popped out of her side, while Ryan and Gretel peeled themselves from their seats. "That was fun," she said. "We should do it again later."

Gretel stomped to the exit mumbling about ripped shorts and bruised shins.

"I hope I didn't offend him," Layne said.

"He's young. He'll bounce back." Ryan bent down to rub his knees. "I may never walk the same, though."

She shot him a flirtatious smile. "I know what'll perk you up."

"Hmm, that sounds promising."

They exited the bumper car arena, and Layne pulled Ryan toward the artichoke stand.

"Not the kind of perking up I had in mind," Ryan said.

"Have you ever eaten an artichoke?"

"Of course. I just didn't like it."

"Really? How was it prepared?"

Ryan's gaze flicked past her to the sign. "Steamed. No. It was grilled."

"How did you eat it?"

"You know...the way you're supposed to eat artichokes."

"Which is?"

"All right, I've never tried one."

"Oh, you are going to love this."

"Doubtful, since I won't be eating it."

Layne put on a pout. "Please?"

He let out a breath. "Let's get this over with."

She placed their order and then handed a cardboard tray filled with various items to Ryan. "I ordered the combo platter," she said.

He inspected the tray. "I don't see the fries."

"No, silly. It's one-half steamed, one-half grilled, a side of mayonnaise, and a side of drawn butter with herbs."

Ryan grimaced. "Drawn butter?"

"It's basically melted."

"Why are food terms so complicated?"

Layne grabbed their sodas, and they selected a weathered metal table in the picnic area. But as they slid onto the bench, a man rushed toward them.

63

Several agents raced to intercept a young man in bare feet, frayed jean shorts, and a smiley face t-shirt.

"What the hell, dudes?" the young man said. "I only wanted to tell her how much I like her show."

Ryan eased back onto the bench. "You have an interesting fan base," he said. "That's a complication I'd forgotten about."

"I try not to think of my viewers as complications," Layne said. "Can they please let him go?"

Ryan signaled to Gretel, who escorted the young man to the table.

"I'm sorry," Layne said to the young man. "I've had, um... some threats recently. They're just being cautious."

"It's cool," he said with a shy smile. "Crap, you're even prettier in person."

Layne felt a blush rise to her cheeks. Likely because the boy appeared to be no older than Dean.

"I love your show," the young man said. "It's by far the sickest on Foodie."

"That's so sweet. Thank you."

"Can I have your autograph?"

"Of course." Layne reached into the beach bag. "Oh, darn it. I don't have a pen."

Another young man wearing a boardwalk staff vest pulled a black marker from his pocket. "Here you go, bro."

"Oh, dude. Perfect." The young man lifted his shirt.

Layne looked at his bare belly. "There?"

"If you don't mind. The bigger, the better."

She signed her name in broad black strokes across his stomach, and he looked down at the ink on his skin. "I'll never wash that part of my body again."

"You can wash all you want," Ryan said. "That was permanent marker."

"Awesome!" He bounded off with his shirt still raised, showing off the brand to all of his friends.

"Please don't take this the wrong way," Ryan said. "But it's difficult for me to think of you as famous. Although, I suppose if I did, that might make me self-conscious. And we can't have that."

Layne chuckled. "I'm having a hard time picturing you as self-conscious."

"What man wouldn't be a little nervous with a gorgeous and captivating celebrity at his side?"

She was too late to stop the embarrassed smile from crossing her face, but then the full impact of what he'd said hit her. "Wait, are you saying I make you nervous?"

"Well, a little bit, yes. I want to make a good impression. Is that such a bad thing?"

"No, no, not at all. I just assumed I was the only one."

He grinned and slid closer to Layne. "I may seem all gruff and tough on the outside, but I'm just a big marshmallow on the inside."

Layne laughed. "A marshmallow, huh?"

"What can I say?" He ran a finger down her arm, and a pulse of electricity shot through her. Then his eyes went to her lips. "Nerves aside, the things I'm thinking about doing right now would get us arrested."

"Me too," she breathed.

He smiled. "Really? Then I like the way your mind works."

He gave her a soft kiss that was way to brief, and then turned his attention to the tray. "So, what do I do with this thing?"

Layne composed herself enough to show Ryan how to pull the leaves off the artichoke, which end to dip, and how to strip the meat from the underside of the leaf with his teeth. He tried the steamed artichoke dipped in mayonnaise and admitted it wasn't all that bad. Then he tasted the grilled artichoke with the drawn butter.

"Hmm. That's pretty good," he said.

Layne would have agreed, except it was difficult to focus on the artichoke with the swell of emotions distracting her. But as they continued to talk and eat, she relaxed. Ryan was so easy to be around. They joked about Gretel in the little pink car, and laughed about the young man with Layne's semi-permanent name imprinted on his stomach. She'd been terrified about this trip, but it was turning into a wonderful day. After eating all the larger leaves from one half of the artichoke, Layne pulled off the smaller, middle leaves, tossed them on the finished pile, and scooped out the choke with a plastic spoon.

Ryan's face puckered. "What are you doing?"

"I'm giving you my heart."

"Pardon?"

"My artichoke heart," she said. "The heart is the best part, but you have to work for it."

"That's an understatement," Ryan said with a grin.

She pretended not to hear him as she cut off the stem and gave Ryan a piece of the fleshy heart.

He eyed it warily. "I may need to ease my way up to this."

"Have I steered you wrong so far?"

"Seriously, Layne. You could've made a toupee with the stuff coming off that thing."

"Come on. If you liked the leaves, I guarantee you'll like this."

He dipped it into the butter and took a small bite. "Hunh."

"Was I right?"

"Yes, you were. Thank you, Layne, for introducing me to artichokes, and for sharing your heart with me."

Gagging noises came from behind them.

"How about we try some arcade games?" Ryan said, using a stern stare to discourage Gretel from providing further sound effects. "I'm decent with a shotgun. Maybe I can win you a teddy bear."

"Oooh, I used to be great at the dime pitch," Layne said.

Ryan threw their artichoke remains into the trash, and they headed for the arcade. Ten dollars and three attempts later, Ryan won Layne the grand prize at the shooting gallery. They both laughed when the arcade attendant handed them a teddy bear all of six inches tall. Layne tried her luck at the goldfish bowls but came up empty. Then she caught a whiff of something that sparked fond childhood memories of time spent every year at the San Bernardino County Fair.

"Corn dogs," she said.

Ryan looked at her. "Excuse me?"

"Do you smell them? The incredible aroma of the ultimate deep fried carnival food."

She grabbed Ryan's hand and dragged him toward the scent. Ryan bought them each a steaming hot corn dog on a stick, and they walked and talked as they ate.

"Mmm," Ryan said, after taking a bite. "Rusk would have loved these."

"Who's Rusk?"

"He's my system's tech. Big fan of corn dogs. And these are exceptional. Crispy on the outside. Sweet, crumbly dough. Perfectly heated on the inside. They don't even need mustard. They're really fantastic. It's too bad he's not here."

Layne lifted a brow. "He's listening, isn't he?"

"Yup," Ryan said with a devilish grin.

"You're a cruel man, Agent Cooke."

As she took her last delicious bite of corn dog, her foot tangled in a long, orange power cord. She reeled, trying to regain her balance, and more than half the arcade games lost power before she landed for the second time in three days on her ass.

"Oops," she said with her mouth full of corn dog and her foot still twisted in the cord.

Ryan hurried to untangle her and help her up, then he moved her aside as an arcade technician charged at them. Gretel and several other agents inserted themselves between the technician and Layne, and the man peered around them.

"Jeez, lady, watch it next time."

The technician reworked the cabling and gave an exasperated wave of his hands as he stomped back to his control booth.

"That cord was very unsafe," Ryan said.

"I appreciate the thought, but I'm getting kind of tired of performing my own stunts. Why don't you hire a stunt double, and I'll be on my way."

"Don't be silly. There's no way a double would pull off these stunts with as much style as you."

"Yeah. Thanks."

As they walked back through the arcade, Layne stopped for fresh, hot corn on the cob slathered in butter and grated Parmesan cheese, followed by a huge scoop of pecan praline and fudge ice cream in a waffle cone, and after that, a warm churro with extra powdered sugar and cinnamon.

"Do you always eat like this?" Ryan asked.

"No. But I figure if this is my last supper, I might as well enjoy it."

"Layne—"

"Wait...do you hear that?"

64

They neared the end of the arcade, and music drifted out of an impressive stone building, adorned by twinkle lights faintly shimmering in the late afternoon sun.

Ryan held his hand out to Layne. "Would you like to dance?"

"Excuse me?"

"The music, I planned it."

"You did?"

"Well, sort of. I knew there would be music here. This is the infamous Coconut Grove Ballroom. Live dance bands play here every week."

Layne smiled as they strolled, hand in hand, toward the sound. In the grand old ballroom, an Elvis cover band performed "Blue Suede Shoes." Thick velvet curtains covered the windows, candles lit the tables, and a disco ball overhead cast reflections across the darkened room. They found an open table and listened to the last part of the song. "Jailhouse Rock" came up next, and Ryan shouted over the band. "Fast dancing isn't my best event. How about I request something slow?"

She nodded.

"Why don't you leave that here," he said, nudging his chin toward the beach bag.

At the edge of the bandstand, Ryan flashed a twenty-dollar bill, and after a short exchange, the bandleader announced they would be slowing things down. With her hand in his, Layne followed Ryan to the center of the dance floor as "Love Me Tender" crooned through large speakers on either side of the stage. He turned to face her, guided her hand to his shoulder and placed his other hand at her waist. They swayed in time to the music, and she enjoyed the warmth and feel of his presence as he tightened his arm around her.

"Do you remember when I said I'd arranged some private time for us to talk?"

She gazed up into his incredible blue eyes. "Yes."

"No one can hear us now, and there's quite a bit I haven't told you."

She waited for him to continue.

"I have reason to believe Agent Rennick falsified a document in your file."

She lowered her brow.

"The document implies you're a foreign operative," Ryan said.

Layne stopped moving. "That's why your team thinks I'm a spy?"

"You'll need to keep dancing. They can't hear us, but there are people watching."

She began to sway with him again, but with little attention to the rhythm of the song. "So, this document has your team convinced that I'm like, what, a German agent?"

"Well, that, and your connection to your uncle. Also your uncanny ability to end up in the wrong place at the wrong time." Ryan grinned. "Our objective is to coerce information from you. The game is, you fall in love with me, you give me what we need, you go to jail."

"The game?"

"To them, it's a game, Layne, not to me. I know it's only been a few days, but..."

"But, what?"

"Layne, I'm..."

She remained silent. Her little voice wasn't as patient. *You're what, damn it?*

Ryan continued. "I know you're not a foreign agent, and I will do anything I have to do to save your life. That includes risking my career."

"But why? Why would you do that?"

"Because I care about you."

"Enough to sacrifice your job?"

His gaze cut away. "Look, I've been told I'm pretty bad at this. Not the dancing, I mean...well...I'm not good at that either. But I've only been in one serious relationship in my life, and I royally screwed it up. But I have never felt the same kind of connection with anyone as I do with you. It's like something I can't control, which is difficult for me, because control is one thing I do very well. Being drawn to you the way I am, it's...it's different. Don't get me wrong. I mean that in a good way. And part of it is a need to protect you—from the agency, from whoever is after the card, from anything that might threaten you. Am I making any sense?"

Layne hesitated. "I...I'm not sure what to say."

"Do you feel the same connection I do? Something more than just interest?"

"Ryan, I..."

He remained quiet.

"You have to understand," she said. "After my husband died, I worked really hard to shut that part of myself off. I never wanted to experience emotional pain like that again. And this is all happening so fast."

"For me too," he said with a still hopeful look in his eyes.

She sighed. "Yes, like you said. I feel something more than interest. And it scares the shit out of me."

He flashed her that amazing smile. This time, it gave away his relief. "Me too," he said, tightening his arms around her.

Layne laid her cheek on Ryan's chest, and they danced for a while in silence. She breathed in his scent, took in the pleasure of his strong arms around her. Then she looked up and studied his eyes. "How can you be so certain we're on the same side?"

"I listened to my gut, did some digging, and came up with the real profile. It verifies you are exactly who you say you are. I don't know how someone pulled it off, but you were not in the wrong place at the wrong time."

"What do you mean?"

"The entire thing was a setup. Someone knew your uncle would come looking for that card. Framing you was part of it."

"Agent Rennick set me up? I knew there was a reason I didn't like her."

"I don't think so. At least, not alone. Rennick's not that good. Someone else is pulling the strings. I just don't know who."

"Can't you come clean? Produce the real document and turn Agent Rennick in? Then maybe we could get some answers."

"It depends on how far up the ladder this goes. If she acted on orders, it won't matter what I say or do, and forcing the issue is likely to get us both killed. If she's working for another agency, then we've shown our hand, which could also get us killed, along with others. I need more time to investigate. More information. And I've got to find out who's involved."

"So, what do we do?"

Ryan spent the next several minutes laying out his plan. When he finished, Layne considered it. She understood it. But she wasn't at all comfortable with it.

"I don't think I can do that, Ryan. This is my life we're talking about."

"Yes, it is," he said. "It might very well mean your life. Your family and friends, they're not safe either. We need to take those chips off the table."

She frowned.

"Trust me," he said. "It won't be long before someone comes after us, then we'll finish it."

"But—"

"I'll be with you every step of the way," he said.

"Except for that part when you're not."

"Well, yes. But I give you my word, I'm not going to let anything bad happen to you."

He kissed her one last time before leading her off the dance floor. She assumed she enjoyed the kiss. She'd barely felt it. They stopped for Layne's bag and then stepped into the bright light of a blazing western sun.

He squeezed her hand. "Ready to hit the beach?"

"Ready as I'll ever be."

Ryan selected a spot in the middle of the crowd, about halfway between the water's edge and the boardwalk, and Layne spread the blanket over the warm sand. She pulled her tank over her head and let her skirt drop to her ankles exposing the dark green, one-piece bathing suit Ryan had picked out for her. Ryan took off his t-shirt and settled in next to Layne on the blanket. He'd told her they would execute the plan at five o'clock.

"What time is it?" she asked.

He glanced at his watch. "Almost four forty-five."

Layne looked back at the boardwalk. It had been a fun day. She hoped they'd have the opportunity to do it again, without the whole lives-in-jeopardy thing. She understood the tremendous risk of Ryan's plan, but the alternatives—life in prison or certain death—weren't all that appealing. And if this would keep the people she loved from harm, then it was her only choice. She could do this. She had to. Ryan's voice tore her from her thoughts.

"I'm sorry, what were you saying?" she asked.

"Your favorite movie?"

"Oh, that's easy, *Defending Your Life*."

Ryan stared at her as though she'd made the title up.

"Meryl Streep and Albert Brooks?" Layne said. "I know, you've never heard of it. Everyone says that. But it's a great film."

"Let me guess. It's a romantic comedy."

She narrowed her eyes. "It's got an excellent message."

"Oh yeah? What is it?"

"That you shouldn't let fear dictate your choices."

"Hmm. That is a good message."

The irony didn't escape Layne, and she used it to bolster her confidence for what lay ahead. No fear, just like Meryl Streep.

Then her damned little voice chimed in. *To hell with Meryl Streep. We need fear, lots and lots of it. Right now, you should be all about the fear.*

"The sun will be down soon," Ryan said. "Want to play in the water for a bit before it gets too dark?"

Bile rose in the back of her throat. That was their signal.

65

Ryan waded into choppy whitecaps, pulling a reluctant Layne with him. The day's weather had been warm for Santa Cruz, but the water was pretty damned cold. He splashed her, and she squealed, then she jumped at him, knocking him over. He pulled her down, kissed her and held her tight as waves toppled over them. They swam farther into the surf. As they played, a large swell came in, and Layne disappeared into the break.

Ryan noted his team ready to act. But when the tide washed back, Layne popped up and lunged again at Ryan. He dodged her, moving into deeper water. She followed. Marco hollered in his earpiece, urging Ryan to pull back closer to shore. Another big wave hit, and Layne ducked under again. This time when it swept out, she didn't surface, and Ryan dove after her. His earpiece erupted as Marco yelled, "Move, move, move." Ryan strained to see through the murk and sand kicked up by the undercurrent. Farther out, visibility improved, but he still didn't see Layne. Damn it, where the hell was she? Diving a little deeper, he spotted her with a man several yards ahead and raced to intercept them.

Both Layne and the man had small oxygen tanks strapped to their backs and masks covering their faces. The man helped Ryan into similar gear, and together the trio slipped into the ocean's depths. They went for some time before the man pointed to a red rope hanging from a boat in the distance. They headed toward the craft and boarded on the side facing away from shore.

Ryan had discarded his earpiece, but he'd anticipated the activities back on the beach. They would scour the break, and Marco would work like hell to get air, Coast Guard, and dive support. But every minute passed meant a fading sunlight that would make the search more difficult for Ryan's team. His former team. All boats within visual range would be boarded and searched, and divers would be sent down at various spots along the shore. They were skilled, but he'd trained them, so he felt confident he could evade them.

Ryan and Layne were shuffled below deck, where several people waited to outfit them in full wetsuits and scuba gear. A helicopter passed low overhead, and Ryan allowed himself a proud smile. "Taught them too well," he said. "Are you ready for this?"

"It's been a while, but I'll manage." Layne sounded more confident than she looked.

The all-clear came from above, and they moved to the upper deck as fast as their equipment would allow. They climbed over the gunwale, and Layne sent him an uncertain glance. He gave her hand a squeeze, nodded, and they rolled into the ocean together. The water was less choppy beyond the reef, allowing he and Layne to insert their regulators with relative ease. Ryan gave a final wave to the boat's captain, and they descended into the black watery abyss under cover of a darkening night sky.

LAYNE HADN'T TAKEN dive lessons in years, and the idea of diving at night never held much appeal. But she stayed close to Ryan and prayed everything would be all right. He'd told her it would take time for agency divers to gear up and gain any depth, so she trailed as Ryan led them deep. He stopped to check his dive watch and adjusted to a heading that, according to the plan, would take them south along the coast.

She'd been worried about the dive. But there, in the peaceful expanse of dark ocean, the familiar comfort of the gear surrounding her...oh, screw it. It would be a fricking miracle if she didn't hyperventilate and die right there—no bus required. Shadowy figures loomed everywhere, and her heart began to race as she struggled to maintain even an ounce of calm. But as Ryan had advised, she focused on him, on her breath, and on maintaining a steady but manageable pace.

Glimmers and vague shapes preyed on them in the murky depths, and eons passed before Ryan changed headings to steer them toward land. Layne continued to fight her unease and concentrated on the course established by Ryan. But ahead of them, a massive form emerged, stalking them with slow deliberation. Layne reached for Ryan, but didn't make contact. She searched for him with her hands, reeled in all directions looking for him. Shit, shit, *shit*. He was gone.

Her respiration grew shallow, and the pressure in her tank oscillated as the regulator attempted to follow her random breathing patterns. She felt something scrape across her back and whirled around, her elbow connecting with something hard. She lashed out, flailing and thrashing, and fatigue set in as the density of the water worked against her. She scrambled to swim away from whatever or whoever was attacking her, but fear and flight gave way to exhaustion and lack of oxygen. Her body succumbed, and her limbs went slack as she allowed herself to be swallowed by the mass of darkness that surrounded her.

SONNY SAT in a low beach chair on the sand and pretended to be engrossed in an anime novel as they walked past him. He found the vivid and graphic imagery of the anime drawings intriguing. But the image right in front of him—Layne and pretty boy holding hands—made him want to upchuck his lunch. Real men didn't hold hands. And if they did, pretty boy sure as hell didn't deserve to hold hers. At least this time the prick had the decency to tell her he was using her as bait.

He watched in disgust as they chatted and settled in close on the blanket. Just another ef-ing day at the beach. He should have trusted his instincts when they went into the water. The bathing suit was a sure tip-off. Who wears a dark one-piece with a high-necked front and a racer back to hang at the boardwalk? Not that Layne didn't rock it, but the only thing missing was the triathlon number. He wasn't sure how much more cheesy water frolicking he could take. And ugh, the kissing. No way she was enjoying herself that much.

A substantial wave rolled in, and Layne went under. He saw it coming, but what could he do? He wanted to dive in, to save her from the surf, from pretty boy, from the bureau. Hell, from The Employer—who was gonna freak. It might be worth it to hear The Employer drop an f-bomb, but this little twist added serious complexity to his task. He would need to take a different approach, one he'd hoped to avoid, not only for his sake, but for Layne's.

His instructions for the day had been to watch and report. So, he had watched, and he would report that Layne Stevens was gone.

66

Marco leveled a fierce kick at the sand, and at the same time invented several new ways to string expletives together. This was not happening. It could not go down like this. He'd called in every team short of the Navy Seals to search for Ryan and Layne, and they'd found nothing. He walked to the waterline one last time. Night had descended, and the ocean's crest merged with the charcoal sky to form one vast fucking black hole.

He turned back toward the beach, and a silhouette approached the blanket. Several tactical agents rushed to intercept, restrain, and search the newcomer. Marco moved closer and took in a tall fit frame, thick blond hair, and angular features. One of the agents pulled a revolver from the back waistband of the man's pants as the man rambled in German. Marco shoved his hands into his pockets and waited.

The man calmed himself, then spoke in careful English. "Please. You contacted us. We will work as a team. We need each other."

Marco bypassed formalities. "Do you know where they are?"

"No. But we will find them. Together."

"What do you mean? Who contacted you? Who the fuck are you?"

"I am BKA. They are my purpose for being here. We need to find the card. We will help each other. Yes?"

Marco stared, for a moment, into the gloom over the coastline, then he considered the man. "Don't take this the wrong way, but your fucking agency got us into this mess. You're gonna help us? I don't think so."

"There is no need to be hostile," the man said.

"Oh good. Then you took it the right way." Marco barked into his radio. "Tell Hawk to remote the doors and windows to Steven's suite. And call housekeeping. Ask them to pack and clean. We've got another fucking guest."

Agents escorted the German man away from the blanket, and Marco bent down to inspect Layne's beach bag. He found both their wallets, their cell phones, sunscreen, a pair of sunglasses, and a set of keys. He kicked at the bag. "Damn it." He had a foreign op in hand. That should be good news. But in truth, with Ryan and Layne missing, it only made his job more complicated. He scooped up the keys. With a black leather, unmarked tag on a brass ring, they didn't appear to be something a woman would carry, but Ryan wouldn't have needed his keys. For that matter, neither would Layne. He shoved them into his pocket, grabbed the bag, and went back to the boardwalk.

On Marco's orders, the team abandoned the search, and he headed back to the surveillance suite. Now in command, he would be expected to check in.

When Marco arrived at the Riede, he was surprised to find just Rusk and a junior level technician manning the equipment and the coms.

"Where is everybody? Marco asked

"There weren't that many of us here," Rusk replied. "But they're helping our German friend settle in."

"Oh," Marco said.

He turned on his laptop and headed for the boxes of coffee. But after picking all three, he came up empty.

"What the hell happened to all the coffee?" He looked around the room. "Is Rennick helping with the BKA agent?"

"Nope," Rusk said. "She went home."

"You're shitting me. She better have had a goddamned bulletproof reason."

"Cramps," Rusk said.

Marco stared at Rusk for a moment, then shook his head, went back to his desk, and opened the top left drawer. "Where are my fucking cigarettes?"

"You quit," the junior tech said.

"Shit. That's right. I really need a cigarette." Out of habit, he patted his pockets and felt the keys.

"You can have mine," the junior tech said. "But they're not your brand."

Marco was already headed for the door. He left for Ryan's condo with the knowledge that Ryan seldom performed an action without a purpose, no matter how innocuous the act might seem. And he rarely made mistakes. If they couldn't find Ryan, odds were, he didn't want to be found. Marco didn't know what to expect, or if the keys would even work, but his instinct told him they were in the bag for a reason.

He pulled his sleek, black sports car into a spot behind the building. Marco had visited Ryan's place only a few times, but he remembered the stairway to the front door off the narrow alley behind Nakamura's fish market. No lights burned in any of the businesses, or in the urban dwellings resting cozily above them. He surveyed the windows of the condo. Nothing. Making quick work of the stairs, he took the keys from his pocket and chose one that might fit a door. It slid in, but the lock didn't turn. He tried the only other key on the ring designed for a door. The key went in, and to Marco's relief, the lock tumbled.

He entered the living area and squinted against the darkness. He wouldn't risk turning on lights, but with only a sliver of moon, this would be tougher than he'd anticipated. His vision adjusted enough to make out Ryan's desk near the windows, and he spotted a stack of items next to Ryan's laptop. That wasn't like Ryan. Everything had a place, and stacks of anything weren't tolerated. But even more odd, an unopened bottle of beer sat beside the stack. He and Ryan often joked about their differing taste in beer. Marco could recognize a Coors Light through a blizzard, and this bottle was meant for him. He twisted open the tepid beer and dug through the pile.

In the moonlight, Marco noted the bottom of the stack held a newspaper, several napkins, and some blank printer paper. A few issues of Sports Illustrated sat on top, but no swimsuit issue, damn it. Then, in the center of the stack—bingo—he found a large manila envelope. Without more light, he couldn't get a decent view inside, and he'd chanced enough time in the condo, so he grabbed the beer and the envelope, and left.

Half an hour later, Marco pulled into his own garage, used the remote to shut the door behind him, and eager to know what he had, turned on the overhead lamp in his car. At first glance, the envelope contents dumbfounded him—the horrendous tie Rennick had purchased for Ryan, a set of papers all clipped together with the receipt from Perfect Picnics, and the profile from Seth exposing Layne as an undercover foreign agent.

Given the rookie assigned to the picnic basket, picking up the profile, and the tie, Ryan was clearly fingering Rennick for something, but what? Ryan had been cryptic in case someone else found the envelope, and it would take some effort on Marco's part to piece things together.

Although he'd seen it before, Marco thumbed through the pages of the profile and noticed the page numbers were off. With the summary marked as page one, the sequence went on to page two, three, and four, and then back to page one. He studied the additional page and shook his head. For twenty minutes, he read and re-read two different versions of the summary. Both were written by Seth. Both showed headers with the same document ID, the same digital password, and the name Layne Stevens. But nothing else compared between them. The extra summary verified Layne as a Foodie Channel host with an unfortunate association to the victim. The one distributed to the team, in its essence, condemned her as a traitor.

Marco gathered the items and got out of his car. From a dark corner of the garage, a figure charged at him.

"What the—"

67

Drawn into consciousness by a steady supply of air and the odd sense of something cradling her, Layne opened her eyes. A cracked dive mask materialized through her daze, and she struggled to free herself, but the diver let go and removed his mask. Relieved to make out Ryan's face in the darkness, she threw her arms around his neck. He held her for a moment, then took her by the shoulders, inched her away, and fumbled with repositioning his fractured mask and mouthpiece.

He checked her equipment, took her hand, and they continued through the shadowy waters toward land. But the giant ghostly form still hovered nearby, and Layne soon realized they were swimming straight for it. By instinct, she pulled away. But Ryan shook his head and tugged her back on course.

As they neared the monster, her heart rate quickened. But it transformed into an enormous boulder, with more coming into view as they navigated the deep labyrinth of jagged reef lining the coast. Ryan carefully guided Layne through spiny crags to an underwater cave just offshore. There they emerged under the safety of rock cover.

"I can't believe we did it!" she said.

"That was impressive," Ryan said. "All except the part where you tried to kill me."

"I guess I did freak out a little."

"A little?"

"Okay, more than a little. I am—"

"Uh huh, so sorry."

Layne grimaced. "Are you all right?"

"Federal agent, remember? We train for these things. Sort of. Other than that, you did great. How long since your last dive?"

"That was my first real dive."

A shocked expression crossed Ryan's face. "But your file said you were certified, and you mentioned diving with your husband."

"Yes, we certified together, but then..."

"You never took your first ocean dive?"

"Nope."

"Wow. You know, there are experienced divers who won't go down at night. You are pretty damned brave, Layne Stevens."

Layne beamed. "I am, aren't I? Who were all those people on the boat?"

"You work in this business long enough, you do a few favors, you earn a few."

"Must've been some serious favors."

She glanced into a large, black duffel bag on the rocks. It contained towels, clothes, a blond wig, a red baseball cap and a stick-on, goatee. Ryan stripped down and began to towel off as Layne hid behind her hand—for the most part—while fending off protests from her little voice.

"What are you doing?" Ryan asked.

"Not looking," she said.

"And not changing."

"My brave spell is over."

Ryan snickered. "Go ahead, I'll turn around."

With his back turned, Ryan dressed and stuffed their gear, towels, and wetsuits into the duffel bag. Layne removed both her wetsuit and bathing suit, patted herself dry, pulled on the men's athletic wear Ryan had packed for her, and planted the wig on top of her head. When she turned to him, she spit out a laugh.

"Thanks a lot," Ryan said. "And can you keep it down a little?"

Layne lowered her voice. "I'm sorry, but you look ridiculous with that pointy little goatee on your face."

"You should see yourself in that wig."

"Is it bad?"

"You always look gorgeous," he said, giving her an irresistible smile.

She picked up a seashell laying on one of the rocks. "Look at this."

Ryan studied the shell. "Hunh. You know my mom told me this legend about sand dollars. Supposedly, if you break one open, you'll find five tiny white doves waiting to spread peace and love."

"What a beautiful story."

"I did it once. Broke one open. All I found was a shrunken shriveled-up urchin body."

Layne frowned.

"But you don't see a lot of sand dollars still intact anymore," he said. "So, this one's a keeper."

"Yeah, not a huge fan of dried up urchin bodies." She placed the sand dollar back on the rock. "Why do we need to keep our voices low? Aren't we at least a mile from the boardwalk?"

"Just being paranoid, I guess. I left Rennick at The Riede to monitor the coms, but I'm worried she'll come looking for us. Let's get out of here."

Layne silently cursed Agent Rennick as Ryan led her up a trail to a dark blue sedan camouflaged by the tall, dense sagebrush so prevalent on Northern California's coast. The scent of it lay thick on the cool night air, and she inhaled deeply letting the heady aroma rejuvenate her. Ryan retrieved a key fob from a side pocket of the duffle, popped open the trunk, and tossed the bag inside. Layne slid into the front seat next to him and peered out the back window, then sighed. No view of the boardwalk from there.

"I still can't believe we did it," she said, replaying the details of their escape in her mind. At the time, she'd been scared to death, but back on solid ground, she felt exhilarated.

"You were amazing out there," Ryan said, pressing the engine start button. Nothing happened.

"What's wrong?"

"The engine won't turn over."

"Do you have your foot on the brake?"

Ryan frowned.

"And it's the right key?" she asked.

His eyes narrowed.

"Just trying to help."

"The key fob worked to unlock the trunk."

"Right," Layne said. "Do we have gas?"

The tightening of his lips sent a clear signal for her to stop helping.

He banged his palm on the steering wheel. "Damn it. We did not just make a life-threatening underwater escape to end up stuck on the side of the road."

He grabbed a flashlight out of the glove box, yanked on the hood release, and got out of the car. Layne followed, standing by as Ryan aimed the light at various parts of the engine. Hmm, did he know what he was looking for? Ryan directed the beam to one particular area. Of course he did. He swept the flashlight to another location. All right, maybe not. She cleared her throat.

"Something you'd like to contribute?" he asked.

"Are you sure?"

"Please."

"Well," Layne said. "It looks to me like the lead wire on the induction coil is missing."

"Excuse me?"

"I said it seems—"

The distinct clack of a shotgun being cocked right behind them pierced the night, and Layne jumped, smacking her head on the inside of the hood.

Then an angry female voice accosted them. "Hands up. Now."

68

Layne winced at the sting on the back of her head, as she lifted her hands into the air. Ryan muttered words that were indiscernible. But she suspected they weren't pleasant.

"Turn around," the woman said.

Layne tried to turn, but her body refused.

"Turn around, now."

"Layne," Ryan said, "she's got a gun. You need to turn around."

"I'm trying," Layne said.

Impatience laced the woman's tone. "What was that?"

Layne turned her upper body hoping her legs would follow. "It's just…my legs won't move."

"What the hell is that thing on your head?" the woman asked.

"It's…it's a wig."

"Turn the hell around or the wig dies, and I won't guarantee my shot."

Layne whispered toward Ryan. "She's going to shoot me in the head."

"Yes, I got that. Take a deep breath, and move one leg at a time."

"Now!" The woman said.

The deep breath worked about as well as it always did, but the one leg at a time thing did the trick. She found her footing and turned, although with no ambient light she couldn't see the woman's face.

"So then," the woman said. "Suppose you tell me what the hell you're doing here with that car."

Ryan squinted at the darkness. "Look, we don't want—"

"Not you. I'm asking about the car, and you clearly don't know jack-shit about cars. I want to hear it from her."

"Oh," Layne said. "Hello. It's a pleasure to meet you Ms...um. I'm Layne Stevens and this is Ryan."

"Yeah, yeah, why the hell are you on my property?"

"I'm so sorry, we didn't realize—"

The woman pointed her flashlight in Layne's face. "Your voice sounds familiar. Did you say your name was Layne Stevens?"

Layne squinted against the glare. "Uh huh."

"As in the Layne Stevens from Food Made Whole?"

"Yes. Do you watch the show?"

"Are you kidding? I love your show. That is, if it's actually you. Take off the wig."

Layne removed her fluff of curly blond hair and managed a weak smile. "See? It's really me."

"Man, the things you can do with leftovers. Makes my mouth water just thinking about it."

"Thank you. Those are some of my favorites too. Could we lower our hands now? You might be aware of my love-hate relationship with exercise, and gravity is winning against my arms."

The woman chuckled. "Yeah, I remember. Mostly hate, right? Sure, put 'em down. Holy crap on a stick. Layne Stevens in my own backyard. Unbelievable. Hey, can you autograph my gun?"

"I'd be happy to. Ryan, do you have a pen?"

Ryan glanced over at her. "Seriously?"

"I got one," the woman said. She pulled a pen from her pocket and gave her shotgun to Layne.

Ryan rolled his eyes as Layne signed it, then carefully handed it back to the woman.

After admiring Layne's autograph, the woman stuffed the gun

under her arm and peered behind them. "So, back to business," she said. "Why are you driving that piece of shit car, and what's it doing on my property?"

"I didn't catch your name," Ryan said.

"I wasn't talking to you."

"I'm sorry about the intrusion," Layne said. "I've had some recent threats on my life, and this man is protecting me. We needed a secluded spot to park the car. We had no idea this was private property."

"You mean, other than the big-ass warning at the entrance to the road that said private property?"

Layne raised scolding brows at Ryan. He shrugged.

"Yeah," the woman said. "Like I thought. Listen, Layne. Can I call you Layne? Never send a boy to do a woman's job."

"Well, again," Layne said. "I apologize. Is there something I can do to make it up to you? Maybe a tour of the studio when my current mess is over-with?"

"Oh, I would love that. I'm kinda glad you trespassed."

"Yeah, me too," Layne said. "It's always great to meet a fellow left-over addict."

"Layne," Ryan said. "We need to go."

The woman dangled the lead wire. "You're not going anywhere without this."

"Can you help us out with that?" Ryan asked.

"Sounded to me like this one right here could handle it herself." She tossed the lead wire to Layne.

"Let me give you my personal email address," Layne said. "Send me your contact information. It may be a few weeks, but I'll make sure you're set up for a tour."

As the woman wrote Layne's email address on the back of her hand, Ryan nudged his chin in the woman's direction.

"Oh," Layne said. "The people threatening me are not very nice individuals. Can we keep this little incident between us?"

"Of course. Anyone comes around asking, they're as good as shot."

Layne chuckled, hoping it was a joke. “Thanks again for being so understanding.”

The woman nodded and headed back through the brush.

“Wait,” Ryan said, “what do we do with the—” His hands clenched. “Shit, she’s gone.”

69

Layne looked at the part the woman had tossed her, then she peered in at the engine. "Ryan?"

"What?" He said, his tone oozing irritation.

"Can you hold the flashlight for me?"

"What are you planning to do?"

"I'm going to re-attach the lead wire so we can go," she said.

"Hunh."

She pointed to the induction coil, Ryan aimed the light, and a few minutes later she brushed off her hands. "Want to give it a try?"

His expression edged precariously close to *yeah, right*. But he took the driver's seat, pressed the start button, and the engine revved. This expression was priceless. She slid back into the car beside him.

"Where did you learn to do that?" he asked.

"My dad. I used to help him fix up old cars."

They drove out the access road, and disappeared into the night, amidst a steady flow of drivers traveling south along the scenic Pacific Coast Highway.

"I know I said this before, but you were amazing back there," Ryan said. "Both in the water and on land, and no stunt double required. Are you sure you're not an agent?"

Layne chuckled. "Thank you, but I never want to do a dive like that again. So, where are we going?"

"We'll worry about that later."

She looked into the back seat. "What's in the ice chest?"

"Human brains. We're transporting them to a bio-engineering facility."

Her eyes grew large.

"I take it back," Ryan said. "You're too gullible to be an agent. It's food and drinks."

"Thank god. I'm starved. Can we eat?"

"Does anything keep you from eating?"

"Not really."

"Would you mind opening one of those sandwiches for me? And I'll take a root beer," Ryan said.

"My favorite," Layne said with a grin.

It was a simple turkey sandwich with lettuce, tomato, and mayonnaise on a French roll, and it was the most delicious sandwich Layne had ever eaten. "There's something about cheating death that makes food taste so much better."

"I'm beginning to wonder if you doubt my ability to protect you."

Layne unbuckled her seatbelt and moved to the center seat.

"Still throwing caution to the wind?" Ryan asked.

"I just wanted to sit next to you."

Ryan put an arm around her, and she nestled beside him. She thought about how they'd ended up there together. In five years, she'd not met a man that seemed worth the threat to her heart. But there was Ryan. No man, not even her husband, had stirred feelings in her like Ryan did. And no man had ever risked his career, much less his life for her. She smiled and rested her head against his shoulder, content until her overactive mind sabotaged her.

"So," she said, "about this termination plan."

"I'd prefer not to use the word termination. We call it an exit plan."

"Right. How does it work?"

"There are dozens of reasons an agent might need to disappear—betrayal, exposure. We all have an exit plan."

"And you just vanish?"

"That's the gist of it."

"What about when this is over?"

"Well, normally, when an agent executes their plan, it's permanent. In this case, it'll depend on how things turn out."

Her stomach tightened. "But—"

"Right now, my main concern is everyone's safety, especially yours. We can deal with the exit plan after we've ended this."

"Well, I don't like it," she said.

"No, neither do I."

As the sun rose over the mountains, the car slowed to a stop, and Layne, having slept most of the trip, woke to a cheek planted in wet shirt. Unfortunately, it was Ryan's shirt. And it was covered in her drool. She groaned.

"You snored a little too," Ryan said. "Is this what I'm in for?"

Her little voice appeared right on cue. *Heh. You are quite the catch.*

"I'm going to fill the tank," Ryan said. "And we need to stock up on supplies. You should probably put on your wig."

They pulled to a gas pump, and Layne got out to stretch. "You're using a credit card?"

"Yes. But give me a little credit," Ryan said, chuckling. "Get it? A little credit?"

But Layne didn't laugh. In fact, she'd barely heard him.

"Tough crowd," Ryan said.

Layne gaped at what appeared to be a salt flat conceding to a substantial body of water, surrounded by a thick forest of magnificent pines and scraggly underbrush. "I recognize this place," she said.

Ryan took her hand and dragged her toward the little store attached to the gas station. The store resembled a log cabin topped by a weathered tin roof, with hundreds of wind chimes hanging from the eves. Situated on the corner of a two-lane highway and a semi-paved road, the sign across the front read Minnow Lake Gas and Market.

Layne gasped. "This is—"

"Uh huh," Ryan said.

"But—"

"Yes, I understand."

Layne stammered. "Ryan, I can't go—"

Ryan lowered his voice. "I'm hoping they don't recognize you, but the disguise would probably work better if the wig was on top of your head instead of sliding down the back."

Layne pulled her wig forward.

"There you go," he said. "Now don't worry, everything will be fine."

He continued to pull her toward the door of the small market, and for a change, Layne's little voice echoed her own thoughts.

The wig is the least of your worries, honey.

70

Marco woke on a cold cement floor and squinted against the bright squares of sunlight beaming through decorative windows in his garage door. How long had he been out? He reached for his head and felt a large welt. "Ouch. Shit." After hauling himself up to a sitting position, he scanned the floor around him for the manila envelope and its contents. His attacker had taken it all. He replayed the prior day's events in his mind. What the fuck was going on? He knew one thing—Ryan had staged his own disappearance, and Layne had willingly gone with him. Ryan controlled the plan, and if anyone could outsmart the team, it was him. But, why? He'd wanted Marco to find the package, and the information looked bad for Rennick. But the puzzle had too many missing pieces, including who'd taken the envelope, and how the hell they'd gotten into his garage. Then he remembered the profile. He looked at his watch. Just after six am. He showered, dressed, and drove downtown to Bureau headquarters to wait for Seth.

"Dude, long time no see," Seth said, strolling into the lobby. "Let me guess, you're here to visit Martha. She's a hot pepper, that one. Totally your type."

"Really? Which one is Martha? Actually, forget that. I'm here to talk to you."

"Cool," Seth said with an easy smile. "It's not often I get visitors. What can I do you for?"

"Can we use your office?"

"Absomundo."

Marco liked Seth. An average looking guy, about six feet tall, with a medium build, he had blond hair, cut a little longer than regulation and course from early mornings spent riding the surf. He wore semi-geeky, nondescript, casual business wear, and had an affinity for Birkenstocks sandals worn over patterned dress socks. His unwavering pleasant nature made him likable. But his uncanny ability to nail every profile handed to him made him a unique asset to the bureau. He led Marco down a long, narrow hallway to his office, and Marco closed the door behind them.

"I'm guessing you haven't heard," Marco said.

"Dude, please don't tell me I'm fired."

"Are you kidding? That would take an act of Congress."

"Whew. What is it then? You're looking mighty serious."

"It's Ryan," Marco said. "He's missing."

"Dude, no way. I just talked to him, like, two days ago. Dang, I hope it's nothing bad. He's one of the good guys."

"Yeah, anyway, I'm following up on the Stevens case, hoping to work this thing through. See if I can catch a lead on Ryan."

"You think this has something to do with Layne Stevens?"

"I'm not sure. I read your profile."

"Don't say it, dude. It's not possible. There is no way Layne Stevens is an op. I'd stake my career on that one."

"What made you think I would question your work?"

"I take a lot of flak. People ask how I know I'm right. I don't know how the heck I know. I just do. It's a gift, dude. And a curse."

"I hear ya. Anyone give you flak on this one?"

"Only Sherry, but she's always nasty. I think she kinda likes me, but she's afraid to admit it."

Marco nodded. "So, what did Rennick say?"

"Called me an imbecile, and told me I had no clue what the ef I was talking about. The usual."

"Anything else?"

"On her way out, she griped about what idiots all men are, and how she would have to handle things herself."

"She stay long?"

"Heck, no. She was in and out of here like a bat on steroids. But that's Sherry for ya."

"Hmm. Anyone else say anything to you about the Stevens profile?"

"Oh yeah. Ryan. He called to have me..." Panic crossed Seth's face.

"It's okay, man. You can tell me."

"I'm not sure if this is against policy or not. I mean, it's a darned encrypted PDF for criminy sake. There's no way anyone could tamper with it. You'd need the password, and the encryption software, and—"

"Seth, what did Ryan ask for?"

"He asked me to send a soft copy of the Stevens summary to his personal e-mail. Said he was working at home and spilled coffee on the original."

"You did the right thing, man," Marco said.

"Dude. You had me scared. Did I help at all?"

"More than you know. And buddy, a word of advice—stay away from Rennick. I'm pretty sure there's a 6-6-6 tattooed somewhere on that blond head of hers."

Marco entered the elevator and pressed the button for the twelfth floor. He didn't like dropping in on Director Hall unannounced, but this couldn't wait. He showed his badge to the Director's assistant, who made a point to be friendly, but direct.

"It must be the director's lucky day," the assistant said. "You're the second person to visit without an appointment this morning. You can stay, but I can't guarantee he'll have time."

Marco sank into an overstuffed reception chair and contemplated the expensively framed black and white historic photos of the city hanging on the walls. They might have been intriguing if he wasn't so damned preoccupied. Twenty minutes later the door to Director Hall's office opened, and Marco's eye's widened.

"Short, what are you doing here? Have you found something?"

Agent Short grew more pale, if that were possible. Then he turned back to Director Hall. "Thank you, sir. It was a pleasure to visit with you."

"You too, Short. Thanks for stopping by," Director Hall said. "Agent Viorantelli, please, come in."

Agent Short gave Marco a tight smile and left.

"What brings you by?" the director asked, gesturing Marco into his office.

"I'd like to speak with you about Agent Cooke, sir."

"It must be my lucky day," Director Hall said.

71

Inside the small market, Ryan grabbed a shopping basket, and Layne sped to the bathroom. Although not incredibly clean, she breathed a sigh of relief at the single bathroom stall with toilet paper and a functional lock. Afterward, she washed her hands, stared for a moment at the stained hand towel that lay on top of the empty paper towel dispenser, and chose to dry her hands on her sweatpants. Then she made use of the small mirror on the wall to situate her curly blond crown.

When she turned to go, she gasped at the sight of a heart carved into the old wood trim on the side of the door. She had etched that heart a lifetime ago. Inside it, the words Layne plus R.C. shown as clear as the day she'd carved them. She shook her head. Raymond Crimble. Her thirteen-year-old crush. He'd never even noticed her. And he hadn't crossed her mind in years. Then it hit her. Were the initials merely a coincidence? Or was the universe conspiring on her behalf? She left the restroom with a wistful grin and picked up a few items on her way to intercept Ryan and his mini cart. The cart contained an ample selection of essentials—toilet paper, a hatchet, ice, and toothbrushes, among other things.

“We can always come back,” Ryan said. “But this should take us through tomorrow.”

Layne flipped over a package, revealing the contents as teriyaki flavored beef jerky.

“I can’t stop at a minimart without buying beef jerky,” Ryan said. “It might be a sickness.”

Layne chuckled. “Well, if we’re exposing our weaknesses...” She held up a canister of ranch-flavored potato chips and a bag of chocolate covered pretzels.

“You don’t expect me to believe those are whole foods, do you?”

“It’s doubtful they’re even part food.”

“You’re not curious about the hatchet?”

“Are you an ax murderer?”

“Nope.”

“Then I’ll settle for blissful ignorance.”

They approached the checkout, where a small television behind the counter showed a news anchor, his voice grim, recounting the incidents leading up to the disappearance of their own Layne Stevens. Layne spun back toward the car maintenance aisle.

“Why don’t you meet me outside, hun?” Ryan said.

Layne bolted out of the store for the car and then sunk low in the passenger seat. Ryan snickered when he slid into the driver’s side.

“What’s so funny?”

“Hiding might be easier if you weren’t channeling the ghost of Marilyn Monroe.”

Layne looked up at her wig, snagged between the seat and the headrest, a bleached blond beacon as to her whereabouts. She growled and yanked it loose. “I am terrible at this spy stuff.”

“Don’t be so hard on yourself. For most of the trip you’ve been great.”

She narrowed her eyes. “I slept for most of the trip.”

“But your few waking moments were really good. Really.”

She shoved the wig back on her head and turned to face him. “Why are we here?”

Ryan coughed out a laugh. “I’m sorry, but we can’t have a serious conversation with that thing on your head. Let's get to the cabin, and I'll explain everything."

They pulled out of the gas station onto an all too familiar, semi-paved road. Layne could still predict every bump and turn with eerie precision. The car wound along the lake, past the tiny town of Minnow with its post office, English Pub, RV park, and a sparse scattering of homes. Farther up the way, cattle grazed lazily in a large green pasture. Layne recognized every inch of the town, and fond memories of spying on cows from her favorite perch on an old wood fence came back to her.

Ryan took a sharp left on what appeared to be a dirt path. She'd never explored this densely-forested part of Minnow, but visions of something like an old cave or a broken-down hunting blind flashed through her head. He had said cabin, hadn't he? After inching for some time through thick brush, the car slowed in front of a patch of trees. If they hadn't stopped, Layne might have missed the dark wooden structure altogether. "What is this place?"

"It's a safe house. Hasn't been used in years. We'll need to get the utilities running, but it's better than camping. Help me unload, then I'll move the car to the barn out back."

Ryan handed Layne a key, and she unlocked the front door of the rustic structure. A musty aroma overtook her, and with the sun shining in, the cobwebbed corners and thick layers of dust were difficult to ignore. She crinkled her nose. "I think I'd rather camp."

Ryan joined her at the door and glanced inside. "Right. Leave everything on the porch, and we'll try to make this place more livable before we move in."

Skeptical, but always up for a challenge, Layne removed dusty, moth-eaten furniture covers, while Ryan opened the windows and located a broom. They swept and dusted together. Ryan battled cobwebs and spiders alone. An hour later the place looked and smelled half decent. Layne flushed the standing water through the faucets, and Ryan went outside to check for firewood.

"Here's our position," he said when he returned.

Layne chuckled. "Our position?"

"The cabin doesn't have electricity, but there's enough wood to last us a while. There should be candles, matches, and lantern fuel in one of the kitchen cupboards. The water seems to be clearing, and the septic tank isn't full, so we can use the toilet, the sinks, and the shower."

"No electricity?" Had he spoken after that?

"There's a wood burning stove inside and a propane stove out back. We'll keep the cooler stocked with ice for perishables, and there's running water. What more could we want?"

Layne grimaced.

"Come on," Ryan said. "It's an adventure."

"No electricity?"

"Why would we need it?"

"Okay," Layne said. "If I can dive at night, I can do this." She scrutinized the room. "I'm not a huge fan of spiders or cold showers, but I can do this."

"That's my girl. And your showers won't be cold."

"I'm your girl?"

"It's not like I'd risk my life and my career for just anyone."

"Aw," Layne said. "That is so sweet. Now tell me about the not cold showers."

Ryan's hands circled her waist, pulling her close. The requisite goosebumps prickled on her arms as she slipped them around his neck, and her breath caught as his lips moved across hers. "There's a propane water heater in the garage, but you'll need to help me get going. I mean get *it* going. The water heater that is."

She gave him a coy smile. "Then you'll have to let go."

His arms wrapped tighter around her, and her body melted deliciously into his.

"Well, gorgeous, I could do that. Or..." He gave her another breath stealing kiss.

Damn, the kiss was tempting, but something distracted her. An odor. An offensive odor. Oh god. Was it her?

72

The call woke Director Braun out of a deep sleep, and his muscles protested at the movement incurred well before they'd had enough rest. He checked the time on his phone—just after midnight. He was far too old for this.

He arrived at BKA headquarters to a conference room crowded with agents and the secure voice transmission line already engaged. Sullen stares filled the room.

"He is here now," one of the agents said, leaning toward the microphone.

"Nice of you to join us, Braun," the raspy voice blared.

Director Braun ignored the condescending tone. "What is going on?"

"I was just explaining that your fucking man, Berger, led us to nothing but dead ends."

"I don't understand," Director Braun said.

"Let me spell it out for you. The locket, your agent's brilliant hiding place, was fucking empty. And Berger played his hand too soon. Now he's in custody."

"What? Where is he?"

"Not my concern, and I can't help him now. My concern is acquiring the card."

Director Braun recognized the smug arrogance in the caller's voice. "You know where it is."

"We have a fair idea."

"Then why did you contact us?"

"Our sources point to your other geriatric guard dogs."

The director's brows lowered. "What do you intend to do?"

"What you should have done on day one."

Director Braun stiffened. "No. You cannot compromise them after all this time."

"You've been warned."

The line went dead.

73

H*oly crap,* Layne's little voice said. *No, really. You smell like crap.*

With Ryan's arms still around her, Layne brought her elbows down, squeezed her armpits together, rested her palms on his chest, and prayed she wasn't the source of the foul stench. "I'll make you a deal," she said.

"It had better be one hell of a deal."

"Let me shower and get cleaned up, then we can do this for as long as you like."

He kissed her again. "How about we shower together?"

Layne lifted both brows.

"Got it," Ryan said. "I'll get the water heater started. There's a dry towel and more t-shirts and sweatpants in the duffel, and you can wear my boxers. Sorry, no bras in my dresser, damn it."

"Boxers?"

Ryan grinned. "They're just like shorts."

She grabbed the toiletries they'd bought at the minimart and headed for the bathroom. The shifting temperatures of the water prompted several shrieks and a record-breaking shower. Afterward, she put on a roomy gray t-shirt, a striped set of boxers, and a pair of Ryan's athletic socks, which drooped at her ankles. She had no makeup, and no choice but to leave her hair wet, falling in curls around her face and shoulders.

"Wow," he said, as she returned to the living room.

Her cheeks grew warm at his reaction.

"Hey," he said. "Do you smell that?"

So much for wow. Gosh darn it. She had just showered. "Nope. Not me. Don't smell a thing."

"I found a dead raccoon under the porch. The odor was driving me nuts. It's gone now, but can you still smell it?"

Whew. "No. Poor thing."

"Tell me about it. It wasn't easy getting under that porch."

"I meant the raccoon, but I guess that goes for you, too."

Ryan approached her and she batted his hands away. "Oh no you don't. Not after you crawled around underneath this place with dead animals and who knows what else."

While Ryan showered, Layne investigated the kitchen and put together a gourmet lunch on old tin plates, giving them each half of a leftover sandwich, a stack of uniformly shaped potato chips, three hunks of beef jerky, several chocolate pretzels, and a root beer.

Ryan emerged from the hallway wearing sweatpants settled low on his hips. And nothing else. Layne's gaze wandered from the day's growth of sexy scruff on his face, to the enticing spray of salt and pepper curls across his bare chest, and down along that scrumptious thin line of hair leading farther south. At that moment, she understood why Maggie called it a happy trail, and she caught herself licking her lips.

He slid his arms around her and grazed the side of her neck with his mouth. "I hope that meant you liked what you saw."

She let her eyelids drop and savored the charge of electricity between them as Ryan kissed and nibbled his way down her throat. "Was I that obvious?" she asked.

"Uh huh. It's one of my favorite things about you."

Ryan's lips found her collarbone, and she responded with a sigh and a wide grin. "Lunch is on the table," she said.

"There's only one thing I'd like to do on this table."

Her damned little voice ambushed her. *How long has it been since you went to the gym? You can't possibly measure up to this chiseled hunk of man.*

Layne's grin dissolved, the charge fizzled, and her eyes flew open. "Wait, I, uh...we should eat."

Ryan stopped nibbling at her neck. "Everything all right?"

"Sure. Absolutely. Yup. Fine. Let's dig in." She angled away from him and took a seat at the table, where they ate for several minutes in silence.

"Earth to Layne..."

"Huh? Oh," Layne said. "I was just thinking about my summers here growing up." That seemed easier than telling him her mind was assaulting her with the thoughts of a self-conscious school girl.

"Pardon?"

"My parents live about a half hour away. I spent all my summer breaks at Minnow Lake. The store, the ranch...nothing has changed."

Ryan looked uneasy.

"Is that a problem?" she asked. "It seemed like you knew."

He didn't answer.

"Ryan?"

"Sorry. I read in your file that your family's home is somewhat nearby. But I didn't realize you'd spent so much time here at the lake. Shouldn't be an issue though."

Something in his tone left her unconvinced. "So, what happens next?"

"We wait for someone to contact us, then we trade the card for answers."

"But we don't have the card."

"Only you and I know that."

Her stomach flip-flopped, and it must have shown on her face because Ryan gave her a sympathetic smile. "I meant what I said at the boardwalk, Layne." He tucked her curls back from her face and let his fingers trail over her cheek. "I would do anything to protect you." He leaned closer. "You know that, right?"

She nodded, and her eyes fell shut again when he kissed her. With each kiss, her breath quickened, and her heart raced. His lips felt soft and warm against hers, and they consumed her in a way she felt to her core. This time, even her little voice was too aroused to object. He pulled her onto his lap, and she straddled his legs with hers. His fingertips brushed up and down her bare thighs, making her skin tingle. She could see the longing in his eyes as his hands slid around her hips to pull her close.

His lips brushed over her cheek and tickled her ear, and she let her head fall back as his mouth trailed down her neck and over the rise of her breast. She gasped when his teeth tugged gently at her nipple through her shirt, and at that moment there was no little voice, no memory card, no danger. There was only Ryan. He scooped her up, carried her to the couch, and with their clothing tossed aside, he took his sweet time to kiss and nibble, to stroke and caress, to explore and savor, to light every inch of Layne's body on fire.

Moonlight sifted through grimy windowpanes as Layne woke on the couch with her back to Ryan's chest. His arm hung over her, and a furry blanket entangled them. He stirred, stroking the underside of her breast with the edge of his thumb. Then his arm slipped around her waist pulling her tight against him. He nuzzled her shoulder, his hips molded to hers, and his toes played with her feet as she exhaled a contented sigh. Then his hand wandered the length of her side, and she smiled, indulging in the feel of his touch, the warmth of his breath, and the heat of his skin against hers. She turned over to face him, and he drew her in, burying his face into her hair.

"You smell so...nice," he said.

"Not like the raccoon?"

"Definitely not like the raccoon." His lips grazed her jaw. "Layne?"

"Hmm?"

His voice grew serious. "There's something I want to tell you. Something you need to remember. No matter what happens."

She tipped her head back to look at him. "What is it?"

His eyes held hers with an intensity she'd not seen before. "I...It can wait," he said. They kissed, and he moved over her, enveloping her, exploring her body with his. Then he filled her. And as she abandoned herself to him, his lips brushed her ear. "I love you, Layne."

74

Gretel stood in his usual position when Rennick entered the suite, but instead of Layne, the German agent, Hans Berger, sat at the small table in the far corner of the room. After a morning debrief on the outcome of the Santa Cruz trip, Rennick knew Berger would be there. But shock spread over Berger's face as she approached.

"Out," she said to Gretel, who, outranked by degree, went for the door.

Aware the suite remained wired for video and sound, Rennick kept her visit short. She gripped the front of the German agent's shirt with both hands and moved her face to within inches of his. "You fucked up. Tell us where they are."

"I have told your people. I do not know."

Careful to avoid the cameras, she dropped a small note into Berger's lap, released her hold on him and straightened. He peered down, and with minimal movement, unfolded the tiny piece of paper and stared at the words written on it. Then he studied her face, crumpling the note before stuffing his hands into his pants pockets.

"You're done," she said, glaring at him to assert her point.

His expression confirmed the message had stung as intended, but it would seem meaningless on video, and would soon be forgotten. The note served as a warning.

"You shouldn't have come," it said. "Give them nothing. From now on we do this my way."

Then she left him. But instead of returning to the surveillance suite, she headed for the stairs.

75

Layne woke up feeling as though she'd run a marathon with a sawhorse between her legs. Ryan made her mind feel young, but her body wasn't buying it. He stirred and brushed gentle kisses across her back.

"Oh no you don't," she said, slipping from his grasp. She wrapped herself in the blanket, leaving Ryan naked and uncovered on the couch as she waddled to the bathroom. Letting the water wash over her, she thought about him. He was easy to trust and even easier to adore; his sense of humor, his loyalty, the things they had in common, and the way he treated her, both out of and under the covers. Holy cow, especially under the covers. She'd never been with a man who was so incredibly attentive and so very...thorough. She couldn't help smiling at the thought. For the last several years she'd resisted the notion that real love found anyone twice. But there she stood, under a sporadically hot shower, in love with Very Special Agent Ryan Cooke.

Bursts of steaming water from the old shower head and a soapy lather enhanced her happy afterglow, but she still had a fair amount of discomfort. She'd forgotten to grab a towel from the duffle bag, but she found one neatly folded in the small cabinet under the sink. Except, the terrycloth covered only a fraction of her body, and it felt course from having been dried in the sun.

Or so you hope, her little voice offered.

She attempted to wrap the towel around herself. Holding the corners together, she snuck across the hall to the bedroom. And darn it, there was Ryan, looking incredible in snug sweatpants that accentuated many of his finer parts. He stepped toward her, and she held out her palm.

"Hey there, gorgeous," he said. "I like that outfit."

"Oh no. No way."

"Are we a little tender?"

She detoured around him to the duffel bag. "*We* won't be riding horseback any time soon, if that's what you're asking."

"Okay, I can take a hint. But can I have one kiss?"

"Nope."

He pouted. "C'mon, I only want one."

Not the damned caramel again.

"Please?" he said, moving closer.

Her brain resisted, but her body acquiesced. He took her face into his palms, and kissed her with a desire so intense, that her hands slid involuntarily around his waist. Her towel dropped to the floor between them, and for a moment, the soreness disappeared. But when he pulled her against him, a stab of pain brought her back to her senses. She broke from his grasp, scooped up the tiny cloth, and ordered him out of the room.

"You're a cruel woman."

She pointed at the door.

"All right, I'm going."

Layne left the bedroom clad in thick sweatpants that were too big and a baggy sweatshirt.

Ryan looked her up and down and made a half-hearted attempt to fight back his grin. "Would you like a chastity belt to go with that outfit?"

She narrowed her eyes. "This is your fault, you know."

"I know, and I'm sorry," he said. "We should have taken things a little slower, but I promise to be good all day." He stood and reached out for her, and again her palm met his chest.

"Is it that bad?" he asked.

"I just need...a break. And as it turns out, I have very little resistance where you're concerned. So, you'll have to be the willpower for both of us."

He moved closer. "I like the sound of that."

"Willpower."

"Hunh. Well, I guess we'll be playing a lot of board games. But first I've made us a fancy breakfast."

Ryan's fancy meal consisted of honey and almond granola cereal with milk, more beef jerky, several strips of red licorice, and bottled water. After they ate, he used his shirtsleeve to clean a small spot on the window and peered outside.

"Looks like it might rain," he said. "I'll bring in some firewood."

Layne cleared the table, while Ryan brought logs and kindling in from the porch to fill an old leather sling next to the wood stove. He nudged his chin toward the stove.

"What's with the hole in the top?"

Layne walked over to inspect the old stove. Made from sturdy black cast iron, it showed a fair amount of rust. But the door was still well-sealed, and the glass window on the front seemed in sturdy condition. She searched the floor near the stove. "It seems to be missing, but you would cook your food on a cast iron plate that fits in this hole."

"Come again?"

"Well," Layne said. "Let's say you wanted to boil water. You'd set your pot on top of a cast iron plate that goes where the hole is. And the missing plate would have heated the water, just like a stovetop."

Ryan grunted as he split a large piece of wood with the hatchet he'd purchased at the minimart.

"But," Layne said, "if you were cooking a chicken, and you wanted to roast it over an open flame, you'd remove the plate and put the meat on a cast iron trivet to cook."

He pounded the small ax into another log. "A trivet?"

"It's like a little round grate with legs so that the flames can reach the meat."

"Sounds unsafe."

"It actually works pretty well. The trivet legs slot into the ridge left by the cast iron plate. See here?"

Ryan inspected the top of the wood stove. "That hole is going to put out some serious heat."

"Being able to remove the plate also makes it easier to clean."

"You, Layne Stevens, are a plethora of culinary knowledge."

"Are you making fun of me?"

"Not in a million years."

Layne lifted a brow.

"Okay, maybe a little." He gave her a sideways grin. "But really, your passion for your job is one of the things I love about you." He grumbled as he swung again. "Cheap thing."

"Excuse me?"

"Sorry, not you, the hatchet. Did you notice any tweezers in the cabin?"

Layne used some duct tape she'd found under the kitchen sink to remove most of the splinters from Ryan's hands.

"I'll bet there are gloves out there on that porch," she said.

"Yup, I saw them."

As she went after the last of the splinters, an old-school analog ring-tone wailed from the kitchen, and she nearly ripped the skin off of Ryan's hand with the tape.

"What the hell was that?"

THE NEUTRAL COLOR SUV Sonny had selected at the rental agency equaled him in its nondescript conformity. He sat, parked in a modest suburban neighborhood, where families left garage doors open, kids in helmets rode bikes in the street, and soccer moms strolled and blabbed into their cell phones as a form of exercise. He hated Los Angeles. Technically, his location placed him East of Los Angeles, in the valley, but he could still see the city smog looming on the horizon.

He'd watched that damn house all ef-ing day. No one went in. No one came out. No curtains opened. He skimmed through the contents of the manila envelope again. He didn't understand the tie. But the profile came in handy. According to the FBI's research, Layne's parents were pretty damned old. Maybe they were dead. Sonny pulled the lid off the ice chest on the passenger seat and noted his dwindling supplies. He'd wait another few hours to ensure they were asleep, then he'd take a break to buy more beer nuts, grab a cherry cola, and use a real bathroom instead of a shitty plastic bottle. Ef-ing geriatrics. If they weren't dead, they were probably snoozing already. His phone honked, and he squelched the urge to ignore it.

"Yup?"

"Anything to report, Mr. Wright?"

"Nope."

A long paused transpired before The Employer spoke again. "You have nothing you wish to communicate?"

"My dislike of the suburbs has reached an all-time high," Sonny said. "Did you know that people here use their dogs as a means of escape, so they can covet thy neighbor behind some bush or in some kid's tree house?"

"Thank you for the enlightening exposé on the doldrums of middle-class existence. Would it be possible to elucidate on the task at hand?"

Sonny let his head fall back on the headrest. "There's nothing to tell. No one came, no one went. If Layne planned to come here, she hasn't materialized yet."

A silver sedan pulled to the curb in front of the house, and a man who looked to be in his mid-forties strolled up the walk.

"I'm gonna have to call you back."

"Mr. Wright, do not dare terminate—"

Sonny snickered as he tapped end on the screen and dropped his phone on the passenger seat. He grabbed his binoculars off the dash and aimed them at the house. Hmm, definitely not what he'd expected.

76

"That's my cell phone," Ryan said, examining his hand as he headed toward the sound.

"You're not going to answer it, are you?"

"I had planned to."

"But what if it's the people that are after us?"

"Isn't that why we're here?"

She shook her head. "I changed my mind."

Ryan smirked and activated the speaker on his phone. "Yes?"

A low male voice responded. "Don't you ever do that again, man. There were a few complications, but I got the Sports Illustrated issues you left me. You were right on that wager, but I need to check on the cap. The max bet may be lower than you think."

"What about the player with the sticky fingers?"

"That's a long shot. But I'll keep you posted."

Ryan ended the call. "That was Marco."

"I gathered," Layne said. "He called to talk about sports?"

"He called to tell me he worked through the clues I left him. I knew Marco wasn't involved in the setup, but including him in my exit plan would have put his career at risk too. Now he can pursue the investigation from the inside and keep us informed. He'll call us back when there's more information on how high up the chain of command this thing goes. But I'm curious about the complications."

"Were we listening to the same conversation?"

Ryan grinned.

"Ah, spy code stuff. Got it," Layne said. "Do men talk about anything without relating it to sports?"

He grinned again.

"What was that about sticky fingers?"

"Forensics found Sergeant Temple's print on the silver tray."

"Dudley Do-Right? You think he's involved?"

"I don't think he's smart enough to be involved, but we can't rule anyone out."

"Hmm," Layne said. "So, how does this phone thing work?"

"I transferred our sim cards to these untraceable phones. They don't have GPS so they can't be tracked, but incoming call content can still be monitored, so our conversations will need to be short and cryptic. I'm sure they're watching Marco's cell, probably Maggie's, and most of your family."

"How are we going to keep them charged?"

"I brought an adapter that draws small amounts of power from the car battery even when the car is turned off."

"You are a man of many talents, Agent Cooke."

"I had hoped that might be evident last night," Ryan said, pulling her to him. "There's something personal I want to ask you."

"Anything."

"Do you know how to play Gin Rummy?"

She pushed him away. "Get the cards, tough guy."

They played several rounds of Rummy, and Layne won almost every hand before Ryan professed boredom with the game. She wiped a little sweat from her forehead and then studied the wood stove. "I know we need it, but this cabin is small, and that fire is really hot."

Ryan nodded. "How about we sit outside on the back porch for a bit?"

"Perfect. I could use some fresh air."

They were headed for the door when "Love Shack" rang out from

Layne's cell phone. She dashed to it, eager to view the caller ID. "Blocked," she said.

"You'll just have to answer it. Remember the rules."

Layne hit the speaker button and adopted a pleasant facade. "Hello?"

"Thank heavens you're alive, baby girl. On the news, it said you were missing."

"Mom? Uh, I'm fine. Can I call you back?" She grimaced and whispered to Ryan, "what happened to AC/DC?"

Helen pretended to choke. "Did you hear that, Karl? I find my missing daughter, and the ungrateful child wants to call me back."

"Tell Layne I said hello," Karl yelled.

A pain stabbed at Layne's left eye, and she covered the microphone with her hand. "So much for brief and cryptic."

"I'm not sure what happened," Ryan said. "Be polite, but you need to hang up."

"It's okay, Cooke," a male voice said. "We're on an untraceable too."

Layne narrowed her eyes at the phone. "Scott?"

"Hey, sis. How's Ryan treating you?"

"How's Ryan...what?"

"I know you too well, Cooke. You lay one hand on my sister..."

"Scott Roberts, how the hell are you?"

"Didn't catch that in the file, huh?" Scott asked. "Gotta admit, I expected more from you."

Ryan frowned. "Frankly, so did I."

"Scott," Layne said. "What's going on? How do you know Ryan? And how did you know he was here?"

"Yeah, I'll explain when we get there."

Ryan's gaze went to the ceiling.

"No worries, Ry," Scott said. "You and I are the only people left who even remember the place. Well, maybe Marco. You're at the lake, right?"

Ryan didn't respond.

"Good," Scott said. "We'll see you in thirty."

Layne gasped. "Wait...we?"

"Sis, come on. You expect me to argue with Mom?"

"Oh god," Layne said.

"I heard that blasphemy, baby girl," Helen said.

"Be there in a bit," Scott added, and the call ended.

Layne gaped at Ryan. "How do you know my brother?"

For the first time since they'd met, Ryan seemed thrown. "This is bad," he said.

"I know. I can't see my mother dressed like this. And I'm still waiting for you to tell me how the hell you know Scott."

He stared at her for a long moment, then let out a sigh. "I'm going to take a shower before our guests arrive. Why don't you pop open a bottle of wine and put on some music?"

Layne suppressed a scream. "This is not a joke."

The back of his hand waved at her as he disappeared down the hall.

THE RUN-OF-THE-MILL SUV served Sonny well as he tailed the silver sedan through the crush of valley traffic. But then the car turned onto a remote two-lane highway, so he followed at a greater distance for about twenty-five miles, and was surprised to see the blinker flash on. If not for the small market on the corner, he might have missed the turn altogether. He slowed to create additional space between the two cars, and an odd scene emerged before him. A fine white powder ceded to huge pines surrounding the edge of a modest-sized lake. Not something you'd see in Florida, where he grew up.

He navigated the natural twists and turns of the bumpy road, losing sight of the sedan several times, but he glimpsed the rear of the car as it turned into the brush. Was it a narrow drive? Or a service path? He couldn't be sure, but he wouldn't risk turning in. He parked at a dirt turnout, wedged a small handgun into the back of his waistband, and hurried into the bushes on foot.

About a quarter mile off the frontage road, Sonny spotted a rundown shack. The sedan he'd tailed sat empty in front. As he approached the cabin, he recognized Layne's voice, and then pretty boy's.

He crept onto the porch and squinted through the only clear spot on one of the filthy windows. The old woman spoke, as did the man who drove the sedan. But Sonny's eyes fixed on Layne. Even in baggy sweats, she looked beautiful, but the conversation seemed tense. He listened a little longer and cursed silently at what he heard. Did they really not have the card? Damn it. They had just decided his next move for him, and it wouldn't be good.

He pulled his gun from the back of his waistband, picked up the hatchet he'd found on the porch, and snuck around to the front of the cabin.

77

Thirty minutes had passed, and Layne managed to find a semblance of calm, but she regretted not buying discount wine at the minimart. She'd learned long ago that her mother went better when paired with a generous glass or three of any type of alcohol. A vehicle rumbled up to the cabin, car doors slammed shut, and footsteps sounded on the porch. Layne braced herself and opened the door.

"Finally, I get to see my baby girl," Helen said, holding out her arms.

Helen carried a robust, well-endowed classically German build. And Layne noted the familiar flower patterned dress with matching apron, thick support hose and utilitarian shoes before her mother pulled her into a stiff embrace.

"Hi, mom. See? I'm perfectly fine. I'm sorry you made the trip for nothing. Why don't you go on home, and I'll call you in the morning."

"Nonsense," Helen said. "I'm not leaving this..." She peered past Layne to examine the small cabin. "...place without answers. And what on God's gracious Earth are you wearing? I tell you, the young people these days. Is that supposed to be—how do you kids say it—goath?"

Layne ignored the tightening in her chest. "I am not a kid, and this is not goth. I'm wearing sweatpants and a sweatshirt."

"In my day," Helen said, "women didn't sweat."

A head of wavy strawberry blond hair and hazel eyes set against golden brown skin hovered behind Helen.

"Mom," Scott said. "Can you please move? I'd like to give my sister a hug."

Helen stepped into the room and sniffed at the air. She ran her fingers over a small table near the door, and tried to shake a thick layer of dust from her hand, but opted to use the back of Layne's sweatshirt instead. "Layne, dear," Helen said. "These accommodations aren't—"

"Hello, sis," Scott said, folding Layne into his arms. "Mom, you promised if I brought you along, you'd let me do the talking."

"Hmph, the way they treat the elderly these days," Helen said.

"Elderly my ass," Scott replied.

Layne followed Helen's gaze to the hallway. "Oh, Ryan," she said. "This is my mother, Helen Roberts. Mom, this is Ryan Cooke."

"Pleasure to meet you, ma'am," Ryan said, extending his hand.

Helen disregarded the gesture and continued her inspection of the cabin.

Scott strode over and gave Ryan a firm handshake along with a burly, one-armed, man hug. "It's great to see you, Ry."

"Nice to see you, too," Ryan said. "You look good. At least one of us gets to spend time in the sun."

"The ladies can't call me tall, dark and handsome without a killer tan, now can they?"

"Oh lord," Layne said.

"I understand you're doing big things at Quantico," Ryan said to Scott.

Layne's eyebrows popped. "At where?"

"Not now, sis," Scott said.

Layne's head volleyed as she listened to Scott and Ryan talk about working the job, special assignments in counterintelligence, and how much things had changed in twenty years. She fought to control the irritated pitch in her voice. "Hello?"

Scott ignored her. "So, let's get down to business, Ry," he said. "Where's the card?"

Layne planted her hands on her hips. "What is going on here, Scott?"

"Sis, I'm trying to talk to Ry. Will you just hold on a sec? Ryan, the card?"

"If I knew where it was," Ryan said, "do you think we'd be holed up in this luxury resort?"

Scott glanced around. "I'll admit, the cabin's matured since the last time we were here."

Layne clenched her fists. "Scott, you told me you were a teacher."

"I am a teacher."

"Then will someone please explain this?"

Like the child Layne knew him to be, Scott looked to Ryan for help. Ryan lifted his shoulders and gestured to Scott. Scott shook his head. Ryan smiled and nodded.

I hope they're not going to mime, Layne's little voice mused. *I hate mimes.*

"Damn it, Scott," Layne said. "Explain yourself."

"Hmm, where to start," Scott said, focusing on the tattered wood floor. "Oh yeah. I'm an agent with the Federal Bureau of Investigation. I've been teaching at Quantico Academy for some time now. Ryan and I were partners straight out of training. He's the best damned agent in the bureau, besides me, of course. And the second best looking G-man at any agency, really."

Layne's hands went back to her hips. "You're an agent?"

"Yup."

"For the FBI."

"Yup."

"How did I not know this?"

"They couldn't call us *secret* agents if we went around telling everyone, now could they?" Scott turned to Ryan. "I've always wanted to say that."

Ryan smirked. "Still the class clown I see."

"So, you lied to me all these years."

"No. Technically, I am a teacher."

"Riiight," Layne said. "And Mom and Dad both knew?"

"Well, yeah."

"But I'm your sister. Why couldn't you—"

"Hold on, sis," Scott said, and he turned back to Ryan. "If you don't have the card, why are you two here?"

"Well," Ryan said. "Rennick set Layne up to take the fall for Schatz's murder and the missing card. I had a gut feeling I was next on her hit list, so I initiated my exit plan. Marco is working the case from the inside, trying to figure out how many floors up this thing goes."

"That Rennick," Scott said. "Always causing trouble."

"Excuse me, but—" Layne said.

"Wait a minute, will you, sis?" Scott's focus stayed on Ryan. "So, you honestly don't have it?"

Layne startled as the sound of a gun barrel clicked behind them.

78

Layne turned toward the sound, and her jaw dropped. Next to her, Scott let out an irritated grunt.

"Mom, for god's sake. Put down the gun," he said.

Helen spoke with a resolve unfamiliar to Layne, as she pointed a large revolver at Ryan. "I watched over this thing too long for the junior boy scout here to tell us he doesn't have it. Layne, where's the damned necklace?"

Layne stared.

Scott lowered his voice. "Sis, why don't you give Mom the locket. I'm not sure I still trust her with a loaded weapon."

"I heard that," Helen said.

"I...I...I don't have it." Layne said. "Uncle Fred swallowed it, then the FBI crushed it during the autopsy."

Helen's tone turned to regret. "That poor old codger. I didn't know about all this when we talked a couple of days ago, baby girl. But that explains why Fred called asking about rumaki. What the hell was he thinking trying to relocate that card all on his own? And why now, after all this time?" She shook her head, then her expression changed. "Hold on, what do you mean they crushed it?"

"Uncle Fred called you about rumaki?" Layne asked.

"I don't give two biscuits about the damned rumaki," Helen said. "What happened to the locket?"

"If I may," Ryan said, inching his way toward Helen. "Might you be the infamous Helen of Troy?"

Helen turned her attention back to Ryan. "You've heard of me?"

"You're somewhat of a legend at the bureau."

Her stance softened, and she let go a sliver of a smile, but she maintained her aim.

"You know," Ryan said. "It would be easier to sort through this if you'd put down the revolver."

"Never did care much for boy scouts, but you seem like a respectable one. All right. But don't make me regret it." Helen lowered her weapon, and Scott rushed to retrieve it.

A vein in Layne's temple throbbed. "Mom, what the hell is going on? Since when do you carry a gun?"

"Damn it, Layne," Helen said. "There's no time for that." She turned back to Ryan. "Am I to believe your candy ass bureau destroyed the card?"

"No. They told us they didn't find it."

"And you bought their story?"

"Well, considering your agent is dead, and someone set Layne up for a fairly heavy fall, yes. If we acquired it, why bother with the setup?"

Layne's eyes ballooned. "Her agent?"

"He has a point, Mom," Scott said.

"Get your father on the phone," Helen said to Scott.

Scott dialed, and Layne gaped at her mother. "What is going on?"

"Not now, baby girl." Helen waved an excusatory hand at Layne. "Could be worse. You could've been adopted by hippies."

Karl answered on the third ring, and Scott put him on speaker.

"Karl," Helen said. "Layne says the card wasn't in the locket."

Karl grumbled. "Where's my damned bucket of chicken?"

"I'll get your damned chicken, just focus with me for a minute. Is that too much to ask?"

"Yep."

"Are you drunk?"

"Nope."

"He's shittier than a fly in gasoline," Helen said, then she shouted into the phone. "Karl, are you sure Fred put the memory card into the locket?"

"Hell, yes, he put it there, but it ain't there now."

"What's that you're yakking about? Where is it?"

"When you told me the old biddy gave Layne the locket, I...er...borrowed the thing, temporarily mind you, and took out the card."

"What? You damned fool."

"You didn't think I was gonna let my Layne walk around with that stinking powder keg hanging off her neck, did ya?"

"So, where the hell is it?"

He didn't respond.

"Karl?"

"What?" Karl said. "You mean the locket?"

"No, you dip shit, the card."

"Don't you call me names, woman. It's here, in the damned—"

A crash sounded on the line, and the connection dropped.

"We need to get back to the house," Scott said. "Mom, you and Layne stay here."

"Like hell we will," Layne said.

"Watch your damned language, baby girl," Helen said. "Or hell is precisely where you'll end up."

"What about your language?"

"I'm an adult," Helen said. "Scott, I will not be left in this filthy shanty. Give me those keys."

"Okay," Scott said. "You can go with us, but I'm driving."

Ryan's head snapped to Scott. "We'll be walking into god knows what. Layne needs to stay here."

"Over your dead body," Layne said.

Sonny finally had all the information he needed. Schatz hadn't found the card, and Layne didn't have it. Layne's mother and brother didn't know where it was, but Layne's father certainly did. He'd been so close, sitting in front of that house. And it had been there the whole time. He just hoped, with the crash he'd heard on the line, that someone else hadn't gotten to it first.

Careful to move lightly over creaky porch boards, he listened to the four of them still arguing inside as he slipped down the steps. Then he allowed himself a smug grin. He'd be halfway back to the house before they stopped yelling at each other. Safely off the porch, he dropped into the underbrush and sprinted to the SUV.

79

Scott pulled the car to the curb at Layne's childhood home, but didn't stay long. Shots rang out from the kitchen window as gunfire from inside the house barraged them. He sped to the end of the block and parked on a side street. Ryan and Scott jumped from their seats and raced to the alley behind the line-up of modest suburban homes. Layne sat frozen in the back seat, uncertain what to do, while Helen dug into her enormous purse.

"Wait for us, goddamn it," Helen said.

Ryan called back to them, "You two stay in the car."

"Bullshit," Helen said as she rifled through her bag. "There's my prize."

Layne's heart thumped as her mother loaded the largest handgun she'd ever seen. "Didn't Scott take your gun?"

Her little voice kicked into gear. *Did you actually just say those words to your own mother?*

"He took my everyday gun," Helen said. "This here's my big daddy. I save it for special occasions. Come on, we've got some ass to kick."

"But Ryan told us to stay in the car."

Helen leveraged herself out of the back seat with a familiar impatience scoring her face. "You coming or not?"

The idea of traipsing into the middle of a shoot-out mortified Layne, but she didn't intend to let her seventy-eight-year-old mother go to a gun battle alone. She attempted to clear that ludicrous thought from her mind as she crept up the sidewalk behind Helen, who paraded in plain sight before stomping straight up the front walk to the house.

Layne ignored the twitch in her left eye and whisper-yelled to her mother. "What are you doing?"

Helen shouted over her shoulder. "The boys took the back, we're gonna cover the front."

Layne's whisper-yell grew shrill. "What do you mean, cover?"

Helen marched up the steps to the porch and assumed *the position.* With her feet spread wide and her knees bent, she leveled her big daddy at the front door. Her green and white flowered dress, pale yellow apron with green bric-a-brac trim, support hose sagging at her ankles, and reading glasses suspended from a gold chain around her neck completed the image.

"Okay, baby girl," she bellowed. "It's show time. You kick the door in, then get the hell out of the way."

Layne let out a squeal. "You want me to kick open the door?"

"Did I really raise you to be this much of a sissy?"

Layne gawked at her old-world German mother gone Rambo.

"Jesus, Layne. Okay," Helen said. "You slide up along the wall, turn the knob, push the door open, then get the hell out of the way."

Scott and Ryan hollered to each other, and more gunfire echoed from behind the house. Damn it. Things were not going well. Layne snuck across the grass, slithered over the porch rail, and plastered herself against the home's faux wood siding.

Her little voice shifted into high. *What the hell are you doing?*

Layne inched toward the door.

Why start listening to your mother now?

She reached for the knob.

This is suicide!

Turned out her little voice had been right all along. This definitely would not end well.

Helen nodded, and in one semi-swift motion, Layne grabbed the door handle and turned. But the door yanked opened from the inside, taking her with it, and Layne stumbled into a barricade.

"What the fuck?" the barricade said before it sent her plummeting backward. She caught herself on the doorframe as her mind strained to process what had happened.

Helen shouted, "Duck and cover, baby girl," and Layne plunged to the floor, shielding her head with her hands. A shot rang out, followed by silence, which turned to...laughter?

From inside the house Ryan chuckled. "You haven't lost it, Helen."

"Damn straight, boy scout."

"Mom," Scott said, "where'd you get that gun? Great shot, by the way."

"No thanks to Layne," Helen said. "You're lucky I didn't shoot your ass, baby girl."

Layne peeked from under her elbows. "Is it safe?"

Scott snickered. "Mom's still got a weapon in her hand..."

"Don't you sass me," Helen said to Scott. "Now, who wants apple kuchen? I made it fresh this morning. Layne, put the coffee on. Where's your father?"

Layne's gaze drifted to the dead man in the entry, and a terrifying realization hit her. "Oh no. Dad!" She leapt over the body and ran into the living room, relieved to find Karl in his favorite chair. But her heart sank as she absorbed the scene. With his body slumped to one side, his head hung tilted and lifeless. His arms draped limp over the armrests. And the newspaper and phone handset lay on the rug. "No!" She ran to him.

Helen moved past Layne to Karl, lifted one eyelid and checked for a pulse. "He was a good man," she said.

80

Layne stared at her father with tears stinging her eyes, as Helen shook her head.

"He was a good man before he started drinking," Helen said. "He's drunker than a priest on Monday. Slept through the whole damned thing."

Helen left the room, and Layne's hand went to her heart. "Oh, thank god. Dad?" She brushed his cheek with her fingers.

Karl stirred. "Huh?"

"Dad, it's me, Layne."

Karl peered at her through slits, then offered a tired smile. "My sweet angel."

"Outta the way, baby girl," Helen said.

Layne moved just as Helen threw a pitcher of water into Karl's face. He leapt from his chair, dripping wet.

"Cursed woman. I hate when you do that." His gaze darted past her to Ryan and Scott. "You didn't tell me we was havin' company," he said. "Where's my bucket of chicken?"

"It's not company, it's Scotty and Layne. And their friend here, the boy scout."

"He don't look like no boy scout."

"It's Ryan, sir." Ryan extended his hand.

Karl wiped his hand on his boxers and gave Ryan a firm grip as he looked around. "Now, what's all the commotion about?"

"Dad," Layne said. "We need you to tell us where the memory card is."

"Do I smell apple kuchen?"

Karl meandered around broken furniture, through shattered glass, and over the dead intruder before he plunked into a chair at the kitchen table. Layne followed him, steering clear of the dead man.

"Dad, the card?"

"All right already. What's the rush?" Karl reached for the cake pan.

"We had a gunfight in your entryway," Layne said. "There's a dead man on the floor. We need that card!"

"I thought the place seemed a little messier than usual," Karl said.

Helen shot him a spiteful glare.

"Dad, did the man attack you? Did he take the memory card?"

"I never saw no man." His hand went to the back of his head. "I got a nasty bump on the noggin. But it's nothing a strong cup of coffee won't fix."

Helen scoffed. "Where is the damned card, Karl?"

"Stop your fussin', woman, it's in the necklace."

"But, dad, the FBI took the locket apart searching for it."

"Not the locket, the diamonds."

"My diamonds?"

"No, the old biddy's diamonds," Karl said. "They're in the house somewhere."

"No, they're not, you idiot," Helen said. "I gave those diamonds to Layne."

"You did what? Damned woman. Why don't you ever tell me these things?"

"I did, but you were having so much fun with your old friend, Jack Daniels, you didn't hear it."

"Well, then, problem solved," Karl said. "Layne has the diamonds, so Layne has the card. Is it too damned much to ask for a cup of coffee?"

"But I don't have the diamonds," Layne said.

Helen glowered at her. "You told me you had them."

"I did. I do. I mean...Maggie has them."

Helen shook her head. "You left your grandmother's diamonds with that red-haired hussy?"

"How many times have I asked you not to call Maggie a hussy?"

"Floozy, then. Is that better?"

Layne gritted her teeth. "Holy mother of—"

"You know god damned well how I feel about blasphemy, baby girl."

"Well," Ryan interjected. "I'd like some kuchen. It smells great. Can someone tell me what it is?"

"It's cake," both women snapped.

Karl leaned over to Ryan. "Ya see, that's the crux of the issue right there. Too much alike I tell ya."

Layne and Helen busied themselves serving homemade German apple cake with coffee resembling motor oil. And it struck Layne that the group was relatively composed given the corpse in the foyer, the disaster made of her parent's home, and the sirens blaring out front.

"This one's yours," Ryan said to Scott.

"But, my kuchen."

"In hiding, remember?"

Scott put on his serious face, pulled out his badge, and met the officers at the door.

Layne adored her mother's apple kuchen. Moist, with just a touch of Fall spice and chunks of sugar-coated apple, it melted in her mouth. So why couldn't she bring herself to eat it? Yes, right. The shoot-out. The body. The sirens. The lies. Oh, the lies. She put her fork down, and while Ryan, Helen and Karl devoured their cake, she watched Scott dole out orders to the officers who'd arrived at the scene—take fingerprints here, wrap the body up over there, pack the automatic weapon in an evidence bag right here. Usual fare, she suspected, for an FBI investigation, but it gave her the willies.

She focused back on her parents. "Let me get this straight. My mother and father are retired German government agents. So was

Uncle Fred. And my brother works for the FBI. Anything else I should know?"

"That about sums it up," Helen said.

"And I've been wearing deadly secrets around my neck off and on for the last three years?"

Helen's eyes pleaded with the ceiling.

Ryan spoke with a mouth full of kuchen. "At least that explains the rumaki." He paused to swallow. "This cake is great, Helen."

"It's Layne's favorite," Helen said.

"Am I the only one disturbed by this situation?" Layne asked.

Ryan continued. "We'll call Maggie tomorrow. See if we can arrange to get the necklace without placing her at risk."

Layne huffed. "Is anyone listening to me?"

Karl looked at Ryan. "What are your intentions here, young man?"

"My intentions, sir?"

"As related to my daughter."

"Hello?" Layne said.

"Forget Layne," Helen said. "What do you intend to do with the card?"

"Thanks, Mom." Layne rubbed at a stab of pain in the back of her neck.

"Okay, let's take one thing at a time," Ryan said. "Sir, you were an agent. You understand what it's like."

"It's been a lot of years, but yeah, I remember."

"He was a good officer," Helen said. "The BKA assigned us here more than fifty years ago as liaison agents to Bureau Counterintelligence. Karl's FBI contact and partner, Martin, was your real father, Layne, and a good friend. He and his wife died in a seven-car pileup. Damned South Dakota fog is thicker than buttercream frosting on the windshield. Anyway, it devastated Karl. He said Martin was angry with him and shouldn't have been driving. Then we adopted you—it seemed like the right thing—and someone had to stay home. So, he retired and raised you kids."

For a second, tears formed in Karl's eyes, but they vanished as he scooped up more kuchen.

"I'm very sorry to hear about your partner, sir," Ryan said.

Karl shrugged. "Comes with the job, don't it?"

"To answer your question," Ryan said. "I care very much about your daughter. But you understand I have some tough decisions to make. I'm not sure I can be true to both Layne and the job. That is, if I still have one when this is over."

Karl swilled a gulp of coffee. "Fair enough. I just don't want to see my Layne's heart get broken all over again."

Layne frowned. She knew circumstances might keep her and Ryan apart, but it made her sad to think about what might happen when all of this ended. She shook her head at the irony.

"Leave it to Layne to meet a nice boy scout with no staying power," Helen said.

"Mom!"

Helen turned to Ryan. "So, what about the card?"

"I honestly don't know. Our agency wants it, as does yours. And Layne is being threatened for it. Someone is targeting her...well, your entire family, if she doesn't find it and hand it over."

"It needs to be destroyed," Helen said.

Layne felt the color drain from her face. "What?"

81

The Employer's gaze flicked from the neat pile of papers to be signed, to the shrill chime of the specialized phone on the corner of the desk. A favorable report from the man attached to the flashing pin number was expected.

"I trust you have satisfactory news," The Employer offered as a greeting.

"Not exactly," the raspy voice replied. "He's out of the picture."

"Please clarify. And be precise."

"I mean Sonny Wright is out. Done. Terminated."

"Terminated? As in deceased?"

"The old bag shot him. Fucking bullet to the chest. Local bureau took the body."

"That is impossible."

"Well, you always said he was a man who could accomplish the impossible."

The Employer expelled a loud breath. "A modicum of respect, please."

"Sure. Hey, I get it. He was supposed to be the hero, but he's gone, and we don't have the card. So, what's our next move?"

"What is Berger's status?"

"Still in custody, but I heard noise about shipping him home."

"Please ensure that does not transpire."

"You're joking, right? He's an irritant at best."

"An irritant with the potential to form a large rash on the skin of my organization if he pursues his inquiry. I will not have that. Am I clear?"

"Damn it, all right, I'll handle it. But what the fuck are we gonna do about the card?"

"With Mr. Wright out of the picture, the task falls to you."

"Without help? No fucking way. Not what I signed up for."

"This is not a volunteer assignment for the local PTA. I am paying you handsomely to do whatever it takes, and your position within the bureau gives you a unique advantage. I don't care how you do it, get me the card."

"We had an agreement. This wasn't part of the deal."

"Did I neglect to mention the sizable bonus for its acquisition?"

"Hey, there. Now we're talking."

82

Layne stared at her mother in disbelief. "Mom, you can't be serious. Destroy it? There are lives at risk here."

Helen turned in her chair and her eyes narrowed at Layne. "Listen up, baby girl. You've never listened to me before, but this time I want you to pay close attention."

Layne folded her arms over her chest. "All right, I'm listening."

"If we find the card, we need to destroy the damned thing."

Layne waited. "Because?"

"That's it," Helen said.

"That's what? Why, Mom? Why do we need to destroy it?"

"Because I'm your mother, and I said so."

"Oh my god. Why would we even consider that? What about Jenny and Dean? Destroying the card would put them at risk."

"You just don't get how this works, baby girl. They're at risk either way."

Layne made tight fists to keep from strangling her mother. "Do you see, Ryan? Do you see what I deal with?"

"Now, ladies," Ryan said.

"I don't care how it works," Layne said. "I care about my kids. And what about the American public? If there's a conspiracy against Americans worth killing over, doesn't the public have a right to know?"

"Screw the public," Helen said. "Of course I don't want to see my grandchildren in danger. But this has got to end. And when it does, that's when Jenny and Dean will be out of harm's way. There's so much you don't understand."

"Then explain it to me," Layne said. "I'm listening, but because you said so is not an explanation."

"Ladies," Ryan said again.

"Why can't you ever just trust what I'm telling you?" Helen aimed a scowl at Karl. "Stop your laughing you old dolt."

Layne let out a frustrated growl. "This is not about you, Mom. It's about—"

"Ladies!" All heads turned to Ryan. "I'd like to remind you that this is my operation. It's my job at risk, my exit plan in play, and my responsibility to make sure no harm comes to anyone—not Layne, not her children, not the American public, not anyone. My op. My way."

Neither woman responded, and Karl chuckled.

"First time I seen them two speechless in years," he said, spooning more kuchen into his mouth.

The two women leveled identical glares at Karl.

"I'm curious, Helen," Ryan said. "If the data on the card is so dangerous, why didn't you destroy it when you had the chance?"

Helen sighed. "I followed orders. We all knew release of that information could do serious damage to the American economy. And this country's financial system is too integral to the global economy to assume there wouldn't be far-reaching repercussions. There isn't one civilized nation that wants what is on that card to go public, but every agency wants it in their back pocket. An insurance policy of sorts. Ours was no different." Helen cast a patronizing glare at Layne. "There, baby girl. There's your explanation. Happy?"

"But how do the other agencies know what the card contains if we don't?" Ryan asked.

"Still wide-eyed, I see. You might not be privy to the contents, boy scout, but somebody above you sure as hell is. Not in detail mind you, but it doesn't take much to get the gist."

"So, the BKA got their leverage, but you had to go dark to protect the data."

"It wasn't just about the leverage. The card was going up for auction. If we hadn't secured it, who knows what the outcome might have been. And we understood what we were giving up. Safeguarding the card meant living in hiding, even from our own government, for the rest of our lives. But we were already pretty damned old, so it didn't much matter."

"I assume you know what's on the card?"

Helen got up from the table, poured everyone more coffee, then cleared plates and silverware.

"Helen?"

"You were right, boy scout. I should've destroyed the thing when I had it in my hand. Then there wouldn't be a damned shooter dripping blood in my entry hall. Do you have any idea how hard it is to remove bloodstains from carpet?"

"You're not going to tell us what's on the card," Ryan said.

"If your own agency doesn't trust you with that information, why the hell would I?"

"Point taken. Do you know who else is looking for it?"

"It's always been a long list—every foreign agency, industry competitors, economic terrorists, and the jackass executives whose necks are on the chopping block if the data leaks. They all have different motives, but the result is the same—public access to the information causes destruction on many levels."

Helen looked over at Layne. "What the hell are you blubbering about?"

Layne sniffed. "I'm not blubbering. It's just that all this time you've guarded this secret, worrying about the future of the entire world. All the things you gave up."

"Oh, poppycosh. We had long since retired when we went after the card, and it was a real kick in the pants to be back in action. I'll admit, I wasn't as light on my feet as the old days, but I still had it. Forty-eight hours of reconnaissance, then in and out. Poor youngin' holding the card never saw us old geezers coming." Helen smirked. "And I wouldn't have had my life any other way, including getting married to that rat bastard sitting there and raising you kids. Now stop your sniveling and help me clean up." Helen turned to Ryan. "As for you, boy scout, I hate to admit it, but tonight's little soiree just about did me in. I can tell you got the metal in you, so I'm trusting you to do right by the card and by our Layne. Do whatever data analysis is needed, then make sure nobody else can, and afterward you can marry my daughter."

Layne nearly spit her coffee all over the table, and her little voice came to the party in rare form.

I can see it now, your mother sitting in the church at your wedding with her big daddy tucked into her purse. Your dad having a few too many high balls before he tries to walk you down the aisle. Maggie, in her transparent madame of honor gown. And Scott, hitting on every woman with a pulse. Fun times.

83

Layne closed her eyes in an unsuccessful attempt to stifle both her little voice and the damned tears she couldn't seem to control. Then Scott strolled back into the kitchen, and Helen regarded him skeptically.

"You have everything sorted in there already?" Helen asked.

"Body's long gone, and the local Fibbies were anxious to get things wrapped up," Scott said. "Intruder ID'd as Sonny Wright, gun for hire. He's got federal allegations up the wazoo. An elusive son of a bitch. Mom, you gave some local bureau guy a major hard on."

"Just what I always wanted. And watch your language you little shit."

"One of his weapons shoots a 7.62," Scott said. "The same caliber that tagged Johnny, right?"

Ryan took in a deep breath. "Yes, it is."

Helen put a plate of kuchen and a cup of coffee on the table in front of Scott, then handed him a dishtowel. "You've got an awful lot of cleanup to do in here."

Scott looked at Layne. "What's up with her? Why can't she do it?"

"I tried," Helen said. "She's useless. Probably her monthly."

Layne grunted her objection through a tissue.

"You clean, Scotty," Helen said. "It builds character."

Scott handed Layne a folded sheet of paper and a small photo. "Found these in the dead guy's wallet. Looks like he was a fan."

Layne's eyes widened as she stared at the image. "It's me, in the black dress." She showed it to Ryan.

"It's a nice picture of you," Ryan said. "But that is disturbing. The man at dinner—you told me his name was Sonny. I can't imagine he used his real name, but that would explain the picture." He unfolded the paper. "And this is the original summary page Seth sent me. I put this in the packet for Marco. How the hell—"

Layne's pocket vibrated and "Love Shack" filled the room. Her head dropped. "Not again."

Scott's brows lifted in question.

"It's a long story," Ryan said. He turned to Layne, but her palm went up.

"I know." She pressed the speaker button on her phone, but didn't get the chance to speak.

"This is an unfortunate turn of events," Siri said to the group. "And a huge loss to me personally, as well as to our organization. Eliminating one of our assets was a severe misjudgment on your part. You should have given us the card. Trust me, Ms. Stevens, what comes next will not be appealing."

The call ended, and Layne stared at her cell.

"Well, ain't that a bitch," Helen said. "Baby girl, you leave my grandchildren to Scotty and me. We'll make certain they're protected. You two just focus on ending this mess."

Scott pulled his phone out of his pocket and sent a few text messages while Helen cleared the rest of the dishes from the table. When he was finished, he put his hand over Layne's. I have people contacting the Chico and San Diego PD's, and we're having Dean and Jenny brought in. You have nothing to worry about.

Layne nodded, but worrying about her kids was rooted in her DNA.

"Scotty," Helen said, "not that I don't think you're capable, but I'm handing this thing over to Ryan here to take the lead. He just seems better equipped to handle this particular situation." She glanced at Ryan. "We talked about this. Why do you look so surprised?"

"You used my name."

"Oh. Well, don't get used to it, boy scout." She let a small grin slip and then turned back to Scott. "Are you okay with that, Scotty?"

"Fine by me," Scott said. "Saves me the trouble of finding a new job, and now I won't have to deal with psycho Siri. No offense, Ry."

"None taken. I'm as good as fired already. And I'm looking forward to dealing with psycho Siri. But I'm still going to need your help."

"Whatever I can do."

Ryan stood, and Layne looked up at him. "What are you doing?"

"We should get going," Ryan said.

"You mean outside?"

"It'll be difficult to get back to the cabin if we don't go outside."

"But Siri's out there. She must be out there. How else could she know?"

Scott answered. "First, sis, I'm pretty sure the caller wasn't actually Siri. And second, the shooter must have had a partner. And since the partner isn't in the morgue with his pal, it means the chicken-shit ran. There were uniforms crawling all over this place. They did a full sweep inside and out. If the person who called was ever here, they're long gone."

Layne weighed the idea of facing a crazed psycho killer over staying with her parents. Facing the psycho killer won.

Ryan put a hand on her shoulder. "You okay?"

She shrugged.

"Scott," Ryan said. "Can you drop us back at the lake house? We'll call you when we get a line on the necklace. Karl, once we have it, I'll need you to help me locate the card. If you don't mind."

Confusion crossed Karl's face for a second, and then he smiled. "Just say the word."

"Well," Ryan said, "it was a pleasure to meet you both. And the kuchen was excellent. Thank you."

Helen walked them to the door and pulled Layne aside, then spoke so everyone could hear. "As boy scouts go, I like this one, baby girl. Don't screw this up."

"Uh huh. I love you too, Mom." She waved back toward the kitchen. "Bye, Dad. Love you."

"Love you too, darlin'. You be careful."

When they arrived back at the cabin, Layne gave Scott a tight embrace. "I always knew you'd do great things, even if you couldn't tell me about them."

Scott kissed Layne on the cheek. "I always knew that about you, too, sis. And don't worry about the kids. Mom and I will handle it. Well, mostly me, because besides fantastic looks and an amazing personality, I've got connections."

"Uh huh," she said, shaking her head. Scott shook Ryan's hand, they exchanged a few words, and then Layne closed and locked the door behind him. She checked all of the locks on all of the windows, drug herself down the hallway, fell backward onto the bed, fully clothed, and lay there staring at the ceiling, unable to move. Ryan climbed on the bed next to her and trailed a finger up her arm.

"Don't even think about it," she said through a yawn.

84

Layne stirred at the sound of someone moving in the bedroom. From under tired lids, she spied bright morning sun, a thin towel fastened around a chiseled waist, and bare skin glistening with the moisture left by a hot shower. She watched firm arm and chest muscles flex, as strong fingers raked through damp hair. And she opened her eyes a little wider when the towel dropped, revealing other rock hard, well-defined muscles.

Her little voice was also awake. *Oh my goodness,* it said. *That should be illegal.*

Layne heard caramel in the recesses of her mind...

"Morning, gorgeous."

Oh shit. Her eyes cut to Ryan's face and she attempted an apologetic grin. "Morning."

He let out a low chuckle. "You know, we have a lot to do today. But if you keep ogling the family jewels like their dessert, we may have to change our plans."

"Oh my gosh. I'm...I...I wasn't—"

"Oh yes, you were. And thank you. It's nice to know you find me tastier than those roasted olives."

She lifted a brow. "It's the roasted figs you have to worry about."

He gave her a mischievous smile as he climbed onto the bed, and she became acutely aware that she lay on top of the blankets with all clothing but a pair of Ryan's boxer briefs stripped off.

"Nice pajamas," Ryan said.

"Darned wood stove. That thing puts out a lot of heat."

He slid close and kissed her bare collarbone. "I can think of other ways to put out some heat."

"But I haven't brushed my teeth," she said.

"I'm not interested in your teeth at the moment."

His lips grazed along her skin and over her breasts. Layne resisted letting her eyes fall shut at the thrill he stirred inside her.

"Didn't you say there were things we needed to do?" she asked.

"We need to call Maggie, but it's probably too early for that."

She grasped at one last attempt to escape the bedroom for a quick scrub with a toothbrush. "You're not hungry for breakfast?"

His hand skimmed across her waist and down over her hip. "I'm very hungry," he said. Then his tongue swirled around her nipple, and she drew in a breath.

It would appear you're the only person in the room concerned about your dental hygiene, her little voice noted.

"Okay, forget breakfast," Layne said, combing her fingers through his hair as she enjoyed *all* of the sensations Ryan was capable of creating with his tongue.

After many deliciously steamy moments in the bedroom, followed by several burning hot moments preparing not so delicious coffee on the wood stove, Layne sat at the kitchen table drinking the god-awful muck, and reveling in her yummiest memories of the last twenty-four hours. But her thoughts were interrupted by the sound of Ryan's voice in the bedroom.

A few minutes later, Ryan joined her in the kitchen with his phone in his hand.

"Who was that?" Layne asked.

Ryan picked up one of the old ceramic mugs Layne had set out for them and poured some coffee. "Who was what?"

"I thought I heard you talking to someone."

He took a sip and winced. "Marco again. Just checking in. Is this coffee?"

"I found it in the cupboard. I read somewhere that unopened coffee will stay good for years. Either good is relative, or it's been a lot of years."

He nodded.

"So, you said something to him about this being the only way?"

"We were talking about the diamonds. In secret spy code, of course." He grinned.

"Ah," she said. Something felt off, but she couldn't place it. "Then, should I call?"

"Might as well get this ball rolling."

Layne put her cell phone on speaker and tapped Maggie's number.

"Maggie Malone, it's your dime, but it's my time."

"Hey, it's me."

"Ohmygod! Where are you? I've been worried sick. Were you kidnapped? Are you all right? Is that scrumptious man with you? Has he taken advantage of you yet? Tell me everything."

"I don't have a lot of time. I need to know if you still have my things?"

"How can you be so materialistic at a time like this? Honestly, I'm surprised at you. Have you been brainwashed?"

"No, and be careful what you say here."

"You mean..."

"Are you with me?"

"I think so," Maggie said.

"Do you remember the things I usually keep in the safe?"

"Yes."

"Do you still have them?"

"Yesssssss."

"All of them?"

"Of course. What kind of friend do you think I am?"

"You are a goddess of a friend. Thank you."

Ryan made a slashing motion across his neck.

"Correct answer," Maggie said. "Now, will you please tell me—"

"Listen, I'm fine, but I've gotta go. Don't do anything with those items. I'll be in touch." She tapped the end button.

"That wasn't too bad," Ryan said. "Excellent work, Agent Stevens."

Layne beamed. "What do we do now?"

"We contact Scott."

"Scott? What about me? I'm right here."

"I need him to help me steal the diamonds."

"Oh," she said. "Wait, why wouldn't Maggie just give us the diamonds?"

"I don't want to put Maggie in that position. If they're stolen, she's not involved."

"Oh," she said again. "But..."

Ryan sent her the look. The man look. The one that said, *if you keep questioning me, my pride might be wounded, and I might start to get upset.*

"Okay, I'll call Scott," Layne said.

"First we'll need a plan. You can help me with that."

Layne smiled. After they'd formulated what she thought was a darned good plan, she sent a somewhat cryptic text message to Maggie. The reply from Maggie read, "10-4," followed by a Latin dancer emoji.

Ryan studied Maggie's response. "Think she got the meaning?"

"Who knows with Maggie."

Next, Layne called Scott.

85

Scott, Karl, and Helen arrived at the cabin at just after seven pm. Ryan explained that, in theory, Maggie had left the necklace for them and would be at her monthly dinner schmoozing network executives until eleven.

"Are we planning to search the whole place?" Scott asked.

"Hopefully not," Ryan said. "Layne sent Maggie a cryptic text message asking her to leave the diamonds in her top dresser drawer. I just hope she understood it."

"Man, I've always wanted to go through Maggie Malone's underwear drawer," Scott said.

"Don't get too worked up there, cowboy," Ryan said. "We've got a job to do."

After a forty-minute drive, Scott parked the car a block away from a series of upscale townhouses overlooking Southern California's coastline.

"I have the address," Ryan said. "We'll need to count them off in front so we can get to it from behind."

"No worries, Ry. I got this."

Ryan raised a brow. "How many times have you been here?"

"Just once. But she's got these bulgy, square wind chimes hanging in the back. Says they remind her of sparkly new condom packages waiting to be unleashed."

"Sounds like Maggie," Ryan said.

"You gotta admit, buddy. She's a temptress."

Ryan smirked. Temptress was one word for Maggie. They headed to the back alley.

"There." Scott pointed to what looked like a slow-motion commercial for wrapped prophylactics blowing in the ocean breeze.

Ryan pulled out a small set of tools to work the lock on the patio door, and when they were inside, he used a penlight to lead them up the stairs to the master suite. The top middle drawer of Maggie's dresser revealed an inviting gap, and Ryan let Scott do the honors while he held the light. A pair of hot pink, liberally feathered thong underwear greeted them. Right under those, black, crotchless bikini panties. And just below that, a red, heart-shaped piece of material tethered by thin strings.

Scott groaned. "She's playing with me, Ry."

"She doesn't even know you're here. Stop screwing around and get the necklace."

Ecstasy danced across Scott's face as he dug his hand into the drawer and came up with a brown velvet jewelry case. He handed it over to Ryan and took his time to re-arrange Maggie's enticing array of lingerie.

"Scott," Ryan said.

No response.

"Scott," he said again.

Then a female voice came from the darkness behind them. "Did you find what you were looking for?"

Ryan began to turn, but the voice warned against it. "Don't you dare move."

"Why?" Scott asked. "Do you have a gun?"

"What if I did?"

He whimpered. "That would be so damn hot."

Ryan turned around. "Maggie, what are you doing here?"

"I live here."

"But you're supposed to be out schmoozing or something."

"Yes, I am. But I was dying to see how you planned to get into my drawers. You made quick work of my back door. I'm equally fascinated and disturbed by that. But bringing Scott with you, well, this is a yummy surprise. Is there something you'd like to tell me, Scott?"

Scott took one more pass around the drawer before extricating his hand from the silky lingerie. "Yes, there is. I can think of many ways to get into your drawers."

A smile spread over Maggie's face, and her lips parted, but Ryan cut her off. "Scott, we've got to go," he said. "Maggie, we were never here."

"Not so fast," Maggie said. She sauntered over to Scott and whispered in his ear.

"Scott," Ryan said.

Scott ignored him.

"Maggie," Ryan said. "Scott and I need to leave."

Maggie didn't acknowledge him either.

Ryan rubbed his forehead. "Would the two of you please holster it?"

No response.

"I'm leaving now," Ryan said as he turned toward the bedroom door.

86

After several rousing games of gin rummy accompanied by her parent's usual bickering, Layne desperately needed a few minutes of peace, and she excused herself to use the bathroom.

Helen shot Layne a scowl. "But we're about to start a hand."

"Mom, I need to go."

"In the middle of the damned game?"

"Let the girl pee," Karl said.

Helen scoffed. "But I'm ahead."

Layne got up from the table and headed toward the hallway. "I promise to let you win when I get back." She grinned with the pleasure of knowing exactly how to get a rise out of her mother.

"You'll do no such thing," Helen retorted. "Ha. Let me win. I tell you, kids today. No respect."

Layne walked the narrow hall to the tiny bathroom and tried to tune out her still squabbling parents. Her dad asked where they kept the whiskey, and her mom called him a stupid old fool not in need of any more booze. He called her an old battle-ax, and she threatened to show him a real battle-ax soon enough. This felt normal to Layne. How had she missed the whole my-entire-family-is-made-up-of-spies thing?

She flipped on the bathroom light, gazed at herself in the mirror, and took in a deep breath of the crisp night air drifting through the open bathroom window. The last several days had taken a toll on both her physical and mental health. She leaned closer to the mirror to inspect the dark circles under her eyes, then she froze as the tiniest creak of the rusty old tub behind the shower curtain filled the room. But before she could run, the shower curtain flew open, the bathroom door slammed shut, and her reflection was no longer alone.

"If you even think about screaming," the intruder said, "I will shoot you where you stand."

The command came with a gun pointed at the back of Layne's head. She froze.

"Here is how this will work. You'll tell me where the card is, then I'm going to kill you."

The initial shock wore off, and Layne responded with as much defiance as she could muster. "If you're going to kill me anyway, why would I tell you where the card is?"

"Well, it's either you who dies, or you and those blathering idiots you call parents. It's your choice."

Layne's voice wavered. "My parents are not idiots."

A strong hand bunched into Layne's hair, yanking her head back, and the gun stabbed at her jaw.

"Tell me where the card is *now*."

Layne's knees weakened beneath her, and she fought back tears. "Do you promise not to hurt them?"

"Cross my heart and hope to die. I've got a fucking piece to your head, do you think I'm going to promise you anything?"

Helen's voice rang out from the short hallway. "Layne, what the hell is taking so long in there? We need to finish the damned game."

Layne's assailant growled into her ear. "Make a decision."

Helen came to the door. "What was that?"

She worked to control the quiver in her voice. "Nothing, Mom. I'll be out in a minute."

"Well, hurry up for christ sake."

"Okay, Mom. Love you."

"Yeah, yeah. Get out here and play already." Layne heard her mother grumbling as she walked back down the hall.

"Good choice. Now, where is it?"

Layne tried to come up with a plan, a way to stall, or a way out, but her brain wouldn't cooperate.

"Where...the fuck...is the card?"

Deadly conspiracy or not, it wasn't worth her parent's lives. "It's hidden in my grandmother's diamond necklace."

"And where is the necklace?"

"Ryan and Scott went to get it."

"You mean the card isn't here?"

Layne's eyes filled with tears, adding frustration at her own weakness to the broad spectrum of emotions roiling inside her. But this time her voice didn't falter. "I believe I just told you Ryan and Scott are out getting the diamonds."

"Shit. Fucking shit. Goddamn it. That's it. I can't take this anymore. You die now."

Voices came from the front of the cabin. Thank god, Ryan and Scott.

"Wait," Layne said. "They're back."

But the grip on her hair tightened as her face was shoved into the sink. And hope eluded her as the cold steel of the gun's muzzle dug into the hollow of her cheek.

87

Traffic thinned on the highway back to Minnow Lake, and Ryan looked over at Scott, who'd spent the entire trip staring at what appeared to be a business card.

"Never pictured you as the sedan type," Ryan said. "But I gotta admit, this thing handles pretty well."

"Uh huh," Scott replied.

He glanced over again. "What did Maggie give you that has you so absorbed?"

"It's her personal card, with her personal phone number on it."

"Didn't you already have her personal number?"

"Oh, Ry. You don't understand. This is her personal, personal number. Many have tried, but very few are granted access to this number. Do you know what that means?

"I'd rather not."

"Would it seem desperate to call her now?"

"Jesus, Scott. A little focus here. You can call Maggie later. And yes, that would seem desperate. What's going on? Is the ultimate player getting soft in his old age?"

Scott let out a sigh. "She might be the one, Ry. *The* one. Know what I mean?"

Ryan kept his eyes trained on the highway. When they arrived back at the cabin, Helen and Karl sat near the roaring fire of the wood stove, arguing over a game of cards.

"Watch her," Ryan said. "If she's anything like Layne, she's a card shark."

Karl chuckled. "Are you kidding? She ain't beat me at Rummy in fifty-seven years."

"That's a lie and you know it."

"Is not."

Ryan scanned the room. "Where's Layne?"

"She's in the damned bathroom," Helen said. "Been in there forever. Screwed up the whole game. And she's acting strange, even for Layne."

"How so?"

"I yell at her to get the hell out of there, and she says she loves me. Odd, I tell ya. Damned monthly."

"Hunh." Ryan headed toward the hallway to find Layne, but Karl got up from his chair.

"So, do ya have the necklace?" Karl asked.

"Oh, right." Ryan went to the table and opened the velvet case. "Here it is."

"That's the one," Karl said. "Take it out for me, would ya? The fingers don't work so well as they used to."

Scott moved in for a closer look, as Ryan removed the strand of diamonds from the case.

"It's darn near impossible to detect," Karl said. "But the card is embedded in the stone thirteenth from the female clasp."

Ryan inspected the necklace. "Clasps have genders?"

"Don't you kids know nothin' these days? This here pointy thing is the male, and this open thing is the female. You insert the male into the female, and the union is sealed."

Scott whispered to Ryan, "Did he just make that up?"

"Hell no, I didn't make it up," Karl said. "And I'm old, not deaf."

Ryan scrutinized the thirteenth gem. "Something must have made you pick the number thirteen for you to remember it all this time."

"Layne's mother and I were married on Friday the thirteenth." Karl revealed a crooked smile. "How's that for an omen?"

"How did you get the card into the diamond?" Ryan asked.

"You sure ask a lot of questions. Before I joined the agency, I worked for a jeweler in Berlin. Taught me a fair piece, like how to hollow out a gem so it was imperceptible to the untrained eye. He would sell it for its regular carat value and use the extra chips to make other jewelry. Not very ethical I s'pose, but it wasn't easy making ends meet in those days."

"Karl, you are full of surprises. How do we get it out?"

"You have to destroy the stone. But carefully, or you'll destroy the card along with it."

Ryan moved to the wood stove for more light and studied the diamond, hoping to discern the tiny card.

Helen edged in next to him. "I changed my mind, boy scout. My vote is we obliterate the damned thing and end this once and for all."

Scott's voice stammered behind them. "Uh...hello, Director Hall."

"I hope you're not talking about the card," the Director said.

Ryan turned, sliding his hands into his pockets, along with the necklace. "Sir, I'm surprised to see you here."

"I could say the same for you," the Director said. "Are you going to introduce me to your friends?"

Ryan cleared his throat. "Director Mitch Hall, these are Layne Stevens' parents, Karl and Helen Roberts, and you know Scott."

"Roberts," Director Hall said to Scott. "So, Ms. Stevens is your..."

"Layne is my sister, sir," Scott said.

Director Hall nodded. "And that makes these two our BKA liaison agents. Am I right?"

"Yes, sir," Scott said.

"Intriguing." The director called over his shoulder, "Okay fellas, you can come in."

Several local FBI agents entered the cabin followed by Marco and Agent Short.

Ryan's jaw tightened. "How did you find us?"

"You always were a creature of habit, Cooke," Director Hall said. "It wasn't difficult to put together."

"I suspected this went higher than Rennick, but frankly sir, I'm disturbed and disappointed by your involvement in this."

"My involvement in what? Explain yourself, Cooke."

"Did you not order Rennick to falsify the Stevens' profile?"

"Of course not. But even if I had, how could Rennick falsify one of our secure documents? Ryan, you've gone too far this time. Marco, take Cooke into custody."

"I'm afraid I can't do that," Marco said. "As much as I respect you, sir, I'm not sure I trust you."

Director Hall shot a glare at Marco. "Are you out of your mind? What about you, Short?"

"I'm with you, sir," Agent Short said. "It's unclear to me whether Agent Cooke's recent behavior has been in the best interest of the agency."

"What the fuck, man?" Marco said. "Sir, Ryan is telling the truth. Either Rennick worked on her own, or somebody here is lying."

A loud sneeze came from the hallway. Then Layne emerged with an arm crooked tight around her neck and a pistol shoved into her side.

"Stop with the fucking sneezing," Rennick said, tightening her hold on Layne's neck.

"Maybe if your cat didn't sleep in your clothes," Layne said.

"Rennick," Director Hall said, "what the hell are you doing?"

"This bitch is a foreign op, sir." Rennick moved Layne further into the room. "She has everyone duped, but not me. I'm ensuring they don't end up with the card."

Director Hall spoke with forced restraint. "Have you all gone insane? Rennick, put your gun down."

"Sir, if I lower my weapon, Cooke and Stevens could escape. He's working with her."

The director cast a questioning stare at Ryan.

"No, sir. My agenda is the bureau's agenda."

Marco shook his head at Rennick. "Man, you are one seriously whacked-out chick."

Director Hall held up a hand for quiet. "Agent Rennick, I am ordering you to relinquish your weapon. Short, we'll need that gun."

Several agents pointed firearms at Rennick, and Agent Short pulled latex gloves from his jacket pocket and closed in on Rennick. She swung her pistol at Agent Short, then at Ryan, then back to Layne.

"But, sir," Rennick said. "Cooke stole the card."

"That's ridiculous. Give Short the gun, damn it," the director said.

Defiance set on Rennick's face, and her arm clamped like a vice around Layne's neck. Ryan stepped toward them, Rennick shifted, and Layne rammed her elbow into Rennick's ribs.

A shot fired, Rennick doubled over, and Layne went down.

88

Everything slowed as Layne watched Rennick stumble backward onto the floor. Time stood still when her gaze met Ryan's, and then lowered to the bloodstain forming on his shirt. And her heart stopped when she realized the bullet from Rennick's gun had barreled straight into Ryan's chest. He fell, and Layne scrambled across the floor to reach him. Scott raced to contain Rennick, while Agent Short grabbed the gun.

With his pain evident and his voice week, Ryan stared up at her. "I'm sorry, Layne. I'm so sorry. I did what I had to do."

"Shhh," Layne said. "Don't try to talk."

"Listen to me, Layne. You deserve the truth."

Her eyes narrowed against a waterfall of tears. "What truth? What are you trying to say?"

"I used you, Layne. I used you to get to the card," he said, struggling for breath. "You're a nice woman, and I hated to do it, but it was my job. I'm sorry."

She shook her head. "What? No. That can't be."

Ryan reached for her hand, but she pulled away from him. "You used me? It was all a lie?"

"Remember, gorgeous. Remember what I told you."

His eyes closed, and tears streamed down her face as she looked up at Marco, but Marco's gaze shifted away from her. When she turned back to Ryan, his labored breathing had stopped, and the hand that had reached for hers lay on the floor at his side, next to the diamonds.

Layne scooped up the necklace, stood, and stared at Ryan's lifeless body. "You son of a bitch," she yelled at him. "You don't get to betray me. I won't go through that. Not again. I won't..." her words turned to uncontrollable sobs as Scott took her into his arms and stroked her hair.

"I know, sis. I know."

She buried her tears in Scott's chest. "Is it me?"

"It's not you, Layne. It's shitty circumstances."

"But first it was...and now...he can't die, Scott, he can't die. I need to know."

"Layne. It's not you. None of it was your fault. Not then. Not now."

Scott moved Layne aside as the paramedics rushed in and set about the work of reviving him. After a short time, one of them turned to Director Hall.

"I'm sorry," the paramedic said. "He's gone."

The room fell silent as they lifted Ryan's body onto a stretcher and wheeled it out to the porch.

Director Hall broke the silence with a question aimed at Marco. "You were working with Ryan on this the entire time?"

"Yes, sir," Marco said.

"What was supposed to happen here?"

Marco's voice seared with anger. "We were supposed to end up with the card. Now we're back where we started, thanks to her." Marco nudged his chin at Agent Rennick.

"That's not true," Layne said. She used Scott's arm to steady herself, but her hand trembled as she held out the necklace. "It's right here."

For a moment, all eyes fixed on Layne with shock and disbelief, except for Helen's. There, Layne saw the familiar flicker of disappointment. But she steeled herself for what she knew had to be done. As several agents rushed at her, she dropped the necklace through the hole at the top of the wood stove and watched it fall into the blazing fire below. The agents shoved Layne aside, and gasps and shouts erupted through the cabin. The diamonds settled into a pile of hot embers, smoldering in the contained heat of the stove. One of the local agents sprinted for the cold pot of coffee to douse the flames. Another stabbed at the coals with a fire poker through the opening on top, trying to hook the strand, but it fell to pieces, and the diamonds turned to dust.

Director Hall's eyes bore into Layne's. "What happened? Diamonds don't melt."

"They don't," Karl interjected. "Not technically. But they'll sure as hell turn to brimstone in a fire that hot."

Director Hall looked at Karl, and then back at Layne. "I assume that necklace contained the card?"

She wiped the tears from her face and sneered at the director. "What card?"

The Director hesitated before he spoke again, then his hands clenched. "Roberts, take your sister and parents to the town car. You ride along with them. Marco, get Rennick out of here. Short, you stay and help me work through this mess."

Helen paused at the door long enough to give Director Hall a spiteful stare. Karl hung his head and followed, but stopped to regard the scene with sadness and regret etched on his face. Layne walked out of the cabin without a glance behind her. They waited in the back of the town car for Scott to finish giving his statement, and her mother looked over at her.

"Your grandmother is cursing like a sailor from her grave over those diamonds. But I'm proud of you, baby girl. You did good."

Layne felt herself detach from the scene as the paramedics wheeled Ryan's body, face covered, to their van. It departed—no blare of sirens, no urgency, no undue grief from the other agents—just another day on the job. Why had she done it? Why had she put her trust in him? She should have learned her lesson the first time. Nothing good ever came from trust.

89

A cool Southern California night sky descended on the safe house as Rennick resisted her escort to a waiting town car. Marco opened the door, and an agent tried to deposit her into the back seat. She scoffed as even in handcuffs she fended him off. Then a taller agent placed one hand on the top of her head, another on her arm, and shoved her inside. Hundreds of crickets chirped into the twilight in unison, and she wondered, briefly, if they were mocking her.

They arrived at the local bureau, and she waited for several hours in a hard metal chair, her wrists still bound behind her, stinging under the tight grip of the steel cuffs. Sweat formed under her clothes, and she struggled to breathe against the sticky odor of urine mixed with smoke. She glanced around. How could she take the local bureau seriously when their interrogation room had been converted from a men's bathroom? Her glare settled on BKA Officer Hans Berger, who sat next to her, his hands also behind his back in cuffs. He turned away. Finally, the door to the small room opened.

"Well, well, well, Rennick. I've had dreams about finding you in handcuffs, but the circumstances were slightly different."

"Fuck you, Roberts."

"Aw. Come on, Sher. Is that any way to treat your favorite academy instructor?"

"I don't have anything to say to you."

"Don't flatter yourself, Rennick. I'm not here for you."

Scott flipped a chair around, straddled it, and looked away from her. "Hans. Can I call you Hans?"

Berger didn't respond.

"Hans, do you understand why we flew you down here?"

Again, no response.

"See, word around the water cooler is that Rennick swings both ways."

Berger's eyebrows jumped, and Scott snickered. "By that, I mean both FBI and BKA. Although what you were thinking makes a great visual, doesn't it? How'd you two lovebirds meet, anyway?"

Berger stiffened. "We are not lovebirds."

Rennick turned to Hans. "You don't have to talk to him. He's a teacher, not a doer. And he carries no weight in this building."

Scott chuckled. "And that is where you're wrong, little missy. Well, that, and just about everything else you've said or done in the last seventy-two hours." He turned his focus. "Hans, please continue."

Berger looked at Rennick. "He believes you are a traitor to your country. We must clear your name."

Rennick shook her head as Hans continued. "Sherry and I met several years ago at the International Cybersecurity Conference in Las Vegas. We attended the same session, and we were placed on a breakout team together. She was the smartest on the team. Versed well above the other participants, including myself. I had questions regarding some of her strategies, and she agreed to review them with me. Afterward, we would periodically email or call. But there was nothing romantic in our exchanges. And there has never been any confidential information given between the two of us. Our relationship was strictly professional—for growth in our respective roles, and sharing of new technologies or techniques. Nothing more. But I was instructed by my superiors to terminate our communications, so we have not spoken in some time. I called her when I learned the card was missing, because I had nowhere else to turn. She attempted to help."

"Techniques, eh?" Scott's eyebrows bounced. "Care to describe any of those?"

Rennick scoffed. "Is that really all you heard?"

"I like to home in on the key pieces of information."

"Here's a key piece of information for you," Rennick said. "Your little secret is out."

"And what secret is that?"

"That the vic in the closet was your uncle."

Scott's lips tightened.

"And I know who killed him."

Scott lifted a brow. "Because it was you?"

"Hell, no. Your sister did it. Little miss cooking show."

"And you know this how?"

"Pull your head out of your ass, Roberts. She's a foreign op, plain as day."

"Let me get this straight, Rennick. You want me to believe that a woman I've known my entire life, who picks up spiders with her ski gloves to take them outside rather than kill them, is a foreign agent. But you're not."

Rennick didn't respond.

"Someone lifted a one-hundred-and-eighty-pound man onto a hook in that closet. You know who has the strength and the height to pull that off, Rennick? I'll give you a hint. It's not Layne."

She directed her gaze to the small window on the far wall.

"But let's suppose for half a second that was true," Scott said. "If Layne was the bad guy, why did you shoot Agent Cooke?"

Her attention snapped to Scott. "I should've capped her when I had the chance."

Berger gaped at her.

"Honestly," Rennick said. "I can't figure if Cooke was in it with the bitch all along, or if he was just too blinded by his dick to notice she was playing him."

Scott slammed his palms on the table and leaned in. "So, you admit to killing Agent Ryan Cooke?"

"Hell no," Rennick said. "My weapon misfired."

"Damn it, Rennick. You were one of the best sharpshooters at Quantico. Are you actually claiming a weapon misfire when you hit your target dead in the chest?"

"You saw it. The bitch elbowed me."

Scott sat back down and waited for several minutes before speaking again. "What about Johnny?"

"What about him?"

"Jesus, Rennick. Can I get you a martini to go with that ice-cold heart?"

"You always did know how to sweet talk the ladies."

He spoke through gritted teeth. "Johnny?"

"Not me. But not for lack of trying. Somebody beat me to it."

"Excuse me?"

"I wanted to scare the bitch. I took a position on the roof across the street, had my sniper rifle aimed at the fricking still life on the wall, and right before I could take the shot, a shooter in the apartment below me tagged Johnny."

"Someone else nailed Johnny," he said.

"Unfortunately, yes," Rennick said. "I almost got to her at the park, too, then that fricking horse appeared out of nowhere. What's a woman gotta do to get off a goddamned shot?"

"You planned to shoot my sister at Golden Gate Park?"

"No, you asshole, listen to my words. I planned to shoot *at* your precious sister. I had every intention of missing."

Scott cast a glance at the mirrored wall, then fixed again on Rennick. "How'd you know about the safe house?" he asked.

"I didn't."

"Holy christ, Rennick. You were at the safe house. I saw you there myself. Are you gonna try to deny that too?"

"I didn't know about the safe house. I had a feeling something was up. So, the day before the beach op, I followed Cooke. He hid some shit ass car in the brush about a mile from the boardwalk, and I put a tracker on it. I checked in with the team the next morning, then faked some nasty PMS shit so I could leave and wait for the tracker to move. It didn't take a genius to figure Cooke was up to no good. And it took even less brilliance to follow him. Why is it, do you think, that I'm the only one who figured it out? Damned idiots."

Scott pursed his lips. "Okay, let's get back to Schatz."

"Do you have a fricking disorder? I already told you. I did not kill that fat, old bastard, and you're either too stupid or too naive to wake up and smell the truth."

"Which is?"

Rennick dropped her head to her chest and then called toward the door, "Guard...next imbecile please."

Scott glared at Rennick and then got up from his chair.

"Roberts," Rennick said.

His hands clenched. "What?"

"I need you to make arrangements for Uzi. My neighbor can't keep her."

Scott shook his head. "Marco was right, you are one seriously whacked-out chick."

"Promise me."

"I promise I will deal with your damned cat."

HE STOOD behind the glass with Director Hall and watched.

"Roberts is good," the director said. "But Rennick's not gonna crack."

"She's a real piece of work."

"We'll try to get a private statement from Berger in exchange for extradition. I don't believe he knows as much as Rennick, but maybe it'll give us something to go on. And she may change her tune when she gets a preview of her new accommodations."

He snickered. "Nothing like solitary confinement to alter your perspective."

Director Hall turned to face him. "How was it, being back undercover after all these years? It can be tough playing both sides. You okay with all this?"

"Chest still hurts like a bitch, but I've lived through worse." He turned his attention back to the glass. He had ducked Director Hall's question, but what the hell was he supposed to say? That he'd fallen for the fucking target and damn near compromised himself? He shoved the thought from his mind.

"Thank god for Kevlar," Director Hall said.

"You can say that again."

"And those new spatter pouches...man, those are realistic."

"Yup, except real blood is easier to clean. That new shit left a nasty stain on my chest."

"I'm sure it'll wash off eventually. Did anyone at the LA bureau suspect?"

"Nah. The paramedics got to the house so damned fast, there wasn't time for anyone to question."

"They're a good team. Hell, I sometimes forget they're not real paramedics." Director Hall said. "Listen, Sonny, I know the Chicago office wants you back, but you need to lay low for a while. Just until we sort out this thing with The Employer. You built a hell of a reputation, and whoever The Employer is, they know your face. Let us bring them in before you go back to the job. I can handle it with Chicago if you want."

"I just appreciate you getting me out of there before I had to make a tough choice. Thanks, but I can deal with the Chicago office."

"I'm serious, Sonny. By all accounts, you're dead, and it needs to stay that way for a while."

"Yep. I get it."

"Still no guesses as to The Employer's identity?"

Sonny watched Scott leave the interrogation room. "Nope. The SOB is annoying, but pretty damned smart."

"Sounds like my ex."

Sonny let out a polite chuckle.

"Well," Director Hall said. "Looks like we're not getting anywhere with Rennick. Thanks for checking in, but you'd better head out before Roberts sees you. Hey, why don't you take a vacation? Go somewhere tropical."

Hell, no. Until they had The Employer in hand, Layne might still need him. He nodded. "Good idea."

90

The interrogation room at the local bureau office matched Layne's expectations—from the uncomfortably hot temperature to the cold hard chairs. After some time waiting for god knew what, her parents were questioned then released. Scott, the super spy, professed important and confidential things he needed to do. That left Layne, alone, with a network lawyer she'd never met. And Mr. Louis Vuitton loafer didn't sugarcoat his message. If Layne refused to sign the statement in front of her, she would likely be arrested for conspiratorial treason; a federal offense that carried a minimum penalty of ten thousand dollars and five years in prison. But, he explained, a minimum sentence constituted a gift, and rarely occurred.

Layne read through the statement prepared by Mr. loafer. It asserted that parties previously unknown to Layne had pursued her diamond necklace for undisclosed reasons. And that Special Agent Ryan Cooke admitted that he'd leveraged her as a resource to draw those parties out. Hmm. Leveraged. Is that what they called it these days? She continued to read. Further, she disavowed any real knowledge of a nano secure digital memory card, and had acted within her rights in destroying the diamond necklace, as it was her legal property.

Mr. loafer advised that with the statement and her witnessed and notarized affidavit, the FBI would have no grounds to charge her. And although he'd carefully crafted it to avoid blatant untruths, it still felt like a lie. But screw them. Screw all of them. They'd certainly done it to her.

That night, just like the damned sand dollar, Layne shriveled up inside. And the feeling seemed hell-bent on staying. It didn't matter how hard she tried, or how many days passed, she couldn't shake Ryan's last words. He had used her to find the card, and it crushed her to accept that she'd let another man into her life, into her heart, only to lose again. And what about her family? The people she thought she knew. They'd been lying to her for years. But why? Because they didn't trust her? Processing it all felt too difficult, so she didn't. She shoved those thoughts behind doors that refused to fully close, and no matter how she distracted herself, the shriveled feeling remained.

She arrived at Ryan's funeral with the hope of showing sorrow. Instead, a barbed wire fence of hurt, resentment, and emptiness squeezed her soul.

Scott approached her. "Hey, sis."

Layne forced a grin.

"You doing okay?" he asked.

"Sure."

"You don't look okay."

What could she say?

Scott held out a small black jewelry box. "Here, I got you something."

Layne opened the box and picked up a cameo locket on a delicate gold chain.

"It's not exactly like the other one," Scott said. "But I think it's close."

He took the chain from her and fastened it around her neck. She touched the locket and made another attempt at a smile.

"It's a nice thought, Scott. Thank you."

The service commenced outside in the despair of a late morning fog, and a chill permeated her clothes. Her black suit, black tights, and low black pumps paralleled her mood. And she couldn't remember if she'd checked her hair or put on makeup before she'd left the house. Did it matter?

At the head of the closed casket, a minister greeted the large group assembled around the grave site. Dozens of people she'd never seen before, members of Ryan's team, hotel staff from The Riede, even staff from Rue de Reves bowed their heads as the minister spoke of fond remembrances and silver linings, a crutch Layne had relied on in the past. But the last few weeks had taught her that silver linings were for the ignorant.

The preacher pontificated comfort from the support of loved ones, and she glanced around. Jenny and Dean had flown in, although they'd never met Ryan. Her parents, Scott, Maggie, Dennis, Chef Degasse, Darren, they had all come. But there was no comfort for Layne. Worse, there was no escape.

After the service, a man started toward her. There was nothing special about him, but he looked vaguely familiar.

Then Maggie pulled her aside. "Are you okay, sweetie?"

"Sure."

"You don't look so hot."

"Yep, Scott mentioned that."

"No, Layne. I mean this really is not good. You look like Morticia on a bad hair day. I'm concerned about you, hun."

"It's a funeral, Maggie. People wear black. You're wearing black."

"There's a difference. I'm rocking black. You are reveling in it. But I must admit, it compliments those dark circles you've got going under your eyes."

"If this is your way of cheering me up, it's not working."

"No, Layne. This is tough love. I've been excruciatingly nice because I believed you needed that from me. But now I think I was wrong. Sadness is understandable. Anger, I totally get. Rage, that would be great. But, this? I don't know what this is. It's not getting any better, and it's not easing your pain, sweetie. Whatever is going on inside your head...it's killing you. You need to do something, or see somebody about this."

Layne glared at her. "You want rage? Fine, here it is, Maggie. Fuck you. Oh, wait. Everyone already has. You don't know what it's like to be abandoned. To have your dreams destroyed in an instant. Not just once, but twice. You, with the world as your one night stand. You can't possibly know what I should or shouldn't be feeling. They betrayed me. All of them. The man I married. Ryan. Uncle Fred. My parents. Scott. They all lied. But I've finally learned my lesson."

She waited for tears, for any emotion other than torment, but nothing else came. She turned and walked away.

"Layne..." Maggie called after her. "Layne, please..."

Layne trudged across the wet grass toward her cab, noting that those in her supposed support system remained to console each other. She knew the loss they mourned wasn't only for Ryan. But, what the hell. The old Layne was dead and buried, too. They could adapt or leave her alone.

Are you sure about this? Her little voice pleaded. *I kind of like our support system.*

"Screw you, too," Layne said to her fucking little voice.

The man she'd seen earlier tried again to approach her. She kept walking.

THREE WEEKS later Maggie watched from just off stage as Layne fumbled with utensils, slurred her words, ignored the script, and showed a little too much personality on camera—not the good kind. Maggie knew the cussing, stumbling, and waving of the middle finger would be edited out. This had become the norm, and the film editors expected to work overtime to give the illusion of a seamless run. But that didn't make it any less disturbing.

Darren Chase moved in next to her and watched for a few minutes, arms folded over his chest. "You realize this cannot continue."

"Yes, I do."

"Let us wrap this up then, while Layne is still vertical." He walked away.

Maggie passed Darren's decree to the set director, then went to her office to make a call. "Okay, Scott. This has to end."

"You're breaking up with me?"

"We only went out once."

"Then I still have a shot?"

"Oh, babe. I'd eat you alive."

"Is that a promise?"

"Stop distracting me," she said. "We need to talk about Layne."

"What's going on?"

"It's been over a month. I stole her phone and looked at her voicemails. Helen has left thirty-seven messages, and Layne isn't calling her back. And poor Karl has visited the station so many times, but she won't see him."

"You've tried talking to her?"

"Sure, because it went so well the last time."

"I'm no expert, but maybe a different approach?"

"I've called the house on the weekend," Maggie said. "Driven over there. I can tell she's inside, but she won't answer the door. She is some deranged form of civil to me at the station, and that's all I get. Mostly she avoids me, and to be honest, I can't talk to her at work, not without making things worse for her."

"At least she's coming to work," Scott said.

"Don't even get me started on the show."

"The last episode did seem a little off."

"A little off? It was a train wreck. We're airing hemorrhoid commercials that are more entertaining. And the ratings are lower than Satan's salami. But I don't give a shit about the show right now. She's scaring me, Scott. I think we've lost her."

"That bad, huh?"

"You know those bureau goons she has stalking her?"

"Yes, for her protection."

"Well, whatever it's for, the only time I see even a hint of a smile from her is after she flips one of them off."

Scott chuckled.

"I know, right?" Maggie said. "Normally, I'd think it's hilarious. I want to laugh, because it should be pretty damned funny. But I can't. I'm too worried. It's just not her, and she's going to lose everything if she keeps heading down this path."

"Where is she now?"

"She just finished taping, and it was a nightmare. She came to work tipsy. She's dropping shit all over the place, swearing, spitting when she talks. She's making Julia Childs look like a frickin' nun. After this run, Darren is sending her home. You need to fix this."

"If I fix it can I have another date?"

"You fix this, darlin', and you can have anything you want."

Scott sputtered out a cough. "Gotta go."

91

Director Braun's cell phone bounced across his nightstand. Groggy, he rolled over to retrieve it, not bothering to read the caller ID. Damned Americans—no one else called at that hour. He prepared himself for the grating voice before answering the call.

"Director Dieter Braun here."

"You sound tired, did I wake you?"

"It is four in the morning in Berlin."

"I know, and I don't fucking care."

The director rubbed his eyes. "What do you want?"

"It's about Berger."

"Is the extradition approved?"

"We have one condition."

Director Braun waited, then let out a weary breath. "What is the condition?"

"He remains in custody until he testifies. We'll have no fucking use for him after that."

"And you will make sure he is well treated?"

"Trust me, I'll take care of Berger."

"What about all the paperwork they said they needed?"

"It won't be necessary."

"You will contact me when it is time for him to come home?"

"Someone will contact you."

"But—"

The call ended.

92

Someone knocked on Layne's front door as she zoned out to mindless reality television. She took a sip of room temperature soda and popped a few cheese balls into her mouth. Another knock, followed by more cheese balls, then a third knock.

Persistent SOB, her little voice said.

Layne turned up the show's volume.

"Sis, I know you're in there. I hear skanky chicks yelling at each other on the damned TV."

"Go away, Scott. I'm tired."

"Me too. I'm tired of standing out here on your front porch."

"I'm not in the mood for company."

"I flew all the way from Virginia to see you. I'm not leaving."

"There's nothing to see."

"Damn it, Layne, open the door."

She scowled and got off the couch. When she opened the door, Scott's eyebrows lurched.

"What is all over your face? Is that... cheese powder?"

"Why are you here, Scott?"

He pushed past her and surveyed the room. "What the hell is going on in here?"

"I was having a snack and watching a show. Is that now a federal offense?"

"There's gotta be at least twenty soda cans on the floor."

"I ran out of wine."

Scott looked her up and down. "Go get dressed."

"I am dressed."

"I'm taking you to dinner. Something without holes would be nice."

"I can't go to dinner. I have plans."

Scott's eyes narrowed, and his hands clenched.

Layne gave him an exaggerated eye roll. "All right. Don't get your boxers in a bunch."

Three minutes later, Layne walked out of the bedroom dressed in the only clean clothes she could find. A dark blue button-down blouse under a white and blue paisley sweater vest, dark blue slacks, and navy flats. She hadn't bothered to comb her hair or put on makeup. Like Scott would even notice.

He watched her enter the room. "Grandma called," he said. "She wants her outfit back."

She glanced down at herself and shrugged.

They were halfway to the restaurant when she finally spoke. "How did the hearings go? That is why you're in town, isn't it?"

"Jesus, sis, I told you. I came to see you. The prelim hearings were over last week, and Rennick's in lockup until the final hearing next month. She'll go through another round of interrogation, but it seems open and shut to me."

"Well, she deserves whatever she gets."

"She deserves to rot in hell."

Several more quiet minutes passed. "Look, Layne, things aren't always what they seem."

"Your point?"

"About Ryan."

Layne flashed her palm, but Scott continued. "I know you don't want to hear this, but I don't believe he meant to hurt you."

Layne glared at him. "All in the line of duty, right? Don't make him a martyr, Scott. I don't think I could take that. Not from you."

"I'm not, but maybe you're looking at this from the wrong angle."

"And what angle is that? The one where Ryan told me he loved me, took advantage of me, used me as bait to find the damned card, and then apologized like that would make everything okay. Or, wait. Maybe it's the angle where my whole frickin' family lied to me about who they are. Which angle is incorrect in your opinion?" She turned to face the window and hoped Scott wouldn't see her tears.

"Not your whole family," Scott said.

"Right. Just you, and Mom, and Dad. The family I grew up with and trusted. No biggie."

They pulled up to the valet station at the new Tajine Morocco, where a woman, draped in colorful jewels and veils, escorted them to a low table.

"Man, I'd like to see Maggie in one of those," Scott said.

"It was one date, Scott. Get over it."

"Correction. One incredible date. A guy can fantasize, can't he? Besides, I may still have a shot."

She sat down and tapped her fingers on the table as Scott shimmied his six-foot-three frame onto a two-by-two pillow on the floor. An awkward reticence settled over the table, and Layne hoped someone would bring alcohol. Soon.

Finally, Scott broke the silence. "You know, sis, if Ryan hadn't said what he did right before he died, you would have gone to prison for the rest of your life. I know it hurt, but what does your gut tell you? Did it feel real? I knew him pretty well. And I've gotta say, I have never seen him behave with anyone the way he did with you. Isn't it possible that he was protecting you, all the way to the end?

"I don't want to talk about this, Scott. Can we please not talk about this?"

More silence fell like a wall between them until Scott spoke again.

"Look, I'm sorry, sis," he said. "I'm sorry about everything that happened. That you had to find out like you did about Mom and Dad. That this all came down on you. But mostly, I'm sorry I lied to you. It killed me to do that. You're my big sis. The person I share everything with. Every time I had to hold something back, it hurt me too. But in my defense, I think you should know that Mom and Dad made me do it."

Layne's eyes widened. "Oh my god. I cannot believe you just blamed our parents for your actions. You're a forty-five-year-old man."

"Well, chronologically, yes. But I still have the heart and mind of a horny teenage boy."

Layne pressed her lips together and tried to suppress her grin. She really wanted to be mad at him.

A tall man in a turban and long silk jacket approached them. He carried a tray with an ornate bronze teapot and two narrow glasses, embossed with gold filigree. He bent to place the glasses in front of them, then stood and poured a light green liquid into each glass from several feet above. Not a drop splashed or spilled.

"Tea," he said, before walking away.

"Kinda not what I expected," Scott said as he stared at the glass.

Layne detected the strong aroma of mint leaves. "I was hoping for vodka, but that is quite a skill."

A curvy young waitress attired in little but sheer scarves arrived with a platter of various foods.

"Excuse me," Scott said to the waitress. "But we haven't ordered yet."

The exotic beauty replied in a thick, sensual, Arabic accent. "I am sorry, sir, for the confusion. Please, let me explain. It is one price for the menu. Chef's choice."

An enticing combination of garlic and cinnamon drifted over the table as the waitress placed the platter between them. "I present here the appetizers."

Layne cringed at the word, as Scott scrutinized the various foods.

"Those look...uh...we don't have any plates or forks," Scott said.

The waitress sent Scott a demure smile. "No individual plates," she said. "We share. And no utensils. You eat like this."

She knelt next to Scott, removed a disk of steaming flatbread from a chimney-shaped basket she'd placed on the table, tore off a piece and used it to scoop up a stew-like substance containing chickpeas, chunks of potato, carrots, and onions. She fed the stew sandwich to Scott, and with her fingertip, wiped a small drop of gravy from his chin, then licked her finger clean. When Scott finished, she dabbed at his lips with a napkin, then placed the napkin on his lap, letting her hands linger. Layne stared, spellbound by the erotic display.

The waitress turned to her. "Would you like for me to help?"

"No! Thank you."

"Very well. When you are done, I will come back to assist with dessert."

"I'll be waiting," Scott said with a sinister smile.

The waitress cast sultry eyes at Scott and left to attend to other tables.

"This place is amazing," Scott said.

"So, the food is good?"

His gaze followed the young woman's veil-covered behind. "What food?"

"Why is it my presence never deters women from hitting on you?"

"The ladies just can't resist me."

Layne laughed. "That was no lady."

He studied her. "It's great to see you laughing, sis."

"It's a pleasant change for me, too. Thank you, Scott. I'm glad you made me come."

"Oh, I almost forgot." He pulled an envelope from his back pocket. "I have a surprise for you."

93

Layne slammed her foot on the invisible passenger side brake as Maggie zipped her Jag through a sea of vehicles, and jockeyed into position along the departures curb at LAX. She parked at an angle between a Hummer and a Porsche, then got out of the car in a gesture to help Layne with her luggage.

"I'm so jealous," Maggie said. "A week on a tropical island with all those incredible, tan bodies. And St. John, of all places. Scott has exceptional taste."

Layne grunted as she hoisted the heaviest of the suitcases over the lip of the trunk. "Well, he certainly has a thing for you, if that's any indicator," she said.

"Oh, the poor dear. He's too damned nice. He wouldn't last a week." Maggie lifted one perfectly sculpted brow.

"I don't want to know what you're picturing," Layne said.

"Let me help you with those bags, hun." Maggie waved for a skycap. "A little help over here?"

Layne set the last of her suitcases on the street, and then looked down at her armpit. It felt...sticky. "Is it unusually warm today?"

Maggie glanced over. "Oh my goodness, Layne. Your cheeks are on fire. Wait...has Aunt Flo finally left the building?"

"What? No! I'm way too young for that."

"Tell that to the hot flash spreading down your neck."

Layne looked down. "I don't see anything."

"Not many of us can see our necks."

"Shit, it can't be a hot flash. Tell me it's not a hot flash."

"It's not a hot flash," Maggie said with an amused grin.

"Just you wait, Maggie Malone. Wait until this happens to you."

"Uh huh. Let's get back to the topic of Scott."

"What about him?"

"Would you mind if I gave him a call?"

Layne smirked. The two were meant for each other. "Go for it," she said. "And tell him I said happy birthday."

"Ooooh, it's his birthday?"

Nope. But Maggie could never resist a special occasion romp, and that would be a perfect thank you gift for Scott.

Layne normally traveled with an action-packed suspense novel, filled with romance and foreign intrigue. This time she opted for a few recipe books. Maggie swore Layne was the only person alive who could scrutinize a cookbook cover to cover and not be bored out of their shorts. And Maggie was right. Layne adored recipes. She loved the pictures, the discovery of a new ingredient or technique, and coming up with ideas for how she might modify them. And she struggled to contain her excitement when she spotted one she wanted to try.

This trip, despite her newly acquired ability to fry an egg on her chest, she found one particular recipe book very intriguing—*Heating Things Up with Lard*. She hadn't used much lard, but as an alternative to other healthy high-heat fats, like pure butter or avocado oil, grass-fed lard could have real potential. The title, however, garnered some strange looks from other passengers on the plane.

She wasn't entirely back to her old self, but she'd made good progress over the last few weeks toward regaining what Maggie referred to as her Layne-ness. Especially when it came to flying. And although the reading had kept her occupied, the last leg of the trip left her feeling restless and unsettled, and somewhat green. She was grateful to deplane at St. Barts, where a leathery man with long dreadlocks and a smooth Caribbean accent took her luggage, then escorted her to a pontoon style boat. The balmy night air greeted her, and with little ambient light, thousands of stars formed a sparkling canopy over the small island. She chose a seat at the front of the boat for the short cruise across the bay to St. John. It was her first trip to the Caribbean, and she intended to take in every minute of it.

Layne surveyed the other passengers and spotted a man at the rail near the back of the boat wearing a dark suit and a dark tie. His face wasn't visible, but had it been daylight, she'd have bet on dark sunglasses. Couldn't they give it a rest? Determined to enjoy her vacation, she pretended this latest FBI stalker wasn't there, and the next time she looked, he was gone.

The small cruiser set out at a fast clip. The wind blew back her hair. And misty sprays of ocean water hit her face. The jaunt invigorated her, and she stepped on the dock to the festive serenade of steel drums. Tiki torches flickered in dots along the beach. And a tall, icy glass of rum punch, complete with a pineapple wedge and purple umbrella appeared in her hand. The boat captain led the group to the open-air hotel lobby, masked by thick foliage that climbed and draped its way up carved pillars supporting an authentic Caribbean thatch roof. Marble floors, handcrafted furnishings, and exquisite sculptures suggested contemporary elegance yet to come.

Layne followed a bellman to her suite on the third floor. Her back tensed as her mind flashed to thoughts of The Riede. But she cast those memories aside as the door swung open, revealing a room comprised mostly of lanai, with a spectacular view of Great Cruz Bay. The bellman placed her luggage just inside and closed the door behind him. She took a minute to absorb the room. There were side walls, but no wall separating her from the outside lanai, and the sweet aroma of exotic flowers filled the space. The faint sound of steel drums washed over her, as she lay back on the vibrantly colored, queen-sized bed and sighed.

"I am so lucky to have a brother like Scott."

"I agree," said a voice from out on the lanai.

Layne jumped from the bed and strained her eyes against the darkness beyond the room. She made out a man in a dark suit and tie.

"This has gone far enough," she said. "I will not be harassed like this any longer. Please get Director Hall on the phone immediately."

The man moved into the light. "I'm afraid I can't do that."

94

It took every ounce of Layne's composure to finally speak. "Get out," she said.

"What?"

She pointed to the lanai. "Get. Out. Now."

"But—"

Her hands clenched. "Out!"

She fought an expletive infused tirade as he left the way he had come, from her third-floor lanai. She wasn't sure how he had gotten off the damned balcony, and she didn't care. But after a few minutes, someone knocked on the door adjoining her room. She stepped close and tested the locked.

"Layne?"

"Leave me alone."

"I wanted you to know where I was, in case you changed your mind."

Layne scowled. Several times during her interrogation, she'd received warnings that until they resolved the case, interaction with Special Agent Marco Viorantelli was strictly prohibited. Shit. She needed chocolate. And rum. Lots more rum. She searched the hotel services binder for a room service menu. Then she overheard Marco talking next door. She strained to listen but caught herself, and continued her quest for a page offering express delivery of rum punch. The sound of Marco's voice stopped, and then her cell phone rang. She glowered at the mighty mouse ringtone before she answered. "Go to hell, Scott." She ended the call.

Mighty mouse sang to her in his hardy tenor voice several more times. "Here I come to save the—"

Decline.

"Here I come—"

Decline.

"Here—"

Decline.

She changed Scott's ringtone to "You Better Run" by Pat Benatar before it rang again, and then accepted the call. "I'm not talking to you, you traitor."

"But you answered."

"You keep calling. I want to be sure you understand that I'm specifically not talking to you." She hit end, and a muffled laugh came from the other side of the adjoining door.

"Get away from that door, Mr. Vermicelli. You don't want to find out what I'm capable of right now."

The laughing stopped. "It's Special Agent Viorantelli," Marco said through the door. "Not Mr. Vermicelli."

"I don't care."

Pat Benatar belted out another verse, and Layne put her phone on speaker so she could yell directly at it. "You asshole."

"Don't hang up," Scott said.

"Give me one good reason why I shouldn't fly to wherever you are and strangle you. How could you do this to me? Your own sister."

"Okay, aren't we being a little melodramatic?"

Layne growled. "Melodramatic? I'll give you melodramatic." Layne threw her phone at the wall, and for the first time since she'd left the cabin that night, her sobs overtook her in uncontrollable waves.

A muffled voice drifted out of the brightly colored area rug. "Layne? Ah, c'mon, sis. Please don't cry."

Apparently, cell phones didn't automatically hang up when you hurled them at a hard surface.

"Talk to me, sis. You know I love you. But you may be in danger. I'm just trying to protect you."

Layne sniffed and dabbed at her eyes with the sleeve of her shirt. Then she picked the phone up off the floor.

"Did you just tell me you love me?"

"I know, I don't say it often enough."

"Shit. That's not fair."

"Talk to Marco."

"I don't think so."

"Please, sis. Do it for me."

After a restless night's sleep, Layne went down to the water for a few hours. She sat in the warm sand, watched colorful sailboats drift in and out of the bay, considered the things Scott had told her at dinner, and thought about the short amount of time she'd had with Ryan. He really had loved her. She supposed she'd always known it. Despising him had been easier than wondering what might have been. But his last words at the cabin had saved her from a life in prison, and she regretted all the horrible things she'd said and thought about him. She gazed up at puffy white clouds drifting across a pale blue sky. "Can you forgive me?"

A wave rolled in, the bubbly fringe tickling her toes and bringing with it a delicate cream-colored disk. Layne smiled and reached for the sand dollar. "Ouch! Shit. What the hell?"

Back at her suite, Layne enjoyed the strong scent of a bright pink lily left on her pillow by housekeeping. She walked out to the lanai and took in the cobalt waters that stretched beyond the bay. Then she overheard sounds coming from Marco's suite. A faint rap on his door, followed by her two favorite words—room service. Her stomach grumbled, and whether due to hunger, or guilt over how she'd treated him, both were good reasons to knock.

Marco greeted her with a hesitant smile. "Perfect timing," he said. "I just ordered lunch."

"No fair using my weaknesses against me," she said.

"I'll do whatever it takes." He glanced down at her hand. "I see you left your room."

She fiddled with the large gauze pad fastened by surgical tape to her right index finger. "We both know I don't need to leave my room to injure myself. But yes, I went down to the beach and tried to pick up a jellyfish."

"Why the hell would you do that?"

"It's a long story. But the man selling shaved ice assured me it wasn't fatal."

"Well, I'm glad you consulted an expert."

She peered around him for a glimpse of the food he had ordered, and another man stepped into view.

95

"Hello, gorgeous."

Warm caramel hit Layne like a wet slap in the face, and her knees buckled beneath her. "Oh my god. This isn't possible. I saw you...you were..."

He moved toward her.

"No! That's close enough. I don't understand this."

Marco reached out, helping to steady her. "I know this must be kind of a shock," Marco said. "Why don't you sit down, let Ryan explain." He helped Layne to a chair near the door, and she fell into it. She closed her eyes, taking a deep, long breath. When she opened them, Ryan was still there.

She shook her head. "This can't be happening."

"I am so, so sorry, Layne," Ryan said. "I never wanted to deceive you."

"Deceive me." Her eyes narrowed. "Deceive me? People don't do what you did. They don't hurt other people as much as you hurt me. They don't use other people, have sex with them, make them feel like they matter and then like they don't, all to find some stupid card. And they definitely don't pretend to die. And to think, I was just starting to believe that you actually did love me. That's just...shitty, Ryan. What you did...it was really, really shitty."

Silence engulfed the room, and Marco interjected. "Well, I've got to get back to San Fran. And I think you two have a lot to talk about. So..."

Neither of them acknowledged Marco's words. He shrugged and left the suite.

"I deserved that," Ryan said. "I deserve everything you've got. You want to yell at me? Hit me? Swear at me? Please, do it. Because leaving you back at the cabin, watching your face when I told you that I'd used you...that was the hardest fucking thing I've ever done in my life. I love you, Layne. I fell in love with you at dinner. And even more that day in the park. And it damn near killed me to watch you suffering these last few months."

Her eyebrows lifted. "You've been watching me? All this time?"

"I had hoped the I love you would be the compelling part of that confession. But yes, I've been keeping an eye on you. Not in a creepy way. I was concerned for your safety. I thought my death would take the focus off of you, but that doesn't appear to be the case."

"What focus? What do you mean?"

"I'm trying to tell you that you're still in danger."

"What? Why would I be in danger? And why did you pretend to get shot? When Agent Rennick attacked me in the bathroom, was all that fake? And why come back now, on my vacation? What the hell, Ryan? Did Scott know about this? I am going to kill that son of a bitch."

"Whoa, there," Ryan said. "I promise I will answer all of your questions, starting with why I faked my own death."

She waited, watching the intense concentration in his eyes as he looked up at the ceiling, then down at the floor, then out to the lanai. Finally, he turned to her. "The easiest explanation is that you are my weakness, Layne."

She thought about it for a moment. "I'm not following."

He sighed. "Marco and I knew that after we recovered the card, we'd need to give it to the bureau, because handing it over ensured the two best outcomes. The first being that no one else acquired it. And the second, that your family would be out of danger, because the card would be out of reach. But we realized that with me still in the picture, you'd continue to be at risk."

"How so?"

"Because if someone threatened you, I would have done anything to ensure your safety. Including stealing the card from my own agency."

"You would have done that for me?"

"If it meant saving your life? In a heartbeat."

Layne's stomach butterflies did little backflips. Then she remembered how irate she was.

"With me out of the picture," Ryan continued, "there was no one to blackmail, so you should've no longer been a target. But for some reason, it didn't play out like we planned."

"Because I destroyed the necklace?"

"No. If anything, destroying the necklace also should have removed the threat."

"Threats like Agent Rennick? Or was she in on it?"

"Definitely not. I don't know how she found us, but she was not part of the deal. Marco was supposed to shoot me. Only he and I knew about the plan. He left a Kevlar vest with the spatter packet behind the cabin, and I put it on before Scott and your parents arrived. Marco arranged the fake paramedics and led Director Hall to us. Everyone needed to believe I was dead."

"Even me?"

"Especially you, Layne. I love you, but you have no poker face at all. If it wasn't real for you, then no one else would have believed it either."

"I guess I can understand that."

"Anyway, Rennick shooting me just saved Marco the trouble, and he ran with it. It wasn't the ideal scenario, but it should have worked."

"What do you mean, it *should* have worked?"

"Well, when we thought the card was destroyed, I intended to come out of hiding. But then one of my...one of Marco's men noticed that you were being followed. And no, not by me. So, I stayed dead to keep an eye on you without raising suspicion. The longer I waited, the more people started following you."

"But I've been perfectly fine. Sort of. At least, from a safety perspective. I hardly go anywhere. And when I do go out, I'm escorted very openly by big men in tight black suits. I don't think being in danger is even an option for me. Are you sure about this?"

"It didn't make any sense to me either, until Scott told Marco about a conversation he had with your father. That's why I'm here."

Layne narrowed her eyes. "I knew it. That bastard! I really am going to kill him."

"Calm down. Scott doesn't know I'm alive. He thinks you're here talking to Marco. And he only helped Marco because he's worried about you."

Layne shrugged. "Maybe death is a bit harsh. But he will pay for tricking me like this."

"I'm sure he will."

"So, what's this about my dad? Please tell me my parents aren't in danger."

"No. At least not at the moment. Why don't we get some food and talk about it over lunch?"

Layne's eyes wandered to the small dining table teaming with vibrant tropical fruits, thinly sliced crispy beef, steamy coconut fry bread, grilled jumbo shrimp, and fried plantains. It all looked and smelled heavenly.

"It would be a shame to let it go to waste."

Layne filled her plate and joined Ryan on his lanai. They ate most of the meal in silence, but when she shut her eyes to savor the sweetness of a fried plantain, she heard Ryan chuckle.

Her eyes opened. "What?"

"I missed that."

"Missed what?"

"Watching you eat. It's captivating. Actually, I missed everything about you, Layne. I don't know how to make up for what I've done, but I'd like to try."

Layne looked down at the table.

"Too soon to talk about this?" Ryan asked.

"Yes. No. Maybe. I don't know."

"All right. I won't push. Right now, we'll concentrate on ensuring you and your family are safe. But whenever you're ready."

Wow, her little voice said. *Why would he ever want to talk to you about it after a response like that? You'd better get your shit together, or you're going to lose him. Again.*

96

Layne took a delectable bite of spicy grilled shrimp and then dabbed her mouth with her napkin. "So, tell me what's going on with my dad," she said.

"He's one smart fella, that one."

"How so?"

"The memory card."

In an unusual act of kindness, her little voice tried to help her. *Don't do it, Layne. Don't board this boat.*

Layne kept her voice casual. "He said something about the card?"

Shit, her little voice said.

"Your father shared an interesting piece of information with Scott after the...um..." Ryan cleared his throat. "After everyone left the cabin."

Mayday. Mayday. It's not too late to abandon ship.

"What kind of information?"

"That diamonds will disintegrate in intense heat, and Cubic Zirconia won't. But you already knew that."

And now we're sunk.

She pushed some crispy beef around her plate. "Is there a point?"

"Your father hid the card in a Cubic Zirconia."

"Did he?"

"Thirteenth gem from the female clasp," Ryan added. "But you weren't in the room when he told me that, so I'm still wondering how you knew."

Layne's throat constricted. "How I knew what?"

"Scott and Marco sifted through every bit of that ash. The Zirconia wasn't there. That is why the plan didn't work. Somebody out there knows you have the card."

"What? That's ridiculous. Why would I take it?"

"Exactly what I've been asking myself for the last few weeks."

Layne stared down at her lap. "Let's suppose, for a second, that in an irrational fit of insanity, I did take the card. What then?"

"We read the data."

Her head popped up. "You can't be serious."

"I'm deadly serious. You're being watched. There are people out there who believe you either have the card, or know what's on it. The best way to neutralize the threat is to understand it. And for that, we have to read the data."

She hesitated. "I'm not saying I took it. But if I did, why would I carry it with me? And how would you access the information?"

He pulled a small USB flash drive out of his pants pocket. "Accessing the data is the easy part."

Her eyes narrowed. "So, you'd want me to just hand the thing over?"

"No. I'd like you to let me install the card into this flash drive so we can look at the contents together."

"We? As in you and me? These are government secrets. Doesn't somebody at the FBI do this sort of thing for a living?"

"They're corporate secrets, and as far as the bureau is concerned, I'm dead, and the memory card no longer exists. Remember? Besides, what little we know of the details points to some type of food conspiracy. Who better to help me analyze information about food than a foodie?"

Layne blinked at him. "Oh no. Food conspiracy or not, the data on that card could get us both killed."

"Then why did you take it?"

"Damn it, to be certain no one else would."

Ryan smiled.

Nice move, Einstein, her little voice said.

Layne frowned. "I was worried someone might find that stone in the ashes. And with good reason, apparently."

"Then help me read it."

She couldn't keep her face from puckering at the thought.

"Come on, Layne. This is about making sure you and your family are out of harm's way, once and for all."

She crumbled a piece of coconut fry bread between her fingers. "What if I told you it isn't here?"

Ryan eyed the locket Scott had given her at the funeral. "That's a very pretty necklace. I noticed you wear it every day."

Crap, her little voice said.

"Look, Layne. Economic terrorists don't just go away. We can pretend this evidence doesn't exist, but if whoever is looking for it can't find the intel another way, you'll eventually get caught in the middle. It's much easier for us to defend ourselves, and to protect you and your family, if we know what they're after?"

"And you want me to help you figure that out."

"Precisely."

A battled waged in Layne's mind.

Then Ryan gave her an adorable grin. "How about I sweeten the deal by ordering dessert?"

Telling him he could take his dessert straight to hell would be the practical thing to do.

"Come on. A food conspiracy worth killing over...aren't you even a little bit curious?"

A loud breath escaped her. "All right. I'll try to help you with the information, but no promises. And it had better be a pretty amazing dessert."

Ryan installed the card into the flash drive while Layne polished off a huge piece of gooey bananas foster covered in whipped cream and chocolate syrup, followed by most of Ryan's passionfruit cheesecake.

He snapped the flash drive closed and glanced over at Layne. "So, how'd you pull it off?"

"What?"

"Stealing the card."

Layne arched a brow.

"Really. It's been driving Marco and me nuts."

She inspected a bumpy white fruit.

"Seriously. How did you even know which stone to take?"

Go on, her little voice said. *You've been dying to tell someone.*

"Oh, all right. Maggie never liked the necklace because one of the diamonds looked flawed. She has an eye for that sort of thing. When my dad told us he'd planted the card in the diamond necklace, I knew. That night, while the paramedics were...anyway, I tore the clasp off the end, slid that section of stones off the strand, stuffed them into my bra, and, well, you know the rest."

"You smuggled them out in your—"

"Yes. In my cleavage. Apparently, I have just enough to hide a handful of gems. And it's a good thing, because they sure as hell searched everywhere else before that interrogation."

"Look at you. Just like a real agent."

Layne held back a smile.

After lunch, they powered up Ryan's laptop and plugged in the drive. Together, they began sifting through the various documents contained on the memory card. Several hours later, Layne finished the task alone. Somehow Ryan had worked his way to the bed and sprawled onto his back, spread eagle, serenading her with a combination of sporadic snorts and throaty gurgles. Kids and puppies are so cute when they sleep. Men, not so much.

Layne shut down the laptop, dropped the flash drive into her pocket, and left a note for Ryan to meet her for dinner at the resort cafe. Over the years, she'd learned some pretty appalling things about the food and pharmaceutical industries, but nothing could have prepared her for what she'd read on that card.

97

Berger tossed and turned on his cot, unable to sleep after yet another grueling interrogation, this time without Agent Rennick. He had laid out, in detail, his agency's interactions with an American federal agent who claimed the card to be at risk. He explained why he had come to the states. And he reminded them of their common goal—to ensure the security of the card.

He described watching as the masked horseman attacked in the park, and then observing from the street as someone fired a shot at The Riede. And later when their agent and the woman disappeared into the sea. He revealed his assignment of years ago to work with Officer Frederick Schatz to ensure the safety of the card. And he spoke of his relationship with Special Agent Sherry Rennick. He told them about his recent course of action in enlisting Agent Rennick to assist him with the task of obtaining the card. And he tried to convince them that while her actions were sometimes misguided, Agent Rennick's intent had been in the best interest of her government. But in the end, he worried all he'd recounted was not what anyone wanted or expected to hear.

Berger had agreed to testify as a witness for the defense, and they'd held him in a cell for what felt a lifetime. Finally, the news had come that he would testify before a grand jury in the morning. What time was it? He didn't know the day, much less the time. He willed himself to sleep, but his eyes refused to close. Dim fluorescent bulbs flickered on and off throughout the cell block, with frequency enough to drive the most stable of men insane. He wanted, no, he needed out of the windowless, life-sucking, claustrophobic cubicle they referred to as his holding cell.

Fortunately, his agency had negotiated an agreement for his return to Berlin after he testified, but things would not go as well for Agent Rennick. It saddened him to think how much she'd given for her country. But she had gone too far—holding a gun to the woman's head, discharging her weapon at another agent. Whether accidental or not, the Americans had all but convicted her. And neither his testimony nor any amount of cooperation on her part would change their minds. Not that she was likely to cooperate. Sherry Rennick was her own worst enemy.

Berger let out a long breath. Damned political posturing. If the two agencies had worked together from the start, the trial, the bloodshed, all of it might have been avoided. The sound of footsteps approaching his cell interrupted his thoughts.

"Hello, Berger."

The flickering darkness distorted his view of his visitor. "Who is there?"

A raspy tone he knew all too well assaulted him. "What a fucking disappointment. You don't recognize my voice?"

"You. This is your fault. The card was not at risk. If you had not contacted us, the card would still be hidden, and no one would be dead."

The man's voice changed. "We'll get to that. First, let me tell you how happy I am to say sayonara to that fucking idiotic voice. I know others appreciated it, in their own way, but it was killing my throat. And second, I only wish I could take the credit for the plan. It was The Employer's fucking genius idea to use your agency to force the card into the open."

"Use us? Your employer? But you were cleared as a federal agent."

"You can hardly blame a guy for a little moonlighting. And here's the best part...who would suspect me? The modest, unassuming lackey who dutifully does their bullshit job. For years, I've had everyone duped. Your government. My government. Even The Employer. And I have no motive. It's a beautiful thing."

"Then why? Why did you do it?"

"For the dental plan. Jesus, Berger, for the fucking money, of course."

Berger moved closer to the bars. "Who is your employer?"

"Really? You were an easy play, but I'll admit I pegged you as smarter than that." His visitor smirked. "As much as I'd like to tell you, I won't. But I do have a message."

"What is that?"

"The Employer asked me to convey that we are still somewhat miffed at the BKA for initially cheating us out of the memory card. Their words, not mine. I don't use words like miffed. Anyway, letting us purchase it at auction would have saved everyone a lot of trouble. But we have credible intel that the card may not have been destroyed. Someone might actually have it. As a matter of fact, I'm planning to visit with her next. So, there you go. One way or another, The Employer will end up with the information."

Berger tensed as he struggled to process what he'd heard.

"Oh," the man said. "The Employer also wanted me to thank you and Agent Rennick for your assistance. I gotta tell ya, bringing Rennick into the mix...that was a fucking gift. I struggled to figure out how I could pin this thing on you. But, Rennick? Well, you know her. It was almost too simple. She buried herself. And I'll make sure she has a nice, long, institutional stay. Don't get me wrong, you were pretty damned useful too, but your services are no longer required."

"What are you talking about? I am scheduled to testify today. Director Braun arranged for extradition."

His visitor chuckled. "Don't you stress over that. I've spoken to Braun. Hey, have you been to The Riede lately? They make a killer grilled rumaki. You gotta love anything on a skewer. Am I right?"

"It was you? You killed Frederick Schatz?" Berger caught a glint of metal flash near the bars of his cell, then a sharp, searing agony took hold of his chest. He clutched the area where the pain felt most intense, and a warm liquid oozed between his fingers.

Officer Hans Berger staggered and then collapsed on his cot. The last sound he heard was the echo of footsteps strolling casually away from his cell.

98

Layne arrived at the colorful, open-air restaurant a little early, ordered a Mai Tai, and enjoyed the sultry ocean breeze. She had the whole destruction of the global economy thing to consider, but she was also on vacation.

Ryan got there right on time and eyeballed her empty tropical drink. "Hope I didn't keep you waiting long," he said.

"No. I've only been here a few minutes."

His gaze fell again to her glass.

"These things never have much alcohol," she said.

The waiter approached, barefoot and dressed in a bright flowered tank with long, plaid, Bermuda shorts. His dark skin set off a thick head of butterscotch hair, twisted into dozens of braids with multi-colored beads smattering the ends. He eyed Ryan with a puckish grin. "You is one lucky mon to be sitting here with such a lovely womon. What you be wanting today, mon?"

"I'll take a beer," Ryan said.

"Ah, Carib. The good stuff." The waiter turned to Layne. "Another Mai Tai for the luscious lady?"

"I'm fine right now, thank you."

"That you are, sister, that you are."

Ryan watched the waiter leave and shook his head. "So," he said, "I'm sorry I couldn't hang in there with you. I hadn't slept in several days. Were you able to make sense of the data on the card?"

"Unfortunately, yes."

"And?"

"I think before you can grasp the depth of the conspiracy, you need to understand how our bodies process what we eat."

Ryan frowned. "Didn't we go over that at the restaurant?"

"Not in this much detail," Layne said. "When you eat, your body uses the nutrients in the food to function, and anything it can't use is handled as a toxin. Toxic overload causes illness, and—"

"Okay, Layne, here's the thing. I may look awake, but I'm still very much sleep deprived. Can we get to the bottom line?"

The waiter came back to their table shouldering a giant tray of fruity, umbrella-garnished beverages, and placed a frosty mug and a thirty-two ounce can of beer in front of Ryan. "I hope you're enjoying your stay with us here on the island," he said.

"This place is amazing," Layne said, gesturing at the surroundings and, in the process, knocking over her glass. The ice tumbled into Ryan's lap, and she winced. "Oh my gosh. I'm so sorry. Let me get you a towel."

Ryan reached for her. "Don't—"

Just as the waiter bent forward with napkins, Layne got up from her chair, turned, and slammed into him. The large drink tray tilted to one side, and the waiter countered. It pitched the other way, and the glasses and bottles toppled. Layne grabbed hold of the waiter's shirt to break his fall, but he stumbled backward. The tray flew over his head, he went down, and Layne fell on top of him.

"Womon," the waiter said. "I'm an easy mon, but even an easy mon likes a bit of foreplay."

"I am so sorry," Layne said. "I can't believe I did that."

"I can," a woman said, rushing at them with her camera. "That was classic. I can't wait to see these on your website." The woman took several shots of Layne still atop the waiter, who donned a broad smile for the lens.

Ryan helped both Layne and the waiter to their feet and thanked the young man for his understanding.

"No worries, mon. That was the most fun I've had all week. Your drinks are on me."

Ryan grinned as he looked down at the waiter's shirt. "Yes, they are."

The waiter followed Ryan's gaze and let out a jovial laugh. "Oh, womon. I like this one. You keep him, okay?" He continued to chuckle as he strolled away.

"So," Ryan said as they took their seats. "Getting back to the information on the card."

"Do you remember where I left off?"

"You were giving me too much detail."

"Oh, right. So, the average American eats a whole lot of crap and gets way too little nutrition. Even what we've been told is healthy generally isn't. And that same average person takes twelve different medications or supplements on a regular basis."

"And there's evidence of that on the card?"

"No. That's common knowledge."

"Then how is it a conspiracy?"

"It isn't. You kind of knew that, didn't you?"

"I guess so. Dr. Hanley is always telling me not to get my meals from a clown or out of a box, and that I'm supposed to eat more fruits and vegetables. I gotta say, I'm not a big fan of vegetables. Although the ones Chef Degasse made were pretty good."

"And you were very gracious to try all of them. But that's a good example of the average American, keeping more processed than fresh foods in the house. Avoiding vegetables. This is where something else comes into play. Many processed foods are engineered to be addictive."

"What? How?"

"Specific taste combinations and certain chemical ingredients have been proven to produce a craving response."

"So, you really can't eat just one." He lifted a brow.

Layne smiled. "Exactly."

"And that's what the card shows?"

"Also common knowledge."

"Who are these people with all this common knowledge?"

"Anyone with an interest and a web browser."

"Right now, my only interest is in finding out what is on that card."

"I'm getting there." Layne took a moment to summarize in her head. "Okay, before I looked at the data, I assumed, like most people, that chronic illness in America was just an unfortunate byproduct of the American lifestyle. You know, busy schedules, lots of stress, too much eating out or buying convenience foods, lack of exercise. But..."

"But, what?"

Layne lowered her voice. "The card contains evidence that—"

"See, honey?" a high pitch voice interrupted. "I told you it was Layne Stevens. Go ahead, ask her. You said you wanted her autograph. We are such big fans of your show, Ms. Stevens. And I got some great shots of you on top of that waiter. Would you mind taking one with the hubby and me? Maybe your friend could take it for us. My gosh, I still can't believe we ran into you like this. Small world, right? We're from Florida, so it's a short trip for us. But I'll bet you came all the way from California..."

As the woman rambled, Layne stole a glance at Ryan.

Uh oh, her little voice said. *Better hope he's not carrying a gun.*

99

Layne noted the unrest in Ryan's eyes as he used the couple's camera to take several photos of the threesome. And as she signed their cocktail napkins, the tapping of his foot grew rapid. When the couple retreated, Ryan held her chair for her and then slid close.

"Will you please just tell me what is on the goddamned card?"

"All right," Layne said in a hushed voice. "No need to get huffy. The card contains proof that chronic illness in America—all those diseases caused by the foods we eat—are actually by design."

Ryan looked pensive. "What do you mean, by design?"

"I'm saying the spread of disease in the US was crafted by the food and pharmaceutical industries. They're working together to create mass chronic illness for their own profit."

His brows pinched.

"Take fats for instance," Layne said.

"I know, fats are bad for you."

"No, not all of them. Remember what the chef said? We need healthy fats to function, but our bodies can't use unnatural fats, like soybean and corn oil. Those become toxins in our system, and without other nutrition to counteract the negative effects, they make us sick."

"But isn't soy supposed to be healthy?"

"Natural soy has some health benefits, but have you ever squeezed a soybean?"

Ryan's brows rose.

"Trust me, if you did, the only thing you'd get is a milky white substance, not fat."

He smirked. "I'm gonna let that one go."

Heat rushed to Layne's cheeks. "We're talking about soybeans."

"Right," Ryan said. "So, if soybeans don't have any fat in them, where does soybean oil come from?"

"Excellent question."

Ryan stared at her.

"Don't ask me," she said. "A lab somewhere?"

He frowned.

"However they do it, those toxic fats are cheap to produce," she said. "And with the processing, they cause all sorts of health conditions—high cholesterol, high blood pressure, heart disease."

"Okay, that makes sense," Ryan said. "And there's a drug for every one of those conditions."

"Yes. This is where the conspiracy comes into play."

"I get it. Because both industries profit from the evil food engineering. But can they really create an exact illness from a specific food?"

"According to the data they can," Layne said. "The corporations form teams made up of food and pharmaceutical engineers to compete for bonuses and prizes. They design great tasting, addictive processed foods that produce treatable illnesses, and pair them with highly effective companion drugs so people can still function. The longer we live, the more money they make. It's like a twisted game."

"Treatable illnesses. Like the flu?"

"Unfortunately, that's the least of it. Cancer is no longer considered a terminal disease. It's now classified as a treatable chronic illness, and is one of the largest money makers for both industries."

"They're causing cancer? On purpose?"

"The financial data details the most profitable programs—cancer, diabetes, arthritis, obesity, heart disease, and a whole list of illnesses that didn't even exist ten years ago. And they haven't limited themselves to targeting adults. We are now a nation of medicated kids. It scares me to think about what life will be like for our grandchildren if we keep heading down this path."

"And there is hard evidence of all of this? Proof?"

Layne nodded. "Test studies, research notes, marketing proposals, signed agreements, bonus payouts—it's all there. The documents prove the health crisis in America is not something that just evolved. It was planned, carefully architected and well marketed. And the American public paid for it, in more ways than one."

"So, all this talk about cures?"

She shook her head. "The practice is so profitable that according to the data the pharmaceutical companies are no longer exploring cures. They talk a good game, and they're fundraising for cures, but that money goes toward helping create the next ailment they can treat. Even worse, once the illness sets in, they can sell medications to treat the side effects of the original medication."

"Jesus. That's insane."

"It makes my blood boil just thinking about it."

"So, what if everyone ate the way Degasse eats?"

"Those industries can't afford for that to happen. Now I understand why someone would kill for the data. If you're a food or a pharmaceutical company, you certainly don't want to be exposed. And if you're a twisted enough human being, you'd know that you could use it for leverage."

"What about the FDA? If it was reported—"

"They already know," Layne said.

"And they're not doing anything about it?"

"Those special interest food and pharmaceutical conglomerates maintain quite a bit of political clout, so that's part of it. But can you imagine what the American public would do if they found out the nation's health crisis was planned? The FDA will need to manage this carefully on both ends. And even then, the hole we've dug for ourselves will be difficult to repair."

"We?"

"All of us. Those companies suckered us in with effective marketing and misleading guidelines for what should be considered healthy. But people choose to eat processed foods because they taste good, they're inexpensive, and they're convenient. Now, with more natural foods, like your tomato, that's just lack of awareness. Most people have no idea how much crap they're ingesting when they eat conventionally raised produce or meats. But they know when they get sick, they can take a pill. It'll be a tough cycle to break."

"And in both directions the FDA is screwed," Ryan said. "So, for those looking to acquire the card, it's Economic Terrorism 101. Leak enough negative information about a government to piss that nation's people off, and those people will handle the rest."

Layne grimaced. "Glad I never took that course. So, now that we understand the data, what do we do with the card?"

100

Layne still had mixed thoughts about their next step. Just like the FDA, it seemed no matter what they did, someone got screwed. But with the topic put aside for the moment, she agreed to take a walk down to the beach with Ryan. They strolled, several feet apart, through a winding maze of brightly flowered pathways adorned by slow-moving iguanas and vibrant exotic birds. And they talked about the weather, and the flowers, and the iguanas, and the exotic birds.

How about we go for something a tad more comfortable, her little voice encouraged. *Like maybe a tooth extraction.*

They arrived at a small beach cove enveloped by lush greenery and thick vines, and Layne had tripped only once, so she had that going for her. She left her sandals near the path and sank her feet into the powdery white sand. When they reached the shoreline, she let her gaze drift out with the sea. But she could feel Ryan watching her.

"Layne," Ryan said.

"Uh huh?" She replied without looking at him.

"I know I said I wouldn't press, but it's making me crazy to have things unsettled between us. I'm not asking for a commitment, or even any kind of decision. I just need to know, do you still love me?"

She looked over at him and held back all the emotions that threatened to erupt. "Of course I do, Ryan, but I..."

"You don't trust me."

She thought about that. "It's not you I don't trust. It's the circumstances. Please understand. My husband's death was devastating. Then when I lost you...I can't explain how deeply that affected me. I felt empty inside. Like I wasn't me. I still don't feel like myself. Not entirely." She took the flash drive out of her pocket and looked down at it. "I can't go through something like that again. It was too hard. And your job—"

"What if I quit my job?"

Her eyes widened. "What?"

"What if I pursued a different line of work so that you and I could be together?"

"I can't ask you to do that, Ryan. I wouldn't want you to do that. It's a huge part of who you are, who I fell in love with."

"Here's the thing, Layne. Not working for the bureau these last couple of months, my entire job focused on you, on ensuring your safety. And being with you now...I just can't imagine losing you again. I love you, Layne, more than anything. This is a new experience for me, and I know I'm not going to be perfect. But I want to be with you. And I will do whatever it takes.

Tears pooled in her eyes, and the walls she'd built began to crumble under his words and the vulnerability in his voice.

"I'm not asking for anything now," he said. "But maybe one day you'll consider giving me a second chance?"

She stared at him for a moment, then threw her arms around his neck and kissed him with all the love and desire she'd tried to lock away when she'd thought he was gone.

When the kiss ended, Ryan wiped a tear from her cheek and looked into her eyes. "Can I take that as a yes?"

She let out a tearful laugh, certain then that any amount of time they could spend together outweighed the risks.

A slow clapping sound came from just up the beach, startling her.

"Such a moving Hallmark moment," a male voice said. "Too bad you're both going to die. Now, since all the mushy bullshit is over with, I'll take the memory card, Ms. Stevens."

Layne turned.

"Not so fast," the voice said. "Hands where I can see them, and move slowly."

Ryan made a weak show of raising his hands. "What the hell are you doing? Put down the gun."

Layne's hands flew into the air, and her jaw dropped as she faced their attacker. "Mr. Tall?"

Agent Short's eyes rolled. "You have got to stop calling me that. I assume the flash drive you're holding contains the card? I gotta admit, that makes my job a hell of a lot easier."

Layne and Ryan stood silent.

"Hand it over," Agent Short said.

"I don't think so," Ryan replied.

"Always the fucking golden boy. Well, the big boy shoe is on the other foot now."

Ryan's brow wrinkled. "Come again?"

Agent Short looked rattled for a moment. "Never mind. And don't press me."

"How did you find us? Damn it, that woman taking the pictures. She must have posted our location online."

Agent Short snickered. "No and no. I thought it might come in handy, so I put a tracking device inside her...you know...her rubber companion, before I gave it back to her."

Layne's eyes bulged. "Oh my god!"

Ryan glanced over at her. "You brought it with you?"

She shrugged.

Ryan turned back to the agent. "What the hell are you doing here, Short? And why?"

"Why? You want to know why? I get shit for pay, and nobody... nobody acknowledges the work I do. You wouldn't solve jack without me. But who gets the fucking credit? Special Agent Ryan Cooke." Agent Short's voice changed to something reminiscent of a drag queen. "Oh, Cooke is so great. Oh, Cooke could solve the case with his eyes shut.

Oh, we'll just assign it to Agent Cooke." He returned to his normal voice. "Well, you can't solve a case without forensics, can you, Super Agent Cooke."

"I don't disagree. In fact, I distinctly remember giving you a commendation in front of the entire team on the last case."

"That case was shit and you know it. You have no comprehension of my capabilities."

Ryan smirked. "What? Like this? You expect me to believe you're going to shoot me?"

"I am going to shoot you. And her too." Agent Short nudged his gun at Layne. "Now, Ms. Stevens. The Employer wants the fucking card, and I intend to be the one who delivers it."

Lane's brow furrowed. "The Employer?"

"You're both trying my patience. Ms. Stevens, give me the card."

She stared at him for several long seconds while a hundred possibilities swarmed through her mind. "No," she said.

"You have got to be fucking kidding me. I'm going to get the damned thing one way or—"

She tightened her grip on the flash drive and took a step back. "You can't have it."

Agent Short closed in, and Ryan lunged at him, grabbing the arm that held the gun. As the two men struggled, Layne turned and heaved the flash drive into the waves. Ryan kneed Agent Short in the gut. The agent lurched, and the gun flew onto the sand, but he pulled a knife from his belt and lashed out, slicing Ryan's arm. Ryan jerked back, grabbing the wound with his other hand, and Agent Short went after him, the knife aimed at Ryan's throat.

Layne scrambled for the gun, pointed, and fired.

101

Despite the events on St. John, the trip had done Layne good. And being back in her work routine helped to lift her spirits. But three weeks had passed since she'd testified before a grand jury, and the verdict was due in.

Maggie approached Layne in the lunchroom with a critical eye and her usual subtlety. "What crawled up your ass today?"

Not at liberty to reveal the source of her anxiety, and absolutely not willing to risk another charge of treason, Layne chose to whine. "I don't know. I guess I didn't get enough sleep."

"Well, you'd better snap out of it. It's your first live show, sweetheart. Screw this up, and we're all out of jobs. But no pressure." Maggie strutted to the coffee.

"Thanks, Mags," Layne said. "I can always count on you for a motivating pep talk."

The main line on the lunchroom phone rang, and Maggie picked it up. "Yes," she said, "go ahead and transfer."

Maggie waited, tapping her foot. "Hey, babe, are you in town?" Her tone became irritated. "Then why are you calling?" She frowned. "It's for you." She gave the handset to Layne and went for the door. "Tell the bastard he'd better get his butt to LA soon. I won't wait forever. I've got places to go and people to do."

"I think you should tell him that yourself." Layne turned to the phone. "Scott?"

"Shit, Layne. You make me swear on mom's future grave that I'll call, then you don't carry your damned cell." The connection broke.

"Crap." Layne ran for her office as Pat Benatar beckoned to her. Fitting, she thought as she almost barreled over a script editor, and then banged her elbow against the door handle. "Ouch," she said, answering the call.

"Playing stunt double again?"

Layne gasped for air. "I ran down the hall to get to my phone, and I hit my funny bone on the door."

"Where'd you run from?"

"The lunchroom."

"What's that, like thirty feet from your office? Jeez, sis, maybe you should take your workouts a little more seriously."

"I'm wearing three-inch heels and a tight skirt. You wouldn't have made it five feet, but never mind that. Did Agent Short get to trial?"

"Yep. You made a clean shot to the ass, sis. He had to stand for his testimony though." Scott snickered. "He said to say hello, by the way."

"Great," she said, feeling her chest tighten. "Well? What happened?"

"Short won the grand prize—a life sentence at casa de nut-job in some godforsaken Arizona hellhole. He'll pull bedpan duty with certified crazies in one-hundred-degree weather, with no opportunity for parole."

"What about Agent Rennick?"

"She still claims shooting Ryan was an accident, but she confessed to falsifying the profile to set you up, and she pleaded out. Same hell-hole, but eight years instead of life."

"But she killed Uncle Fred."

"Turns out, she didn't. Short made a full confession to avoid the death penalty. Told us about somebody called The Employer who paid him to do it. We think that may have been your psycho Siri caller. Short didn't have much information on The Employer, but he did confess to killing Uncle Fred and a German agent who'd been helping him. On orders from The Employer, of course. Oh, and get this. Remember there were three rumaki skewers on the silver tray?"

"I'll take your word for it."

"Short requested an extra one. The sous chef at The Riede confirmed that he laid a fourth one on top. Short ate the damned rumaki off the top skewer, and then stabbed Uncle Fred through the heart with it. He took it with him and used it again on the German agent, Berger. We found the skewer in Short's utensil drawer."

Layne puckered. "Ewww, Scott, I did not want to know that."

"Sorry."

"Yuck."

He chuckled.

"Why do you tell me stuff like that?"

"To hear your reaction."

"Of course you do. So, Agent Rennick wasn't involved at all?"

"She had ties to the German agent, and it's likely she and Short worked together. But If she was connected to the murders, we can't prove it. Still, as far as I'm concerned, eight years is about thirty shy for Rennick."

"What about Sergeant Temple? Wasn't he a suspect?"

"He claims he kept showing up at the crime scenes because he was bored. But I think he had some weird kind of agent envy thing going on."

"But didn't they find his fingerprints on the silver tray?"

"Yep. Turned out the dumb shit was just hungry. But, he admitted under oath, like the true professional he is, that he thought twice before actually eating the evidence. They released him when they realized he was too lazy and too stupid to have committed a murder. But the SFPD forced him into early retirement for almost tampering with a crime scene."

"So, who shot Hansel?"

Scott smirked. "You mean Johnny? Short and Rennick both deny taking the shot. But it could've been the guy who stained mom's carpet. There's something sketchy about him."

"Oh yeah. What was his name?"

"Sonny. Sonny Wright. I'll never forget it."

"Why?"

"Because mom had to replace her carpet, and I'm the one who had to hear about it. Over, and over, and over."

"The name sounds so familiar. What was sketchy about him?"

"He disappeared."

"How does a dead man disappear?"

"That's the sketchy part. The body is just gone."

"Why would anyone want to steal a dead body?"

"Who the hell knows? It's a freak show out there, sis."

"Weird. So, there aren't any terrorists?"

Scott coughed out a laugh. "Good one, sis. There are plenty of terrorist organizations that would kill to get their hands on this kind of data. And The Employer, whoever they are, is still at large. But with the card buried at sea, there's nothing for anyone to go after. The FDA is still claiming denial, and it would take years to recompile all that evidence. So, things seem to have settled down, and I'm sure The Employer is long gone."

Layne shivered with a mix of emotions. "Well, at least it's finally over."

"Sis—"

"Okay, Scott. Thanks for calling."

"Sis, don't hang up. I need to talk to you about a cat."

Layne shook her head and tapped to end the call.

102

Director Braun fell back onto his couch, took off the black dress shoes constricting his feet, and loosened his tie. The memorial service had moved him, but he still angered at the circumstances. Such a needless waste.

His phone vibrated in his pocket. He pulled it out and stared at the caller ID. At least someone from the states had the decency to call during the daytime hours.

"Director Braun here."

"Dieter, I'm glad I caught you. I wanted to personally give you my condolences. They were good men. It's a loss to both our agencies."

Director Braun's jaw tightened. His counterpart in San Francisco would not navigate through this so easily. "Hello, Mitch. I appreciate your kind words. And the urgency given to my request for return of their remains."

"I'll help in any way I can," Director Hall said.

"I am heartened to hear it. Because I do not consider this matter closed."

"I'm sorry, Dieter. I don't understand. Our agent confessed to both murders. He'll never be released from prison. If you're pushing for the death—"

"You and I know, Mitch, that Special Agent Short was nothing more than an errand boy. And the real perpetrator is not in custody. Frederick Schatz was a friend. And Hans Berger, well, to me he was more than an agent. He was like a son. Twenty-two years invested not only in his career, but in his life and his happiness. He was my family. While Special Agent Short may have been the weapon, someone else commanded those executions. I will not rest until that person is apprehended."

Director Braun heard a sigh on the other end of the line. An unusual occurrence for seasoned Executive FBI Director Mitch Hall.

"You're right," Director Hall said. "Confidentially, Short fingered someone known as The Employer for ordering the hits, along with the acquisition of the card through any means. We've been watching The Employer's organization for some time, under suspicion on various fronts—everything from data leaks, to lobbyist tampering, to illegal transport of goods, but nothing violent until now. Whoever The Employer is, they're clever, and they're elusive. And our inside man was compromised, so we'll need to start over there. But it's a joint effort across bureau territories, and I assure you, we are doing everything in our power to nail the son of a bitch."

"As will I," Director Braun said. "I recognize this information is unofficial, but I appreciate your candor, Mitch. With that, we can begin an investigation of our own."

"Actually, I think I can do one better. I'll have your agency read in, and get you everything we have. Hell, the more people working on this, the more likely we are to catch a break."

The tension in Director Braun's chest eased a bit. The offer gave little consolation for such a tremendous loss, but the ability to take formal action provided some amount of solace. "Thank you, Mitch. That means the world to me. And we'll begin our own research tomorrow."

"Glad to have you on board. And Dieter, I truly am very sorry."

Director Braun ended the call, then stared down at the wrinkles and veins protruding from his hands. For this, retirement would wait.

103

Disconcerted, Layne put her phone on her desk. Then she sat down and opened her email, but barely scanned the messages. She couldn't focus, couldn't take her mind off the call from Scott. She chewed on the news that Rennick may only have been guilty of trying to incriminate her, and that Mr. Tall had confessed to everything. But it didn't make sense. He just didn't seem like an evil mastermind type of guy. Then she remembered what he'd said to them on the beach—that The Employer wanted the card. Mr. Tall...Agent Short had simply been a pawn. And this person calling themselves The Employer had abandoned him, letting him take the fall on his own. What kind of sick bastard would do that to someone?

Her cell phone blasted "Love Shack," and she nearly fell out of her chair. Each time she'd dared to answer a call with that ringtone, a harmless telemarketer had accosted her. And Scott had assured her The Employer was long gone, but a small shiver zipped through her just the same. She sent the caller to voicemail and made a mental note, which she would likely forget for the hundredth time, to choose a new general ringtone.

Maggie popped her head in the door. "There you are. It's almost time. Hold on. Is that what you're wearing? Why did I let you dress yourself for this?"

Layne looked down at her outfit. "I've had this on all day."

"I assumed you were going to change."

Still distracted, Layne locked her office and allowed Maggie to shuffle her down the hall to the side of the set. But when she peeked around the curtain, all thoughts of the card and The Employer evaporated.

"There are a lot of people out there, Mags."

"Yes, sweetie. It wouldn't be a live audience without them." Maggie fluffed Layne's curls and undid one more button on her blouse.

Layne slapped at Maggie's hand. "Stop that."

"For christ sake. It's a cooking show, hun, not a bible study."

The president of the network, Darren Chase, approached them. "There's my favorite celebrity chef. Are you apprehensive, my dear?"

"Yes, I am," Maggie said. "Do you see what she's wearing?"

Layne ignored Maggie and offered Darren a big smile—probably too big. "Not nervous at all," she said.

He chuckled. "You look lovely. And I'm certain you will be splendid, as always."

"Thank you, Darren. That's very nice of you to say."

"I have complete confidence. If you can arrest an extended alcoholic binge and Pteromerhanophobia, I am positive you can manage this."

"Pardon me?"

Just then the show's announcer boomed over the speakers, "And now, please join me in welcoming your host, Layne Stevens!"

The audience applauded, whistled and cheered. Darren gave Layne a reassuring pat on the shoulder. And Maggie nudged Layne onto the stage. The show went flawlessly—no stumbling, no grease fires, no men in dark suits. And Layne felt a renewed sense of purpose. She'd vowed to use her role on the Foodie Channel to help turn the nation's health crisis around. And for the first time in months, she eagerly anticipated her next show, her next topic, even her next trip.

Before the taping concluded, Layne blew a kiss to the front row where her parents were seated along with Scott, Jenny, and Dean.

There had been a moment when she'd taken their love for granted. She wouldn't allow that to happen again. And before the curtain closed, she dedicated the episode to an American federal officer and a hero, Special Agent Ryan Cooke, shot in the line of duty.

It was late when Layne said her goodbyes to her audience. She hugged Maggie, thanked Darren and her crew, and headed back to her office, exhausted from the emotional twists and turns of the day. Halfway down the hall, she stopped. Hadn't she shut her office door? Goosebumps prickled on her arms as she tried to recall.

I told you this wouldn't end well, her little voice said.

As usual, Layne ignored it, but her pulse rose as she snuck down the hall.

True to its job on her payroll, Layne's little voice let her have it. *You absolutely closed that door. Do I need to recap our last open door incident?*

"Shut up," Layne whispered to her little voice as she peeked her head around the door frame and peered inside.

Dim light flickered from an antique green tiffany lamp, playing tricks with her vision, and her eyes fought to adjust. Then her gaze fixed on a floral arrangement—tall, and full of vibrant color—that someone had placed in the middle of her desk. Oh, thank god. The receptionist must have delivered the flowers and left the office door open.

She stepped inside and pulled a notecard from a plastic holder in the center of the bouquet. Then she caught a movement in the far corner of the room. A rush of nausea and dread threatened to bring up her lunch, and she froze as a man moved in the shadows.

"Hello, gorgeous. Great show tonight."

Layne lifted a brow. Was that...caramel?

A tingling sensation danced up her spine, she smiled, and her world was complete.

THANK YOU!

There's a big wide world of books out there, and I feel truly honored that you chose to read mine.

For more great reads

that entertain and inspire please visit

www.cliffhousebooks.com

SOCIAL STUFF

Recipes

For recipes from the novel (can you say Candied Bacon Creme Brule?) and more of my favorites, please visit my website **www.carietoeller.com**

Coming Soon

Second Corpse: The Soup

Ride along as Layne drags Maggie through the sweltering Arizona summer heat in search of killer clam chowder (and Ryan).

Want to Connect?

facebook.com/CRToeller
twitter.com/carie_toeller
instagram.com/carietoeller
pinterest.com/foodmadewhole

www.ingramcontent.com/pod-product-compliance
Lightning Source LLC
Chambersburg PA
CBHW050858250626
47155CB00001B/11

* 9 7 8 0 9 9 7 0 6 4 7 1 1 *